# A SACRIFICE

Hadji fitted the pieces of wood together, connecting them by means of screws driven into the pre-drilled holes. He had assembled and disassembled his portable shrine so often that he could have done it now in the dark, if need be.

A low moan escaped from Mrs. March as she slowly rose back to consciousness. *Good*, Hadji thought. *Her awareness is necessary.* He ignored her pleading eyes and muffled cries. He opened the suitcase and drew forth a small obsidian statuette of a man with the head of a jackal—Anubis.

Hadji placed the statuette upon the flat surface of the altar and turned to Mrs. March. She tried to struggle against her bonds, but her fear had bound her more strongly than any rope.

Hadji lifted her to her knees and leaned her frail body over the front of the altar. Chanting, "Anubis, prince of eternity, deliver me from death," Hadji pulled the knife from his back pocket.

# STOLEN SOULS

## JEFFREY SACKETT

**BANTAM BOOKS**
TORONTO • NEW YORK • LONDON • SYDNEY • AUCKLAND

STOLEN SOULS
*A Bantam Book / December 1987*

ISBN 0-553-26937-2

*Published simultaneously in the United States and Canada*

---

*Bantam Books are published by Bantam Books, Inc. Its trademark,*
*consisting of the words "Bantam Books" and the portrayal of a rooster, is*
*Registered in U.S. Patent and Trademark Office and in other countries.*
*Marca Registrada. Bantam Books, Inc., 666 Fifth Avenue, New York, New*
*York 10103.*

---

PRINTED IN THE UNITED STATES OF AMERICA

KR        0 9 8 7 6 5 4 3 2 1

This novel is dedicated to my dear mother, with thanks for her support and encouragement; and to the memory of my father.

# AUTHOR'S NOTE

All hieroglyphic texts and phrase combinations used in this book have been checked and double-checked with authoritative texts in the field of ancient Egyptian language, and I believe them to be grammatically and syntactically correct. Those readers who are to any degree familiar with ancient Egyptian may object to the occasional use of plural verb and enclitic constructions with singular subjects and predicate nominatives. I can only ask such people to read until they reach the point at which such usages are explained. Any other errors in grammar or construction are both unintentional and entirely my fault.

As with many ancient writing systems, Egyptian hieroglyphs allow us to discover the consonants used in their spoken language, but not the vowels. Thus the romanization system used herein, while standard among contemporary Egyptologists, should not be regarded as accurate. It merely represents the sound of spoken Egyptian to as great (or little!) a degree as we can surmise.

Those readers who do not know that the English language once employed polite/plural and familiar/singular second person pronouns may incorrectly assume that in using the latter I am attempting to ape Biblical speech. I urge such people to dig their old high school English notebooks out of the back of the closet, assuming that they went to school back in those distant days when such things were still taught.

Interested readers can delve somewhat more deeply into the sequence and nature of the historical events to which reference is made in this book by consulting J. H. Breasted's seminal work, *A History of Egypt*, and R. K. Webb's *Modern England*.

This is a work of sensationalist fiction. All non-historical characters and contemporary events recounted in this book are therefore fictional as well, thank God.

J.S.

Homage to thee, O my divine father!
Do thou embalm these my members, for
I would not perish and come to an end,
but would be like unto thee, who never
saw corruption. Come then and strengthen
my breath, O lord of the winds! Stablish
me, stablish me, and fashion me strongly,
O lord of the funeral chest! In truth it
hath been decreed that in me shalt thou
see thy likeness, and that my face shall
look forever upon the face of the god!
How long, then, have I to live?
  Millions of years.
  A life of millions of years . . . .
                            —*The Egyptian Book
                              of the Dead*, XLV
                              and CLXXV


For I know that my redeemer liveth,
and that he shall stand at the latter
day upon the Earth; and though after
my skin, worms destroy this body,
yet in my flesh shall I see God.
                    —*Job* 19 : 25–26


Credo quod absurdum est. —Tertullian

# P R O L O G U E

Winter comes unbidden and largely unnoticed to the hill
country of Upper Egypt. The Nile, that ancient lifeline of the
ancient land, drifts lazily down from the uplands of the Sudan
and the mountain vastness of Ethiopia, following its eternal
path toward the Aswân High Dam through the largely
unpopulated wasteland of desert. The Nile has seen much in
its immortal meandering. It has seen pharaohs and caesars,
caliphs and sultans, kaisers and tsars, emperors of France and
kings of England. Its banks have resounded to hymns of praise
to Allah, to Christ, to Osiris. And when winter comes, the Nile
is as impervious to its arrival as are the red hills and pitted cliffs
of the empty land which stretches out on both sides toward the
barren sands of Libya on the west and the warm blue waters of
the Red Sea to the east. Winter means nothing to Upper
Egypt. It means no change of climate, no alteration of the
ocher cast of the endless sand, no particles of ice in the warm,
sluggish river. It is but a date on the calendar, a reminder that
the mountains of Ethiopia are busy freezing next spring's
floods in their icy wombs. It means nothing to the river. It
means nothing to the hills.

The warm January breeze wafted gently over the rocks and
sand, lifting occasional wisps of dust up into the clear blue sky.
Small lizards and beetles scurried hither and yon from the
sunlight to the shade afforded by the infrequent slopes. The
world of Upper Egypt was silent but for the intermittent
scraping of scales and spindly legs upon pebble and stone; but
for the low moaning whisper of the wind; but for the distant
cries of birds gliding gracefully through the boundless blue

vault of heaven; but for the occasional splash of a frog
returning from the banks to its river home.

These were the only sounds.

Except for the chanting.

From a distance the ruins of the ancient holy place were
indistinguishable from the rock mounds and sheer cliff faces
which interrupted the monotony of the desert. The roof of the
predynastic mastaba had collapsed thousands of years before,
and the rays of the sun beat mercilessly down upon the
exposed interior of the small temple, reflecting an almost
painful brilliance from the smooth surfaces of the external
walls. Once these walls had been faced with the purest,
smoothest white stone, but the facing had been removed long
before, in the days of the later Ramesids, to be used in the
construction of other buildings far to the north. The walls were
still smooth now, but the smoothness came, not from human
effort, but from the incessant desert wind which had caressed
the mastaba continuously for thousands of years.

Within the interior of the ruined temple were forty-two
people, standing rigidly in obviously predetermined positions.
The temple had been designed and built to accommodate
precisely this number, its floor plan devised to provide specific
places for each one of the forty-two people. There had always
been forty-two, never one less, never one more, since before
the days of Nasser and Sadat; since before the days of Islam
and Christianity; since before the days of Alexander of
Macedon and Cambyses of Persia; since before the days of
Rameses the Great and Amenhotep the Magnificent. When
Menes created the Kingdom of Egypt by uniting the hill
country with the land of the delta, this religious community
was already old beyond memory. When the priests of Egypt
invented a calendar and gave History its first date, 4241 B.C.,
centuries before Menes, this religious community could already look back upon a past as far distant from that calendar as
Rameses was from Hitler.

And they had always numbered forty-two, for there are
forty-two judges in the Hall of the Two Truths where Isis,
Osiris, and Thoth preside over the judgment of the souls of the
dead. Each judge is a god. Each of the forty-two people
standing motionless beneath the Egyptian sun on that warm
January day was the priest of one of the forty-two gods.

The people were dressed simply, almost austerely, in clean,
unadorned white linen. Each wore a medallion upon a golden

chain, fixed close to the throat. Each medallion bore upon it four simple hieroglyphs, and three of the four were identical on each of the forty-two medallions. Each bore the ankh, the loop-topped cross which was the symbol of life; the head of a jackal, symbol of the god Anubis, guardian of the grave; and the tekenu, an armless human form seated upon a narrow platform.

The fourth hieroglyph was different on each of the medallions. An old woman who was the priestess of Isis wore a medallion which bore the head of a cow, which was both the symbol of Isis and her visage. A much younger woman's medallion displayed the head of a cat, the animal of Bast, goddess of pleasure. Here the baboon of the mood god, Thoth; there the falcon of the war god, Montu. The bull of Ra and the ram of Amon, the hawk of Horus and the crocodile of Sobek, the wolf of Wepwawet and the beetle of Khephra— each found a place on the medallion of their respective priests. But the ankh, the jackal, and the tekenu were on each of them, for the ankh symbolized their hopes, the jackal symbolized their primordial god, and the tekenu symbolized their bridge to eternal life.

Not that they possessed eternal life: no, these were human beings, not gods, and they would pass from this world at the end of their measure of days. But successors would be chosen, examined, taught, and initiated, and the cult would continue as it had for countless thousands of years. Each generation of priests hoped that it would be the last generation, that the fulfillment of the promise would grace their priesthood, that they would be the ones to escape from the gloom of the grave. This each generation hoped for. And each generation had died.

But the cult survived through the centuries, through the millennia. It survived Christianity and Islam, foreign conquest and revolution—always furtive, always cautious, always disguised. Always there.

The cult survived because its memebers knew things which the world had forgotten. They knew that the spirits of the ancient gods still roamed through the ruins of their ancient temples. They knew and practiced the ancient rituals in the ancient tongue. And they knew the secret before which even kings had once trembled.

The forty-two priests and priestesses stood in a triangular formation. At the head of the assembly, who faced an empty recessed cubicle which once, long ago, had contained a statue of the god Anubis, stood a bent, frail, wizened old man. The gentle wind seemed almost to unbalance him as it caused his linen robe to flap slightly around his skinny legs, as it drifted over his bald head and through the long, wispy white bread which hung down from his wrinkled, pallid face. His voice was soft and tremulous, but his tone bespoke an authority born of long accustomation, for he had been the high priest of the cult for the past threescore years and had been the priest of the god Set for a decade prior. Of late he had resigned himself to the approach of death, for he had become shorn of hope that his would be the generation to defeat the passage of time.

But his hope had been reborn just three days before, given new life by, of all things, a small advertisement buried in the back pages of a foreign newspaper. And so he had sent out word to his people and called them to this hasty assembly. It was the age-old custom for them to meet on this spot on the night of each new moon and conduct their rituals beneath the black sky in the midst of darkness so deep that the flickering stars could not relieve it. But no one had objected to this meeting at midday in midmonth, for the rebirth of the old man's hopes had breathed new life into their own. They had come eagerly to this spot, each one repeating the same words silently within: I shall not die, I shall not die. Millions of years. A life of millions of years.

*"Anet hrauthen neteru,"* the old man chanted in the long-dead tongue of ancient Egypt.

*"Anet hrauthen neteru,"* the assembly chanted in response. Homage to you, O gods.

The old man nodded a signal to two guards who stood in the shadows of the eastern corner of the mastaba. They were not priests, not members of the cult. They were from the poor dregs of Egyptian society, recruited and paid well for their service and their silence, given food and women and comfort and, unbeknownst to them, periodically killed and replaced. The two guards walked forward, bringing with them a terrified girl in her early teens who screamed and kicked with futile desperation against her captors. The guards dragged her before the cracked and pitted altar which stood a few feet removed from the eastern wall of the mastaba, and pulled her arms outward, twisting them up so that she leaned her upper body over the surface of the block of broken stone. Her pleading cries and tears seemed to be unnoticed and unheard as the old man lifted the ceremonial dagger from the center of the altar and placed its tip against her throat. *"Anet hrauthen neteru,"* he repeated.

*"Anet hrauthen neteru,"* the assembly answered. Homage to you, O gods.

The old man drove the blade into the girl's flesh and her warm lifeblood spurted out onto the altar, captured and held in the bowl-shaped depression which had been carved into the center, as the excess flowed freely down the front and sides, seeping into the spaces between the ancient stones of the mastaba floor. The girl's trembling body soon grew still, and the light in her eyes flickered and then went out. The guards removed the sacrifice from the altar and tossed it unceremoniously back into the shadows of the corner. The old man then immersed the already bloody knife in the warm pool of sanguine liquid upon the altar top. *"Anet hrauthen 'Anpu,"* he chanted, lifting the knife high as if in offering.

*"Anet hrauthen 'Anpu,"* the assembly chanted. Homage to you, Anubis.

The old woman who wore the symbol of Isis upon her medallion walked slowly to the front of the assembly. She knelt awkwardly and raised her flabby arms upward in a gesture of praise as the old man touched the bloody dagger to her forehead and chanted, *"Anet hrauthen Auset."*

*"Anet hrauthen Auset,"* came the chanted reply. Homage to you, Isis.

The priests approached the altar one by one, each in turn kneeling before the high priest and receiving a drop of the sanctified blood upon the forehead. *"Anet hrauthen Nebtkhet,"* he chanted as he touched the blade to the forehead of the priestess of Nephthys.

*"Anet hrauthen Nebtkhet,"* they chanted. Homage to you, Nephthys.

*"Anet hrauthen Tekhuti."* The priest of Thoth knelt before him.

*"Anet hrauthen Tekhuti."* Homage to you, Thoth.

*"Anet hrauthen Kheru."* The priest of Horus knelt before him.

*"Anet hrauthen Kheru."* Homage to you, Horus.

*"Anet hrauthen 'Ausar."*

*"Anet hrauthen 'Ausar."* Homage to you, Osiris.

They moved in a slow and regular cadence, approaching, kneeling, receiving the bloody dagger, rising, returning to their places. When the last of the priests had resumed his place, the old man turned once again to the spot where long ago had stood the statue of Anubis. He raised his arms outward, the palms of his hands facing the sanctum and his fingers pointing toward the sky, and bowed his head.

*"Au arina neterhetepu en neteru. Perchkheru en khu,"* he chanted. I have made offerings to the gods. I have sacrificed to the spirits.

*"Anet hrauthen neteru,"* they responded. Homage to you, O gods.

*"'Anpu kheq tetta, nekhemkua ma aterit."* Anubis, Prince of Eternity, deliver me from calamity.

*"Anet hrauthen neteru."*

*"'Anpu neb nest, nekhemkua ma 'aputat utetiu themesu."* Anubis, Lord of Thrones, deliver me from the messengers of evil.

*"Anet hrauthen neteru."*

*"'Anpu neb Ut, 'Anpu chent neter het, 'Anpu neb nifu—"* Anubis, Lord of the City of Embalming, Anubis, Dweller in the Tomb of the Gods, Anubis, Lord of the Winds—

He did not chant the final supplication. It burst from his throat, a frenzied, desperate cry. *"'Anpu, nekhemkua ma ab!"*

Anubis, deliver me from death!

As with one voice, the priests and priestesses cried, *"'Anpu, nekhemkua ma ab!"*

*"'Anpu, nekhemkua ma ab!"*

*"'ANPU, NEKHEMKUA MA AB!"*

Then they were silent. They stood motionless as the old high priest turned slowly and faced them. He spoke in his normal Arabic tongue as he said as loudly as his feeble old voice could manage, "You have all heard some part of the truth, but allow me to lay all rumors to rest." He paused dramatically, and then said, "The holy ones have been found!" An excited buzzing arose from the assembly, and the old man raised his hand to quiet the noise. When silence had returned, he continued. "We must prepare for the ceremony. We must repair the holy place and make ready to receive the gift of the god. And we must send a member of our company to escort the holy ones ôn their long journey back to the land of their birth."

A number of eager voices issued forth from the assembly to volunteer for the mission, but this was not a democracy. It was an autocracy, in the tradition of the ancients—a theocracy, as it had been in olden times. The old man raised his hand once again, and the voices died away. "The priest of Thoth shall go," he said quietly.

A young man standing close to the front of the triangular formation lifted himself to his feet and stood proudly amid the kneeling priests and priestesses. The old man motioned him forward, and he approached the front of the ruined mastaba with slow, measured steps. He knelt once again before the altar, as he had done a few minutes before. The old man placed his hands upon the young man's head and said, "Ahmed Hadji, may the gods bless you and give you success in your mission."

The young man muttered, "I am unworthy of this honor."

"You are worthy of more than this," the old man replied, "and great will be your reward when you return. But listen carefully, my son! Guard yourself against eagerness, for haste gives birth to error. You are charged to return to Egypt with the lord Sekhemib and the others, but you must not seek a tekenu in that distant land. Here shall we prepare for the ceremony, and here shall the tekenues be brought forward. Here shall we bask in the radiance of the god. Here shall we see the old promise fulfilled."

Ahmed Hadji, the young priest of Thoth, bowed his head submissively. "I shall obey, my master."

The old man smiled warmly down at the young priest. Had it been so recently that he had envied his protégé the smooth olive skin and the strong young arms? Had it truly annoyed him that Hadji's thick black moustache and curly black hair contrasted so starkly with his own bald head and thin white beard? Had he really thought with such sorrow that before he had become bent and shrunken with age he had been taller than the short man who now knelt before him? Foolishness, such foolishness. Age means nothing, nothing. The old man's eighty years of life and the young man's thirty years of life were but leaves drifting upon the surface of the eternal river, and decades, centuries, millennia awaited them both. Millions of years. A life of millions of years.

"Arise and go hence, Ahmed Hadji," the old man said kindly. "May the gods go before you on your journey.

"*Anet hrauthen neteru,*" Hadji whispered. Homage to the gods. He arose and returned to his place among the priests. The forty-two worshippers stood in silent meditation for a few moments, and then turned to leave the ruined mastaba, walking away in contemplative quiet. By the evening they would all have returned to their otherwise normal and uneventful lives, blending unnoticed into the teeming population of the modern Arab Republic of Egypt.

Soon the ancient ruin was empty once again but for the beetles and the lizards and the floating wisps of dust. The pitted stone hills in the distance caught and exchanged the last faint echoes of the pleading cry as it faded into the deepening stillness of the desert waste: *'Anpu, nekhemkua ma ab*. Anubis, deliver me from death.

And then there was silence but for the low moaning wind which drifted over the sands.

# I

# THE PRIESTS

▲

Verily I, even I, have come!
I have overthrown mine enemies
upon the Earth, although my
body lieth a mummy in the tomb.
—*The Egyptian Book of
the Dead*, LXXXVI

# CHAPTER 1

▲Reginald Fowles, fourteenth Earl of Selwyn, could be described in many ways to someone so ignorant of twentieth-century Britain as never to have heard of him. He succeeded to the peerage at the age of twenty-six, upon the death of his father, the thirteenth Earl. He did not take his seat in the House of Lords until three years thereafter, for his combat service in the First World War seemed a more pressing responsibility at the time. Wounded at the Battle of the Somme, the fourteenth Earl returned to England and involved himself cautiously in the internal politics of the Conservative party. Although it was true that for a brief period he was friendly with Oswald Mosley, the leader of the British Union of Fascists between the wars, the general public assumption that the Earl was himself a right-wing radical was untrue. He served His Imperial Majesty George VI as a colonial administrator in Africa and was being spoken of as a possible choice to be viceroy of India when Churchill called him to the War Office after the German conquest of France in 1940. The Earl remained in London throughout the war, and when his wife and only son were killed in a German bombing raid during the darkest days of the Blitz, he took the morning off to attend the funeral, stiffened his lip, and carried on with his job. After the defeat of Hitler's Reich, he retired to his vast estate at Chudley, and but for an occasional social engagement connected to the political life of the Conservative party, he never left it. His pithy and insightful articles were not unfamiliar to readers of *The Times*, but he himself was familiar to almost no one at all. When Queen Elizabeth paid him a courtesy call on his eightieth birthday, he behaved in the respectful, grateful, and decorous manner which his breeding and convictions engendered. The Queen could tell that she had best keep her visit brief, however, by the way he kept glancing at the clock during their conversation.

Brave soldier, loyal monarchist, servant of the Crown, world traveller, member of the cabinet—the fourteenth Earl of Selwyn was all of these things. But at the moment his most significant attributes were that he was an eighty-six-year-old man, and he was dying.

The prospect of his imminent demise upset many family friends and menials. The servants went about their tasks at Chudley with hushed deliberation as if already in mourning. Fredericks, the butler, grew to expect the daily phone calls from Downing Street and Windsor, inquiring after the old Earl's condition. Tessie, the cook, kept a handkerchief near her at all times, so as to be able to dab away the tears which kept threatening to erupt. The local notables visited frequently, not to see the Earl (who would not have received them anyway), but to let themselves be seen showing concern. There were only two people who were not concerned, only two people who hoped that the old Earl's death would come soon. One of them was the old Earl himself. The other was his nephew Roderick, the fifteenth Earl of Selwyn-to-be.

The old Earl did not fear death. As a devout member of the Church of England, his belief in the saving grace of God through Christ (a belief born more of habit than conviction, to be sure) provided him with whatever solace and comfort he may have needed. But beyond that, the old Earl was tired of living. He had seen the Empire which he had helped govern disintegrate. He had seen the old European order which he had known and loved destroy itself in two insane, suicidal wars. He had seen politics, once the dignified reserve of privilege, degenerate (in his eyes, at least) into a brothel of sycophantic careerism. He had seen his wife and son laid to rest, too soon, too soon.

And he had spent his entire adult life guarding a horrible secret, burdened with the knowledge of the terror which lay locked and bound in seven oblong crates in the attic at Chudley.

He was tired, worn out. He welcomed the approach of the end.

The old Earl's end was also going to be welcomed by his

nephew, Roderick Fowles, a young man as unlike the old Earl as could be imagined. The old Earl had devoted his life to the service of the Crown and the kingdom. Young Roderick was devoted with equal intensity to his stomach and his palate. The old Earl had pursued a vision of order and justice. Young Roderick pursued women. The old Earl had thought rarely of himself. Young Roderick thought of nothing but himself.

Roderick was not a bad fellow, actually. He was just an example of the degree to which a life in which there was no pressing need to do anything could create a rather genial personality which contained no vision. Roderick was generous to a fault, primarily because it had never occurred to him that money was a finite commodity. He had the easy air, so attractive to women, which was born of an almost total absence of responsibility. His conversation was glib, charming, and devoid of content. He had hundreds of friends and made new ones easily and frequently, because his friendship had no depth. Though only twenty-two, he was already beginning to show signs of portliness, which would doubtless in another decade turn into obesity, the result of too much rich food, too much wine, consumed in quantities too great, too often. Roderick knew he was putting on too much weight, but he reacted to this fact with a smile, a sigh, and a shrug, as if it were a matter beyond his control. He simply did not care.

Nor, in one sense, need he care. He had been destined since his birth to be the fifteenth Earl of Selwyn. He had been wealthy and pampered and catered to. As the sole family member of the new generation, the entire future of the family rested with him, and he knew it, and his old uncle knew it, and his parents had known it while they were still alive. He was irreplaceable. To be sure, his uncle could have remarried and sired another heir, but that was unlikely. The old Earl's devotion to the memory of his late wife precluded such an action on his part. He was to live and die a childless widower.

Roderick Fowles thus grew to young manhood secure in the knowledge that all he need do for the rest of his life was enjoy himself, and enjoy himself he did, expansively, cheerfully, charmingly. He knew nothing of importance, did nothing of significance, thought nothing of relevance, and had no goal other than the immediate satisfaction of every momentary desire.

His uncle could not stand him.

He did not dislike his uncle, however: quite to the

contrary, he found the old Earl to be a fascinating and diverting old fossil. The fact that he could not even begin to understand the attitudes which had structured the old Earl's life and actions served merely to make him all the more intriguing to young Roderick. He almost enjoyed the (to him) inexplicable rages to which his exploits drove the old Earl.

And he did not desire the old man's death in any personal or vindictive sense. He merely wished to inherit Chudley and the enormous fortune attendant thereunto. It was really quite inconsiderate for the old fellow to have lived so long beyond the average life span. Why, Roderick should have been the Earl of Selwyn over a decade ago!

Becoming Earl meant money to Roderick, nothing else. The allowance he received from his uncle, coupled with the money he derived from his father's bequest to him, was huge by any rational standard; but there can never be too much of a good thing, according to Roderick. He could not be fairly described as greedy, because greed is a result of an inadequate supply of funds, not an overabundance. But Roderick equated money with fun, and he liked to have fun—the more fun the better. Thus, the more money the better.

It was his preoccupation with possessing more and more money which had led him to contemplate selling some of the fourteenth Earl's "old rubbish," as Roderick described it. And it was this which brought him this day to the deathbed of the fourteenth Earl of Selwyn for what, Roderick hoped, would be one last tirade.

The old Earl lay tucked and bundled upon the canopied bed in a room already too hot and stuffy for everyone but him. He glowered as his nephew bent over him and asked solicitously, "How are we today, Uncle?" The old Earl's lip curled in distaste as he regarded young Roderick. The countenance which confronted him was pleasant enough: the sandy hair which fell in almost coquettish curls upon the unlined forehead; the clear green eyes which strove at this moment to display such concern; the thin aristocratic nose whose delicate upsweep gave an illusion of asceticism to the somewhat pudgy cheeks; the carefully manicured fingernails; the dapper tailored jacket; the unostentatious yet obviously expensive jewelry—all of this might have made Roderick a pleasant sight to anyone who did not know him as well as did his uncle, who did not hold him in such low esteem.

"How are we today?" the old Earl echoed sarcastically. "We

are dying today, you young idiot." His voice was feeble, his breathing labored.

"There, there, Uncle. No need to be so pessimistic." Roderick smiled, patting the cold and boney hand which rested on the bedcover. "I'm sure you'll be up and about in no time at all."

"I'll be up, all right. Up in a box on the shoulders of six men." He paused to catch his breath. Talking was an obvious source of discomfort to him. "And don't try to flatter me with your crocodile devotion, you insect! I know that you are practically salivating over your inheritance."

Roderick assumed an air of injured innocence. "Really, Uncle! Must you be so unkind? You know that I am sick with worry about you."

"Ha! If you are sick with worry about anything, it's about the inheritance taxes hanging over your head." The old Earl peered myopically past his nephew at the small man standing in the corner. "Who's that?"

The small man approached timidly. "It's Pearson, Your Lordship. Remember me? Your solicitor?"

"Of course I remember you, you little fool. I'm not senile, you know. I'm just dying. What are you doing here?"

"When you asked me to fetch Master Roderick from London, I took it upon myself to accompany him and pay my respects." Pearson, a servile and nervous fellow, clasped his hat to his chest as he spoke.

"I would prefer being shown respect, not having it paid to me," the old Earl coughed. "Very well, since you're here anyway, perhaps you can assist Roderick in explaining this!" He grabbed a folded newspaper from his night table and struck his nephew in the face with it. The unflappable Roderick merely smiled innocently.

"Wh-whatever are you referring to, Your Lordship?" Pearson stammered.

"You know damned well what I am referring to, you lickspittle!" the old Earl bellowed, his anger drawing forth reserves of hitherto unsuspected strength. "There, in black and white, on the back page."

Oh, Lord, he's seen it! Pearson thought with despair. But to maintain the fiction of his noninvolvement, he turned to the back page of the newspaper and took a moment to read the advertisement which he himself had composed.

NOTICE TO SELL

His Lordship the Earl of Selwyn wishes to make known his willingness to dispose of certain objets d'art and antiquities which form part of the private Selwyn collection. Grecian urns, mediæval armor, Egyptian mummies, paintings by Gainsborough and Turner, and other valuable pieces are included in this offer. Interested parties should contact Mr. Horace Pearson, Esq., 37 Saville Row, London.

Pearson licked his lips and muttered, "Oh dear. Oh dear."

"I do not recall contemplating such a sale, Mr. Horace Pearson Esquire," the old Earl shouted. "But the explanation is of course obvious. It is not the fourteenth Earl of Selwyn who is interested in selling off the family collection, but the fifteenth." He grabbed the paper away from Pearson and struck Roderick with it once again. "Well, the fourteenth Earl is still breathing, thank you very much. And nothing, not one piece of that collection is to be sold, not now, not ever!"

Roderick sat down gently on the side of the bed and patted his uncle's hand once again. "Now don't upset yourself, Uncle. You shouldn't be worrying about such trivial—"

"It isn't trivial, damn you! It is a matter of the most vital importance. Roderick, how could you take it upon yourself to place this notice without consulting me. Is this a sense of propriety? And you!" he said, turning his wrath on the cowering Pearson. "Who is your employer, I or my worthless nephew?"

"Now don't be yelling at Pearson," Roderick interjected hastily. "I placed the notice myself without discussing it with him. He knows nothing about it."

God bless you, Master Roderick, Pearson thought.

"Do you think I'm foolish enough to believe that?" the old Earl muttered, seeming to lapse back into lassitude. "On your own you couldn't place a golf ball on a tee, let alone a notice in a newspaper." He sighed.

"Listen, Uncle," Roderick said, "I admit I was a bit precipitous. But, really, why should we keep all that old rubbish up there in the attic? It serves no purpose. It isn't displayed. No one ever sees it. Why not just sell it so that people can at least enjoy it all?"

The old Earl laughed humorlessly. "Oh, I see. It's altruism, is it? Philanthropy?"

"Of course it is."

"Then why sell it? Why not just donate it?" Roderick smiled sheepishly and shrugged. "Bah!" the old Earl grumbled. "You have more money than you know what to do with, and still you want more." He shook his head. "Thank God your parents didn't live long enough to see what you've turned into."

"Really, Uncle," Roderick said, his tone one of hurt and wounded pride.

"Don't 'Really Uncle' me, Roderick. You don't know what you're doing. You couldn't know . . ." He seemed to sink back into the pillows, suddenly once again weak, old, ill.

Pearson coughed softly and muttered, "If you will excuse me—"

"Come back here, Pearson," the old Earl said. "I want you to hear this." He turned to Roderick and said, "Listen to me carefully, nephew. You were indeed precipitous, and not so much as you may think. I will be dead soon, Roderick, and you will be the Earl of Selwyn, and you—stop grinning, you young idiot! This is important!—and you will have responsibilities. Life is not one long cocktail party. Your family have been loyal and useful servants of the Crown since the days of Henry II . . ."

As the old Earl commenced upon his labored and uninteresting account of the family, Roderick plastered a look of rapt attention upon his face and promptly allowed his mind to wander. The fifteenth Earl of Selwyn. What a nice sound that had to it! He pictured himself entering the House of Lords in his robes (he loved to dress up) and could barely suppress a smile of anticipation. Chudley would belong to him, along with the stables, the yachts, the investments, the banks. Though he had only a vague idea how much money the old Earl had and where it came from (never having interested himself in such boring and mundane matters), he knew that it ran into the hundreds of millions of pounds.

"RODERICK!"

He snapped suddenly back to attention. "I'm listening, Uncle. Truly I am."

The old Earl pounded his fist feebly on the bed and muttered, "If only Richard had lived."

The reference to the dead cousin he had never known did not bother Roderick. His ego was so well insulated that nothing could bruise it. "Yes, yes, I know," he said soothingly.

"But be at peace, Uncle. I shall discharge my responsibilities in such a manner as will do well to the family honor."

The old Earl gazed at him piercingly. "I wish to extract a promise from you, nephew, in the presence of this witness." He nodded in the general direction of Pearson.

"Certainly, Uncle. Anything you wish." A promise is just words, after all, he thought.

"When you become the Earl of Selwyn, all of the property I now hold will be yours. That is your right as an Englishman and a peer. Even after the government takes its booty, you will be wealthy beyond your wildest dreams. There will be no need to sell any of the collection."

"Of course, Uncle. I—"

"Shut up and listen! I repeat, it will all be yours. I do not believe that it will be necessary to sell anything, but that will be your decision to make." He took hold of Roderick's hand and squeezed it hard. "But not the seven boxes."

Roderick was momentarily confused. "You mean the mummies?"

"Yes, the mummies." The old Earl furrowed his brow. "How did you know that the boxes contained mummies, by the way? I don't recall ever telling you that. I don't recall ever telling anyone that."

Roderick shrugged. "Oh, I just opened one of them up and had a look."

"You what!?" The old Earl's face grew suddenly panicked. "You opened the boxes!?"

"Just one of them, Uncle."

"What in God's name for?"

"I was curious. They've been up there for as long as I can remember, and I just wanted to see what was in them, that's all."

"Did you touch it?"

"The box?"

"The mummy, you idiot, the mummy!"

"What, touch a mouldering old corpse?" He laughed. "I rather think not."

"Tell me the truth, Roderick, please! No games, now, please!"

He was somewhat perplexed by his uncle's sudden agitation. "That is the truth, Uncle. I opened one of the boxes, took a peek inside, and then shut it again. Honestly."

The old Earl heaved a sigh of relief. "Then listen to me,

my boy, and give me your word, in front of this witness." As if it were an afterthought happily had, he said to Pearson, "Get the Bible from the dressing table. Give it to the boy." Pearson complied, and the old Earl said, "Place your hand on the book, Roderick, and listen to me very carefully. I want your solemn oath, your word as a Christian gentleman."

Roderick, who had never given religion a moment's thought and who had no idea what it meant to be a gentleman as the old Earl used the word, said, "Certainly, Uncle."

"I want you to promise me that you will never sell the mummies, never donate them, release them, or in any other way relinquish ownership of them. Promise!"

"I promise, Uncle."

"I want you to promise me that you will never open the boxes, never touch the mummies in any way for any reason."

"I promise."

"I want you to promise me that if any circumstance ever arises, any circumstance at all, which necessitates the selling of the manor and the lands, you will not leave the mummies here. I want you to promise that you will take them with you from this place and bury them, deeply, very deeply, secretly, with no marker, no publicity, no knowledge of the act by anyone save yourself."

"I promise."

The old Earl held his gaze. "Swear by Almighty God."

"I swear by Almighty God."

The old Earl nodded, somewhat, though not fully, contented. "Roderick, there is a teakwood box from India in the safe where the family documents are kept. After my death I want you to read the materials in the box. Pay careful attention to them. There is a document written by your great-grandfather which contains information which each successive Earl of Selwyn must know. Read it carefully and then put it back. When and if you marry and have an heir, be certain that he reads the document as well. And you must extract from him the same promises I have just extracted from you. Is that understood?"

"Yes, Uncle, I understand perfectly."

He nodded again. "Good. Now get out of here, both of you, and let me die in peace." He sank deeper into his pillows and closed his eyes.

Roderick and Pearson left the room quietly and closed the door softly behind them. "Master Roderick—" Pearson began.

"Shhh," the young man silenced him, motioning the solicitor to follow him down the hall and away from the old Earl's door. They walked in silence through the corridors of the old mansion which was soon to be Roderick's possession. They came at last to one of the upstairs sitting rooms. "Well," Roderick said at last, "what on earth was that all about!"

"Master Roderick," Pearson gushed, "thank you ever so much for denying my complicity in this. I don't know what I would have—"

Roderick dismissed the solicitor's gratitude with a wave of his hand. "Oh, it was nothing. From the looks of him, he's not going to be around long enough to cause any trouble anyway." He smiled with a small degree of genuine sadness. "Poor old bugger."

"Still, I am deeply appreciative. If there is ever anything that I can do—"

"Well, you can tell me how the negotiations have been going."

Pearson seemed not to understand. "Negotiations. What negotiations?"

"The offers to buy all that old junk Uncle has stashed away upstairs." He smiled at the look of incredulity on Pearson's face. "Oh, come now, old fellow, you don't seriously expect me to be bound by a promise extorted from me by a half-dead old man, do you? Why, I doubt the old boy is in possession of his faculties anymore."

"But—but—you gave him your word. You swore." Pearson, a devout Methodist, seemed unfamiliar with Roderick's brand of religious indifference.

Roderick shook his head. "An act of kindness to a dying man, nothing more. When a man on his deathbed asks you to promise something, you promise it. No one would seriously expect you to abide by such a thing." He laughed. "And what a promise. My God, you'd think those boxes contained chemical weapons or something, the way he talked."

"Yes, but still"—Pearson was troubled by his part in so egregious a deception—"His Lordship's wishes were quite clear on this point."

Roderick patted Pearson sympathetically on the shoulder. "I know how you feel, Pearson. I really do. You've served Uncle for—how long has it been?"

"Thirty years, sir. And my father served His Lordship's

father before him, and my grandfather your great-grand-father."

"Yes, well that's my point exactly, don't you see? Soon I shall be the fifteenth Earl of Selwyn, and I expect you to be as faithful to me, to the new Earl, as you and your family have been for generations."

"But His Lordship—"

"Is not long for this world. And then I shall be His Lordship." Roderick smiled. "So let's not waste time on this foolish regret, shall we? The rubbish up in the attic—"

"Antiques and works of art are hardly rubbish, sir!" Pearson pointed out deferentially.

"Eye of the beholder, my good fellow, eye of the beholder. They are useless to me; therefore they are rubbish. I have no need of them, no desire to possess them. And better to sell them than to toss them away."

"Begging your pardon, Master Roderick," Pearson said tentatively, "and meaning no disrespect, but if that's the way you feel about the collection, why not just leave it as it is, where it is, I mean, and leave it intact to your heir?" He shifted nervously. "When there is an heir, I mean. I mean—"

Still affable but obviously verging on impatience, Roderick shook his head. "Really, old boy. The matter is closed. Now tell me: have there been any responses to the notice?"

"Oh, yes, certainly," he replied, fumbling in his briefcase for a folder. "I brought the offers with me to show to you in the event we had the opportunity to discuss them." He paused. "Still, after His Lordship—"

"Now, now, no more about the old Earl. Just tell me who has been offering how much for what."

Pearson extracted a few sheets of ledger paper from the folder and looked at them quizzically. Then he clicked his tongue and muttered, "Damn!"

"What's wrong?"

Looking up, he said, "Oh, uh, nothing of moment. You know that the contents of the collection are numbered—inventory purposes, or something of that nature—and when I instructed my secretary to prepare a list of the offers, she did so as if the pieces were to be auctioned rather than sold privately."

Roderick sighed. "Pearson, whatever are you talking about?"

"Well, sir, I have the offers and the amounts, but they are

listed by item number, not by item description. What I mean is, I know what has been offered by the prospective buyers, but not what the offers are for."

"Let me see that." Roderick took the papers from Pearson's hands and glanced over them quickly. "No problem. We'll just go up to the attic and match the offers with the numbers."

"Oh, that's hardly necessary, Master Roderick. I can simply have Gladys do this over tomorrow by item and not by number. There's no need—"

"Yes, but I don't want to wait until tomorrow. I'm dying of curiosity." He strode to the door and Pearson followed unwillingly behind him.

They encountered Fredericks, the butler, at the foot of the stairs leading from the fourth floor of the mansion to the attic, and the old servant bowed slightly and asked, "May I ask if your meeting with His Lordship went well, Master Roderick?"

"Oh, yes, certainly. As well as might be expected under the circumstances."

"I fear he will not spring back from this latest illness with the same alacrity he has shown in the past." The butler's tone was regretful.

"Well, we can always hope, Fredericks," Roderick said cheerfully. "But you must excuse us. We have some inventory to examine up in the attic."

Fredericks did not move from the foot of the stairs. "May I assume that you are referring to the collection, Master Roderick?"

"Yes, indeed," Roderick replied as he walked past Fredericks, Pearson in his wake, and began to mount the stairs. Then he stopped, realizing that the old butler might have some notion as to the cause of the old Earl's peculiar preoccupation with the seven mummies. "By the way, Fredericks," he began, turning to him, "how long have you been with the family?"

The butler drew himself up proudly and replied, "I began to serve His Lordship the same year that King Edward VII passed away."

Pearson gasped slightly. "My God! How old are you, man?"

"What year was that, Pearson?" Roderick asked.

"Edward VII died in 1910! I do not mean to impugn . . ."

Fredericks smiled slightly. "Allow me to explain. I had the honor of being His Lordship's whipping boy when we were children."

"Whipping boy!" Roderick was astonished. "Are you trying to tell us that my uncle had a whipping boy!?"

"Oh, most assuredly, sir. The thirteenth Earl was a very old-fashioned gentleman. My father was butler to the thirteenth Earl, and he counted it a singular honor to have his son appointed to that post." He paused slightly. "As did I, of course."

"So it was your childhood association with my uncle which led to your becoming his butler?"

Fredericks seemed surprised, and slightly annoyed, at the question. "Surely you know, sir, that my family has been providing service to your esteemed family for over three hundred years!"

Roderick realized at once that he had been told this sometime or other, but he had paid no attention to it. "Oh, yes, of course. How silly of me."

Fredericks seemed slightly mollified. "As I am certain you are aware, your chauffeur, Geoffrey, is my nephew."

"Yes, yes, of course, of course," Roderick said, though he had no idea this was the case. "Let me ask you something. You've been with my uncle for so long, you might know the answer."

"If I can be of help, it would be my pleasure."

"I just had the most bizarre conversation with him about certain pieces in the collection. Uncle seems to have an almost obsessive concern about the mummies. Do you know of anything which might explain that?"

Fredericks looked at him uncomprehendingly. "The mummies, sir?"

"Yes, the mummies. In the collection upstairs."

The butler shook his head. "To the best of my knowledge there are no mummies in His Lordship's collection."

"But of course there are. I saw one of them myself, not two weeks ago." Fredericks continued to stare at him in confusion. "Surely you have seen those seven crates up there, haven't you?"

Fredericks's face lit up with sudden understanding. "Oh, the crates! Yes, certainly. I'm sorry, sir. I had no idea what was in them. Mummies, you say? That's very interesting."

"Yes, well, do you know anything about them?"

The butler shook his head. "No, sir, not a thing. They were there the first time I ever had occasion to go into the attic. To the best of my knowledge they've been there for generations. At least, I don't recall anyone ever having said anything about the time or means of their acquisition." He stopped and his brow slowly furrowed.

"Something?" Roderick asked. "Do you recall something?"

"Perhaps," Fredericks said pensively. "You have stirred a memory in me, sir, about an incident a long time ago. Back during the war, it was."

"Which war?" Pearson asked. With men as old as Fredericks one had to ask such questions.

"The second one, Mr. Pearson," he replied. "I remember thinking at the time how odd it was, but of course I never asked, and, well, so much else was happening—"

"What is the incident?"

"Well, sir, you know that His Lordship's late wife and son died when a German buzz bomb hit the estate in—let me see—late in 1941, I believe. It fell to me to call His Lordship at the War Office in London with the news, and . . ." He stopped speaking, as if seeking to clear away the cobwebs of memory.

After a few moments Roderick asked, "Well? What happened? Get on with it, man!" This mild irritation was as angry as Pearson had ever seen Roderick.

"Well, sir, I recall that when I finally reached him, I told him that the estate had been hit, and before I could say another word he ordered me, almost in a frenzy, to check and see if any damage had been done to the seven crates in the attic. I tried to tell him about Her Ladyship and Master Richard, but he wouldn't allow me to speak. In fact, as I recall, he shouted at me, 'You goddamned bloody fool, get up to the attic and examine those crates!' He was quite agitated, sir, and I hadn't even informed him of the death of his wife and son."

Roderick listened pensively. "Then what?"

"Well, sir, I did as I was instructed. I examined each of the seven crates and found each to be securely sealed and locked, as always. Then I returned to the phone and told him so. He said 'Thank God,' or words to that effect. Then I discharged my less happy obligation." He paused and shook his head. "I never did understand that, Master Roderick. I would think that if a bomb hits a man's home, his first concern would be for his family, not his artwork."

"Yes, one would think so," Roderick replied. "Well, thank you, Fredericks. You've been most helpful."

"My pleasure, sir," Fredericks said, bowing slightly.

Roderick proceeded to ascend the stairs, Pearson following

two steps behind him. As they rounded the landing which separated the two flights, Pearson said, "A most peculiar tale."

"Yes, but Uncle is a peculiar fellow. I don't really understand it at all." He paused for a moment. "Say, Pearson."

"Yes, Master Roderick?"

"You don't think there's something valuable locked up in those crates, do you? Gold or silver or something?"

Pearson shook his head. "It isn't likely, sir. Precious metals could be more easily and safely stored than by packing them away in the attic."

"Yes, but what if it isn't coins or bars? What if it's jewelry or loose gems? What if it's something we can't even imagine?" He was obviously relishing the possibility of unexpected treasure. "What if—"

"But sir, you opened one box yourself. You found nothing in it but a mummy."

"Yes, but I only opened one of them." He proceeded to leap up the stairs eagerly. Pearson heaved a sigh of regret and followed after. He reached the attic door just as Roderick, who had turned the key in the lock, was pushing it open. "Come on, Pearson, hurry up. Isn't this exciting?"

"Yes, Master Roderick," he muttered.

The two men moved through the attic which housed the Selwyn collection. To call it a collection was technically accurate, but the implication of an organized, displayed, cherished private museum was totally misleading. The Earls of Selwyn had been accumulating works of art for generations without the slightest urge to do anything with the pieces they acquired other than to lock them away in the attic. The pieces were numbered and listed, of course, as was everything else of value at Chudley; but once their presence had been registered, they were stored haphazardly. Paintings leaned in thick stacks against the wall. Urns, statues, busts, and boxes of miscellaneous objects lay everywhere. Enough armor was present to outfit a cortege of knights.

Roderick walked quickly through the room, knocking over a Renoir, hopping over a bust of Caracalla, to get to the seven crates which rested upon the floor near the south wall of the room. He was impervious to the effect the room had upon most people who entered it, such as Pearson at that very moment. The room smelled of age and ancient dust. In its dimly lighted atmosphere an aura of some strange sanctity seemed to pervade everything, even the most mundane of objects.

Pearson stood motionless, drinking in the antiquity, allowing waves of romanticism to wash over him.

"Pearson! Come, help me with this!"

Roderick's command interrupted his reverie. "Oh, yes, sir. Coming."

Pearson found him struggling to insert the edge of a crowbar under the top plank of one of the crates. "Get that other tool and work on the other end, will you? That's a good fellow." Six of the crates were stacked one atop another, with the seventh crate lying beside them. It was this seventh crate, the one offering the easiest access, which Roderick had opened previously. He seemed determined now to open the rest, already having cut the binding ropes.

Pearson went to work on the crate with a shrug of resignation. This somewhat silly man was soon to be the fifteenth Earl of Selwyn, and as such represented the source of a sizeable percentage of the income of Pearson's firm. One of the earliest lessons he had learned in his law career was that eccentric clients must be catered to.

They managed to loosen and then remove the crate cover in a few minutes. Much to Pearson's chagrin, another box lay within the one they had just opened. "Oh dear," he sighed. "Is this nailed shut also?"

"No, not the coffins." He grinned at Pearson's discomfort. "Well, they are dead people, after all. You don't just dump them in a hole, then, do you? They must have coffins." He reached into the box and drew open the coffin lid, which was apparently much lighter than one might expect. Pearson knew enough to know that coffins of any age or nation would be built rather sturdily. But Roderick had flipped up the lid without the slightest difficulty. He could tell from the sigh which issued forth from the young man that the treasure of Croesus had not found its resting place in the crates in Chudley's attic.

"Damn," Roderick muttered. "It's just like the other one!"

"How do you mean, sir?"

"Well, come here and look."

Pearson smiled nervously. "I'd rather not, if it's all the same to you, sir."

"Don't be silly. It can't hurt you."

"With all due respect, Master Roderick, that's hardly the point. I'm not particularly fond of the—shall we say, the grotesque?"

"Very well, very well. It doesn't matter." He reached into

the crate and pulled out a small golden medallion. "Here, take a look at this." He held it up for Pearson to see.

"Was the—" he paused, "the late gentleman wearing this, sir?"

"At one time, apparently. Now it's just lying beside him in the box. I found a similar medal in the other box I opened. Think it's worth anything?"

Pearson shrugged. "I'm no expert on such things, but I would assume it has some value. I tend to think, however, that its presence in the crate with the other object would make it valuable more as part of the same sale item than as a separate piece."

Roderick nodded dejectedly. "Probably correct. I don't suppose there's really any point in opening the rest of them, do you?"

Daring to hope for the best, the solicitor eagerly agreed. "Oh, I'm sure there isn't, Master Roderick. I think we had best just proceed as originally planned." He pointed at the briefcase which he had leaned against a Byzantine icon. "I do have the price offers and the item numbers, if you would like to—"

"Oh, yes, of course," Roderick said, remembering why they had begun to ascend to the attic in the first place. "Well, let's get to it."

"I took the liberty of bringing the list of insurance amounts on each item as well, for purposes of comparison."

"Oh, they're all insured, are they?"

Somewhat taken aback at Roderick's lack of practicality, he nodded. "Of course they are, sir. Everything of value is insured."

"How comforting." Pearson could not tell if Roderick was being sarcastic or simply honest in his ignorance. He chose to assume the latter.

They worked their ways through the lists for well over an hour. Pearson would read off the item number from the insurance list and the amount for which it was insured; Roderick would search about for the object so numbered. Realizing the inefficiency of this procedure, they soon switched roles. Roderick would read off the item number from the object itself, and Pearson would leaf through the pages in an attempt to find it.

The names and descriptions rolled off like a museum inventory, which is what in a sense it was. Gauguin, Holbein, Dürer, busts of the Caesars, armament from the Wallenstein

army in the Thirty Years War, first editions of Milton and
Goethe . . .

They were finished at last, and Roderick was well pleased
with the offers Pearson had received for each of the items
offered for sale. "Wait a moment," he said. "What about those
mummies?"

"Wait a moment. . . . wait a moment. . . ." Pearson
went over to the crates and knelt down beside them. He ran
his hands over the wood, looked around the sides, even
struggled to move the lone crate so as to look at its back. He
bent, craned, crawled, and delved, but to no avail. "I'm sorry,
Master Roderick. There doesn't seem to be a number on these
crates."

"Really? How irritating."

"You don't seem to understand, sir. We've gone though the
entire list. That, plus the fact that there are no numbers,
means that these pieces are not insured."

Roderick seemed slightly surprised, but not shocked.
"Hm. How unusual."

Pearson was only half listening to him. "These crates are
apparently more important to His Lordship than anything else
in the world. I can't believe that they were never insured."

"Perhaps they aren't worth very much," Roderick mused.
"That would explain why they aren't insured, wouldn't it?"

"Yes, but it wouldn't explain why they are so important to
His Lordship." Pearson shook his head. "There is something
here I do not understand."

"Well, I'm not going to worry about it. I plan to sell them
anyway. I don't suppose it really matters that they weren't
insured, does it." It was a statement, not a question.

"No, no, I suppose not," Pearson replied, nodding. "Still,
if we have to ship them somewhere, we had better get some
insurance on them."

"Why waste the money? If we have a firm offer to buy, why
not put the burden of insurance on the buyer?"

Pearson considered for a moment explaining to Roderick
the ways in which business was conducted, and then thought
the better of it. It would be a waste of words. "Yes, well, we
can look into that."

"You do that, Pearson, by all means." Roderick straightened his back uncomfortably. "All this hopping about and
lifting things has quite tuckered me out. Will you join me for a
brandy before calling it a night?" He smiled. "You will spend
the night, won't you?"

"Thank you, no. I must be in London early tomorrow morning. I will join you in a brandy, though."

"Fine, fine." Roderick proceeded to engage Pearson in the easy small talk at which he excelled admirably. They returned to the sitting room, where Roderick poured a brandy for each of them. Raising his glass, Roderick said, "To your health, Mr. Pearson."

"And to yours, sir," was the reply. "And to that of His Lordship."

Roderick laughed. "Oh, yes, fine. Certainly." Still laughing, he sipped. Pearson, not at all amused, sipped from his glass also. "Tell me, Pearson, what shall we do with those damned crates? If no one knows we have them, no one will—"

"Oh, gracious! We have an offer for them also."

"We do? Why didn't you mention it to me upstairs?"

"Well, I was waiting until we got to their item numbers on the insurance list. Of course, we never did, because they aren't insured."

"Oh. Well, no harm done. What is the offer?"

"Well, sir," Pearson said, sipping another bit of his brandy, "I received a phone call the day after the notice appeared in the press. A young lady named—wait a moment." He put his glass down and shuffled through his briefcase before pulling out an obviously handwritten memo. "Ah, here it is. Yes, yes, this is it."

"Another brandy?" Roderick was holding the bottle aloft.

"Oh, no, not for me, thank you, Master Roderick." He restrained his urge to comment on the extent of Roderick's drinking. "Shall I?"

"Oh, yes, yes, please continue." Roderick took a large gulp of brandy.

"Well, the day after the notice appeared in the press I received a phone call from the United States, from a young lady named—" he glanced at the paper, "Dr. Harriet Langly. Miss—I mean *Doctor* Langly told me that she is the curator of a museum in a small college—" another glance at the paper, "Winthrop College in Greenfield, the state of New York. She was quite excited about the mummies." He paused. "Odd thing for a young girl—"

"How young is she?" At last, a subject in which Roderick showed some normal interest.

"Oh, I don't know. I just mean she seemed to sound young on the telephone. She has a doctoral degree, so I don't suppose she can be too young."

"Probably a wrinkled old hag." Roderick laughed. "Go on."

"She says that her budget is not large, but she has been authorized to make some expenditures for the purpose of upgrading the college's museum collection."

"What level of expenditure did she mention?" He poured himself another brandy.

"She suggested five thousand dollars per mummy, a total of thirty-five thousand dollars, to be paid at the rate of thirty-five hundred dollars per year for ten years."

Roderick nodded. He took another drink and then asked, "Tell me, Pearson, how much is that in real money?"

"Real money, sir?"

"Yes, real money. Pounds and pence."

"Oh, I'm sorry, sir." Pearson searched about in his pocket for a calculator, but had not brought one with him. "Well, I can estimate the amount roughly, if that's all right."

Roderick waved his hand expansively. "Certainly. Go right ahead."

"Well, let me see. . . ." He did a bit of mental multiplication. "It would be approximately thirty-five hundred pounds for each mummy, for a total of twenty-four thousand five hundred pounds, paid at the rate of twenty-four hundred pounds per year for ten years."

Roderick was crestfallen. "Is that all? That's absurd!"

"I'm sorry, sir, it isn't. In fact, it's the best offer we have received. I'm afraid that there is something of a glut on the market. Every little museum apparently has its own mummy. I called the British Museum, the Louvre, and the Metropolitan Museum in New York—to see what price they might be willing to offer, you understand—"

"Yes? And?"

"They all gave the same answer. They would accept the mummies as a donation to the museum, but none of them would pay a brass farthing for them."

"Hm! No wonder they aren't insured. They aren't worth anything!"

"Begging your pardon, sir, but they are worth twenty-four thousand pounds to Dr. Langly."

"Well . . ." He seemed unwilling to accept the facts. He had hoped to realize a good deal more than the amount mentioned from the sale. "Why can't she pay us all at once? Why over ten years?"

"Budget problems on her side. As I said, it's a small

college. I don't imagine they have much of a museum budget. Besides, it might be to your advantage to receive payment over an extended period."

"Howso?"

"Taxes, sir. The longer the period of payment, the less the tax burden."

"Oh, really?" Roderick was as innocent of the tax law as he was of almost everything else in the world of finance. "Well, I suppose we'd best do it, then, eh?"

"I do think that it's the best offer we're likely to receive."

"New York. Is that anywhere near Orlando?" He pronounced it AwLAHNdo.

"I don't think so, sir. I believe that—"

"You know, Pearson, I've always meant to go to that Disney fellow's place over there in America." He poured himself yet another drink. "I do believe I shall! Listen here, old boy. As soon as Uncle passes away, you fix up the deal with this Langly woman and book me on the Concorde to America along with the crates."

"I don't know if the Concorde carries freight, sir."

"Well, whatever, whatever. You handle the details. I shall deliver the pieces personally and then go to this amusement park everybody seems so enthusiastic about."

"Master Roderick, I don't believe that New York is anywhere near—"

The entrance of Fredericks the butler interrupted their conversation. "Excuse me, gentlemen. I think you had better come, Master Roderick."

"Come? Come where?"

"It's His Lordship, sir. I fear that he is sinking."

"Really? Strange. He seemed strong enough a little while ago. I'll certainly, but—"

Fredericks did not propose to debate the point. "Please come now, sir."

Roderick sighed. "Oh, very well." He drained his glass, placed it on the table, and followed Fredericks out of the sitting room. Pearson followed at a discreet distance.

They walked down the long corridor toward the old Earl's room, and Roderick was made slightly uneasy by the servants who lined the hallway on both sides. Some damned death ritual, no doubt, he thought. The servants looked at him kindly and sadly, trying to express sympathy with a grief he did not feel.

They entered the bedroom silently. A nurse was bending

over the old man, listening to his heart and lungs with a stethoscope. Fredericks whispered, "I've summoned the doctor, but . . ." He left the sentence unfinished, but his meaning was clear.

The old Earl turned his head painfully in the direction of the open door. His body was trembling, and his breathing loud and liquid. He raised one weak hand and gestured for Roderick to approach. The young man did as he was bidden, and sat down beside the old Earl, taking his hand and holding it gently. "Relax, Uncle. Everything is going to be all right." The old Earl muttered something weakly. "What? I can't understand you, Uncle."

"Remember . . . remember . . ." Remember your promise, the old man was thinking. Remember what I told you to do.

"Remember what, Uncle?" Roderick had already forgotten.

A wave of rage washed over the old man's face, and he raised a fist as if to strike his nephew. Then, suddenly, he dropped back upon the pillow and, with a long, labored breath, he died.

The room was silent as the nurse applied the stethoscope once more to the old man's chest. She looked at Roderick and shook her head sadly. "I'm sorry." She gathered up her equipment.

Roderick felt nervous for some reason, but it passed almost as quickly as it had come. This was one advantage of superficiality. He turned to find Fredericks and Pearson facing him. Both bowed slightly as Fredericks said, "Your Lordship."

He acknowledged their salutation with a curt nod, and head high, back straight—the epitome of noble dignity—he exited the room and walked slowly down the corridor.

Pearson turned to Fredericks and said, "I'll make the funeral arrangements and begin probate proceedings. We shouldn't burden Master—I mean, His Lordship at such a time."

"Yes, yes, of course." They watched him as he strode slowly away. "A great responsibility to be thrust on such young shoulders. He must have enough on his mind right now without having to fret over such things."

"Yes, yes, indeed." Pearson sighed. "The late Earl was all the family the poor boy had. I can imagine what he must be feeling and thinking just now." Fredericks nodded sadly.

As he walked down the corridor, the fifteenth Earl of Selwyn was thinking, I'm going to go to Disneyland!

# CHAPTER 2

▲ When the phone rang at three in the morning it did not find Harriet Langly sleeping. She had been awake most of the night, though she had retired somewhat earlier than usual. She had reasoned that the approaching day was to be probably the most important day in her professional life, and she wanted to be well rested. Having told herself this, of course, she caused her own insomnia. She had lain tossing and turning since ten in the evening, and now, five hours later, she was still awake.

Thus, when the phone rang she picked it up on the second ring and said "Hello?" in her customary clear, precise voice, no differently than if it had been three in the afternoon.

"Hi! did I wake you up?"

"Don't be silly. I've been up all night counting canopic jars."

"Counting what?"

"That's an Egyptologist joke."

"Oh. Good one, Harriet."

"Where are you calling from?"

"We're at Kennedy Airport. Got here about a half-hour ago. Your friend with the truck was here waiting, and the exhibits are all loaded, safe and secure."

"Fantastic!" Harriet said as she hopped from the bed, phone in hand, and began to search with her toes for her slippers beneath the bedside. "That's great. No problems at all, then, right?"

"Not a one. We got through customs without a hitch. They didn't even open the crates. They just examined the papers and our credentials." Suzanne Melendez laughed on the other end of the phone line. "The Earl kind of greased our way through."

"You don't mean he bribed the officials! There's no need—"

"Oh, no, nothing like that. He just talked our way through. I think that man could charm the tusks off an elephant."

"Oh, good." Harriet repressed a brief surge of panic. She wanted nothing questionable done which might jeopardize the transfer of ownership from the Selwyn collection to the museum. For an instant a headline flashed through her mind: Earl of Selwyn Arrested in Bribe Attempt. Shipment Secured in Government Warehouse. She was relieved to hear that nothing improper had been attempted, especially because nothing improper was necessary. "Don't scare me like that."

"Relax, honey. Everything's fine and we'll be on our way in a few minutes. I just called to tell you because I knew you'd be worried."

"Thanks, Suzie. You know me pretty well. I've had butterflies in my stomach all week."

"Well, take it easy. I'll be there with the Earl and the seven late gentlemen in about four hours."

"The who?"

Suzanne laughed. "That's what his lawyer, Mr. Pearson, calls the mummies. The 'seven late gentlemen.' Isn't that a scream?"

"Cute." Harriet smiled. "What's he like?"

"Who, the Earl?"

"Yeah."

"He's a dream. I adore him. You'll hate him."

"You mean I'd better hate him, because you adore him?"

"Damn right."

She laughed. "Okay, I promise to detest him thoroughly."

A pause on the other end as Suzanne spoke to someone near her. "Harriet? I have to sign off now. Your friend Mr. Foster wants to hit the road. He says he's afraid of hitting rush hour traffic."

Rush hour traffic! Harriet thought. Will Foster is such a pain. When rush hour begins, four hours from now, it will be heading toward Manhattan, not away from it. But it was good of him to drive down with his truck to pick up the exhibits, so Harriet decided not to make any remarks about him. "Okay, Suzie. We'll be waiting for you at the museum. You think you'll get here about seven?"

"Better make it eight. We're going to stop for a bite to eat in New Paltz."

"Don't leave the truck unguarded!" Panic rose again.

"Relax, Harriet. Jesus! I'm the one who underwrote the insurance on these things. Do you think I'm going to take any chances with them?"

"No, no, of course not. Sorry. It's just that I'm—well—"

"Yeah, yeah, I know. I understand." Her voice was kind, though just a bit condescending. "Look, I gotta go. Bye."

"Bye." She heard the click on the other end and then put down the receiver. Harriet sat back down on the bed and glanced at the clock. The numbers 3:12 blinked on and off at her. She considered for a moment trying to go back to sleep, and then decided against it. She could put this time to much better use. She wouldn't be able to sleep anyway. Though she had already spent weeks getting the museum ready for the arrival of the exhibits, she figured she might as well go there early for one final check.

Harriet walked out of her bedroom and into the kitchen. She put some coffee on and dropped a few bread slices into the toaster. The phone rang again and she ran into the bedroom to answer it, praying that it would not be Suzanne telling her that a plane had just crashed on top of the truck. "Hello?" she said breathlessly.

"Hi, sweetheart. I knew you'd be awake, so I decided to call and calm your nerves."

She heaved a sigh of relief. "Tommy! Thank God it's you."

Dr. Thomas Sawhill laughed. "Hey, I think that's the nicest thing you've ever said to me!"

"Don't be too flattered," she said, laughing also. "I just meant—"

"I know, I know. You're waiting for a call telling you the exhibits have been hijacked, right?"

"Something like that. Jeeze, are my paranoias that obvious to everybody? Suzanne just called to tell me that they arrived okay, now you call to calm me down—everybody seems to know that I'm wide awake at three in the morning!"

"We just know you, babe, that's all. If your roommate from college and your husband-to-be didn't understand how your mind works, then nobody would."

"I guess that's true," she replied, smiling. "I can't help but be a bit nervous."

"Of course. There'd be something wrong with you if you

weren't. This is a major step for you. It will look great on a résumé."

"That's not why I'm doing it, Tommy, and you know it."

"I know. But it doesn't hurt to be able to say that you managed to create a legitimate museum out of a dumpy college warehouse."

"Tommy, it already was a legitimate museum when they hired me as curator. It just had a severely limited collection."

"Well, you've made it grow."

She accepted the compliment. "Want to come over for breakfast? I have some coffee going."

"Are you kidding? I'm going back to sleep."

"How can you sleep on a day like this?"

"Hey, they aren't my mummies! I just called to tell you not to worry, that the exhibits will get here all right, and that I'll see you at the museum at seven."

"You can be a little late. Suzie says that they're going to stop for breakfast when they reach New Paltz."

Thomas Sawhill's rather groggy voice became suddenly serious. "I hope they know enough not to just leave the truck in some parking lot while they eat. I mean, those pieces are valuable, and—"

She laughed. "Now who's being paranoid? I don't think anyone's going to break into the truck and steal dead bodies!" She knew that he pretended not to have any interest in the exhibits, but she also knew that, for her sake, he was as excited about the acquisition as she was. This was one of the things which endeared him to her, the fact that he took her career seriously. All too many men in the past had regarded it as a hobby. "Suzie assured me that they'll keep the shipment secure."

"Well, that's good. Ever since you told me what she was like when you went to college together—"

"That was fifteen years ago, Tom. She's changed. And besides, I was the exact same way back then. If you can't be irresponsible and self-indulgent in college, when can you be?"

"Well, I never was."

"Your loss."

"Don't be nasty." He chuckled as he spoke. "I'm going back to bed. I'll see you about seven. Bye."

"Bye."

Harriet went back out to the kitchen to find her toast burned beyond redemption, but the coffee smelled good. Just as well, she thought. I couldn't eat anything right now anyway. She poured herself a cup of coffee and walked back into the bedroom.

As she sat down in front of the mirror which was the upper part of the rear panel of her vanity, she gazed at her reflection and thought contentedly about her current situation. She had everything she had ever really wanted out of life. All the work she had put in at the University of Chicago, where she earned her doctorate in Egyptology at one of the world's best departments dedicated to that arcane discipline, had been worthwhile. Oh, Winthrop College was not Yale or Harvard, that was obvious. But it was a good school, small, serious, high standards, exclusive in the purest academic sense. Her dual role as professor of cultural anthropology and curator of the small but, under her guidance, growing Winthrop Museum afforded her all the professional satisfaction she could possibly want. She had scored quite a personal triumph in beating whatever competition there may have been in the purchase of the seven mummies, and she contemplated the expanded, increasingly well known little museum with no small degree of delight.

And there was Tommy. It is difficult enough to find an intelligent, sensitive man under any circumstances, but to find one who understood and encouraged her fascination with the long dead civilization which had been her field of study—that was an incredible stroke of luck. She reflected briefly on the numerous ignoramuses she had dated, and their stupid, childish jokes about Egyptology ("So! You're studying to be a Mummy!"), and felt pleased that Thomas Sawhill contrasted with them so well.

As she looked at her face in the mirror, she smiled. She had always assumed, with the absurd ignorance of childhood, that the body started to decay at thirty. Well, she was nearly half a decade beyond that, and she felt that she had never looked better. Her light blue eyes were unencumbered by crow's-feet, her smooth white skin was still smooth and white. Her long light-brown hair was softly layered around her heart-shaped face and highlighted with subtle streaks of blond. And if she had taken recourse to the color bottle of late to hide those few inevitable hints of gray, what of it?

She stood up and examined her figure in the mirror with the same objective precision she applied to archeological artifacts. I'm no artifact yet, she thought. Her waist was slim, her stomach flat, her breasts high. She had always felt that she was a bit too busty, but it didn't seem to bother Thomas Sawhill. She grinned. Not at all!

She sat down again and sipped from her coffee. It's amazing to think that just three years ago she had been so depressed that she had even, in a moment of alcoholic depression, considered ending it all. She had been unattached and unemployed (there being very little demand for Egyptologists in today's high-tech economy); she had been overweight and deeply in debt.

And then came the job offer at Winthrop College. She had applied for it as a matter of course, but at the time, living in Manhattan and hoping for a position on the faculty of some at least half-way decent college, the idea of moving to a small town like Greenfield up in New York's hinterland to teach at a hole in the wall school like Winthrop seemed like a sentence of professional death. Her first impression of the town had done nothing to alter her opinion. Greenfield was small, pretty, and friendly, but there was nothing in the town other than the college, one short business street, a movie theater, and two bars, one for the college kids and one for the townies.

She almost prayed that the college would not offer her the position, and when they did, it was only the dire economic situation in which she found herself that made her accept it. Her old friend, Suzanne Melendez, with whom she had roomed for four years at the state college at New Paltz, had counseled her to decline the appointment. Of course, Suzanne was a devoted urbanite and regarded any population center of under a million people as a bastion of barbarism.

Well, Suzanne was wrong, and Harriet had made the best decision of her life by accepting the position. She found, much to her surprise, that the school was very selective in its admissions policies, so that the quality of students whom she taught was far above average. The school was generouly funded by a private foundation bequest, thus being able to avoid the kind of financial pressures which so often led small colleges to accept anyone who could pay the tuition. She was given the additional appointment of museum curator after her first year at Winthrop, and she met Thomas Sawhill, the town physician, at a barbecue at the college president's house that summer. It wasn't quite love at first sight, but it came close.

And the town of Greenfield itself had proven to be an extremely pleasant place to live and work. There was an air of calm, of ease of friendliness, of safety here which she had never known, not in New York City, not in Chicago. It was the normal small-town atmosphere, but it was all new to her. She loved it.

Everything was going great. Everything.

And when she saw the notice in the London *Times*, which Suzanne had thoughtfully sent her, she began to think that she had been born under some sort of lucky star. She dared to hope that the modest offer would be considered. She was flabbergasted when it was accepted. Seven mummies from a private collection! Unexamined, uncatalogued, unphotographed, untouched. According to Mr. Pearson, the lawyer she spoke with over the phone, the mummies had been acquired by a previous Earl of Selwyn sometime in the past, no one knew when, and had lain untouched and unopened in the attic of the family mansion. It was almost as if she had discovered them herself. She smiled at the foolishness of the thought. She glanced at the clock.

Harriet shook her head as if to clear it. Stop wasting time, she thought. You have a big day ahead of you. Five o'clock already!

She took a quick shower, put on her makeup a bit more quickly than usual, and dressed. She put on a black ruffled blouse and black slacks. She chose black because she anticipated having to do some crawling around on her hands and knees to examine the cases the mummies would doubtless be stored in.

Harriet left her apartment, climbed into her vintage Volkswagen Beetle, and drove the short distance to Winthrop College. She waved as she passed the statue of Montgomery Winthrop, the nineteenth-century tycoon whose largess had created and posthumously sustained the college named for him. Good old Monty, she thought. She pulled into her parking space in the faculty lot and walked the few hundred yards to the Museum.

Tom was joking when he referred to the museum as a dumpy college warehouse, but there was an element of truth to the description. What was now the museum had until only five years before been precisely that, a storage building. It had been her predecessor, now curator of a larger museum at a larger college, who had first sorted through the boxes and piles in the warehouse and discovered that the nucleus of a small

museum collection already existed at Winthrop. True, much of
it consisted of American Indian artifacts and paintings by some
of the lesser luminaries of American brush and canvas, but it
was a start. He, and Harriet after him, had been steadily
accumulating exhibits, a piece here and a piece there, slowly
creating a decent, though somewhat eclectic, collection.

She surveyed her domain from without. The eager and
unpaid labor provided by the students at Winthrop had turned
the warehouse into an attractive little museum. Harriet knew
that museums were generally constructed of brick and stone,
but the pleasant wood with its fresh white paint and red trim
not only preserved the old American atmosphere; it also
seemed to radiate a pristine hominess which could be regarded
as a welcome relief from the austere Gothicism which seemed
to be the impression made by most museums.

She unlocked the door and entered, switching on the light
beside the doorway. She looked around, pleased at the
arrangements she had made for her new exhibits. (Careful,
girl, she thought. They're the museum's exhibits, the college's, not yours. Let's not get territorial.) After checking the
fire alarm circuit, she shut the door.

The Winthrop Museum was housed in one very large room.
The students had made one significant structural change a few
years back, under the watchful eye of a local carpenter who
had donated his time and skills to the project. The building
was two stories in height but had only one floor. The students
had constructed a catwalk which ran along all four sides of the
room, at a height one third of the way up the wall. This
preserved the airiness which the tall, open center of the room
provided, and also allowed the display of exhibits on a second
level. Harriet had placed the Indian artifacts against the west
wall of the ground floor. The south wall was reserved for the
East Asian sculpture which a patron of the school had kindly
provided. The north wall, which contained the entrance way,
was still largely unused but for the table upon which lay guides
and brochures about the college. The walls along the catwalk
were filled with paintings, mostly early twentieth century, a
few nineteenth, a few modern. A long display case along the
west wall catwalk held a collection of vintage swords and other
weapons which had been rusting in the museum when it was
still a warehouse.

The east wall of the lower section was completely empty. It
was here that Harriet intended to place the mummy cases,

resting against the wall. The center of the large, spacious room was at present occupied by seven glass cases, lined in red velvet. The cases were empty. She smiled at them. *You won't be empty for much longer.* It was her intention to display the mummies themselves in the glass cases, not in their own coffins. The coffins were themselves an exhibit, and she reasoned that she was in a sense making two acquisitions for the price of one.

She felt a wave of nervousness fighting its way out of her subconscious, but she repressed it. True, she had no idea what condition the mummies were in, but that was unavoidable. It was the fact that they had never been examined or researched which made them such a fascinating find. She hoped that they were largely intact. She remembered how startled she had been at the lifelike visage of Rameses II in the Cairo Museum, and how sad she felt when she looked at the broken, rotted face of Tutankhamen. *I hope the embalmers who worked on our mummies were the ones who worked on Rameses, not young King Tut!*

As for the coffins themselves, the mummy cases, she was reasonably certain that they would be of decent display quality. No mummy buried in a substandard-quality coffin would have received an embalming which would enable it to survive for so many thousands of years. Even in death the Egyptian class structure had an impact. The fact that the mummies existed at all indicated that they were not paupers, and that their coffins would thus be worth displaying.

She turned her head when she heard a soft knock on the door. Sam Goldhaber, the president of Winthrop College, was smiling at her and half leaning into the room. "Can I come in, boss?" he asked.

Harriet laughed. "Good morning, Sam. You're up bright and early."

The elderly man strode into the room. "I've had this date circled on my calendar for weeks. I wouldn't miss this delivery for anything." He brushed a stray lock of thinning white hair off his forehead. "Are you excited?"

"Oh no," she laughed. "I take possession of ancient Egyptian exhibits every day of the week. Of course I'm excited! I haven't slept a wink all night!"

Goldhaber chuckled kindly. "You've done a splendid job with this project, Harriet. We're all very, very proud of you."

"Thanks, Sam. Thanks for giving me the chance to try."

"My pleasure." He glanced at his watch. "Seven o'clock. When are they scheduled to arrive?"

"I would think sometime between now and eight. Suzanne called me about three—"

"Who?"

"Suzanne—oh, I'm sorry. Suzanne Melendez, my friend with the Surity Insurance Company, who handled the insurance for the shipment."

"Oh, yes, yes, I remember. She called you?"

"Yes, at about three this morning. They were just about to leave Kennedy Airport, and it's about a four-hour drive, and she said they were going to stop for some food—so I figure anywhere between now and eight o'clock."

"I see," he said needlessly. "Well, what shall we do until then?"

"I think I'll just putter around here," Harriet replied. "There's still a lot of things I have to do in here before we can display the exhibits properly, and—"

"Listen, young lady," Sam said with mock avuncularity, "there isn't a damn thing you have to do in here, and if you don't take it easy, you're going to develop a nice little ulcer for yourself."

"Oh, Sam, don't be ridiculous!" she laughed.

"I'm not," he said, his tone serious now. "You're too much of a workaholic."

"I'm not a workaholic at all," she said, a bit defensively. "I just take my job seriously, that's all."

"So do I, but I remember to eat breakfast." He peered at her knowingly over the rims of his glasses. "Did you eat breakfast today?" Her slightly sheepish grin answered his question. "That's what I thought. Let's go to the cafeteria. I'll buy you breakfast."

"Sam—"

He shook his head firmly. "I don't want any undernourished faculty members fainting in the classroom. Now, those are your boss's orders!"

"Doctor's orders too," Thomas Sawhill said from the doorway. "I like my women with some meat on their bones."

"Tom!" she said cheerfully. "You're early."

"Not by much," he said, walking into the room and joining them. "After we spoke on the phone I couldn't get back to sleep anyway."

"I'll bet," she laughed. It was her opinion that Sawhill would be able to sleep through a nuclear war.

"Well," he said, smiling, "I didn't sleep deeply, anyway, so I got up and came over." He extended his hand to Sam Goldhaber, who shook it with friendly enthusiasm. "How are you, Sam?"

"Fine, Tom, fine. And yourself?"

Sawhill took Harriet's arm and smiled, saying, "Okay, unless I'm going to end up married to an anorexic."

Harriet sighed and said, "Okay, okay, we'll go get something to eat. But let's not dawdle. I want to be here when the exhibits arrive."

As they walked from the museum to the cafeteria, Harriet took a position between the two men. She glanced left at her boss, who often called her "boss" jokingly, and then right to her lover, and smiled to herself. After years of career frustration and personal loneliness, everything was finally going well.

Emotional and physical reactions mingled in her as she looked at Thomas Sawhill. Tall, broad-shouldered, with intelligent, flashing brown eyes, he was the essence of adolescent female fantasies made flesh in the reality of adulthood. The bushy but carefully clipped moustache and the flecks of gray in the sideburns beneath his sandy hair lent him an air of dignity which offset the dimples which emerged with each smile. God, he's good-looking! she thought.

She had to look up to gaze into Sawhill's face, but she was able to look Sam Goldhaber right in the eye—well, when she was wearing heels, at least. Sam was the gentlest, warmest person she had ever known, the kind of man who immediately put everyone at ease and made each person with whom he spoke feel as if he or she were someone special. This accounted both for his numerous friendships and his school popularity. A born teacher, Harriet thought. I wonder if he regrets taking the job of chief administrator? Maybe all those decades of teaching at various colleges and universities had grown wearisome to him. Maybe when I'm in my sixties, I'll want to forsake the classroom for the office too.

Sam noticed her smiling at him and he smiled at her in return. His rather watery blue eyes and snowy white hair combined with his gentle smile and the twinkle which peered out over his bifocals to give him the appearance of a Jewish Kriss Kringle. I couldn't ask for a better boss, Harriet thought. Or a better mentor and friend.

The old cafeteria of Winthrop College was one of the few stone buildings at the school. The incinerator smokestack rose up from behind the low, narrow structure with the ornately carved coats of arms (whose, no one seemed to know) in stone above the heavy oak doors. Sawhill pulled the door open and held it for Harriet and Sam.

They entered the cafeteria and made their selections of food and drink. She was going to limit herself to orange juice and toast, but Sawhill heaped some scrambled eggs and sausages onto her plate as well. There was no waiting line. Indeed, no one else was in the cafeteria other than the cook and the two student servers. This was to be expected, of course. No college student in his right mind would be up at seven o'clock in the morning unless he had to, or unless he had not yet been to bed since the previous night.

"So tell me about the mummies," Sam said as they sat down at one of the long wooden tables.

"I've already told you everything I know about them," Harriet replied, buttering her toast.

"I know, but I like to hear your voice. So tell me again." He poured some milk into his tea and stirred it.

She laughed and shook her head. "Wait a few weeks, and you can attend my lecture on them." She bit off a piece of toast, ignoring the eggs which she had not wanted in the first place. "I found out a few things about the earls of Selwyn, though."

"Tell us, by all means."

"Well," she said, swallowing, "I looked up the name, the title, I mean, in Brookfield's *Heraldic Registry*. The first Earl of Selwyn was a falconer for King Henry II. I suppose the family name, Fowles, comes from that."

"When was Henry II?" Sawhill asked, sipping his coffee.

"Late twelfth century." They looked impressed. "I suppose you could consider it an old family."

"You don't?!" Goldhaber was mildly surprised.

She smiled. "The word *old* has a different meaning to an Egyptologist than it does to most people. Anyway, one of the earls—the eleventh one, I think—was a British representative in Egypt during the early nineteenth century, maybe late eighteenth. I forget."

"Some historian," Sawhill chided. "No memory for dates."

"The British were interested in Egypt, the Suez area, ever since they established themselves in India during the 1700s," she said, ignoring Tom's remark. "It's a natural trade route, and an ideal place for a canal. That's one reason that Napoleon invaded Egypt." She took another bite of toast. "Try to strangle trade with the east."

"And this earl was the one who first brought the mummies to public attention?"

She shook her head. "No one *ever* brought them to public attention. I'm assuming that he's the one who brought them back to England, but there has never been any mention made of them anywhere, by anyone, anytime."

"Well, that's damned peculiar!" Goldhaber said.

"Sure is, but it's a hell of a break for us," Harriet replied through a full mouth. "It means that they've never been examined, never been photographed. God knows what kinds of information we might be able to obtain from investigating them. Oh, I know that the chances of anything of great importance coming out of this is remote to say the least, but every bit of knowledge, no matter how small—" She stopped abruptly, blushing slightly.

Goldhaber turned to Sawhill and laughed. "She's just realized that she's launched into the same harangue that she hit me with a few months ago when she came begging for the money to buy her mummies." He patted her hand paternally. "She was right then and she's right now."

"Well, it's true," she muttered, amused but slightly defensive. "And don't forget, this is a good bit of publicity for the school. What do they call it in politics—a photo opportunity? Well, when we officially unveil the exhibits, we'll have photographers and reporters all over the place."

"Don't fantasize about that aspect of it too much," Sawhill warned. "It isn't like a major archeological find."

"Oh, I know that, Tommy, but it doesn't have to be. All it has to be is unusual to attract the press. And it certainly is unusual."

"Yes," Goldhaber agreed. "It is the publicity aspect of it which sold the idea to the board of trustees. Of course they all protest their devotion to the advancement of knowledge, but they are all practical people, business people. I doubt we could have gotten the money from them to buy a regular old run-of-the-mill mummy about which nothing remains to be learned."

"True," Harriet said, "though I take issue with your term, 'run-of-the-mill mummy.' No mummy is run of the mill. Each and every one of them is a priceless piece of our human heritage."

"You're starting to lecture, Professor." Sawhill laughed.

"I'm serious, Tom." She pushed the plate with the uneaten eggs and sausages away from her. "And we should remember that they are more than exhibits. Oh, I know that I call them that too, but they were human beings once, living people. They loved and laughed and wept, they had parents, friends, children, hopes and dreams. We're waiting for seven *people* to arrive here today."

Harriet's intensity had been one of the things which first attracted Sawhill to her, and he smiled slightly at the quiet thoughtfulness which underlay her last statement. "I'm sorry, Harriet," he said. "I wasn't being flippant. I understand what you're saying, and you say it very well."

"Well, they're ours, in any event," Goldhaber said. "And I'm sure that we will make the most of them."

"I can hardly wait to examine them," Harriet said eagerly. "Do you realize that this will be the first time I'll have the opportunity to examine an Egyptian artifact which hasn't already been worked over by dozens of other people? If there is a funerary text inscribed on the coffins, I may even be able to publish a recension and a translation." She paused. "If it's something new, of course."

"Wait a minute," Sawhill interjected. "Didn't you tell me that you went on an archeological dig in Egypt?"

"Oh, sure. About eight years ago."

"Didn't you have the opportunity—"

"No, no," she interrupted. "We didn't find anything, really. The site had been worked on. Egypt has been combed by archeologists for well over a century. I can't help but think that the major finds have all been found."

The cafeteria door opened as Harriet was speaking, and Jasper Rudd, the town's chief of police, sauntered in. "Mornin', folks," he said cheerfully.

"Hello, Chief," Harriet and Goldhaber said simultaneously.

"Jasper!" Sawhill exclaimed. "What are you doing up at this hour?"

"There's nothing wrong, is there?" Goldhaber asked, suddenly the concerned college president.

"Relax, Sam. I called him," Harriet said. "I wanted to have some armed security here when we unload the exhibits."

"What for?" Goldhaber asked. "No one is going to try to steal the mummies."

"That's probably true. But we are committed to an insurance policy on these exhibits, a policy which my best friend arranged for us, and I don't want to take any chances."

"Besides," Sawhill added, "it doesn't hurt to have an officer of the law present at the delivery, just in case there is any damage."

"Or if the exhibits are not as they were advertised or described over the phone," Harriet said. "Don't forget, this is a sight unseen purchase."

"I hardly think the Earl of Selwyn would try to defraud the college!" Like many Americans, Goldhaber had an inbred and totally irrational respect for the titled aristocracy.

"Not intentionally, no. But why take for granted that he or his lawyer know what they're talking about? Neither of them are archeologists."

"Well, I suppose that's true. You don't think the Earl will take offense, do you? I mean—"

"Oh, Sam, don't be silly!" Harriet said. "He's a man of the world. He knows the way business is conducted."

"Of course he does," Sawhill agreed. "There's nothing wrong with having an official present at the delivery, especially since the stuff is so valuable."

"And so heavily insured," Harriet added.

"Right. We're not waiting for a package from UPS, you know! In fact, I think it'd be pretty unusual for there *not* to be a law officer present." He slapped Jasper familiarly on the back. "And old Jasper here is our resident gendarme."

Jasper grinned. "You see, Professor Goldhaber just gets nervous whenever he sees me. He always thinks that his college kids have been raising hell in town or something."

"Like last year, when they painted jack-o'-lanterns on the gravestones in the cemetery for Halloween?" Harriet asked, smiling.

"Yeah. Or when they managed to steal that statue of Winthrop during Homecoming Week."

"Found it wearing a bra and panties, didn't you?" Sawhill asked.

"Yeah, right in front of the Methodist Church two days later."

Goldhaber raised his hand to silence them. "Please, please, don't remind me of all this. You'll give me ulcers!"

Jasper laughed. "Don't worry about it, Professor. Old Doc Sawhill can fix you up if that happens. Just take it easy and let *me* get the ulcers."

This elicited a wave of laughter from all present, for no one was less prone to nervous tension than Jasper Rudd. Though he and Sawhill called each other Chief and Doc most of the time, they had known each other most of their lives, and Sawhill knew that the statue of Montgomery Winthrop had a better chance of developing ulcers than had Jasper.

Jasper Rudd was a bit older than Thomas Sawhill, and they had come to know each other decades before through Jasper's younger brother Gus. Growing up as they had in a small town, everyone of course knew everyone else, but Sawhill had always enjoyed Jasper's company in particular. He had even worried about him when Jasper was drafted and shipped off to Vietnam while Sawhill rested comfortably behind a student deferment. He had no such worries for Gus when the latter joined the navy a few years later.

Sawhill and Jasper lost touch with each other after that, for while the doctor finished medical school and went into practice in his home town, Jasper moved to New York City and joined the police force. He spent twenty years on the force before retiring on a comfortable pension and moving back to Greenfield. But at age forty he was really much too young to retire, and he jumped at the chance to become the town's chief of police when old Chief Gutersloh retired. His two years in Vietnam, coupled with his twenty years as a New York City cop, had prepared him for almost anything. Jasper Rudd took everything in stride. Nothing bothered him.

Indeed, after his experiences in Southeast Asia, the South Bronx, Manhattan and Brooklyn, Jasper tended to regard his job as chief of the Greenfield police force as something of a paid vacation. He only had one other officer to supervise, and that was his brother Gus. He had taken the job in Greenfield casually, a nice retirement job for a man not really of retirement age. He spent most of his time walking around town and talking to the residents or playing cards in the police station with Gus and Will Foster. Sure, he had to roust a drunk now and then, and the college kids were always up to some mischief or other, but to a man with Jasper's urban experience this barely even qualified as law enforcement.

"I appreciate your getting up so early to come and supervise, Chief." Harriet smiled.

"No problem, Miss Langly. I'm an early riser anyway. Always used to work the early morning shifts back in the City." Jasper looked over at the student server, who was lounging tiredly behind the empty cafeteria service area. "Hey, sonny. Bring me a cup of coffee. will you?" He sat down at the table beside Goldhaber.

"You're supposed to serve yourself, Jasper," Sam observed. "This is a cafeteria."

Jasper Rudd shrugged. "Never knew a college kid who didn't want to be on the good side of a cop." He smiled. "Besides, a cup of coffee ain't much of a bribe."

"How did you know we'd be here?" Harriet asked. "I asked you to meet us at the museum at seven."

"I know, I went there. Left Gus there to wait for Will's truck. I figured you'd be here"—he shot an amused glance at Sawhill—"moochin' a free meal, so I came over to join you."

"How come you came over so early?"

The student walked over and handed Jasper a cup of coffee. "Thanks, sonny," he said. "I ain't early. It's seven-thirty."

"Seven-thirty!" Harriet looked at her watch. "Good grief! Where the hell are they?"

"Come on, now," Goldhaber said. "Knowing Will Foster, when they stopped for breakfast he sat down to clean the diner out of pancakes."

"Sure, honey. Try to calm down. They'll get here when they get here. Maybe they hit traffic. Maybe the Earl wanted to sightsee."

"Sightsee! Don't be ridiculous. There's nothing to see on the New York State Thruway!"

"Not to you, maybe, but to somebody from another country there might be sights of interest." Sawhill paused and considered his suggestion. "On the other hand—"

"The thruway is just a big long road." She felt her anxiety beginning to surface. "God, I hope that nothing—"

Goldhaber and Sawhill laughed gently. Jasper just smiled. "Don't worry, Miss Langly," the policeman said. "Will's a reliable man. The stuff'll get here safe, soon enough."

"Yeah, I'm sure it will," Harriet nodded. "I can't help but be a little tense. I know I'm being silly."

"You're not silly, honey," Sawhill said. "You're just showing appropriate professional concern."

She smiled at him, but glanced furtively at her watch once again. Get here! she thought, as if a mental command could speed them on their way. Get here! She kept the smile on her face as her stomach slowly began to tie itself up in knots.

# CHAPTER 3

▲ "So damned inconvenient!" Roderick Fowles, fifteenth Earl of Selwyn, was saying as he stared out the window of Will Foster's truck, watching the endless line of trees speed by on the thruway roadside. "I shall sack that idiot Pearson straightaway, you mark my words!"

"It really wasn't his fault, Your Lordship," Suzanne Melendez said. "When you told him you wanted to come to the States with the exhibits, he must have assumed that you wanted to go to Greenfield with them."

"I told the old fool that I wanted to go to Orlando!"

"Yes, and you will, as soon as all the paperwork is done at the Museum and you've had a day or two to rest up. You can't enjoy Disneyworld when you have jet lag."

"But three days!" Roderick shook his head. "I just can't believe that there were no available seats on a plane to Orlando."

"You do have a reservation, Your Lordship, for next Wednesday. And you'll enjoy Disneyworld much more if you've gotten some rest."

"Yes, but really! I told that idiot at the airport who I was. Why didn't he just chuck someone off the reservation list?"

Suzanne laughed. "I'm afraid that you won't find too many Irish Americans who are impressed with your title. And it is the peak season to Florida."

"Yes, but really!" Roderick was furious. He had never had to bow to the necessity of waiting his turn for anything except his peerage, and he was not reacting well.

Suzanne patted his hand sympathetically. "I promise, Your

Lordship, that I'll personally escort you on a tour of Disney-world. Okay?" She smiled. The act of patting his hand had nothing in truth to do with sympathy. Any excuse she could find to touch him, she seized upon as a cat might leap upon a mouse. Her overtures would have been obvious to anyone less obtuse than Roderick.

He turned to Will Foster, who was watching the road intently as he drove, doing his best to ignore the Earl, to whom he had taken an immediate dislike. "I say, Foster, are you certain it takes that long to drive to Florida?"

"Two days, easy. Three, if you drive normal."

"Damn!" Roderick sniffed petulantly. This evidence of the frustration of expected privilege endeared him to Suzanne. It made Will Foster want to pull over and throw him out of the truck.

Will was a virile and independent twenty-five, and he made no secret of the fact that he thought Roderick was a "namby-pamby mama's boy fag," which is how he referred to him when speaking privately to Suzanne. Will Foster was a physical, not intellectual, young man, and his frequent fistfights were among the major reasons behind his expulsion from Winthrop College seven years earlier. (The fact that his grade-point average rarely met the minimum required for continued matriculation did not help, either.) He had managed to remain in Greenfield by getting a job as a grounds keeper at the college, and this allowed him to remain in an environment he had come to like while earning a living at physical outdoor tasks. He was healthy, young, confident, outgoing, uncompli-cated.

This background and personality made him all the more disgusted with Roderick, who lacked even the intellectual acumen which might excuse his pampered, easy-chair life. How Suzanne Melendez could find this chubby pansy attrac-tive was beyond Will's comprehension. He stole a quick glance to his right at the woman sitting beside him in the cab of the truck. Older than he, but attractive. Long black hair, dark brown eyes, thin but not unpleasantly so. Suzanne Melendez struck Will Foster as a sexually aggressive career woman, someone too preoccupied with her job to commit herself to a relationship with any one man. He glanced down at her long legs, ran his eyes up her lithe form and wondered what she would be like in bed.

His opinion partook partially of truth, but the reality of

Suzanne Melendez was something a man like Will Foster could never understand. She was indeed devoted to her career, but her unattached status was similar in origin to the problems her friend Harriet Langly had always faced, until she met Thomas Sawhill. Suzanne was unwilling to take a backseat to anyone, and her dislike of the demand so many men had made that she surrender her career goals and subordinate her life to theirs had made her wary of commitments. Unfortunately, it had also bred into her an assumption that sexism was present even in its absence, and she had thereby ruined a number of relationships which might have blossomed over time into the type of marriage she quite openly wished for.

There was enough of an adolescent romantic in her nevertheless to be instantly infatuated with the Earl of Selwyn. His easy charm, dapper manner, and obvious affluence seemed suddenly of greater importance to her than the actuarial charts with which she was accustomed to spend her time. What Foster regarded as an effeminate manner was to her nothing less than the haughty confidence born of breeding and wealth. She envied both, for she had neither.

"We should be in Greenfield in a few minutes, Your Lordship," she said.

"Jolly good," he muttered morosely.

"You know," Suzanne said almost tentatively, "it's really been quite a thrill for me to be able to get to know you so well in such a short time. I'd been dying to meet you ever since we spoke on the phone last month."

A distracted "Hm" was his only response.

"I've spent a good deal of time in England, but I've never had a chance to meet any of the peerage. It's really quite a thrill," she repeated.

Roderick shot her a bored, perfunctory smile and reached into his jacket pocket. He withdrew a silver cigarette case and took out a custom rolled cigarette. Allowing the hand holding the case to drift languidly in her general direction he said, without looking at her, "May I offer you a cigarette?"

"No, thank you," she gushed.

Foster glanced over at him as he lighted the tip of the cigarette. "Gonna kill yourself with those things," he muttered.

Roderick sighed. "Beg pardon?"

Foster laughed. "On second thought, never mind. Go right ahead."

Their conversation, such as it was, continued in this desultory fashion until Foster moved the truck to the right and pulled off the thruway at the Greenfield exit. "We're here, Your Lordship," Suzanne said cheerfully.

"Splendid," he muttered.

They drove down Route 15 in silence, Foster irritated, Roderick bored, Suzanne trying to think of something to say. The drive down the main street of Greenfield occupied but a few minutes, and they soon found themselves passing the statue of Montgomery Winthrop at the entrance to the college. As Foster pulled the truck up as close as possible to the door of the museum, he waved in the general direction of Gus Rudd, who was leaning casually against a tree near the entrance. After putting on the hand brake and turning off the ignition, Foster alighted from the truck and walked over to the deputy chief.

"Mornin', Gus," he said. "Where is everybody?"

"Dunno. Jasper went looking for them. I guess I better go look for him now."

"Okay. I'll start getting things moving."

Gus frowned. "I think you better wait 'til Dr. Langly's here. I kinda think she wants to check stuff out. That's why me'n Jasper are here, to help supervise and check stuff out."

Foster grinned. "Yeah? Well, you better be here to give me a hand movin' these goddamn crates."

"Yeah, yeah, sure, Will. No problem." Gus knew that he only had the job he held as deputy because his brother was chief, and he always went out of his way to be accommodating to the locals. "Look, why don't you just relax for a few minutes while I go and round everybody up. Okay?"

"Okay. I gotta go get a forklift out of the grounds building anyway." As Gus departed to search for his brother, Foster returned to the truck. He hopped up onto the mounting step and leaned in the window on the driver's side. "Listen," he said to Suzanne and Roderick, "I'm goin' over there"—he pointed at the grounds building—"and get myself a forklift to move this stuff with. You two hang out here for a while." He jumped down and began to walk quickly away.

"'Hang out'?" Roderick asked.

"It means wait around," Suzanne explained. "He has to get some equipment to unload the truck with."

"Oh, I see." Roderick sighed. "Well, we might as well stretch our legs. Damned long drive!"

"Yes, it certainly was," she agreed readily. "We've both—"

Her comment was cut off by the fact that Roderick had opened the door and was climbing ungracefully out of the truck.

He stretched and yawned and then looked around him distastefully. So this was what they called a college in this country! It compared very poorly, both in size and beauty, to the schools he had attended in England, all of which he had been asked to leave. But inasmuch as he had no use for a university degree, his frequent expulsions upset no one but his late uncle. It certainly never upset Roderick.

"It's kind of pretty, isn't it?" Suzanne asked, gesturing around at the wood and brick buildings.

"Quaint," he replied, smiling thinly. He looked over to where Will Foster was approaching them, the forklift he was driving emitting a load, rusty roar. As Foster pulled up and climbed down from the seat, Roderick asked, "What on earth is this contraption?"

"It's a forklift, pal," Foster said impatiently.

"Oh, I see," he replied, not seeing at all. "What's it for?"

Foster glanced at him impatiently as he walked around to the back of the truck and, withdrawing a key from his pocket, unlocked the padlock which had held the rolling door shut during the long drive. "It's for unloading the crates. What did you think?"

Roderick shrugged. "No idea, actually."

"Suzie!" He heard a voice cry from behind him. He turned to see five people approaching, one of them, a woman, practically running toward them. The woman embraced Suzanne Melendez and said, "Thank God you're here! I've been going crazy!"

Suzanne returned her embrace. "Why? We're not late, are we?"

"No, but—well, you know."

She laughed. "Yeah, I know. Patty Paranoia. Well, here we are safe and sound."

"No problems?"

"Not really. Well, the back door of the truck opened up while we were driving here and we left a couple of mummies scattered on the Thruway, but other than that—"

Harriet Langly grimaced. "That's not funny, Suzie!"

She laughed again. "Take it easy, Harriet. Everything's fine." She turned to Roderick and said, "Your Lordship, may I present my dear friend, Harriet Langly." Then, to Harriet, "The Earl of Selwyn."

Harriet extended her hand to him and he took it without shaking it, barely touching his fingertips to hers. "How do you do?" she said. "I must say that this acquisition is quite exciting for me."

"The—oh, the mummies. Yes, of course." It was clear that he did not share her interest in them.

The other four people approached at paces considerably less rapid than Harriet's had been. She took Sawhill's arm and said, "May I introduce to you to my fiancé, Dr. Thomas Sawhill. Tommy, this is the Earl of Selwyn."

"My pleasure," Sawhill said, holding his hand out. Roderick shook it, somewhat more firmly than he had taken Harriet's hand a moment before.

Harriet continued her introductions. "Dr. Samuel Goldhaber, president of Winthrop College. The Earl of Selwyn."

"Hello. Welcome to the United States."

"How do you do."

"Jasper Rudd, our chief of police."

A nod. "Earl."

"How do you do."

"And I believe you've met Gus, Jasper's brother?"

"Hiya," Gus said, grabbing Roderick's hand and pumping it enthusiastically. "It's real nice to meet you."

"How do you do."

"Well," Harriet said, obviously very pleased to have gotten that over with, "let's get to work. Your Lordship, you can discuss the details of the transfer with Dr. Goldhaber while we see to the unloading."

"Details? Oh, my solicitor, Horace Pearson, handles all such matters. I'm just eager to get done with this and get to Florida."

"But there are papers to be signed, aren't there?"

Roderick shrugged. "I have no idea, actually."

"But—"

Suzanne cut her off by saying, "I have all the necessary documents. Mr. Pearson and I arranged the whole thing back in London. Once you've made an initial examination of the shipment we can effect a transferal of ownership. How long will that take, by the way?"

"I plan to make a superficial examination today. Authentication won't take more than a day or two."

"Good." She turned to Roderick. "You see, Your Lordship?

We'll be able to wrap this up in plenty of time for us to get you back to Kennedy to catch your plane to Orlando."

"Yes, wonderful. Fine." Roderick was making a tired effort to be pleasant.

"You want me to get started, Dr. Langly?" Will Foster asked.

"Yes, Will, please. I'd like you to remove the crates one by one and bring them into the museum. There are seven glass cases in there. If you could lay one crate beside each glass case?" As Will nodded and walked back toward the truck, she turned to Roderick. "You see, we plan to display the mummies and their coffins separately. Once we've put the crates next to the display cases, we'll open them one by one and eventually remove the mummies from the coffins. I don't plan on doing that today, though."

"Oh," Roderick said, not caring one whit.

"Hey, Gus. Come on up here and give me a hand," Will called. He had driven the forklift over to the rear of the truck and had positioned it with the fork inserted into the storage compartment a few inches above the floor.

"Sure thing, Will," Gus said. He climbed up into the rear of the truck. "How you wanna do this?"

"You take one end of this crate and I'll take the other. When I get it over to the door, help me carry it in."

"Okeydokey." They moved one of the crates over toward the fork and carefully lifted it up. After placing it on the flat extended prongs, Will leapt out of the truck. He turned to Harriet.

"According to the instructions Miss Melendez brought with her, six of the crates were stacked by twos and this one was by itself. I don't know if that means anything, but she said to try to keep 'em in the same order." He shrugged. "Dunno why."

"No need, I'm sure," she said. "But we might as well start with this one. Be careful, now."

"You bet." Will returned to the forklift and slowly raised the fork. He backed away from the truck. Harriet suppressed a gesture of warning as the crate seemed to sway slightly, balanced as it was upon the two narrow prongs. There was, of course, no need for concern, she reminded herself. Will knew what he was doing.

Foster turned the forklift around and slowly drove the short distance from the truck to the museum. When he reached the door, he stopped the machine and lowered the fork to the ground. Harriet had already opened the door, and she stood there eagerly, biting her lower lip as Will and Gus carefully lifted the crate and moved it inside, their feet shuffling under the weight of the old, heavy wood. They placed the crate beside the farthest glass case. Will turned to Harriet and asked, "You want me to open it up?"

"Yeah, but listen carefully. I want the crate dismantled, not just opened."

"Huh?"

"I don't want to risk damage to the coffins by lifting them out of the crates. What we have to do is remove the nails and sort of peel the wood away from the contents. Then we can open the coffin and relocate it without risking damage."

Foster shrugged, slightly annoyed at the added work which he regarded as unnecessary. "You're the boss," he muttered. "I gotta go get a crow bar and a hammer. Hold on." He walked out, shaking his head disgruntledly.

Sawhill and Goldhaber had walked in, followed by Suzanne and Roderick. Jasper and Gus remained outside, keeping casual watch over the truck. "Well, what's the procedure?" Goldhaber asked.

"After we dismantle the crate, I'll make a transcription of whatever is inscribed on the coffin lid—Sam, did you bring the camera I asked you to bring?" He nodded, pointing to the brochure table where he had deposited his camera earlier. "Good," she continued. "Then we'll open the coffin and I can make a cursory examination of the mummy. After we're done with all seven crates, you and the Earl can sign whatever needs to be signed, and from then on I just have my own research to do with the exhibits. I can authenticate them in a few days, but I'm hoping that they'll provide me with enough work to occupy my time for quite a while."

"Aren't you going to put them in the display cases right away?" Sawhill asked.

Harriet shook her head. "Not just yet. We can keep them in the coffins for the time being. If they've survived a damp English attic for a century or so, they can survive a day here." She looked nervously at the crate which rested on the floor beside her. "God, I hope they're in good shape."

"Well, gee, honey," Sawhill said, "they were made to last, weren't they?"

"Sure. But the climate in Egypt, especially Upper Egypt, is considerably different from that of England. Egypt is hot and dry. England is cold and damp." She smiled at Roderick. "Meaning no offense, Your Lordship."

"Oh, no, you're quite correct, actually," Roderick said. "Absolutely beastly weather. I much prefer the south of France."

"Yes, so do I," Suzanne chimed in. "If only it weren't so frightfully expensive!"

"Oh, is it expensive?" he asked innocently.

"I just hope that the bodies are intact," Harriet said, distracted.

Will Foster strode in, his arms burdened with a variety of tools. As he entered he called back over his shoulder, "Hey, Gus, gimme a hand in here, will you?"

"I'm guarding the truck," Gus's voice replied.

"I think Jasper can handle it by himself," Will observed sarcastically. "Come on, gimme a hand. The quicker we get this done, the sooner we can all go home."

"Okeydokey," Gus said reluctantly. He walked over to the museum, leaving his brother yawning beside the truck.

As the two young men positioned themselves on either side of the crate, Harriet told them, "Now look, be real careful. I don't want the tools to go through the crate and into the contents. Just kind of slide it in between the planks and—"

"Dr. Langly," Will interrupted her with gentle amusement, "I know how to use a crowbar."

Harriet blushed at the grins Will and Gus were exchanging. "I'm sorry, fellas. Go on, do your jobs. I'll shut up."

"No need for that, ma'am," Gus said. "Just don't worry. We'll be careful." He and Will began to pry open the lid (which Roderick had once opened, and Pearson had made certain to have nailed shut.) Will pulled out the nails on his side, and with a mighty shove he and Gus tore the lid, and the connecting nails, away from the crate. Moving to the front and rear of the crate respectively, Will and Gus began very carefully to separate the planks which formed the body of the encasement. Once Gus allowed his hand to slip, sending the crowbar careening across the floor of the museum and sending a chill up Harriet's spine, but he just grinned and said, "Sorry. No harm done." She returned his smile without conviction.

Once the nails were removed from the front and rear, leaving the crate dismantled but for the sides, Will and Gus began to pull down on the two remaining sides which connected to the bottom of the crate. After a few moments and some piercing squeaks as the slips of metal were ripped free of their century-old housing, the sides of the crate came down, leaving the ancient sarcophagus resting in plain view.

They all stood in silence for a moment, each of them in some way affected by the solemnity of the moment—each save the bored and blank-faced Earl of Selwyn, that is. Will pushed the side panel away with his foot, and Harriet slowly approached the coffin. She knelt down beside it and gently stroked the smooth surface. "Thousands of years," she murmured. "Millennia."

"What did you say, honey?" Sawhill asked.

She glanced over at him. "Come here, Tom. I want to share something with you." He dropped to his knees beside her and she took his hand and placed it upon the sarcophagus, moving it slowly across the rounded contours of the lid. "A human being carved this stone. Maybe he was a slave, maybe he was an artisan; there's no way to know. We'll never know his name, but he was a living, breathing human being, and he lived thousands of years ago. Here, feel this." She ran his fingers over the rows of hieroglyphs upon the coffin lid. "Look at it, the graceful carving." She gazed at the ancient writing and then looked up at Sawhill. "Someone *made* this, Tom. Someone who died thousands of years ago created this, and left it after him." She shook her head. "I'm not saying this very well. I can't explain how it makes me feel, to be in the presence of something like this. It's as if the past never really passes away, and we all leave something of ourselves, something of our lives, in the things we touch." She flushed slightly at the smiling people who were listening to her. "I probably sound silly."

Sawhill resisted the urge to embrace her and merely said, "You don't sound silly at all." He turned to Goldhaber. "Does she say things like this to her students?"

"Sure," the college president smiled. "That's why we give her morning assignments. She's the only teacher we have who can keep them awake."

The ripple of friendly laughter restored Harriet's businesslike manner, and smiling, she said, "Well, enough of this. Let's get to work. Sam, if you'd be so kind as to photograph the sarcophagus from all angles? Tom, I'm going to make transcriptions of the hieroglyphs on the lid. Would you hold the pages when I'm done with each of them, keep them in the proper order?"

"Gee, okay, if you think I can handle it!" he said with amusement.

The room was suddenly a bustle of activity. Sam Goldhaber was walking around snapping photographs as Will and Gus brought in the second and then the third of the crates. Harriet placed a sheet of plain white paper in a clipboard and leaned over the one exposed sarcophagus. She squinted her eyes in an attempt to read the worn hieroglyphs, and her brow furrowed. "Tom, get me the whisk broom over there on that display case, will you?"

Sawhill fetched the whisk broom and extended it to her handle first, but she did not take it from him. She continued to frown and muttered something unintelligible, and then began to run her fingers along the inside of one of the indentations in the coffin lid created by the carving of the pictographic figures. "That's odd," she muttered.

"What's odd?" Sawhill asked.

"I don't think this is made of stone. It seems to be some sort of lacquered wood, but for the life of me I can't identify the lacquer." She ran her hand over the surface of the lid. "It sure as hell feels like stone. It doesn't have the smoothness or the grain that wood should have."

"Well," Sawhill paused, trying to think of an explanation. "You can lacquer a wood to hide the grain, can't you?"

She shook her head. "The Egyptians couldn't, or at least they never seemed to want to. They might paint wood or overlay it with gold, but this is some sort of lacquer." She stared at the sarcophagus, frowning.

"Does it make a difference?" he asked.

"No, probably not. It's just odd, that's all." She turned to him and took the whisk broom. "Thanks, hon." Harriet swept the broom across the hieroglyphs with quick, strong, yet somehow delicate movements, and then leaned forward over them once again. Sawhill stood back and watched her with interest, contrasting the motions of the attractive young woman with the austere dignity of the grayish-brown coffin over which she was so intently bending. He had always assumed that Egyptian sarcophagi bore carved representations of the deceased on the lid, almost as if the entire body of the inhabitant were reproduced as the lid itself, but this was not the case here. The coffin did have the characteristic shape of the mummy sarcophagi he had seen in museums—six sides, with the bottom two sides drawing away from the feet at an ever increasing distance from each other, joining the shorter upper two sides two thirds of the way up the box, where the upper two sides swept inward to attach to their respective ends of the head of the coffin—but it lacked the ornateness which he had assumed was customary. Perhaps these people were not wealthy enough to get a funeral with all the trimmings. Perhaps this was the ancient Egyptian equivalent of the plain pine box of the pauper's graveyard. I just hope Harriet isn't disappointed, he thought.

Harriet gazed at the hieroglyphs for a for a few more moments and then, taking pen in hand, began to transcribe the figures onto the white paper on the clipboard. Her hand moved with a slow precision and her tongue insinuated its tip out of the side of her mouth as she concentrated. She seemed oblivious to the noise of screeching nails and splintering wood as Will Foster and Gus Rudd reduced another of the crates to kindling wood. She paused in her writing and glanced back and forth from the paper to the lid, as if to verify the accuracy of her transcription. Then she removed the paper and handed it to Sawhill. She placed another piece of paper onto the clipboard and began to transcribe another line of hieroglyphs.

Sawhill looked at the paper in his hand and read:

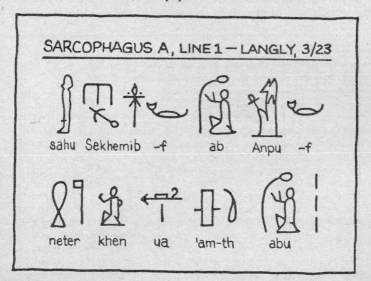

SARCOPHAGUS A, LINE 1 — LANGLY, 3/23

sahu Sekhemib —f   ab   Anpu —f

neter   khen   ua   'am-th   abu

"Honey?" he asked.

"Hmmm?" She was busily transcribing the second line.

"What does this say?"

"Hmmm?"

"What does this say? This first transcription."

She glanced at the page he held. *"Sahu Sekhemibf, ab 'Anpuf, neter khen ua 'amth abu."* His laughter distracted her from her transcription, and she asked irritably, "What's so funny?"

"I don't mean how does it read in Egyptian," he laughed. "I can read the vocalization myself. I mean, what does it *mean*, in English."

"Oh, Lord, I'm sorry," she said. She shook her head as if to clear it. "I wasn't paying attention to what you said. It means, 'The body, or mummy, of Sekhemib, the priest of the god Anubis, a prophet among the priests.'"

He emitted a low whistle. "Sounds like an important fellow."

She nodded doubtfully. "Could be. But if he was, I can't understand why he was buried in a wooden sarcophagus."

"What does the rest of it say?"

"Patience, my dear, patience." She returned to her work as he watched her with interest and amusement. After a few moments she handed him the second piece of paper.

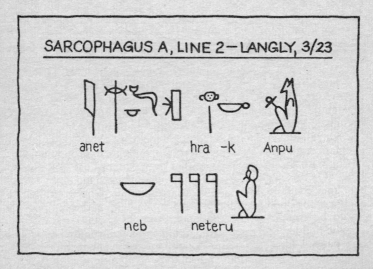

"And this line? What does it mean?"

She sighed. "It means, 'Homage to you, Anubis, lord of the gods.'"

Her tone of voice surprised him. "You don't sound happy with this text. What's wrong?"

She thought for a moment. "Let me put it this way. You've read some classical mythology, right?"

"Sure."

"I mean, you know something about the Greek and Roman gods, don't you?"

"Of course. Just general knowledge, of course, but—"

"Okay. Let's say that we were translating a text from what we thought was an ancient Greek hymn, and we came across the line 'Praise to you, Poseidon, king of the gods.' Would that strike you as strange?"

"Sure it would, because he was the god of the sea. Zeus was the king of the gods." He paused as what she was saying dawned on him. "You mean—"

"Right. Anubis was the god of the grave. Ra, or later Amon-Ra, was the chief deity in the Egyptian pantheon. I've read thousands of texts in graduate school, and never, not once, have I ever read anything which described Anubis as the lord of the gods."

Sawhill considered this for a moment. "What do you think it means?"

She shrugged. "I'm not sure. You know I tend to be pessimistic."

"Well, what *might* it mean, then. Speculate."

Harriet thought for a moment. "It could mean an unauthentic sarcophagus. It might be an error made by the mason. It might be a special compliment given to Anubis by his priest, though I doubt it. Or . . ." She paused.

"Or what?"

Harriet glanced over at Roderick, who was trying to avoid flirting with Suzanne. Satisfied that he was out of earshot, she said, "Or this whole damn thing might be a fraud."

"You're kidding!" Sawhill was astounded. "Who would try such a gambit? I mean, they have to know that the exhibits would be examined by someone who could spot a fraud."

She nodded in agreement. "You'd think so, wouldn't you?" She paused for a moment. "Look, I don't want to jump to conclusions here. Let me finish the transcriptions and then examine the contents. Even if the coffin is not authentic, that doesn't meant that the mummy isn't." She paused. "If there's a mummy in there, I mean."

He smiled. "I thought you weren't going to jump to conclusions!"

She shook her head. "I'm not, I'm not. Let me get back to this."

A few more increasingly tense moments passed. Then Harriet tossed the next piece of paper to him and said, "This is nuts!" He looked at the page and read:

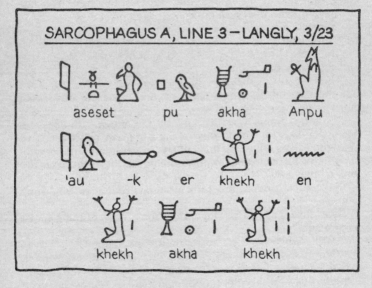

"This is nuts!" she repeated.

"Why? What's it say?"

"It's a question and an answer. He says to Anubis, 'What is my duration, Anubis?' In other words, 'How long do I have to live?' The answer is 'Millions of years, a life of millions of years.'"

"And that's wrong? I mean, what makes you seem so upset by this? Is it an unusual prayer, or what?"

Harriet sighed. "This is a very famous quotation from the Papyrus of Ani, the Book of the Dead. But in the book it is the god Thoth who is asked this question, not Anubis. Anubis is a death god, not a life god." She shook her head again. "It's a hodgepodge. Ra's titles, a prayer to Thoth, all recast to Anubis."

"But he's a priest of Anubis, right? I mean, he *was* one, right? Isn't it reasonable to think that he would only have prayers and references to Anubis on his coffin?"

She was growing irritated. "I know you're trying to help, Tom, but don't speculate like that. Egyptian religion didn't work that way. It didn't make any difference whose priest or priestess someone was. You just don't shift things around like this. They just didn't operate that way. Believe me!" Her last few words were snapped out.

"I believe you, I believe you. Don't get mad at me, Harriet. I didn't write it!"

She rubbed her eyes and then scratched her forehead. "I'm sorry, Tommy. I really am. It's just that—" she sighed, "something just doesn't *feel* right about this."

"Well, the mummies are the important things, right? Why don't you just skip the transcriptions and examine the mummy?"

She smiled. "Because there are proper procedures in archeology, just like medicine. Besides, the lid of this particular sarcophagus is unusually sparse, and there's nothing on the sides. There's some sort of circular design on the lid I want to copy. I've never seen anything like it."

"Is it another problem?"

She laughed. "I hope not. I don't think so. Let me copy it, and then we can open the sarcophagus and see what we have."

Sawhill looked over her shoulder and watched as she drew. Harriet was muttering unintelligibly to herself all the while, shaking her head, with a look of the utmost concern on her face. She carefully drew a circle, as it stood on the lid, and copied in the hieroglyphs.

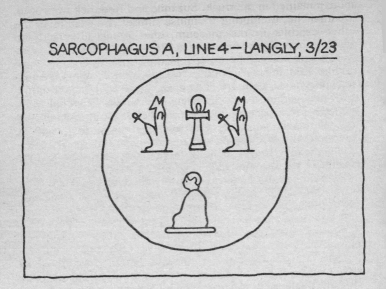

SARCOPHAGUS A, LINE 4 — LANGLY, 3/23

"Well? Problem?" Sawhill asked.

"Not exactly," Harriet replied. "I just don't understand the meaning of this particular series of figures."

"You mean you're unfamiliar with them?"

"Well, the top three, *Anpu ankh Anpu*, literally mean 'Anubis life Anubis.' But that doesn't mean anything, syntactically or logically."

"Could be a prayer, or a bit of praise. No?"

"Possible. I don't know."

"What about the bottom figure?"

She shook her head. "It looks familiar, but I can't quite place it. I'll have to look it up in my copy of Gardiner's *Grammar*. It must not appear in the standard texts with any great frequency." She sighed. "Oh, well, we'll see." She looked up. "Are you ready for the unveiling?"

Sawhill nodded enthusiastically. "I sure am. Your fascination with this stuff is contagious. I'm dying to see what's inside."

Harriet turned from the sarcophagus to the other people in the room. Will and Gus had just finished tearing down the wooden planks which made up the third of the crates. Four more remained in the truck. Suzanne and Roderick were off in a corner, he attempting to amuse himself by examining the other exhibits in the museum, she trying desperately to awaken some spark of interest in him. Sam Goldhaber, having used up a roll of film, was reloading his camera. "Folks," Harriet said in a low voice, "we're going to open the first sarcophagus now, if any of you are interested."

They gathered around her immediately, Roderick with somewhat less alacrity than the others. Having already opened this particular coffin, he was less than eager to review its contents. But the inbred dictates of class and social station demanded politeness, and he feigned interest.

"Now, I'm not sure what we'll find in here," Harriet began. "I think we can assume that the body is in a state of decay. I'm pretty sure that this sarcophagus is made of some sort of wood, not stone, and a conclusion we can draw from this is that the mummification procedure used here was either inferior or rushed. Couple that with at least a century of storage in a climate much more damp and cold than Egypt, and we have a situation not at all conducive to preservation." As he listened to her speak, Sawhill got the impression that she was speaking pessimistically so as to dim her own hopes. The lower you are, the less far you have to fall, he thought.

The doubts she had expressed on the basis of the inscriptions disturbed him. He had no particular interest in Egypt or archeology, but he had a deep and abiding interest in Harriet Langly. He knew that she had built up her hopes regarding this purchase, that it represented to her a major opportunity in the career she had always wanted but never really been able to have. If the sarcophagus is empty, if the mummy decayed, if there is fraud or even innocent misrepresentation—if any of these conditions exist, the disappointment will crush her. He found himself holding his breath.

"Will, Gus, will you lift the lid?" Harriet asked. "Be careful. It's heavy." Roderick knew that it was not, but he held his tongue. Will Foster and Gus Rudd moved to either side of the sarcophagus and, bracing themselves, pushed in and up against the lid. It sprang up into the air and fell, clattering loudly, onto the floor.

"Hey, Dr. Langly, I'm sorry," Gus said.

"Yeah. Shit, that was as light as balsa wood," Will added. "We're sorry, ma'am." Harriet did not reply. "Ma'am?" She seemed not to hear him.

She was staring at the mummy.

It was perfect.

Sekhemib, the priest of Anubis, "a prophet among the priests," was just a shade over six feet tall. He was wrapped in the traditional burial linen, which was yellowed, faded, rotting, but his body appeared to be completely intact. The linen had adhered to his face and hands, and the contours of his countenance were clearly visible through the thin, decaying cloth. His brow was high and his nose hawklike. His lips were thin and wide, his shoulders broad and regal. His powerful-looking arms were folded across his muscular chest. In life, Harriet thought, he must have been an impressive man, majestic and lordly.

She allowed her eyes to drift over her exhibit from head to foot, and then she noticed a yellow disc resting on the floor of the coffin just beside the mummy's head. She reached in carefully, not wishing to touch the exhibit or in any way disturb it until it had been properly photographed. She knew from her studies that while the complex embalming methods of the ancients preserved the body, the linen in which it was wrapped became very delicate and prone to disintegration over the millennia. So as she reached in and grasped the yellow disc, she took care not to allow her hand to brush against the head of the long dead priest.

She held up the yellow disc. It was a medallion upon which had been engraved the same four hieroglyphs which were enclosed in the circle upon the lid. Everyone in the room had the same unspoken thought. Gold. It must be gold.

Harriet Langly leaned slowly, almost reverently forward and gazed down at the priest of Anubis. She stared enraptured into the dusty face and whispered, "My God! He's beautiful!" No one laughed at the statement, for it seemed in some strange way to be true.

A loud voice broke into the silence. "GET AWAY FROM THERE!"

They spun around toward the voice and saw a small olive-skinned man walking quickly into the room. Harriet, startled, stepped away from the sarcophagus, and the man positioned himself between it and her, his stance and aspect bespeaking protectiveness and possession. He turned to Roderick. "Are you the Earl of Selwyn?"

Roderick seemed taken aback. "Yes. Who the devil are you?"

He inclined his head in a curt bow. "I am Ahmed Hadji, Your Lordship. You cannot sell these mummies. There has been a terrible mistake!"

# CHAPTER 4

▲ Jasper Rudd leaned tiredly against the side of the truck and glanced at his watch. Where the hell are Will and Gus? he thought irritably. They have four more of these damn things to unload before we can get out of here. He had no objection to lending an element of security to the delivery—indeed, he rightly regarded it as part of his job—but he abhored time wasted. He shook his head sadly as he considered his younger brother. Nice kid, but never able to do anything right. God only knows what Gus would have done if Jasper had not been able to get him a job as his deputy. The town council had not been too pleased with the idea when Jasper suggested it, especially considering Gus's dishonorable discharge from the Navy and the fact that he had washed out of the State Police Academy, but Jasper's highly satisfactory tenure as police chief had made them willing to wink at their doubts and the obvious nepotism. Ever since he had been hired, Gus had knocked himself out to do a great job, but his performance was only passable. Jasper shook his head again. Where the hell is he?

The sound of a gunshot answered his question. Drawing his service revolver, Jasper ran to the museum, his adrenaline pumping. He had seen the diminutive stranger enter a few minutes earlier and had given it no thought. Perhaps he should have questioned him. This was but a passing thought, for all of Jasper's years of combat and law enforcement experience had taught him the futility of hindsight. He was, as if a switch had been thrown, now the consummate professional responding to the sound of the gunshot as a race horse would to the sound of the bell.

He rushed into the museum, ready for anything, and found the eight people standing as if in shock amid the dust of floating plaster. Gus was standing in the midst of them, smiling with self-satisfaction. "What's going on here?" Jasper demanded, breathing heavily, his gun still drawn.

"Everything's under control, Chief," Gus said. "These folks were getting into a pretty heavy argument here, and I decided I had better settle them down before things got out of hand."

Jasper looked up at the hole in the ceiling, and down at the rubble of plaster and paint on the floor right beneath it. "So you took a shot in the air?"

"Yup." Gus grinned.

"You fucking asshole!" Jasper bellowed. "Where the hell do you think you are, in a goddamned Western?!" The grin departed from Gus's mouth immediately. "You discharged a firearm in an enclosed room filled with unarmed civilians just to stop an argument?! What the hell's the matter with you?"

Gus was crushed. "Gee, Jasper, I just thought—"

"Shut up!" he snapped. Turning to Sam Goldhaber, he asked, in a more civil, though authoritative, tone, "What's the problem here?"

Goldhaber pointed to the small man facing him. "This person says he has a legal claim on the exhibits."

"It is true," Hadji replied. "I am Ahmed Hadji, of the Egyptian National Institute of Reclamation. I contacted Lord Selwyn's solicitor in London and concluded an agreement for the repossession of these mummies on behalf of the institute."

"But that's impossible," Suzanne countered. "I worked out the details of the sale with Mr. Pearson myself, not one week ago. He never said anything about a Mr. Hadji or any institute!"

"Nevertheless, I am here to claim rightful possession of these exhibits, as you call them. I was unable to reach Heathrow Airport in time to stop their removal from England, but I was able to get here before any damage was done to them. I now demand that they be turned over to me." He drew himself up haughtily.

Jasper suppressed a laugh. "What do you plan on doing, carrying them out of here?"

Hadji flushed at the sarcasm. "I shall make arrangements for their return to Egypt as soon as this matter is settled. You are obviously a law enforcement official. I demand that you assist me in claiming my property."

"Uh-huh," Jasper said, not at all impressed with the imperious manner of the stranger. "You know this guy, Earl?" he asked Roderick.

He shrugged. "No I don't, actually."

"Uh-huh," Jasper repeated. "You got a bill of sale?" he asked Hadji.

"Well, no," Hadji replied. "The documents were to be signed by His Lordship once the negotiations were completed."

"The negotiations have been completed!" Harriet said loudly and with great agitation, tinged with fear that she would lose possession of the exhibits. "I completed negotiations with Mr. Pearson myself, on the phone."

"The phone!" Hadji laughed derisively. "You don't even know if you spoke with Mr. Pearson. You don't even know the man."

"Well, His Lordship knows him," Suzanne said. "Why would he be here, if we hadn't completed a deal with his lawyer?"

"Beside the point," Hadji waved his hand in dismissal. "How much did these people offer you for the mummies?"

"Well, I'm not certain. I don't quite remember," Roderick replied.

"We have a firm agreement of thirty-five thousand dollars for the entire group," Suzanne reminded him.

"Oh, yes. Yes, indeed. That's right," Roderick said.

"Your Lordship," Hadji said meaningfully, "I am prepared to pay, on behalf of the institute, one hundred thousand dollars for each of the seven mummies. That is nearly three quarters of a million dollars for the group."

Roderick was stunned. "Oh, I say!"

"Your Lordship, I can have a cashier's check in your hands within twenty-four hours," Hadji said.

"Hold it! Wait a minute!" Harriet yelled. "We have an agreement. We have taken delivery of the exhibits, paying for the insurance ourselves, and the Earl's presence here testifies to the fact that we own them. Possession is nine tenths of the law, right, Jasper?"

Jasper nodded slowly. "I think that would apply here, yes."

Hadji turned on her bitterly. "Do you have a bill of sale, madam?"

"Not yet, of course not!" Harriet was shaking with rage. "I have to authenticate the mummies first, before the documents are signed."

"Well I do not!" He turned to Roderick. "Will you cooperate with the institute?"

"It's not his choice to make! We have a verbal agreement which we can substantiate in court, and that constitutes a contract!"

"Shut your mouth, woman!" Hadji snapped.

Will Foster, who had been leaning casually against the wall, straightened up menacingly. "You watch your mouth, you little fuck, or you're gonna leave here with one of those mummies shoved up your ass!"

"Easy, Will," Jasper said, amused. To Hadji he said, "Look, Mr. Hadji, if you have some sort of legal claim to these things, then you should get yourself a lawyer and take your case to court. As far as I can see, the museum here has a clear right to retain possession. Nobody's gonna just hand these exhibits over to you on nothing more than your own say-so."

Hadji was turning red, trembling. "There is a law against the illegal transportation of Egyptian artifacts claimed by the Egyptian government. You must enforce the law!"

"He's lying, Jasper," Harriet said quickly. "There's no such law."

Hadji grabbed her by the shoulders and shook her. "Shut your mouth!" Jasper began to move toward them to pull Hadji away from her, but Will reached them first. He spun Hadji around and put all his weight and muscle behind the closed fist which drove into the Arab's mouth, sending him sprawling on the floor.

"Will!" Jasper said loudly as he grabbed the younger man by the arm. "Cut it out! Stay out of this!"

Hadji rose unsteadily to his feet, blood pouring from his mouth. He looked dazed and angry. "I'll kill you for this, you bastard," he said thickly.

Will smiled coldly and without humor. "Why don't you just try to, buddy? Give me an excuse to pound you into the ground."

"Will, I'm not kidding!" Jasper was dead serious. "I'll run you in if I have to."

"But he—"

"He's my problem, not yours. Now just go stand over there and stay out of this. Now, Will!" Foster walked sullenly away. Jasper turned to Harriet. "What's this about a law?"

"There's a law prohibiting the smuggling of artifacts out of

Egypt," Harriet explained. "But these mummies weren't in Egypt, they were in England."

"They were stolen from Egypt!" Hadji shouted. "They are Egyptian property and must be returned!"

Jasper shook his head. "I'm a cop, not a lawyer. If you have a case, get yourself a lawyer and let a judge straighten this out."

"I demand that you—"

"You're not gonna demand anything," Jasper said, growing increasingly irritated. "This is the United States you're in now, my friend. We have laws and procedures for settling disputes over property, and you had better follow them."

"I'm warning you, you fool!" Hadji spat. "These mummies are mine. If you keep them from me, you'll pay dearly, dearly."

Jasper had had just about enough. "I think you'd better leave." There was a tense moment as Jasper and Hadji stared hard at each other. Then Hadji walked slowly to the door, saying, "This is not finished. I shall have the mummies. And you shall be sorry for this." He left the room. Jasper went to the door and watched him walk away.

"Gus," he said over his shoulder, "get to the truck and keep an eye on those crates while that guy is still hanging around here." Gus nodded and walked quickly out. He met Hadji a few yards away from the museum.

"The chief told you to beat it," Gus said sternly.

But Hadji, almost meekly, said to Jasper, "Sir, please accept my humble apologies for my behavior. I hope you understand that my concern for these artifacts has upset me greatly."

Jasper nodded warily. "Sure. I understand."

Hadji walked slowly back toward the door of the museum. "I hope that you will all be reasonable about this." Leaning so as to be able to see around Jasper, he said to Harriet, "Perhaps we can come to some mutually satisfactory arrangement? Our institute would be more than happy to generously endow this charming little museum of yours." He was suddenly all sweetness and reason.

Harriet shook her head firmly. "No. I'm sorry, but no."

Hadji entered the room. Jasper did not obstruct him, but he was watching him closely. "There are perhaps other artifacts in which you may be interested? We have many connections and an almost limitless supply of funds. We could—" He stopped in mid-sentence and stood, a look of horror frozen on his face. "Get away from there!" he shouted.

Will Foster was sitting on the edge of the sarcophagus. "You talking to me?"

"Yes, you ape! Get away from there! Instantly!"

Will folded his arms. "Who's gonna make me?"

"Will," Harriet said, "please don't sit on that. You may damage it."

Reluctantly, Will stood up. "Okay, sure, Dr. Langly."

It might have ended there, but Hadji was not satisfied. The sight of Will Foster so close to the mummy of Sekhemib seemed to fill him with anger and apprehension. "Get away from the mummy! Don't touch it!"

Will glowered. "You ain't giving orders around here."

"Do what I tell you, instantly! Get away from it!"

Will smiled pleasantly and, in a spirit of pure orneriness, reached down and placed his hand on the mummy's hand.

"You IDIOT!" Hadji exploded, rushing at Will. He attempted to push him away from the sarcophagus, but Will easily deflected Hadji, who went once again sprawling on the floor. He was weeping when he rose to his feet. "You stupid ass! You stupid, stupid fool!"

Jasper grabbed Hadji by the arm and dragged him to the door. "Okay, that's it. Get out of here. If I see you around this museum again I'll arrest you for criminal trespass. Now beat it!"

Hadji was still trembling as Jasper pushed him out the door. "You'll pay for this, all of you!"

"Get out of here," Jasper said firmly. Hadji walked past Gus and disappeared around the corner of the nearby grounds building. "Gus, get back to the truck," Jasper ordered, and Gus immediately complied.

Jasper turned and walked back toward the others in the museum. "Well, don't that beat all!"

Harriet was shaking, seething with anger. "Who the hell does he think he is?"

Jasper shook his head. "Damndest thing. You know, Miss Langly, I don't know a whole lot about international law. Are you sure this transaction is legal?" He saw her furious eyes beginning to glower at him, and he hastened to say, "Now, now, I'm not going to confiscate your exhibits or anything. I think the courts'll have to settle this, if he wants to go to that trouble and expense. But are you sure about that law he talked about?"

Harriet breathed deeply, trying to calm down. "Look, Chief, during the past century European and American archeologists took an awful lot of stuff out of Egypt for their museums back home. A few decades ago—I think King Farouk was still ruling Egypt at the time—they passed a national law prohibiting any further removal of artifacts, and most countries entered into treaty agreements with the Egyptians, accepting the law. But it only refers to *further* removals. They can't claim anything taken out of Egypt *before* the law and the treaties." She shook her head. "It's absurd. This guy might as well go to the mayor of New York and demand the return of Cleopatra's needle."

"The return of what?" Suzanne asked.

"Cleopatra's needle. It's an obelisk from Egypt in Central Park, behind the Metropolitan Museum. It was a victory monument of King Thutmose III."

"Then why do they call it Cleopatra's needle?" Suzanne wondered.

"Because people are stupid," she said angrily. "The point is, these mummies were taken out of Egypt well over a century ago, at least. There is no law prohibiting the transfer of ownership of artifacts from a private British collection to a private American museum."

Jasper nodded, wanting to believe her. "Well, all I can say is that you should proceed as if the mummies are yours, and—"

"They *are* ours!" Harriet shouted.

"I know, I know," Jasper said soothingly. "I'm sure they are. Just try to forget all this and let Professor Goldhaber and the college's lawyers worry about it."

"Of course," Sam Goldhaber said. "We clearly have the better claim."

This did not mollify Harriet, who was upset that anyone else might have any claim at all. "I will *not* give up these exhibits!"

"You won't have to, I'm sure," Sam said.

"Of course not," Sawhill agreed. "Don't pay any attention to that nut. Let's just get back to work."

She was not listening to him. "And what's this National Institute of Reclamation? I've never even heard of it."

"Harriet," Sawhill said insistently, "forget it, will you? Don't worry about it. The mummies are here, and here they will stay. Okay?"

She nodded impatiently. "Okay, Tom, okay." She sighed softly. "But I don't think we should store them in the museums until everything is settled."

"You think he might try to steal them?" Jasper asked.

Sam shook his head. "I don't know if we need worry about that."

"I don't know," she replied. "He seemed pretty determined."

Jasper considered it. "I suppose I could lock them up in the cell down at the station. No, wait, that's no good. They wouldn't all fit, not in those coffins."

"How about the grounds building?" Sam suggested. "We keep our heavy equipment in there, tractors, trucks, and so forth. It's pretty secure, probably the most difficult building in town to break into. What do you think?"

Jasper nodded. "Maybe. Maybe. It'd be more secure than this place, that's for sure." He turned to Will Foster. "You got room enough in there, Will?"

Will was rubbing his hand distractedly. "Huh?"

"You got room in the grounds building to store these exhibits?"

"Oh, yeah, sure. No problem." He continued to rub his hand.

"What's the matter? You hurt yourself?"

"No, it's nothing. Feels like a pulled muscle or something, probably from all this moving and driving and stuff."

"Well, I'll help you get these crates back onto the forklift and into the grounds building."

"That's okay, Chief. Gus'll help me."

Jasper walked over to the door and leaned out. "Gus? Get in here," he shouted. Gus scurried in a few moments later. "Me and Will are gonna move the exhibits into the grounds building and lock 'em up nice and tight. You—"

"Hey, I'll help him, Jasper. No need for you to do it."

"No, you'll get some wood and some plaster and some paint and fix that hole you put in the roof."

Gus looked dismayed. "Gee, I don't know anything about fixing roofs."

"Then you shouldn't have shot a hole in it!" Jasper said angrily. "Now get going."

"Chief," Harriet said, "we have to leave at least one of the mummies in here. I still have to examine it carefully to make certain that it's authentic, and the lighting in the grounds building just isn't good enough."

"Fine with me. Let's get at it, Will." He looked at Will Foster, who was still rubbing his hand. "Hey, you okay?"

"Yeah, yeah, sure." He winced slightly. "Jesus, I hope I'm not getting arthritis."

Sawhill walked over and said, "Here, let me see your hand." Will extended it to him and Sawhill gently probed with his fingers. "This hurt?" Will shook his head. "This? Or this?"

"Nope."

Sawhill grinned. "You were right the first time, Doctor. You probably pulled a muscle." Will smiled, relieved but uncomfortable.

"Will," Jasper asked, "you want me to get somebody else to help me move the exhibits?"

"No, no, it's no big deal," Will replied. "Probably do me good to use it."

"Just be careful with it," Sawhill warned.

"Yeah, sure, Doc." Will and Jasper walked over to one of the two as yet unopened sarcophagi and began to move it toward the door.

Sawhill turned back to Harriet and smiled. "One hell of a morning!"

She shook her head. "It figures, it really figures. I should have known that this whole thing was too good to be true. I knew that something just had to happen to screw it up."

Sawhill laughed. "Come on, nothing's been screwed up. You still have the exhibits." He glanced over at the opened sarcophagus. "You want to get back to work?"

"No." She shook her head. "All of a sudden I feel exhausted. I think I'll go home and take a nap."

"Sounds good to me," Suzanne said. "Look, why don't we all meet for an early dinner, say about five o'clock? Give us all a chance to rest up. I've got a terrible case of jet lag."

"Great idea," Sawhill agreed. "Why don't we meet at five at Bottadio's, on Bouton Street? Best Italian food in town."

"Good. I love Italian food," Suzanne said. "What do you think, Your Lordship?"

"Eh?" Roderick had not been listening to anything for the past few minutes. Seven hundred thousand dollars! he was thinking. Seven hundred thousand dollars! In real money that must be quite a bit!

"Dinner at five. Okay with you?"

"Oh, yes, most certainly."

Suzanne took Roderick's arm. "Come on, then. I've booked us rooms at the Huguenot Hotel in the old section of town. Let's go get a cab."

"Oh, no, I wouldn't hear of it," Sam said quickly. "I'm parked nearby. Let me drop you off."

"Hey, thanks, Professor. See you later, Harriet. Bye, Tom."

Harriet smiled as the three of them left the museum. Turning to Sawhill, she said, "If Suzie doesn't show up at Bottadio's, maybe we should call her boss and tell him that she resigns."

"Huh?"

"Nothing." She laughed. "I'm going to go home and take a nap. I wasn't expecting all this nonsense this morning. I'm bushed."

"Okay. I'll drive you home."

"No, Tommy, I have my car, remember?"

"Oh, right. All right then, I'll follow you home. Make sure you get there okay."

She smiled disbelievingly. "Hey, this is Greenfield, not Brooklyn. Nobody's going to—"

"Mr. Hadji is in Greenfield, not Brooklyn," he reminded her. "I don't like the looks of that guy. And I don't like his attitude."

"You don't think he might do anything, do you?" She sounded less frightened than merely concerned.

Sawhill shrugged. "Who knows? He seemed pretty upset to me. And getting slugged in the mouth by Will certainly didn't help his mood. I'd just like to be careful, for a while at least."

Harriet raised her eyebrows. "You sure you don't have an ulterior motive?"

"Honey," Sawhill said, grinning maliciously, "when it comes to you, I always have an ulterior motive; but that isn't the point. I don't believe for a moment that Hadji is going to pack up and go back to Egypt or go to a law office and seek professional advice. He doesn't seem the type. I think he's going to hang around Greenfield for a while and try to cause trouble."

Harriet considered this. "Really?" He nodded. "Well, then, maybe I wouldn't mind your tagging along."

"Good." He smiled and took her in his arms. "In fact, I

think I'd better stay over tonight, just to be safe." Laughing, Harriet punched him lightly in the stomach.

As Harriet Langly and John Sawhill stood talking, as Will Foster and Jasper Rudd engaged in relocating the exhibits, as Gus Rudd disgruntledly began to repair the roof, and as Suzanne Melendez, Sam Goldhaber and the Earl of Selwyn were nearing the Huguenot Hotel, Ahmed Hadji, still dabbing the droplets of blood from his mouth, was seating himself before a desk in the real estate office of Jack Lewis. Clearing his throat and wiping his brow with the sanguine handkerchief he held in his trembling hand, he said, "I am seeking temporary lodgings in the general area of this town."

Jack Lewis, a man of florid face and down-home demeanor, grinned and nodded his head idiotically. "Yeah, yeah, sure, we got listings, lots of 'em. Whatcha have in mind?"

Hadji paused briefly and then said, "I have an unfortunate tendency to nervous tension. I am concluding a business arrangement nearby, and I require a residence where I will not be disturbed. I prefer a room in a private home in which there are no other boarders and only one owner in residence, preferably someone elderly, and thus quiet."

Lewis thought for a moment. "Well, old lady—I mean, Mrs. March down on Pine Lane has a room available, but there is another person living there, her son Edgar."

Hadji shook his head. "That is unacceptable. As I explained, my nerves—"

"Yeah, yeah, right, sure." He thought again. "Well, I can't really think of any other . . . Wait a minute, wait a minute. Egar's gone off to Oregon for a month or so." Lewis shook his head sadly. "Old Ed never really amounted to much. Builds those suspension bridges here and there. Can't seem to hold down a job."

"And he is absent at the moment?"

"Yeah, but only for a month or two, like I said."

"Then the site is acceptable. I will require it for no more than a week."

"Well, you see, Mrs. March rents her room by the month, not by the week. I doubt she'd—"

Hadji waved away the objection. "I will pay for the month. Money is of no matter."

Lewis stared at him for a moment and then, shrugging, reached over to the Rolodex. "Let's see, Macable, Maranofsky, ah, here it is. March." He kept one hand on the Rolodex card as he dialed the phone number with the other. He waited as the phone rang on the other end.

"Hello? Mrs. March? Jack Lewis here. Yes. Yes, fine. How are you? Heard from Ed? Uh-huh . . . uh-huh . . . Well, isn't that nice. Listen, Mrs. March, I have a gentleman here, a Mr.—" He looked up quizzically.

"Hadji. Ahmed Hadji."

"Mr. Hadji, who would like to rent your room. He only needs it for a week, but he says he'll pay the month. . . . Uh-huh . . . Uh-huh. Okay. Okay, fine. I'll bring him right over."

"It is settled, then?"

"Sure, if the price is okay with you. You see, I work on a commission when it comes to rentals. One month's rent. She wants two hundred a month for the room, so that'll be four hundred." Lewis paused. "You know, Mr. Hadji, you could stay in a hotel for a week for a lot less than that."

"No. I know what I require."

"Okay, if you say so. I just don't want you to think that I'm trying to cheat you or anything."

Hadji smiled coldly. "I am quite certain that your honesty is above suspicion." He reached into his pocket. "Shall I pay you or the lady?"

"Well, just give me the commission, two hundred. You can give Mrs. March the rent." Lewis's eyes widened as he saw the thick stack of hundred-dollar bills which filled Hadji's wallet. Hadji drew two bills from the wallet and tossed them on the desk before him. Lewis picked them up and grinned as he stuffed them into his pocket. "Well, that's fine, fine."

Hadji rose to his feet. "If you are ready, I wish to go there immediately. I have some important phone calls to make."

"Oh, yeah, sure, sure." Lewis rose also and led Hadji toward the door of the office. "Marjorie," he said to his secretary, "I'll be back in about ten minutes." They walked outside to where Lewis's car was parked at the curb. Lewis opened the door and held it for the diminutive Egyptian, who climbed in and sat rigidly in the front seat. Lewis walked around the car and took his own place in the driver's seat. Turning to Hadji, he said, "You know, you'll like Mrs. March. She's a dear old lady."

"I'm sure," Hadji muttered.

Lewis started the car and pulled away from the curb. "She's been renting that room of hers for as long as I can remember.

She don't need the money, really. Got a pension from the phone company and Social Security. But I think she likes meeting people and making a few extra bucks now and then. Know what I mean?" Hadji stared ahead of him without speaking, and Lewis decided to abandon any further attempt at conversation.

Hadji smacked his forehead in consternation. "Ah, I forget. My luggage is at the train station. Can we stop there first?"

"Sure, sure, no problem," Lewis replied. "It's not too far out of the way." He made a sudden turn, throwing Hadji against the passenger door. Hadji strove to appear unruffled, and failed.

Lewis drove a few blocks and then pulled in in front of the Greenfield train station. Hadji scurried out of the car and ran inside. Lewis sat patiently, drumming his fingers on the steering wheel, giving an occasional glance at the train station door. After a few minutes had passed, Hadji emerged from the station, carrying two large, obviously very heavy suitcases. Lewis got out of the car and opened the trunk as Hadji came panting over. "Whatcha got in there, rocks?"

Hadji did not understand the joke. "Pardon?"

"I say, whatcha got in there, rocks?"

He shook his head slowly. "No."

Rather than try to explain, Lewis heaved the suitcases into the trunk and then shut it. When they had resumed their places in the front seat, he began to back track along the route to Mrs. March's house. They drove the short distance in silence, Lewis attending to the road and Hadji gazing impenetrably out the window.

Lewis pulled the car to a stop in front of a small cape cod which, though aging, had been very lovingly cared for. The white picket fence which girdled the property displayed a fresh coat of paint, and the carefully tended garden which ran along the front of the house rested attractively beneath glistening clean windows.

Hadji removed his suitcases from the trunk and insisted upon carrying them himself, even though Lewis had made an attempt to take one of them. Lewis preceded him up the steps and rang the doorbell.

An elderly white-haired woman opened the door with one hand as she wiped the other on her apron. She squinted at Lewis through her bifocals and then smiled. "Oh, hello, Jack. That was quick."

"Woulda been quicker, Mrs. March, but we had to get his bags from the station first." He stepped inside. "This is Mr. Hadji. Mrs. March."

Hadji extended his hand and bowed slightly. "My pleasure, madam."

"Well, I'm pleased to meet you, Mr. Hadji. Won't you come in?"

"You two go ahead," Lewis said. "I have to get back to the office." He shook Hadji's hand. "Pleasure doing business with you, Mr. Hadji." Hadji grunted and then picked up his bags and carried them through the door, which Mrs. March was holding for him.

She shut the door and asked, "Where are you from, Mr. Hadji? Not from around here, I'm sure."

"I am an Egyptian," he replied, inspecting the interior of the house. Small foyer, somewhat larger living room, kitchen off to the left, small dining room adjoining it. Stairway against one wall of the living room, doubtless leading to the bedrooms upstairs.

"From Egypt! Isn't that exciting." She smiled maternally. "Are you here as a tourist?"

"No, I am on business." He turned and looked at her, noticing the gentleness of the somewhat watery blue eyes and the face which, wrinkles and the ravages of time notwithstanding, bespoke a kindly and caring personality. "In fact, I decided upon your room because I need peace and quiet while I engage in my business. Mr. Lewis tells me that your son is the only other resident, and that he is not here at the moment?"

"Oh, yes, that's right. Eddy is out in Oregon. He's an architect, you know. He's working on the design for a bridge." She was obviously very proud of her son.

"That's good. I shall be here for less than a week, and I need solitude and privacy. I hope you do not frequently entertain guests?"

She laughed. "Oh, my, no. Most of my friends have passed beyond this veil of tears. Reverend Sloan calls on Saturdays—that's his visiting day—but other than him nobody ever comes by." Smiling, she added, "That's one reason why I rent the room. I like the company."

"Excellent," Hadji muttered. "Perfect."

"Well, if you will follow me, I'll show you the room. I hope—"

"If you please," he interrupted, "I would like first to make a very important phone call. It is long distance, but I shall reverse the charges. May I please use your phone?"

"Oh, yes, of course. It's right in here." She shuffled slowly into the kitchen and gestured toward the wall phone which hung beside the kitchen table.

"Thank you," Hadji said. Picking up the receiver, he dialed "0" and waited for a moment.

"Operator," the tinny voice said on the line.

"Operator, I wish to place a call, a collect call to Mr. Haleel Haftoori in Cairo, Egypt. The number is 46–687–5344."

"Thank you. Please spell the name." He did so. "Thank you. And your name, please?"

"Ahmed Hadji—that's H-a-d-j-i—and please emphasize to the person who answers that I am calling from the United States."

"Thank you. Please hold."

Hadji waited impatiently as the various connections were made and the several operators passed their charge on to one another. At last the connection was made to the number he had given.

"Reclamation," the lightly accented voice said in English.

"Is this Cairo 46–687–5344?" asked the overseas operator.

"Yes, National Institute of Reclamation. May I help you?"

"I have a collect person to person call for Mr. Haleel Haftoori from Mr. Ahmed Hadji in the United States."

"One moment please." There was a pause, and then the institute receptionist said, "Mr. Haftoori is on the line. Go ahead, please."

Hadji spoke now in Arabic. "This is Hadji."

"Hello, my son," said Haftoori, the aged high priest of the ancient cult. "What is the status of your mission."

"I have found the Lord Sekhemib and the others."

"All seven? Intact?"

"I have seen only the Lord Sekhemib. But he is whole and uninjured."

"Praise the gods!" the old man said, his voice shaking with emotion. "Praise the gods!"

"But master, wait." Hadji licked his lips. "There are problems. I arrived too late to prevent the sale of the lords to a museum here in the United States."

"The United States! You are not in England?"

"No, my master. I arrived too late. They have been sold to a museum in a small town here."

"You must acquire them by any means! You must!"

"Yes, I know I must. I shall! But . . ." He stopped speaking.

Haftoori waited for him to continue, and then said angrily, "Yes, yes, go on."

Hadji sighed. There was no way to avoid stating the unpleasant truth. "One of the Americans placed his hand upon the head of the Lord Sekhemib."

Hadji thought he heard a gasp from the other end of the line. There was a long pause, and then Haftoori said, "There is now no choice. You know what must be done."

Though Haftoori could not see him, Hadji inclined his head in respectful submission. "Yes, my master."

"Proceed with caution, but with haste. I shall make the travel arrangements. What phone number can you be found using?"

Hadji looked at the phone housing which hung from the wall. "Area code in the United States 315, number is 642–1119."

"Good. Proceed as you must." Haftoori paused and then added, "Do not reproach yourself, Ahmed."

"I am to blame."

"No, you are not to blame. The tekenu has chosen himself."

Hadji nodded. "Yes, my master."

"The gods bless your labors. *Anet hrauthen neteru.*"

"*Anet hrauthen neteru.*" Homage to the gods.

The phone clicked dead and Hadji replaced the receiver. He turned to Mrs. March, who was standing over the stove, saying, "I've just made some bran muffins. Would you like one?" She moved the hot muffin tin from the stove to the work counter beside the sink and closed the oven door with her knee.

"No thank you, madam. But there is something I wish to show you, if you don't mind."

"Oh? And what's that?"

"Come, it is in my suitcase." Hadji went back out to the foyer and, putting one suitcase on its side, opened it and drew out a small leather toiletry case. Mrs. March shuffled in behind him and watched with curiosity as he drew a glass bottle and some cotton from the case.

"Why, whatever is that, Mr. Hadji?"

"I believe, Mrs. March," he replied as he opened the bottle and, holding it some distance from his face, poured some of the liquid contents onto the cotton, "that in English it is called chloroform."

He was on her in an instant. She was too startled to struggle with any success as he pressed the drug-soaked cotton down over her nose and mouth. The old woman attempted to push him away from her, but he forced her to the ground and held her immobile with his weight until by degrees she ceased to struggle. When he was certain that she was unconscious, he released her and returned to his suitcase. He drew a length of rope and a strip of cloth from the side pocket.

Once he had bound and gagged the old woman, he made a quick inspection of the house. He drew the curtains on the side and rear windows but left the front curtains open so as not to arouse the suspicions of the neighbors. He went down into the basement and found it unfinished, a mere storage area, dimly lighted and rather dank. It would do.

He returned to the foyer and dragged Mrs. March to the steps of the basement. She was still unconscious but was beginning to move her hands spasmodically as the small dose of chloroform began to lose its effect. He dragged her down the stairs to the basement and left her lying on the cold stone floor as he returned to fetch his suitcases. He brought them both down with obvious effort and stood for a moment, wiping his brow and trying to catch his breath.

Hadji then opened one suitcase and took out a series of highly polished wooden planks, each one approximately three feet in length and two feet in width. He also took out a screwdriver and a small plastic bottle filled with screws.

He fitted the pieces of wood together, connecting them by means of screws driven into the predrilled holes. He was thinking of other things as he assembled the portable altar. He needed to pay very little attention to his current task, for he had assembled and disassembled and reassembled his portable shrine so often that he could have done it now in the dark, if need be.

A low moan escaped from Mrs. March as she slowly rose back to consciousness. Good, Hadji thought. Her awareness is necessary. He glanced over at her to find her staring at him in confusion and terror. He ignored her pleading eyes and muffled cries, and opened the second suitcase. He drew forth a small obsidian statuette of a man with the head of a jackal. Anubis.

Hadji placed the statuette upon the flat surface of the altar and bowed before it. Mrs. March felt her heart pounding, and she struggled against her bonds as she tried to make out the words she heard Hadji chanting in a high singsong voice.

Then Hadji rose from his knees and walked over to Mrs. March. He took her by the arms and dragged her over to the altar. She tried to force herself to struggle, but she found that fear had bound her more strongly than any rope, and she lay limp. Hadji lifted her to her knees and leaned her frail body over the front of the altar. Then, drawing a knife from his back pocket, he slit her throat.

The blood gushed over the lacquered wood, the severed artery shooting spurts of warm liquid upon the statue of Anubis. Mrs. March's eyes grew glassy, and then ceased to see.

Hadji propped her body against the altar with a nearby milk crate which he had seen, tossed apparently at random into the basement. As the blood poured out of the woman's throat, Hadji prostrated himself before the altar and chanted, *"Au arina neterhetepu en neteru, perchkheru en khu."* I have made offerings to the gods. I have sacrificed to the spirits. *"'Anpu kheq tetta, nekhemkua ma aterit."* Anubis, Prince of Eternity, deliver me from calamity.

*"'Anpu neb nifu, nekhemkua ma ab."*

Anubis, Lord of the Winds, deliver me from death.

The dark, damp basement echoed to the words of his chant. The only other sound was the sound of the blood running off the altar onto the floor. It ran as if it were a river. Then it dripped. Then it stopped.

# CHAPTER 5

△ Much to his surprise, Roderick had been finding the conversation fascinating. Knowing so little about almost everything, he had sat in rapt attention as Harriet expounded upon the process, techniques, and varieties of mummification, and he found himself reluctant to tear himself away from the table at Bottadio's restaurant when the maitre d' told him that the call he had been trying to place all afternoon and evening had finally gotten through. He playfully enjoined Harriet from continuing her exposition until he returned to the table.

He stood casually with the phone in his hand, one knee bent, one hand thrust in his pocket. If he noticed the curious looks the locals cast in his direction as they passed, he gave no indication. Resting the receiver between his jaw and shoulder, he drew a cigarette from his cigarette case and lighted it. He tapped his foot impatiently and blew smoke rings as he waited.

"Lord Selwyn?" the London operator's voice asked.

"This is Selwyn," he replied testily. "What the devil is the problem now?"

"Terribly sorry for the delay, Your Lordship. We've gotten an answer on the line. Please proceed."

Pause. "Horace Pearson's offices. Are you there?"

"Yes, hello, Gladys?" What's wrong with her voice, he wondered.

"Speaking."

"Selwyn here. I've been trying to get hold—"

"Oh, Your Lordship, it's been terrible here, terrible. Are you returning to England?"

"Return! What on earth for?" He was suddenly concerned.

"The damned Commons haven't raised the inheritance tax again, have they?"

"Oh, no, Your Lordship!"

"Well, thank God for that! What's the problem?"

She paused. "Oh, my gracious, haven't you been informed?"

"Damn it all, Gladys. Informed of what?"

"It's Mr. Pearson, Your Lordship. He's dead. He's been killed. Murdered."

Roderick was stunned. "What—what are you talking about?"

"I *am* sorry, Your Lordship. I thought you'd been contacted."

"No, no, I had no idea. What happened?"

"No one seems to know. Poor Mr. Pearson left the office to accompany you to the airport yesterday, and he told me that he had an evening appointment with an Eastern gentleman. That was the last time he was seen alive. When I came to the offices this morning, I found him lying on the floor in a pool of blood. His throat had been cut!"

"My God!"

"Yes, it was horrible. I've been at Scotland Yard all day."

"Pearson," Roderick muttered. "Poor old bloke."

"The police want to question the Eastern gentleman, but I have no idea who he was, and poor Mr. Pearson's appointment book is gone. All of his files have been rifled."

"Do the police think this fellow killed him?"

"They don't know. No one seems to know anything."

"Bloody wog!" Roderick spat. He actually had no idea what a wog was, but his uncle had always said that whenever Easterners were discussed, so he felt it to be an appropriate comment.

"Oh, Your Lordship, what are we going to do?"

"Eh? Do? Whatever do you mean?"

"All of Mr. Pearson's records are disorganized, strewn about the office! I've been here for hours, trying to sort things out. I don't know where anything is!"

"Well, what do you expect me to do about it?" Roderick was annoyed at the question, but realized as soon as he spoke that his voice had been harsher than intended. More gently, he said, "Gladys, I'm certain that you will persevere. For now, just go home and get some sleep."

"Perhaps I should," she sighed. "I've been here all evening."

"What time is it there?"

"About ten-thirty. I've been trying to reôrganize the files since five!"

"Well, then, you certainly had a long enough day. Take tomorrow off," he added expansively.

"Yes, Your Lordship," she replied with relief, even though she was not his employee.

"Goodnight, now," he said. "And don't worry about Pearson's files."

"Goodnight."

Roderick tossed the receiver to the waiting maitre d' and then walked back to the table. Why didn't they call me? he wondered, and then answered his own question. Of course, if they had the itinerary which he had submitted to his people, and not the one which Pearson had written up for him, Scotland Yard would expect him to be in Orlando with his chauffeur, his butler, and most of his luggage. Roderick frowned. Those bloody twits were enjoying Disneyworld, and he was stuck in this rural backwater. "Damn!" he muttered. And then he thought, Poor old Pearson.

He resumed his seat with Harriet, Suzanne, Sawhill, and Goldhaber and stared distractedly off into space. He was suddenly uninterested in the conversation.

"Great food here," Suzanne was saying as she stuffed another fork of lasagna into her mouth.

"Ummmph," Sawhill agreed through his veal in wine sauce.

"I just adore the Romance languages, don't you, Your Lordship?" she asked. "The name of this place is so pretty."

"Bottadio," Sam said savoringly, rolling the vowels off his tongue.

"Bottadio," Suzanne repeated in the same manner. "Our language seems so hard and, well, I don't know, unappealing. Don't you agree, Your Lordship?"

"What? Oh, yes. Yes, indeed." Roderick's mind was miles away.

"It's an interesting name for many reasons," Harriet added. "Have you ever heard the old legend about the wandering Jew?"

"Ten colleges in thirty years," Goldhaber mused. "Must be me."

"Oh, shush. Seriously, do you know the legend?" It was a general question, not directed to any one person at the table.

"Doesn't it have something to do with an eternal man?" Sam asked.

"Immortal, not eternal," Harriet corrected him. "The story was that one of the people who mocked Christ at the crucifixion was condemned by him to remain alive until the Second Coming. His name was Salathiel, I think, and the legend has it that he popped up every once in a while throughout the ages."

"So what does this have to do with Bottadio?" Sawhill asked.

"Well, the same story is told about the Roman soldier, an Italian, of course, who pierced Christ's side with a spear while he was on the cross. He was condemned to the same fate, to wander eternally until the end of the world."

"And his name was Bottadio?" Suzanne asked.

Harriet shook her head as she took another forkful of ziti. "Nickname. *Bottadio* means 'God striker.'"

Sawhill smiled at the others as he nodded at Harriet. "College professor. Ask her the time and she tells you how to build a clock."

"But I'm sorry we drifted off the topic," Suzanne said. "This whole mummification thing fascinates me. Please go on."

"Sure," Sawhill moaned. "Perfect dinner conversation."

"Get this! A doctor with a weak stomach!" Harriet took a sip of the deep, rich red wine in her glass. "Where was I?"

"How they got the idea," Suzanne prompted, glancing at Roderick. He had seemed so interested before, but now he just sat there pensively.

"Oh, yeah. As I was saying, the predynastic Egyptians generally just buried the bodies in the sand, unembalmed and unenclosed. The earliest known mummies are just dried out corpses which were accidentally preserved by the dry heat and sand of Upper Egypt, far south of the Nile Delta. We assume that they got the idea of preservation from coming across old bodies which had not decomposed."

"No embalming and still no decomposition?" Sam asked. "That's hard to imagine."

"Well, they weren't well preserved. They looked rather like prunes. But the point is they demonstrated that the body could escape the reduction to dust which happened to bodies buried in the north."

"But how did that lead to the whole process of mummification? I mean, mummification as we use the word generally, with the wrappings and everything?" Suzanne seemed very absorbed in the topic.

"Nobody knows the exact development, but it's easy enough to guess. Trial and error, different solutions for embalming, different types of coffins, different types of wrappings. Eventually, by the period we call the New Kingdom, they had perfected the technique."

"And when was that?"

"Traditional date is about 1570 B.C., after the expulsion of the Hyksos." She took another sip of wine and laughed lightly. "Don't get me started on the Hyksos, by the way. I did my master's thesis on them."

"Okay," Sawhill said. "I for one have no idea who they were, and I can probably live without the knowledge."

"So when they perfected the process, what exactly was the process they perfected," Suzanne asked.

"Well," Harriet said, a hint of warning in her voice, "it sounds a little grisly."

"I think we can stand it," Goldhaber said, smiling.

"Okay. You asked for it." Harriet placed her wine glass down on the table. "When someone with money died—"

"This was expensive, right?" Suzanne asked.

"Damned expensive. When someone with money died, his body was taken to the undertaker, as we would call him. The first step was the removal of the organs of the body, a process called evisceration. The undertaker made an incision in the abdomen and took the lungs, intestines, and the rest out through the incision. The heart was left in place."

"Why the heart?"

"The Egyptians believed the heart to be the seat of thought and memory, so it had to be left in the body."

"What about the brain?"

Harriet took another sip of wine. "Drawn out through the nostrils with a hook."

Suzanne threw her napkin down on the table. "Wait a minute. I don't think I want to hear any more of this."

"You asked for it," Harriet said wickedly. "Anyway, the body and the organs would all be placed in natron for what tradition says was seventy days. Natron," she added before anyone could ask, "is a type of salt. For reasons which I do not understand, it dehydrates much more rapidly than regular salt."

"Sounds sort of like salting pork," Sawhill observed.

"Pretty much the same idea," she agreed. "Incidentally, if

the body was that of a woman, especially a young one, the family didn't bring the corpse to the embalmers for a while."

Suzanne seemed perplexed. "Why not? Wouldn't it start to rot?"

"Sure it would. That was the idea. It was a way of making sure that the embalmers didn't have sex with the corpse."

"Okay, okay, that's enough," Suzanne said. "This is getting disgusting."

"The worst is over," Harriet assured her. "After the natron treatment, the body and the organs were taken out of the chemical and wrapped in linen strips. The organs were placed in receptacles called canopic jars and were stored near the sarcophagus in the tomb. The body itself, of course, was placed in a sarcophagus. And that's about all."

"And all mummies went through this procedure?" Sawhill asked. "It sounds like a hell of a lot of trouble."

"Oh, it was. Only the royalty and nobility could afford that kind of treatment. The poor were still just dropped in holes in the sand. There was a small—well, what we might call middle class, and they got a cheap version of the full procedure."

"What did they do, leave the liver in?" Sam asked.

"Good one, Sam," she said. "Very funny."

"You said this was done during the—the New Kingdom, was it?" Suzanne asked. Harriet nodded and Suzanne continued, "So what about the mummies you just bought? Are they from that period?"

"I assume so," Harriet replied, "because the mummy of old Mr. Sekhemib is so well preserved. But I can't be sure until I examine it fully."

"Fascinating," Sam Goldhaber said.

"It really is," Harriet agreed. "I know some people think it's kind of a strange thing to be interested in, but it fascinates me. I'm really looking forward to examining the bodies in depth."

"Did you translate all that stuff you copied off the coffin lid?" Suzanne asked.

"Oh, sure. I did that this morning while Will was unloading the others." She frowned, remembering her misgivings. "There're a lot of things that don't quite made sense to me, though."

"Like what?"

She looked at Sawhill. "I told Tommy already, because he was helping me do the transcription."

"Some help!" Sawhill grinned. "I held her paper for her."

"I don't suppose it could do any harm to tell the rest of you. I'm certain the mummy is genuine, but there are problems with the coffin itself and with the hieroglyphs."

"You mean hieroglyphics, don't you?" Sam asked.

"No," Harriet replied, holding her wine glass up as Sawhill filled it from the bottle. "*Hieroglyphic* is an adjective. The individual characters are called hieroglyphs. That's the noun form."

"You mean they aren't hieroglyphs? They're fakes?"

"No, no, not at all. It's Egyptian writing, all right. But there are inconsistencies. There's a prayer addressed to Anubis on the lid, but he has Ra's titles. And a section of the Papyrus of Ani, a very famous work, is reproduced with the name of the god changed to Anubis from Thoth."

No one else at the table seemed particularly impressed with these revelations. "So?" Suzanne asked. "So what?"

"I know it doesn't seem important," Harriet said patiently, "but the Egyptians were a very consistent people, especially when it came to funerary ritual and formalized religious ceremonies. I'm not saying the sarcophagus is a fake, but there certainly is something out of the ordinary about it. It may take a while to figure it out."

"Well, if that's all there is that's strange—"Sam began.

"I haven't really examined the mummy yet," Harriet reminded him.

"Yes, but it looks authentic to me. I mean, I haven't made a study of Egyptian mummies, but it certainly looks like one." Sam glanced around the table for support, and got nods of agreement from Suzanne and Sawhill and, cautiously, from Harriet. "If there's nothing else amiss, it doesn't seem to me that there is anything for you to worry about."

"Oh, I'm not worried. Not really. But inconsistencies bother me. There's this, for example." She reached into her purse, which was leaning against the foot of the chair, and took out the golden medallion which she found lying in the coffin beside Sekhemib.

"Harriet!" Suzanne exclaimed.

"What?" she asked innocently.

"You shouldn't be carrying that around with you! That's a damn foolish risk!"

"Oh, don't be silly. Nobody's going to snatch my purse in Greenfield!"

"You should keep that locked up in the museum," Sam said kindly but firmly. "It isn't your property. It belongs to the college."

Suzanne seemed annoyed. "I wrote the policies on these exhibits, remember. If that were lost or stolen—"

"Hey, come on, all of you. Cut it out. It's not only common practice for curators to remove pieces from a museum for research purposes, it is absolutely necessary. I had to check something about it."

"Well . . ." Sam was skeptical. "I don't know—"

"Oh, for Christ's sake, Sam, I wasn't stealing it!"

"No, no, I know that. Of course not. But I can't help but feel that museum pieces shouldn't be stored in a lady's purse."

Harriet understood the concern Suzanne and Sam were voicing, so she said, "Look. If it will make you happy, I won't bring the mummies home with me at night. Okay?"

The ludicrousness of the image she had just suggested caused a ripple of laughter. "Okay," Sam said. "So what's with the medallion?"

"Couple of things." She turned the medallion over on its face and pointed to a line of hieroglyphs on the back.

"Hey, I didn't see that when we open the coffin," Sawhill said.

"That's because we didn't turn the medallion over," Harriet explained. "I certainly would have if the Hadji creep hadn't come storming in."

"What does it say?"

"Well, that's the problem. It says *'Anet hrauthen 'Anpu,'* which means 'Homage to you, Anubis.'"

"So? Sounds okay to me," Sam said.

"Yes, but you've never studied Egyptian. *'Hrauthen'* is a plural form. It *should* say *'Anet hrak 'Anpu,'* using the singular form. In other words, it is grammatically incorrect. If you were a man who engraved tombstones nowadays, you'd be careful enough not to carve something like 'He were a good guy' on a tomb."

"Hmm," Sam said, nodding. "That's odd, isn't it."

"Sure as hell is. It really makes me doubt the authenticity of this medallion."

"What about the evolution of the language?"

"What do you mean?"

"Well, might this be an earlier form of the language? I mean, I know enough about Egyptian history to know that its civilization lasted for thousands of years. There must have been changes in the language during such a long period."

"It is possible that there was an ancient usage of this sort, but it was not used during the New Kingdom period. For that matter, I'm pretty sure it wasn't used during the Middle Kingdom or the Old Kingdom either."

"It could be an honor usage," Sam mused.

"What's that?" Suzanne asked.

"An honor usage? If I remember my lessons from Hebrew school, the Bible uses a plural noun form for the word 'God' when applied to the Supreme Being. The Hebrew word for 'god' is *el;* but when they wrote of *their* god, the God of Israel, they wrote *elohim,* which really means 'gods.' They pluralized the noun to exalt the deity."

This confused Sawhill. Languages had never been his best subject. "But then how can you tell when the plural *means* a plural and when it means a singular?"

"Verb form," Harriet muttered. To Sam she said, "It's possible. I may have to write to Professor Craigo back in Chicago about that. I just don't know."

Suzanne reached over and took the medallion from the table. She handled it gently, turning it over in her palm and stroking the smooth metal. She ran her fingers over the four images on the face, and asked, "What does this say?"

"It doesn't really say anything," Harried answered, frowning again. "The cross in the middle—"

"The ankh?" Suzanne asked.

Harriet seemed surprised. "How did you know that?"

Her friend laughed. "If you paid more attention to jewelry that living people wear and less to the jewelry of the dead, you'd know. Honestly, Harriet! Everybody knows what an ankh is! People wear them on necklaces all the time. It's fashionable."

"Really!" She nodded approvingly. "Good symbol to wear. It means 'life.'"

"I thought it meant fertility."

"That too, originally, anyway. The hieroglyph looks like a cross to us because of our Christian culture. It's really an idealized combination of the male and female genitals."

"No kidding!" Suzanne grinned lasciviously at Roderick. He ignored her.

"What about the others, Harriet?" Sam asked.

"Well," she went on, "the two seated figures on top—the seated figures with jackal heads, holding ankhs—are images of Anubis, god of the grave. Sekhemib apparently was a priest of Anubis, so that makes sense as a badge of identification, but the three hieroglyphs don't really form a sentence."

"What about the fourth one?" Sawhill asked. "That's the one you didn't recognize this morning."

"Yeah, I had to go and look it up." She turned to Sam. "That's why I had to bring the medallion home with me. I wanted to have it to refer to as I leafed through my dictionary."

Goldhaber nodded, smiling. "Explanation accepted, professor."

"Good." She turned back to Sawhill. "This figure is called a tekenu."

"And it means?"

She shrugged. "No one knows. It appears in many funerary carvings, but Egyptology has still not figured it out. It looks like a man sitting on a sled, and I read that sometimes it is written as a man lying on a sled. Some scholars have speculated that the reclining form is a depiction of the fetal position, so that the tekenu symbolizes the rebirth of the dead man. Others have said that it is a predynastic hieroglyph referring to some form of human sacrifice."

"I can't see how this could symbolize human sacrifice," Sam said.

"Well, it could in a number of ways. The figure lying on the sled may be dead, his blood shed to give life to the deceased. Or perhaps the sled, which of course implies movement, represents some manner in which the tekenu gives new life. No one really knows. This is all speculation."

"So its meaning might turn these three other figures into a sentence?" Sam asked.

"Possible, but unlikely," she replied. "This is just one of ancient Egypt's mysteries."

"Like the pyramids," Suzanne said softly.

Harriet shook her head. "There's nothing mysterious about the pyramids. They were enormous tombs for absolute monarchs built with slave labor, nothing more."

"But I thought we didn't know how they built them? I mean, I read that they couldn't have built them with the technology they had at that time."

"I've heard that too," Sawhill said. "And things about the angles of the sides having some numerological significance."

"Please, please, don't do this to me," Harriet said, putting a palm on her forehead. "I thought only high-school kids paid any attention to that crap. We know exactly how they built the pyramids, and exactly why. There's no mystery. It's things like this—" and she tapped the figure of the tekenu on the medallion which Suzanne had replaced on the table, "which constitute the mysteries of the past. No aliens, no black magic.

Just hieroglyphs we can't interpret, gaps in dynastic lists we can't fill, chronologies we can't piece together satisfactorily."

"That's kind of depressing to hear," Suzanne muttered.

"Depressing! Why?"

"Well, I think people get a kick out of things like that. I mean, mysterious, dark things from the distant past, you know? They're fun to think about."

"Sure, I understand that," Harriet said. "I have a thing for vampire novels myself. But we shouldn't confuse history with fiction. I mean, I get a kick out of *Dracula*, but I don't for a moment believe that vampires are real." Suzanne did not seem mollified, but Harriet ignored her. "Egypt is ancient enough for many real mysteries to exist, the kind that obsess scholars. The tekenu image, for example. There was an Egyptian civilization long before there was an Egyptian writing system, and figuring out what exactly it was like is a major task. Maybe this tekenu figure refers to something so far distant in the past of Egypt that even the dynastic peoples didn't really understand it. It seems to occur at random in tombs and on sarcophagi, but it's never explained, never used in sentences."

"But if they didn't know what it meant, why would they use it?" Sawhill asked.

"Well, let's say that over a period of thousands of years the language of ancient Greece was lost to learning. There would still be Christian communities and Christian churches, and they would follow the tradition of using the symbols for alpha and omega in their churches without knowing what they meant. They might put the Chi-Rho on their altars without knowing what it meant."

"The what?"

"The Chi-Rho. You've seen it, Tommy. It looks like a P superimposed on an X."

"Oh, sure. I've seen that in churches. That's Greek?"

"Of course. It's the first two letters of the word *christos*." She turned to the others. "See? Perfect example. Tommy is a well-educated man coming from a civilization rooted in the culture of ancient Greece, and he doesn't know what the symbols mean."

"Be fair, honey," Sawhill said. "Greek civilization was a long time ago."

She shook her head in disagreement. "Two thousand years separate us from ancient Greece. Three thousand years separate the New Kingdom of Egypt from the preliterate period. See?"

Sam laughed. "I can see why you impress your students, Harriet."

She blushed. "Hey, I'm sorry I've been monopolizing the conversation. I get carried away whenever I talk about Egypt. It's been my passion since childhood."

"Don't apologize!" Suzanne exclaimed. "We asked you to explain mummification. And it was fascinating. Don't you think it was fascinating, Your Lordship?"

Roderick had been sitting in silence, paying absolutely no attention to the conversation. He looked up at Suzanne. "Hmmm?"

The expression on his face concerned her. "Is something bothering you?"

"Oh, no, no, nothing." He paused. "Well, there is, actually. I called my solicitor before to ask him about this Hadji fellow."

"Oh." Harriet was immediately on her guard, feeling her prize exhibits threatened anew. "And what did he say?"

Roderick shook his head. "I spoke to his secretary. My solicitor has been murdered."

Silence hit the small group. No one spoke for several minutes. Then Sawhill said, "That's horrible!"

"You mean Mr. Pearson?" Suzanne whispered. Roderick nodded. "Oh my God! I just saw him yesterday at the airport. What happened?"

"The police aren't certain," Roderick replied. "His secretary found him in his office this morning with his throat cut."

"Oh, that's terrible, terrible," Sam said, shaking his head. "The poor man. I'm so sorry, Your Lordship."

"Yes, me too," Sawhill said. "Please accept my sympathies. Did he have a family?"

Roderick shrugged. "I have no idea. I never asked."

The festive mood which had existed earlier in the evening had dissipated. Sawhill looked around at the others and asked, "Does anyone want coffee or dessert?" Those who chose to respond shook their heads, and he called for a check.

"Hey, Tommy," Harriet said pensively, "didn't that Hadji person say that he had been negotiating with Lord Selwyn's lawyer?"

Sawhill's head, which had been bowed in the direction of the money he was removing from his wallet, snapped up. "Shit, that's right! Your Lordship, do the British police know about him?"

"No, but by God, Gladys—Pearson's secretary—said he had an appointment with an Easterner. Do you think it was Hadji?"

"It makes sense. You'd better call London again, Your Lordship. They have to know about this guy." He turned to Harriet. "And we'd better tell Jasper."

"Yeah, right away. If he killed the Earl's lawyer, he might very well steal the exhibits."

"Harriet, for God's sake, I'm not worried about the mummies! He might do something to you!" He took her hand when he saw her face blanch. "Easy, easy. Let's get to Jasper's right away."

"Yeah, don't worry, Har," Suzanne said with assurance. "There's nothing to get upset about." The look that she and Thomas Sawhill exchanged indicated that neither of them believed that last statement.

"Perhaps I should go back to the hotel and place the call to Scotland Yard?" Roderick suggested.

"No, wait," Sawhill said. "Let's all go to see Jasper. He's going to want to talk to your police anyway, and I'm sure they'll have a few things to discuss with him too." He tossed some money down on the table, and they all rose to make their ways to the door.

It was a bit chilly outside, and they all drew their collars tight around their necks. Harriet got into Sawhill's Saab while Suzanne and Roderick followed Goldhaber to his battered old station wagon down the street. "Maybe we should call the state police," Harriet said as Sawhill slid into the driver's seat and shut the door.

"Let Jasper decide about that. I'm sure that there are standard procedures he has to follow when stuff like this happens." He paused. "Let's not jump to conclusions. For all we know, Hadji has nothing to do with what happened in London."

"God, I hope not," she muttered. Harriet nervously chewed on her nails as Sawhill pulled away from the curb with Goldhaber's car a few yards behind him. "I know that museums can be competitive, and the Cairo Museum's people are almost fanatical because of all the things the West stole from Egypt. But murder!"

"The more I think of it, the less sense it makes to assume a connection," Sawhill said. "I mean, what purpose would be served by killing the lawyer?"

"Get rid of a witness?"

"Not when the next day he identifies himself to seven people, two of them police officers." He shook his head. "I think we're just acting a little skittish because of the way Hadji acted."

"But we're still going to see Jasper, right?"

"Oh, yes, of course. Better safe than sorry." They drove the rest of the way in silence. Sawhill stole an occasional furtive glance to his right and was disturbed by the obvious worry which was furrowing Harriet's brow.

They reached the police station in a few minutes. The small town hall was of late nineteenth-century design, and the police station (which was added years later) seemed conspicuously out of place attached to the side of the building. The steeple-topped wooden town hall contrasted unpleasantly with the squat red-brick annex which, Jasper always joked, had been thrown up in haste by the lowest bidder.

They alighted from their cars and gathered before the door of the police station. "Now listen," Sawhill cautioned them. "Let's not act too paranoic. Jasper has a ton of experience with serious crime and serious criminals. He'll know what to do, and he'll also know if we're acting foolish, so let's not embarrass ourselves. Okay?" His warning was greeted with nods of assent all round.

Sawhill opened the door and found Jasper sitting behind his desk. Will Foster and Gus Rudd was seated in front of the desk. The scattered poker chips, beer cans, pretzels, cigarette and cigar butts, and playing cards told Sawhill immediately that it had been a slow, quiet night in Greenfield.

"Hiya, Jasper," he said. "Will, Gus."

"Hey, Tom, come on in." Jasper looked behind Sawhill and saw the others trudging in nervously. "Hi there, folks. Something wrong?" He stood up. "It isn't the museum, is it?"

"No, no," Harriet said quickly. "At least not yet. It's just that—well—" She turned to Sawhill.

"Lord Selwyn called London a little while ago to talk to his lawyer. He was informed that his lawyer was murdered. The police over there don't seem to have any leads, not any that he heard of on the phone anyway."

"Yes?" Jasper asked. His tone of voice said "So what?"

"His lawyer's secretary told him that Mr. Pearson—that was the lawyer's name—had an appointment last night with what she described as—an Easterner?" He looked at Roderick for confirmation of the description.

"Yes," Roderick said. "An Easterner. Like that boorish

fellow who caused all that unpleasantness this morning. It could be he."

Jasper Rudd placed his poker hand on his desk and leaned back in his chair. "Any reason to think they're one and the same?"

"Well, he did say that he had been negotiating with Mr. Pearson, didn't he?" Harriet said. "And you saw yourself how excitable that man is."

Jasper nodded. "Have any of you seen this guy since this morning?" They all shook their heads. "Hmmm. Well, it's possible. Anyway, the London police should be informed." He reached over to the telephone and dialed for the operator. "This is Chief Rudd in Greenfield. I want the overseas operator. Yes, I'll hold." He cupped his hand over the mouthpiece and said, "I wouldn't worry about this, folks. Calling somebody an Easterner could mean anything. Coulda been a Hindu or a Chinese, coulda been a Russian."

"There are many Indians in London," Roderick said, nodding. "Many Pakistanis and Chinese as well. I hadn't thought of that, actually."

"Sure," Jasper said. "It doesn't necessarily mean—Yes, operator. I need to be connected with Scotland Yard in London. No, I don't know the number. Please look it up. Yes, this is official business. Yes, I'll hold." He looked back up. "Yeah, it doesn't necessarily mean that this Hadji is dangerous."

"Shit," Will muttered. "That little asshole couldn't scare a mouse away from cheese."

"He doesn't seem dangerous to me," Jasper concurred. "I don't—hello? Scotland Yard? Oh, I'm sorry, operator." He looked up. "London operator." Sighing, he repeated, "This is Chief Rudd of the Greenfield Police in New York State, U.S. of A. I need to be connected with Scotland Yard. Yes, yes, I'll hold." He shook his head. "Goddamn phone companies."

Sawhill's medical eye noticed Will Foster rubbing his hand. "Hey, Will, that hand any better?"

Will shook his head. "No, Doc, it's worse. I can't hardly move it."

Sawhill walked over to where Will Foster was sitting. "Here, let me have another look at it." Sawhill extended his hand and Will placed his own in it. Sawhill frowned as he ran his experienced fingers over the injured member, turning it over and examining it carefully. Will's hand seemed to have stiffened and grown cold. The skin seemed to be stretched tightly across the bone, and the veins stood out clearly, blue against the white. "You can't move it?"

"No. You know what it feels like when you fall asleep on your arm and it's all numb when you wake up? It's sorta like that, 'cept it isn't limp. It's all stiff."

"Well," Sawhill said with a certainty he did not feel, "it's probably just a severe muscle strain. Look, Will, if it doesn't feel any better tomorrow, drop over to the office and see me, okay?"

"Yeah, sure, Doc."

Sawhill turned his attention back to Jasper, who had already begun to explain to the London police what the situation was in Greenfield. "So when Mr. Selwyn—yes, I'm sorry, Lord Selwyn—told us what he'd heard on the phone, I figured I'd better get in touch with you." Jasper paused for a moment and then laughed at something said on the other end of the line, prompting Sawhill to reflect that police officers, regardless of nationality, speak a common language born of similar experiences. "Yeah," Jasper went on. "His name is Hadji."

"Ahmed Hadji," Goldhaber reminded him.

"Of the Egyptian National Institute of Reclamation," Harriet added.

"Ahmed Hadji," Jasper said into the phone, "of the Egyptian National Institute of Reclamation." Pause. "Beats the hell out of me. Something to do with archeology." He paused again, a very, very long pause which he interrupted only with an occasional "Uh-huh." Then he said, "Well, I really appreciate that, Inspector Sheldon, I really do. Yeah, my number here is U.S. area code 315; number's 682–9696. Thanks again." He replaced the receiver.

"Well?" Harriet asked.

Jasper did not reply immediately. He was staring pensively off into space, his eyes narrowed with concentration and concern. At last he said, "Real polite people you got over there, Earl."

Roderick smiled. "We endeavor to be cooperative."

"I'm not interested in their manners!" Harriet snapped. "What did they say?"

Jasper sighed. "I think we got a problem here, folks."

"You mean Hadji?" Sawhill asked.

The policeman nodded his head slowly. "That guy may be a foreigner here on a legitimate passport for legitimate purposes, doing nothing illegal. But everything in my experience as a cop tells me that there's more to it than that."

"Oh, Jasper, for Christ's sake!" Harriet said with annoyance. "What did they tell you on the phone?"

"Well," he said slowly, "for one thing this Pearson fellow wasn't just killed. His throat was slit and he seems to have been drained of blood. There was blood at the murder site, but not enough to account for the body's blood loss. They said it looked to them like some sort of ritual murder."

"Good God!" Sawhill said.

"Yeah," Jasper continued, "and there's more. While I was talking to Inspector Sheldon he had a quick computer check run of this institute. No record of it exists in their files."

"You mean it doesn't exist?" Harriet exclaimed. "Hadji's a fraud?"

"Not necessarily," Jasper said. "You can't expect their computers to have entries for every little organization in every country of the world. But it doesn't look good to me, that's for sure. Since the possibility exists of this murder being connected to an Egyptian national now in the United States, Sheldon says they can call on the help of Interpol. He's gonna keep in touch with me and let me know whatever they let him know, if anything."

"What should we do?" Sam Goldhaber asked.

Jasper turned to his brother Gus. "You go to that grounds building at the college and camp out there. I want those exhibits kept a close watch on. And keep your gun at the ready, you hear?"

"Okay, Jasper," Gus said.

Jasper Rudd turned to Harriet and Sawhill. "It isn't any of my business, but I know that you two are engaged. Can I assume that you're, well, real close, if you know what I mean?"

Sawhill was amused by Jasper's attempt at delicacy, and he repressed a grin. Harriet was in no mood to be amused by anything, and she simply replied, "Yes. So?"

"So I think tonight might be a good night for you to stay over at Miss Langly's, Doc. On the couch, of course."

"Of course," Sawhill laughed softly.

"I'm not trying to imply anything—" Jasper began.

"Oh, cut it out," Harriet said, clearly irritated. "You're not a dorm mother! Besides, what do you think we do at night, shake hands?"

"Yeah, right," he said, turning to Sam. "Professor Goldhaber—" he began and was interrupted by the ringing of the phone. "Gus, get that, will you?" As Gus picked up the phone, Jasper continued, "Professor, I don't know what your budget is at the college, but I suggest you hire somebody full time to guard those exhibits."

Sam seem surprised. "Well, Chief, isn't that really your job? I mean—"

Jasper shook his head. "I can have Gus keep an eye on them tonight, and they'll probably be safe tomorrow during the day. But I'm short of manpower. It's just me and Gus. I'm sure you understand. You folks at the College have to see to your own long-term security."

"Yes, I suppose so," Sam said dejectedly. He knew the school's budget quite well. There was no money for security guards.

"Earl," Jasper said, turning to Roderick, "I don't know if this Hadji fellow was involved in your lawyer's murder, but it may be that he was. I don't think it would be wise for you to spend the night alone in a hotel. Savvy?"

"Pardon?" Roderick asked. He did not notice Suzanne's eyes widen as a small grin spread over her face.

"Do you catch my drift?" Roderick's look of utter incomprehension caused Jasper to sigh with annoyance. "Stay someplace else, for your own safety."

"Oh!" Roderick said as he caught the meaning of Jasper's suggestion. "Oh, yes. Very well." Then he muttered, "I'd rather not," but was ignored.

"Jasper?" Gus said seriously. "We got another problem."

"What now?"

"That was Mrs. Lewis on the phone. You know Jack Lewis, the real estate guy down on Elm?"

"Yeah. What's happened?"

"He's been killed."

There was a deep quiet in the room for a moment. Then, before he rose from the seat behind his desk, Jasper Rudd opened a drawer and took out his gun. "You folks go home," he snapped. "I got work to do."

"You want I should come with you?" Gus asked.

"No. You get your ass over to that college and do what I told you to do." He thrust the revolver into the holster which had been hanging empty from the belt around his waist. "If I need you, I'll call you on your radio." To the others he repeated, "You folks go home, and stay there."

They muttered their assent and stood back as Jasper walked out of his office, a look of grim determination upon his frowning face. Gus coughed and said, "Well, I guess I'll go over to the college now. You folks gonna be able to get home okay? I mean, does anyone need a lift or anything?"

"No," Sam said, "I can drop Miss Melendez and the Earl off at their hotel. Thanks anyway, Gus." Sam held the door for the ladies and followed them out, followed by Roderick and Thomas Sawhill.

The five of them stood outside in the slightly chilly night air for a few moments before Harriet said, "Well, I guess I'll see you in the morning."

"Yeah," Suzanne replied. "See you, Har. Night, Tom."

"Sleep well," Sawhill said, and then extended his hand to Roderick. "Sorry again about your friend, Your Lordship."

"Yes," he said as he shook Sawhill's hand. "Ghastly thing, absolutely ghastly."

"Yes, terrible," Sawhill agreed. "See you, Sam."

"Good night." Sam walked over to his automobile and unlocked the doors for Suzanne and Roderick. As they entered he said, "One hell of a night."

"Yeah," Suzanne said. "I thought this kind of thing didn't happen in small towns."

"So did I!" Sam laughed grimly. "But you know what they say. The big cities get the junkies and the street crime, and the small towns get the axe murderers and the chain-saw massacres."

"Charming!" Roderick muttered. I'll bet my chauffeur and butler are watching Disney's fireworks right now, he thought dejectedly.

Sam drove the few miles to the Huguenot Hotel and bade his passengers a good-night which was cherrier than he was. He had known Jack Lewis fairly well for the past few years. Indeed, he and Jack Lewis had assisted new faculty members, Harriet included, in finding housing in Greenfield, and not a few students had availed themselves of the Lewis Agency when the dorms at Winthrop were filled to capacity. Poor guy, Sam thought. What a terrible thing to happen.

Sam Goldhaber watched as Suzanne and Roderick entered the old colonial building which had once housed a Dutch patroon, but which was now one of the regions best known country inns. They're both so young, he reflected. So many years ahead of them. Lord knows what their futures will hold.

Poor Jack Lewis was probably looking forward to a good many more years, and look at him now. Poor bastard.

Sam sighed as he began to drive back to his house on the other side of Greenfield. Life is so sad, sometimes, he thought. You make your plans and have your hopes and dreams, and then some damn thing like this happens. "Man proposes and God disposes," he mutered aloud.

No, not God, he thought. You can't chalk life's vicissitudes up to some arbitrary deity, some patriarchal superbeing dredged up from the imagination of the prescientific mentality. There is no fate, no destiny, no providence, no divine hand in the universe. There's just one damn thing after another.

It had been quite a long while since he had last given any thought to religion, to that system of beliefs imparted to him by his aged, bearded, yarmulked father back on the Lower East Side of Manhattan over a half a century ago. The all-encompassing Orthodox Judaism of his parents and grandparents had been the central fact of their lives, a structure of faith and practice within which a complex and unmanageable universe was given meaning and significance. It was this religious system which had enabled them and their ancestors before time to survive the thousands of years of exile and persecution and segregation which separated them from the ruined temple in Jerusalem.

Sad, in some ways, Sam thought, that mythology has such deep roots.

He had rejected the religion of his parents early in life, but still felt oddly tied to it. He was a scholar and a skeptic and had no belief in deities. He had not set foot in a synagogue since the day he left home for college, decades ago. He was irritated by devoutly religious Jews, more irritated even than he was by the Christian radicals who seemed to be proliferating in the United States recently, possibly because he felt their arcane preoccupations reflected unfavorably upon him, but perhaps at least partially because he felt a residue of parentally implanted guilt that he was not one of them. He had no connection with any synagogue or Jewish group, and yet he had made the study of the Semitic languages—Hebrew, Arabic, Aramaic, and the other old tongues—the focal point of his academic career. He believed the kosher tradition of his parents to be foolish and atavistic, but he still never ate pork. He observed no holy days, but felt a tug of nostalgic sadness at the approach of each Passover. None of this made any sense, but it was all so deep as aspect of his personality that he had learned to live with it long ago.

Know thyself, the philosopher had said. A next to impossible objective. Sam laughed softly and drove on.

There was less self-knowledge than carnal knowledge on the mind of Suzanne Melendez at that very moment. After saying what she hoped would be a temporary good-night to Roderick, she rushed into her hotel room and proceeded to take one of the quickest showers she had ever taken. Then as she manipulated her hair dryer with one hand, she rummaged with the other through her suitcase. She drew forth, examined, and rejected three negligees before settling upon one of sheer white silk. Grinning, she switched off the hair dryer and tossed it onto the bed, after which she brushed her hair furiously. Hurry, hurry, she told herself. It won't matter how sexy I am if jet lag gets to him before I do.

She slipped the negligee over her head and felt a slight tingle of pleasure as the cool, smooth fabric slid over her nipples. She slowed her pace a bit to carefully apply her makeup, and then stood back and examined herself in the full-length mirror with which the hotel owners had considerately furnished the room. Heels, she thought, that's what's missing. She chose a pair of white spike-heeled pumps from the shoe collection which was bulging her other suitcase, and reexamined herself in the mirror. She smiled. Perfect, she thought. I could give an erection to a eunuch!

She quickly brushed her teeth and then walked across the hallway to Roderick's door. She knocked softly and asked, "Your Lordship? Are you still awake?"

The door opened a few moments later, and the young nobleman greeted her with a languid smile of passive surprise. "Oh, Miss Melendez!"

"I'm sorry to bother you," she said, "but I'm just so upset about poor Mr. Pearson. Do you mind if I come in for a moment?"

It was not Roderick's habit to refuse half-naked women entrance to his rooms, so he said, "Oh, of course not, of course not." He stood aside and allowed her to enter. "I was just thinking of the poor old fellow myself, actually. I found a letter from my uncle in my luggage, and I assume that Pearson gave it to my butler to pack. Here," he said as he picked a sheet of cream-colored paper up from the night table. "Have a look at this."

Suzanne was not the slightest bit interested in the letter, but any topic could serve as a preliminary to what she hoped would be a night of passionate lovemaking, so she took the page from his hand and read it silently.

Nephew (the late Earl began):
The fact that you are reading this means that I have finally been released from this miserable world, and that you are now the fifteenth Earl of Selwyn. I hope to have been able to speak to you personally before this letter comes into your hands, but in the event that I have not, there are a few things I wish to communicate to you. Kindly give them your attention.

Roderick, you know that I have never had much use for you. I regard you as an ignorant, spoiled idiot without the common sense of a ploughboy and with a standard of morality only slightly more elevated than a common tart. You are the last person to whom I wish to leave the title I have cherished all these years, not to mention the estate and properties thereunto attendant. But the law is the law, and for better or worse you are now the Earl of Selwyn. God help the Realm.

Roderick, you must, you *must* develop an understanding of what it means to be a British nobleman. I have tried over the years to instill a sense of honor in you, and I know that my efforts have been ineffective. I pray that the passage of years will cause you to grow up. You have responsibilities, Roderick, and I refer not only to your current status. You have a responsibility to your ancestors and a responsibility to your descendants. Yours is an old and honored name. I pray to God that you will not disgrace it.

Suzanne looked up without finishing the letter. "I don't think that you and your uncle got along very well, if you'll pardon my saying so, Your Lordship."

"No, not well at all," Roderick replied, yawning. "I feel a bit sorry about that, actually. He seemed so concerned that I would bring the family name into disrepute!"

"You would never do that," she said cloyingly as she tossed the letter back onto the night table.

"I hope not," he said. His face was serious as he added, "I know that I'm not the most responsible fellow around, but actually being the Earl of Selwyn makes me think a bit more about myself. About what I should be doing, I mean." He laughed lightly. "Of course, having never had to do anything, I'm not entirely certain what it is I'm supposed to be doing." He yawned again.

"Well, right now you should be relaxing," she said, sounding for all the world like a libidinous schoolmarm as she pushed him firmly but gently down upon the bed. "You've had a long day, what with the flight and the terrible news and everything. You just lie back and relax and let me massage your muscles."

"Well—I, uh—" Roderick allowed himself to be guided down upon his back. How delightful! he thought, as Suzanne began gently to knead his upper arms and shoulders. She stood over him as she worked his muscles, bending stiffly at the waist so that she was certain he could see her small, firm breasts beneath the cupping fold of her bodice and the sensuous outline of her thighs and buttocks against the clinging silk. She slid her hands beneath his pajama top and continued to knead his soft arms and shoulders, working her way as unobtrusively as possible down past his slightly flabby midsection.

Roderick smiled and closed his eyes as her hands found his flaccid organ and began slowly but firmly to stroke it. She tossed him an eager, licentious grin, and then pulled his penis free from the opening in the front of his pajama bottoms. She placed her lips around the tip and deftly enveloped it, lubricating it with her saliva and running her lips and tongue up and down the shaft.

Roderick Fowles began to snore.

"Your Lordship?" she said softly. No response. "Your Lordship?" she repeated, somewhat more loudly. An increase in the level of his snoring was his sole reply.

Suzanne stood up and placed her hands upon her hips and repeated angrily, "Your Lordship!"

Roderick mumbled something unintelligible and smiled as he rolled over onto his side.

Suzanne Melendez turned and opened the door of the hotel room. She cast one last offended look at the insipid grin on the young nobleman's face and then closed the door behind her.

"Shit!" she muttered, and then went back to her own room to go to sleep.

# CHAPTER 6

▲ The sound of the crickets made Ahmed Hadji nervous. His mission was one of stealth and caution, and even the minor noises made by the insects filled him with a fear of discovery. He stood motionless behind a large old elm tree which stood upon the campus quadrangle at one end of which the museum was located. The museum was locked and dark, but the grounds building, which rested on an adjacent side of the quad, was the site of some activity. Hadji could take no chances. He stood pressed against the back of the tree and glanced over at the grounds building carefully, awaiting an opportunity to make his way toward the museum.

Gus Rudd and Will Foster were standing in front of the grounds building, looking cold, tired, and speaking in hushed, serious tones. Hadji could not make out their words, but he was reasonably certain that their conversation revolved around one of three possible topics. They could have been speaking of the afternoon's events, of the arrival of the ancient dead and the subsequent confrontation. Or they could have been speaking of the strange feeling of discomfort which Hadji knew the large, boorish idiot who had dared to touch the Lord Sekhemib must be feeling. Or they might very well be discussing the murder of Jack Lewis. Hadji was certain that they could not have been speaking of the death of the old woman. They could not have known about it.

Hadji thought back to the events which had transpired a few hours before, when he had decided that it was unsafe for Lewis to be alive. For his mission to be successful, no one could know where he was staying or (needless to say!) what his true purposes were. He had gone to Lewis's office that evening, waiting in the diner across the street until he saw the secretary leave for the day. He peered through the venetian blinds and saw Lewis sitting at his desk, quite alone. Excellent, Hadji had thought. Quite fortuitous.

He had walked across to the real estate office as inconspicuously as possible, looking from side to side. He saw no one whom he recognized, which meant of course that he was seen by no one who would recognize him. Entering the office, he had greeted Jack Lewis in a friendly manner, holding out his hand in greeting. Amazing, Hadji thought, how these American simpletons can be so easily disarmed by the common civility which the rest of the world uses to mask private motives. When Lewis, smiling, had risen to return the handshake, Hadji had quickly thrust his knife upward into Lewis's abdomen and tore it across, disemboweling him with the precision of a surgeon. Ahmed Hadji was well trained.

As the body of Jack Lewis lay twitching on the floor of his office, Hadji had stepped over it as if it were merely a piece of wood, rather than the remnants of a human being, and had taken Mrs. March's address card out of the Rolodex on the desk. He had searched quickly through Lewis's file cabinets and desk, making certain that no record of the brief encounter earlier that day existed anywhere other than in the memory which Hadji had just severed from the world of living expression. He was sure that nothing remained to link him to the residence on Pine Lane. He knew that Lewis's secretary knew neither his name nor the details of the supposed rental of the room. All was secure.

As he stood pressed up against the tree, watching Gus and Will, Hadji wondered if the murder had been discovered already. Possible. But unimportant. He watched as Will attempted to remove something from the pocket of his coat. His inability to do so prompted Gus to reach into Will's pocket and pull out the small bottle from which first he and then Will took long draughts. Alcohol, Hadji sneered. He knew that his ancient ancestors had brewed and enjoyed malt liquor, but the long centuries of Islamic rule had bred a disapproval of alcoholic beverages into the Egyptians, even into someone as decidedly non-Islamic as Hadji.

He watched and waited for over an hour, forcing himself to be patient, restraining the urge to dash toward the museum when the two men had their backs turned to him. Wait, he told himself. You must not risk being seen. Too much depends upon you. Wait.

At last Will Foster took his leave and Gus Rudd leaned back against the door of the grounds building. Hadji watched him closely. After a few moments Gus drew a large ring of keys from a clip on his belt and unlocked the door. He took a perfunctory look around and then disappeared into the grounds building, closing the door behind him. Ahmed Hadji watched as Will Foster's form grew distant and then invisible in the darkness, and then he ran to the museum.

He reached the museum and ran into the shadows at the side of the building. He stood again motionless in the darkness, his heart pounding, his breath coming quickly. Then he took a small utility knife from his pocket and began to cut the pane of the window beside which he was standing. His dagger was sheathed on his belt, with the catch undone for easy and rapid access if the need arose. He cut the square hóle in the window pane and, replacing the utility knife, took a suction cup mounted on a locking device from the deep pocket of his overcoat. He placed the mouth of the suction cup against the outline of the cut in the glass and proceeded to press gently against it. It was his intention to hold the glass segment secure as he carefully separated it from the window, thus allowing him access to the room without running the risk of attracting attention by breaking the glass.

But he had cut too deeply. As he pressed the suction cup against the glass, he dislodged the segment and sent it cascading into the museum. It shattered loudly when it hit the floor, breaking the silence of the evening with its startling shrillness.

Hadji repressed the urge to panic. He withdrew into the shadows and waited. No one approached, no voices were heard. He leaned slowly forward and looked in the direction of the grounds building. There was no motion and no sounds, and Hadji released a relieved sigh, certain that the sound of breaking glass had gone unnoticed.

He walked back over to the window and put his hand through the hole which gaped near the interior window lock. He gently pressed the lever to the left and then, finding it immobile, pressed it to the right. The lever moved immediately, releasing the window. Hadji pushed the window up and gingerly clambered through into the museum.

It was of course pitch black within, and he had no intention of in any way illuminating the interior. He stood immobile for a moment as his eyes adjusted to the darkness, and he soon realized that he had broken into a storage room. He almost tripped over some indeterminate shape resting low to the floor in the darkness but was able to find his way to the door of the room without significant difficulty. He turned the door knob and pulled it open.

Hadji moved carefully into the large central room of the museum. It was lighter in the main area than it had been in the storage room, and he was able to see well enough by the moonlight and stray beams from the lampposts outside. He saw the sarcophagus resting in somber solitude on the same spot it had been earlier that day. With chagrin he noticed that the other sarcophagi were missing. It suddenly occurred to him what that foolish drunkard of a policeman was doing at the college near the museum so late at night. They must have removed the other lords to the building, he thought. Stupid idiots.

He walked over to the sarcophagus and slowly, reverently, lifted the lid. Ahmed Hadji stood for a moment gazing down upon the long dead face of Sekhemib. When he had arrived just in time to prevent the profaning of the lord high priest he had had neither time nor the peace of mind to contemplate the splendor of the moment, nor had he been able earlier that morning to offer the prayers of thanks so appropriate to the circumstances.

Sekhemib! he thought in awe. The lord Sekhemib himself, his mummified body lying before him, untouched by the blade of time, uninjured by the merciless passing of the years, the centuries, the long millennia. "Sekhemib," he whispered and felt a thrill course up his spine at the very vocalization of the name. Sekhemib and the others, Yuya, Meret, Senmut, Khumara, Herihor and Wenet, the seven lords, the beloved of Anubis. For thirty-seven centuries their mummies were hidden, stolen, lost, and the priests of the cult, and their successors, and their successors' successors down through the long ages, searched in vain for them. And now, here was Sekhemib, and the others were resting nearby. And he, Ahmed Hadji, was the first living man to gaze upon the awesome countenance of the lord high priest and to know and understand exactly what it was he saw.

Hadji dropped to his knees, bowed his head, and raised his hands upward. *"Anet hrauthen 'Anpu,"* he whispered, *"neb pet neb ta, suten khert, neb neteru, xeper tesef qeman unenet—*" Homage to you, Anubis, Lord of Heaven, Lord of Earth, King of Heaven, Lord of the Gods, self-created, Creator of the Things Which Shall Be—

He heard voices from outside, growing suddenly louder. He tensed. When he heard the key being turned in the lock of the entrance door, he bolted from his knees and scurried back to the storage room. Hadji shut the door behind him, quickly but quietly, and knelt down before the keyhole, hoping that he would be able to see what transpired, but the keyhole offered no view of the area around the sarcophagus. He forced himself to breathe slowly and once again he waited, tense, motionless.

Harriet Langly opened the door upon the interior of a museum with which there was apparently nothing amiss. She walked in, followed by Thomas Sawhill and Gus Rudd, who was saying, "I dunno 'bout this, Miss Langly. Jasper kinda wanted me to stay over there with the other boxes."

"I know, Gus," she replied, "but I didn't want to walk in here all alone, not with all the other things that have been happening."

"All alone!" Sawhill said. "Hey, thanks a lot."

"Shut up, Tommy," she said, not unkindly. To Gus, "I'm not trying to take you away from your guard duty. I just wanted you here until we got the lights on."

"So I can go back now?"

"Sure. And thanks again."

"Oh, that's okay." As he turned to go back to the grounds building Gus said, "I'd be happy to stay with you, but I got my orders and—well, you understand."

"Of course I do."

"Okay. 'Night now."

"Good-bye, Gus."

"Be sure to lock up," was his parting official reminder.

Harriet smiled at Sawhill. "As if I'd forget to lock up my museum."

"He means well, honey. His brain just has a little synapse trouble." Sawhill walked into the center of the room and looked down at the mummy. "I have decided to disagree with you."

"Huh? Disagree with me about what? I haven't said anything."

"This thing isn't beautiful. It's hideous."

"Oh," she laughed as she took the golden medallion from

her purse and then placed the purse upon a nearby table. "I see. Well, beauty is in the eye of the beholder, as they say."

"Yeah, but look at this thing! A dried up old corpse!"

"No, a perfectly preserved mummy."

"I know how much you love Egyptian history and all that, but I can't help but think that it takes a pretty fucked up culture to have a preoccupation with death so obsessive that they would go to all this trouble to preserve the bodies of the dead."

"You don't understand," she said as she placed the medallion carefully onto the floor of the coffin. "They were preoccupied with life, not death. This is a denial of death, an affirmation of life."

Sawhill shook his head. "It still seems unhealthy to me."

"Such ethnocentricity! Look at how screwy our funerary customs are."

"Oh, come on! There's no comparison!"

"No? Isn't the United States the culture which invented the steel-lined, concrete-encased coffin, guaranteed worm-proof for centuries?"

"Well, sure, but—"

"Don't we have cemeteries for pets? And what about cryogenics!"

"Yeah, but that's a California thing. What do you expect?"

"Do you know the average American family spends more on a funeral than on a wedding?" She laughed grimly. "Talk about inverted priorities!"

"It still doesn't compare."

"Wasn't it our culture which came up with places like the Playboy Club?"

He was momentarily nonplussed. "What's that got to do with death?"

"Nothing. But it doesn't have anything to do with emotional health, either. I mean, think about it."

"Come on, Harriet. It was just an innocent night club."

"It was a place where men went to ingest intoxicating substances served to them by half-naked women dressed like animals." She grinned. "You see? All a matter of perspective."

"Well—"

"And he isn't hideous. He's beautiful." She knelt down beside the coffin and smiled into the ancient face. "Look at the condition he's in, Tommy. He's a perfect specimen. Absolutely flawless."

"I suppose," he conceded. "Still, I'm glad I don't look like that."

Harriet laughed. "Hey, three thousand years from now you won't look this good. You won't look like anything."

"Yeah," he said distractedly. "Look, you want to go home now?"

"In a minute. I just want to look at him for a little while."

Get out of here, Ahmed Hadji thought. Go home! He was pressing his ear up to the crack between the door and the frame. He could hear them clearly in the stillness of the dark night.

"Honey, you wanted to come by and check on things, to make sure nothing had been taken. Okay, we're here, and nothing has been taken, okay? So let's get going. It's been a long day."

"Okay, okay." She rose to her feet. Then she paused, frowning. "That's funny."

"What's funny?"

"It just occurred to me. I could have sworn that I closed the sarcophagus this morning."

"Well, you probably forgot. You were pretty upset, remember."

"Yeah," she agreed. "I probably forgot to close it up. Give me a hand with the lid, will you?"

Ahmed Hadji heard the sounds of the lid being replaced. He listened to the footsteps as they moved toward the entrance of the museum. When the light flicked off and the door shut and he heard the locking of the door, he sighed and wiped his brow.

Hadji opened the storage room door slowly and carefully. Satisfied that he was alone, he went back into the large central room and once again removed the lid of the sarcophagus. He reached into his deep pocket and took out a pair of rubber gloves. He would not place his bare hand upon the body of Sekhemib. To do so would be to profane the Lord High Priest as well as to endanger his own life.

Hadji put on the gloves, picked up the medallion and put it in his pocket, and then slid his hands beneath the shoulders and thighs of the mummy. It was lighter than a living man would have been, lighter even than a conventional corpse, but it was still heavy enough to cause him some discomfort as he lifted it from the sarcophagus. He carried the mummy into the storage room and placed it upright against the wall. Hadji removed his coat and draped it over the window sill to serve as a buffer and then moved the mummy to the side of the window. He climbed out of the room through the open window and then reached in, grabbing the mummy by the shoulders. After pulling it toward the opening, he pressed his hands together against the mummy's arms and lifted. It moved upward a few feet. With a quick motion, Hadji moved his grip down to the waist. He pulled down and the mummy's torso came level to the ground upon the fulcrum of the window sill. Hadji pulled the stiff form out through the window and leaned it against the outside wall of the museum. He crept stealthily to the edge of the building and peered around the corner. The policeman was nowhere in sight.

Ahmed Hadji smiled. He lifted the mummy in his arms once again and walked quickly, though a bit awkwardly, away from the small museum. He ran over to the automobile he had rented early that day, under a false name, of course, and placed the mummy upon the hood of the trunk. He unlocked the car and opened the rear door. Hadji was looking around nervously all the while, for this was the most dangerous part of his evening's enterprise, when he was most visible, most exposed. But he saw no one. He slid the mummy into the back seat, finding to his chagrin that it was too long to rest flat upon the seat. He had no choice but to leave the stiff, linen-enshrouded corpse propped up on an angle against the opposite door.

He shut the rear door and climbed into the driver's seat. He did not depress the accelerator pedal as he turned the key in the ignition because he was afraid that the sudden racing of the engine might attract attention. There was fortunately enough gasoline in the fuel line to enable the car to start without difficulty, and he drove off, not turning on the headlights until he reached the main road just beyond the college entrance.

"Ha!" he laughed aloud. I've done it! I've done it! I've done it!

His timing had been better than he knew, for he had not been gone more than ten minutes when Harriet Langly and Thomas Sawhill returned to the museum. "If it isn't here, then I don't know where it could be," Harriet was saying as she opened the door.

"You could have left your purse at the police station," Sawhill said.

Harriet nodded as she switched on the light. "Yeah, that's possible. I know that I had it when we left Bottadio's." She looked to her left and saw her purse lying on the brochure table. "Oh, thank God, there it is! I remember now. I put it down there when we were here earlier."

"Good," Sawhill said wearily. "Now let's go home and go to sleep."

"Okay. Sorry, Tommy. I just—" Her eyes went wide with shock. "Tommy! Oh my God!"

"What? What's the matter?"

"Look!" She pointed at the sarcophagus and Sawhill saw the lid, which he knew he had helped her place back on top of the coffin shortly before, lying on the floor. Harriet ran over to the sarcophagus and gasped. "Goddamn it! Goddamn it!"

Sawhill was a step behind her. "Gone," he said angrily. "It must have been that goddamn Arab."

Harriet ran to the door and started screaming, "GUS! GUS! Come here quick!"

Gus Rudd's head appeared in the distance from within the doorway of the grounds building. "You say something, Miss Langly?" he called.

"There's been a robbery! Come here, *please*!" Gus slammed and locked the grounds building door and came running over to her. "Somebody stole the mummy."

"Shit," Gus muttered. "Did you see anything? Hear anything?"

"No, of course not," Harriet screamed. "He didn't just walk by us carrying it!"

"Harriet, calm down," Sawhill said.

"Don't tell me to calm down! Goddamn it!" She pounded her fist against her thigh in frustration.

"Gus," Sawhill said, "you'd better go call Jasper."

"Yeah, yeah, right." Gus nodded. "Miss Langly, I'm gonna go call Jasper now. You try to stay calm." He opened the museum door and began to leave.

"Where the hell are you going?" she asked.

Gus stopped short. "To call Jasper, Miss Langly."

"There's a phone right next to you on the table, Gus!"

"Oh. Sorry." Gus picked up the receiver and began to dial.

Tears began to well up in Harriet's eyes and then burst forth, cascading down her face carrying with them most of her mascara. "That son of a bitch!"

"Take it easy, honey," Sawhill said. "This must have just happened. He can't have gotten far. Jasper'll get him."

"Miss Langly?" Gus said. "Jasper wants to talk to you."

Harriet took the receiver from his hand. "Hello, Jasper? You have to catch him. He stole the mummy we left in the museum."

"Now listen carefully, Miss Langly. I'm gonna call the state police and have some roadblocks set up. Problem is, we don't know what kind of car he's driving or where he's going. We don't even know where he's staying."

"What about hotels, motels?"

"No," Jasper's voice said firmly. "He ain't gonna waltz into a hotel lobby carrying a mummy. I think he's probably staying here in town somewhere. We'll start searching in the morning."

"In the morning! Listen, Chief. Tommy and I were here not fifteen minutes ago, and the mummy was still here. He must have just stolen it, and he must be around here somewhere, somewhere in town. You *can't* wait until tomorrow."

"Ma'am, I'm investigating a murder right now. In fact, I think the crimes are related."

This statement startled Harriet. "You mean you think Hadji killed Mr. Lewis?"

"Yup. Look at the facts here, Miss Langly. This Hadji says he's been talking to the Earl's lawyer, and the lawyer ends up dead with knife wounds. Then he shows up here, making all sorts of threats, demanding that we give him those exhibits. Then he disappears, and the one man in town who might have rented or sold him a place to live winds up dead, also with a knife wound." He laughed grimly, without humor. "One hell of a knife wound. Now. I'm gonna call all the hotels and motels within a thirty mile radius, but I'll bet by my next month's salary that I won't find anything. He's here in town with your exhibit, or else he's on the road in a rented or stolen car. Either way, we'll find him. But not tonight. You got me right in the middle of questioning Marjorie Granitto, Lewis's secretary."

"But can't Gus look for him?"

Sure, if you want to leave the other six boxes unguarded." He paused, awaiting her reply. There was none. "I didn't think so. Now take my advice. You lock up that museum and go home. Call up your insurance lady friend and Sam Goldhaber, let 'em know what's happened. But don't go looking for this guy yourself."

"The hell we won't! I'm—"

"Miss Langly, if I'm right in my suspicions, this man has killed two people. It won't bother him to kill two more. Do you understand me? Now, go home and try to get some sleep." He hung up without saying good-bye.

Sawhill stood beside her, waiting to be informed as to the substance of the conversation. When she did not speak, he said, "Well? What did he say?"

She sighed. "He said we should go home and go to sleep."

"What?!"

"Yeah, it makes sense, what he said. He's got a murder on his hands and he can't come over here now." She turned to Gus. "I think you're supposed to keep watch on the other exhibits for the night."

"Sure thing. I'll be back over there if you need me for anything." He turned and left the room.

Sawhill shook his head angrily. "Well, we can't just go home and go to sleep. We have to do something."

"I now, I know, but what? Jasper said he thinks Hadji killed Mr. Lewis. If that's true, we can't do anything even if we find him."

"We could tell Jasper where he is," Sawhill suggested. "If we see him with the college's property, we can have him arrested."

"Who knows where he is?" she asked rhetorically. "This guy may be a murderer, Tommy. Are you and I going to make a citizen's arrest of a man like that?"

"Well . . ." The idea did not appeal to him.

"Oh, Tommy, this is horrible," she wept.

He took her in his arms, but she resisted his embrace. He was confused by her reaction, but tried to hide the fact. "Well, what should we do?"

Harriet shook her head. "I don't know. I just don't—" She drew her breath in suddenly. "Jesus! You don't think he took the others also?" They stood staring at each other for a few moments and then without another word they bolted from the room and ran madly toward the grounds building. When they reached the door Harriet began to pound on the door frantically, screaming, "Gus! Open up! Gus!"

"What's wrong, ma'am?" Gus asked from behind her.

Harriet and Sawhill spun around. "Good grief!" Sawhill exclaimed. "What the hell—"

"Why aren't you inside with the rest of the shipment?" she demanded.

Gus laughed. "Shit, Miss Langly, you didn't even give me chance to get back here. You two ran right past me."

"That's impossible!" she yelled. "I didn't see you!"

"Harriet," Sawhill said soothingly but a bit condescendingly, "it's dark out here. And we were running and very apprehensive."

"So what?" she snapped. "I didn't see him. I'm not blind, dammit!"

"I was right over there, ma'am," Gus said, pointing to the trees between the grounds building and the museum. "I was taking a leak."

Harriet looked at him for a moment and then laughed despite her emotional upset. "I'm sorry, Gus, I really am. I'm just so—I don't know—angry, annoyed, frantic. I'm really sorry."

"Hey, no problem," Gus said, all smiles. "But what's wrong? Why'd you come running over here?"

"We want to check the other crates. Just to be sure that nothing else was stolen."

Gus seemed hurt by the implication. "Gee, Miss Langly, I been here all night. I been watching 'em."

"I know you have, Gus. Nobody's doubting you. But we don't know what might have happened before you got here. We just want to check. Okay?"

He shrugged. "Yeah, sure. Don't matter to me." He was clearly not placated by her explanation. Gus unlocked the padlock and led them into the pitch blackness inside. Harriet saw four crates stacked against the wall with two uncrated coffins, identical to the one in which Sekhemib had laid, resting beside them, as soon as Gus had switched on the lights.

"Would you guys please lift the lid on one of them?" she asked.

"Sure," Gus said, waving Sawhill back. "I don't need no help. These lids are real light." Harriet followed him over to the wall and watched nervously as he easily lifted the wooden lid and placed it with exaggerated caution on the floor. She took Sawhill's hand nervously and looked inside.

"Thank God," she muttered, grateful for two things. There was indeed a mummy in the sarcophagus, and it was, like Sekhemib, in absolutely perfect condition. "Thank God," she repeated.

"You want to open the others too?" Gus asked.

"Just the other uncrated one, please." Gus lifted that lid as well, and Harriet heaved a sigh of relief. A third occupied sarcophagus, a third perfect mummy. "Tom, when photographs of these mummies hit the papers, museums all over the world are going to be kicking themselves for not beating us to this purchase."

"Are they really that good?"

"They're unbelievable! I haven't seen mummies this well preserved anywhere, ever. Not even in Cairo."

"I'll have to take your word for it," Sawhill muttered. He squinted at the body in the sarcophagus. "Is that a woman?"

"Uh-huh," she said, kneeling down to look at the lid. "This lid has pretty much the same inscriptions as the other one, except for the name. This is—" she paused as she studied the hieroglyphs inscribed on the top line, "Meret, priestess of Isis." She shifted in the direction of the other lid, moving there on hand and knee. "And this is—" another pause, "Yuya, priest of Set." She frowned and shook her head.

What now, Sawhill thought. "Another problem?"

"I'm not sure. Gus, you got a flashlight?"

"Sure, Miss Langly. Ain't it bright enough in here for you? I got all the lights on." He handed her the large heavy flashlight which hung from a strap on his belt.

"Oh, sure it's light enough. I just want to check something." She clicked on the light and brought its beam to bear upon the lid. "Same phrases," she muttered. *"Anubis, Set, ankh, tekenu—"*

"Same medallion," Sawhill added helpfully. He was standing over the mummy Harriet had identified as that of Meret.

"Don't ogle the dead, Tommy," she warned. She rose to her feet, brushed off her hands and knees, and looked down at the medallion which rested upon the breast of the woman. "Not quite the same."

"Does this one make sense?"

"Maybe," she muttered. "I think I understand."

He waited for the explanation which was not forthcoming. "Well? Want to let me in on it?"

She looked up. "Sorry. I was thinking." She paused, deep in thought. "Do you remember the hieroglyphs on the first medallion?"

"No," he said with amusement. "They all look the same to me."

"Well, there were four of them: two figures of Anubis, the

cross of life, and the tekenu. This one has ōne figure of Anubis, the cross, the tekenu, and the fourth hieroglyph is the symbol for Isis."

"Makes sense, doesn't it? You said she was a priestess of Isis."

"Yeah, that's the point. This isn't supposed to be a sentence. It's some sort of badge of identification. In fact, I'll bet that the other fellow over here has a figure of Set on his medallion."

"He has one too?" Sawhill had not noticed.

"You know, Tommy, for a doctor you're pretty unobservant. Sure he does. See?" She pointed down at the medallion around the neck of the other mummy. "And there it is, the symbol for Set."

"So what does this mean?"

"I'm not certain, but these three people may have been part of some retinue burial."

"What's a retinue burial? I mean, I know what a retinue is—"

"It was not uncommon for a dead king to be buried along with his wives, advisors, generals, and so forth. They are called the retinue corpses. They were supposed to thus be with him in the next life."

"Jeeze, Harriet," Sawhill said, "how common could that have been? Unless there was some mass assassination, how often would all those people have died at once?"

"Tommy," Harriet said, as if she were explaining something to a child, "they didn't necessarily have to be dead to be buried."

"Are you serious? Buried alive? That's horrible!"

"Yeah, but I don't hink they were buried alive. Their facial expressions are too peaceful. Still . . ." She paused again, obviously bothered by something.

Sawhill was pleased that she had immersed herself in her speculations once again. It had apparently calmed her down and taken her mind off the theft. He said nothing, not wishing to break into her thoughts, grateful for her apparent ease.

"It's just strange," she said at last. "I can't think of any reason why three people who were priests of different gods would be together in identical caskets, wearing virtually identical medallions, unless they were part of a retinue burial. But I've seen retinue mummies. If they're well preserved enough for facial expressions to be evident, they look like people who died very unpleasantly. But these three look peaceful."

"Maybe they weren't buried together," he suggested. "I mean, the ancient Egyptians didn't bury them in the Earl's attic."

She laughed. "Can't argue with that. Wait a minute." She leaned into the casket and moved the flashlight beam slowly over the midsection of the mummy. "Yeah, look here. No scar on the skin."

"Skin! What skin?"

She looked at him, astounded at his lack of knowledge. "Tommy, this is a mummy, not a fossil. There's skin under these bandages. And the linen adheres to the skin so closely that even minor details can be made out."

"No kidding!" He nodded his head, impressed. "So what about scars?"

"There aren't any."

"Should there be?"

"Of course, if the body was eviscerated before mummification. There aren't any scars, meaning that the organs were not removed, meaning that these people were not mummified according to standard procedure."

"Maybe they got the quick job, like you mentioned?"

She shook her head. "No, not priests. They got the best embalming possible, better sometimes than the kings, because it was the priests who were in charge of the whole thing. They didn't do it themselves, of course, but they were in charge of it." She shook her head. "No scars."

"If they were dead before evisceration, there couldn't be scars," Sawhill observed. "Scars result from healing. Corpses don't heal."

"Don't be picky," she said irritably. "Okay, not scars. No cuts, then. No incisions. The point is, they weren't eviscerated. And that's damn strange."

"Well," he said, "there must be an explanation."

She nodded. "Wish I new what the hell it was." She sighed and turned to Gus, who had been standing quietly. "Do me a favor, will you, Gus? Put the lids back on before you lock up the building? I have to go home and try to forget this night."

"Sure thing, Miss Langly. And don't you worry. We'll find the thief and get the other mummy back."

"Thanks, Gus. Good night, now."

"Good night. See you, Doc."

"Night, Gus." Harriet Langly and Thomas Sawhill walked out of the grounds building. Gus watched them leave and, yawning, he turned back to the sarcophagi. Lifting one of the lids, he dropped it gently into place atop the casket.

Gus looked down at the face of the one Dr. Langly had referred to as the priestess Meret. The face of the corpse which had lain upon its funeral bier four millennia ago was frozen into an impassive expression which bespoke neither pain nor joy, neither hope nor fear, but merely dust, darkness, and death. I wonder if she was pretty? Gus mused. I wonder what girls were like back then. Kind of sad, when you think about it. I guess it's true what Miss Langly said this morning, that these bodies were alive and thinking and stuff like that, all those years ago. It really is kind of sad. Nothing left of this lady but this dried up prune of a mummy.

Almost kindly, Gus reached down and stroked her cheek.

# II

# T H E  T E K E N U

▲

Hail, Soul, thou mighty one
of terror! Verily, I am here!
I have come!
        —*The Egyptian Book of the
                Dead*, IX

# CHAPTER 7

▲ Dr. Thomas Sawhill yawned and shook his head briskly as he sat pensively behind his desk. Good Lord, what a day yesterday had been! Life seems to crawl along slowly in this little town, and then suddenly rushes like a river. So many events in one day! The arrival of the shipment, the confrontation with that Arab, a murder, a theft—Good Lord, he repeated to himself. What a day!

He straightened and then tensed his back. If Harriet and I ever get around to tying the knot, we're going to have to do something about our mattress problem, he thought. Harriet Langly liked to sleep on a mattress so soft that the sides practically enveloped the sleeper, but such softness wreaked havoc with Sawhill's back. He needed to sleep on a mattress so stiff that a board might almost have done the job.

But there are compensations, he thought, smiling. Sawhill looked at the framed photograph of Harriet which he kept on his desk in his medical office, and reflected upon his good fortune. When he had graduated from Stanford Medical School it seemed almost his destiny to return to his hometown of Greenfield to begin his practice. Internship and residency at Greenfield's small but well-equipped Harrison Hospital, followed by the retirement of his old mentor, Dr. Wilburforce, and a ready-made medical practice just tossed into his lap—what other choice could he have made?

And he was content. Affluent, well-respected, engaged to a fascinating and beautiful woman with a mind equal to his own, all of this combined to make Thomas Sawhill a very happy man.

He knew that Harriet was not particularly happy this morning. The theft of the mummy had given her an attack of insomnia which, while of course understandable, was equally purposeless. As a medical man Sawhill knew that people who suffered from insomnia could not control it; indeed, that itself was the problem. As Harriet's lover he naturally sympathized with her. But as an individual who never had any trouble sleeping, no matter what the circumstances, he had to admit to himself that he really couldn't understand the problem.

And so he had struggled to keep his eyes open and his mind alert that previous night as Harriet rambled on about God knows what into the wee hours of the morning. He must have fallen asleep despite his efforts to the contrary, and when he awoke this morning it was to find Harriet, wide awake and exhausted, sitting at the table in her kitchen, staring morosely out at the still-deserted streets of the small town. Poor Harriet, he thought. Such a buildup for so many weeks, and then one of her exhibits is stolen from right under her nose. Poor kid.

Sawhill rose unsteadily from his desk (damn, his back hurt!) and walked over to the coffee pot which was sitting on top of a file cabinet. As he poured himself a cup of coffee, his secretary, Millie Rowland, knocked on the door and opened it simultaneously. She was still wearing her overcoat. "Good morning, Doctor."

"Hello, Millie. Coffee?"

"Oh, no thanks. Gee, you're here early today."

"Yeah, well, I woke up early. Any appointments?"

"Yes," she nodded. "They should be coming in—" she glanced at the clock on his office wall, "in about fifteen minutes. Shall I pull the files?"

"Yes, please. Let me see the appointment calendar."

And so his day began, as it began every day. His life was orderly, measured, slow, pleasing. He went through his morning's task of attending to the usual assortment of runny noses, fevers, chipped bones, arthritic arms, and stomach pains.

It was nearing twelve noon when Millie leaned her head into his office. "Only one left, Doctor," she said.

"Good," he replied. He rubbed his eyes and yawned. Not enough sleep, he thought, and too much excitement. I think I'll go home and take a nap after seeing this patient. "Who is it? Give me his file."

"He doesn't have one, I'm afraid. I'll start one for him after he fills in the patient info card." She paused. "Unless you want to see him first?"

He looked up. "Any reason? Is it an emergency?"

She shrugged. "I don't know. But he looks terrible and he's very upset."

"Okay, send him in. Who is he?"

"It's Will Foster. He said you told him to drop by, but there's no appointment made for him."

"Oh, yeah, Will. Yeah, I told him to come by today if his hand wasn't any better."

"His hand?" She shook her head. "I don't think it's a problem with his hand."

"Well, what else could it— Never mind, just send him in, Millie."

As Millie looked behind her and ushered Will into the office, Sawhill rose to greet him. He put his best professional smile on his face, but it dropped to a look of surprise and concern as soon as he saw the condition of the young handyman.

Will Foster did not walk so much as limp and shuffle into the room. His right hand, which had been cold and stiff the evening before, seemed today to be a frozen reptilian claw. The skin was stretched so tightly across the bone that it seemed to be cracking and blistering as he moved. Will was wearing a short-sleeved shirt, and Sawhill could see that whatever had afflicted his hand had spread up his arm. It was beginning to affect his face as well, for Sawhill immediately noted the stiff, taut right cheek and the eyelid which seemed as it were being pulled upward, away from the eyeball. He surmised from Will Foster's gait that whatever disease he had was spreading to his right leg as well.

"Doc," he rasped. "What's wrong with me? What's happening to me?"

"I don't know yet, Will," he said, motioning for Foster to seat himself on the examination table. "But we'll find out. Tell me what's been happening with your hand, what you've been feeling."

"I ain't been feeling nothing, Doc. That's the scary thing. I went to bed last night, feeling weak and chilly, but it was only my hand that was all numb. I woke up this morning and I couldn't hardly get out of the bed. My right arm don't work. I can't even move it." He required Sawhill's assistance to hop up onto the examination table, and was also unable to remove his shirt unaided. "I don't mean I couldn't make it move. I mean it feels like it's made of cement or something. I try to move it with my left hand, and it feels like if I push hard enough it'll snap off. And my leg don't work right, it's all cold, and my face feels funny." He grabbed Sawhill's jacket sleeve with his left hand and looked at him with desperate, terrified eyes. "You gotta help me, Doc. I'm scared shitless!"

"Relax, Will," Sawhill said as he placed a thermometer in his patient's mouth. "We'll soon get to the bottom of this." He proceeded with the standard preliminary examination, and was not pleased with his findings. Blood pressure was very low, pulse was erratic, temperature, 96°. Will's breathing was labored, but there was no fluid in his lungs. As Sawhill listened to his heart through the stethoscope, he heard what sounded disturbingly like creaking. No motor responses in the right arm whatsoever, minimal response in the right leg. Whatever disease Will had contracted, it was affecting his right side from temple to toe. Sawhill poked, squeezed, and probed Will's skin gently with his fingers. There was no elasticity. The skin felt rough and scaly, like the skin of a desert lizard which had somehow died of the cold.

"Well?" Will Foster asked hopefully.

"There are some tests we need to run, Will." He reached into his supply cabinet and took out a small plastic bottle. "Go into the bathroom and urinate into this. We'll need a urinalysis, and a blood test also, and a few other tests. I'm going to call the hospital and arrange to check you in. Okay?"

Will gulped. "The hospital? Can't you treat me here?"

"Maybe I can, Will, but I have to be sure what I'm treating you for first, and that requires hospitalization and a series of tests."

"But can't you figure it out here and now? Don't you have any ideas?"

It was apparent to Sawhill that Will was one of those quite common individuals who had an insurmountable dread of hospitals. Probably a childhood experience, death of a parent or something similar. Associates hospitals with death, not recovery. "I have suspicions, Will, that's all. I can't be sure of anything until we've done some tests."

"Well, what do you suspect?" Will was shaking in fear.

"I don't like to speculate until—"

"Goddamn it, Doc, what the hell do you suspect?"

Sawhill could see that Will was growing hysterical. Poor

guy, he thought. He must be terrified. Nothing, nothing in the world, is more frightening than having something go wrong with your body. There's nowhere you can go to escape the problem, nothing you can do to take your mind off it. It is with you, within you, constantly. "Listen, Will, I'm not at all certain about anything here, and my suspicions may be one hundred percent wrong. I don't want to upset you unnecessarily. Do you understand?"

"Are you nuts?" Will shouted. "Don't you think I'm upset now? For Christ's sake, Doc, what the hell is wrong with me? Tell me!"

Sawhill disliked giving a diagnosis without certainty, but he feared that further refusal would reduce Will to unmanageable panic. "Okay, okay. I'm not sure about this, because I have no real experience with the disease, but it looks to me like it may be scleroderma."

"Sclero—what the hell is that?"

"It's a degenerative tissue disease, also called progressive systemic sclerosis. It involves a degeneration of the skin and the nerves."

"How the hell did I get it?" Foster seemed a bit calmer, as if being able to give a name to his malady somehow made it easier to accept.

"I don't know," Sawhill said kindly. "No one knows what causes it. We don't know if it's something in your metabolism, something hereditary, a virus, a bacterium—we just don't know. And," he added pointedly, "I don't even know for sure if you have it."

Will didn't listen to the encouraging reminder. "Scleroderma," he said quietly.

"Maybe. Maybe not. That's why we have to go to the hospital."

"If I have it, what can you do about it?"

"Well, there's really no cure, just palliative treatment to minimize its effects. Are you allergic to penicillin?"

"No."

"Good, because standard treatment involves a good deal of it. We also employ chemotherapy and corticosteriods . . ."

"What? What?"

"Corticosteriods. Chemicals used by the adrenal cortex to regulate its own functioning." Will began to ask for a more enlightening explanation but Sawhill cut him short. "Listen,

Will, there's no point in discussing this before we know the facts. You may not even have scleroderma. But we have to get you into a hospital to find out. Okay?" Foster nodded glumly. "Now go and fill that bottle, and then we'll draw some blood. I can have the fluids sent on ahead for analysis. It'll save time."

Sawhill watched as Will shuffled out into the bathroom to fill the specimen bottle, and he then took the phone and dialed the hospital. "Hello? This is Dr. Sawhill. . . . Yes, fine, Janice, fine. How are you? . . . Good. And Billy? . . . Good. I want to send a patient in for a full battery of tests. . . . No, all preliminaries indicate progressive systemic sclerosis. . . . No, he doesn't need a private room. The ward will do fine. . . . Okay. Thank you." He hung up as Will shuffled back into his office. "Six o'clock tonight, Will. I'll take you over there myself."

"Okay," he muttered. "Doc, is this gonna kill me?"

Sawhill always dreaded that question, especially when the answer was in all likelihood an affirmative one. "Will, let's wait until we know for sure what we're dealing with here. I told you that I couldn't make a firm diagnosis. Besides, scleroderma is more common among women than men, and it rarely attacks anyone under thirty. So don't assume the worst." His phone rang. "Excuse me for a moment." He picked up the receiver. "Dr. Sawhill," he said.

"Hiya, Doc," said Jasper Rudd.

"Oh, hello, Jasper. What's up? Anything on the robbery?"

"No, not yet. I've been so goddamn busy with the Lewis murder that I haven't been able to do anything about the theft yet, 'cept get the state police to keep a look out for Hadji."

"That's too bad. It never rains but it pours, right?"

"Yeah, shit. You know there hasn't been a major crime in this town in its whole damn history? And then in one night, two big ones."

"Well, you can handle it. That's why they pay you the big money." Sawhill laughed, and Jasper chuckled slightly. "Why'd you call, Jasper? Anything I can do?"

"Well, I'm going over to the museum now to have a look around. I called Miss Langly and the Earl and her insurance agent friend, and they're meeting me there. I'd kind of like you there too. Save you a trip down to the station. I need a statement from you."

"Sure, sure. I have my last patient here with me now. I can be there in a few minutes."

"No hurry. Just come over when you can."

"Okay. See you soon." He hung up and turned to Will. "What was I saying? Oh yes, don't automatically assume the worst. We'll run some tests and then figure out what to do. Okay?"

"Yeah, sure, Doc," Will muttered. He looked down at the urine bottle he was holding and handed it to Sawhill.

"Fine, fine. Now let's take some blood, and we'll send both samples over to the hospital." He corked the bottle with a plastic cap and placed it in a plastic bag, upon which he wrote Will's name. After sealing the bag, he said, "Make a fist. We'll take the blood from your left arm."

"Don't you want it from the side that's got the problem?"

"No. I don't want to break the skin until we know what we're dealing with." He tied a thin rubber cord tightly around Will's upper arm and then gently plunged a syringe into a vein. He drew out the necessary amount of blood and then, releasing the cord with a quick tug, wiped the puncture with alcohol. "Okay, all done." He placed the bottle of blood in another plastic bag and called out, "Millie. Come here for a moment, please."

His secretary leaned in the door. "Yes, Doctor?"

Sawhill was writing Will's name on the second plastic bag. "Run these over to the hospital on your way home, will you? Mr. Foster is checking in there tonight for a series of tests, and I want them to get the blood and urine analysis done before he gets there."

"Sure thing," she said. "Anything else you need before I leave?"

"No, that's all. Thanks." She took the two plastic bags and closed the office door behind her as she left. Sawhill turned to Will. "Look, Jasper wants me to meet him over at the museum to give him a statement about the theft."

"Theft?" Will asked with an obviously low level of interest. "What theft?"

"Oh, you don't know? One of the mummies was stolen last night."

"No shit? Hey, that's a damn shame." He shook his head. "Dr. Langly must be frantic."

"Yeah, she was very upset. Anyway, I'm going over there now. You want to come along? Might help take your mind off things."

"Sure, why not? Got nothing else to do." Sawhill held the

door for Will, who shuffled painfully out, nervously rubbing his right cheek as if the action might restore sensation.

Sawhill attempted to make light, banal conversation as they drove to the museum, and Will tried to respond as if nothing were amiss. Neither man succeeded. Sawhill's feigned cheerfulness did not cheer his patient, and it was of course impossible for Will to forget that one half of his body seemed to be rotting on the bone.

Sawhill parked his car as close to the museum as possible out of consideration for Will. They walked slowly to the doorway. Sawhill made an instinctive attempt to assist Will by taking his arm, but Will waved him away. "I can still walk, Doc," he said. "I ain't no cripple, not yet."

"Sorry, Will. I didn't mean—"

"Yeah, skip it. Listen, I don't really want to stand around in there, have everybody stare at me and stuff. I'm gonna hang around out here, maybe sit down under a tree and relax."

"Sure, Will, of course. I understand." He left Will near the grass of the campus quad and entered the museum alone. He found Jasper and Gus dusting the empty sarcophagus for fingerprints as Harriet, Roderick, Suzanne, and Sam looked on with obvious concern. "Good afternoon," Sawhill said.

"Tommy!" Harriet exclaimed. "I didn't know you were coming here."

"Yeah, Jasper called me and asked me to drop by." They kissed perfunctorily. Harriet's mind was on the theft of one of her precious exhibits, and he was concerned about Will. "How's it going, Jasper," he asked. "Any clues?"

"Not a damn thing," Jasper Rudd spat. "Not here, not at Lewis's office, either. Whoever did this was goddamn careful." He pointed to the storage room. "The thief came in through a window in the back. Must have left the same way. Door's okay, no damage to it. Seems to me that he was probably hiding in there when you and Miss Langly showed up here last night."

"Isn't that creepy?" Harriet said.

"It's infuriating," Sawhill replied. "If we'd only known—"

"If you'd known, you'd both probably be dead right now," Jasper said. "We ain't dealing with kids stealing hubcaps."

"Do you still think the theft is connected to the murder?"

"Can't prove it. Right now I can't prove a goddamn thing, but every instinct I have tells me that they're related, and that Ahmed Hadji committed both crimes."

"No word on his whereabouts, either?"

"No, but that Inspector Sheldon from Scotland Yard called me back. He did a little digging, called Interpol and the Egyptian consulate over there. Got a little background on our suspect."

"Really?" Suzanne and Harriet said simultaneously. "You never mentioned that," Suzanne added.

"Didn't want to have to repeat myself when the doc showed up. It seems that this Mr. Hadji is a multimillionaire connected to some import-export company called Luxor Limited. Deals in antiquities and manufactured copies. Apparently they import the antiquities and export the copies."

"And the institute?" Harriet asked.

"Exactly what he said it was. Egyptian National Institute of Reclamation. It's a private organization, though. No connection with the Egyptian government. They try to get back museum pieces from all over the world. It's a nationalist thing, I suppose."

"That's discouraging," Sam Goldhaber muttered.

"Why?" Sawhill asked. "If he's legitimate—"

"If he and his institute are legitimate," Sam finished for him, "then it reduces the likelihood of his having stolen the mummy or killed Mr. Lewis. And that leaves us worse off than we were before, if we lose our only suspect."

"There's some funny things about that institute of his, though," Jasper added. "Sheldon told me that the board of directors for the institute are the same people as the board of directors for Hadji's import-export company. That's the info he got from the Egyptian consulate's computers, anyway. They're both run by a man named Haleel Haftoori, and neither of them has what Sheldon called a tradition of hereditary devolvement."

"What the hell is that?" Harriet asked.

"Hereditary devolvement," Suzanne explained, "is the passage of property ownership from father to son or mother to daughter—parent to child, basically."

"Right," Jasper said. "According to the records he was able to dig up, none of the people involved in the business or the institute—and they're the same people, remember—are married or have any kids. The business goes back about a hundred years, the institute about seventy years, and no one has ever left any of their interests in either of them to an heir. None of them has ever *had* an heir."

Harriet thought this over. "Do you think that means anything?"

Jasper shrugged. "Beats me. It's weird, though, ain't it?" He resumed dusting the sarcophagus. "I wish I could get my hands on Hadji. I can feel in my bones that he did all this, whether it makes sense or not. I have a lot of questions to ask that little man."

"Then perhaps you should begin to ask them," Ahmed Hadji said.

They spun around, startled by the sound of his voice. Hadji, dressed in a plain blue business suit, strode casually into the room. "Hold it right there," Gus said, drawing his gun. "You're under arrest."

Hadji ignored him. To Jasper, he said, "I have come to reassert my right to the ownership of these mummies. I have spoken to the Egyptian embassy in Washington, and our ambassador plans to—"

"Where were you last night, Mr. Hadji?" Jasper asked. To Gus he said sharply, "Put your gun away." Gus reluctantly complied.

"I see no reason why I should respond to such an impertinent question!" Hadji snapped.

Jasper moved slowly, threateningly closer. "You're gonna respond to it because I'm the one who asked it, you understand? Now, where were you last night?"

Hadji shrank slightly from the close proximity to Jasper Rudd. He was clearly intimidated. "Well—at what time?"

"All night, Mr. Hadji. The whole goddamn night."

"I was in my hotel room, but for the brief time I went out to eat."

"What hotel?"

"The papier-mâché monstrosity on your Main Street."

"You mean the motor inn?"

"I believe that is its name."

"And where did you eat?"

"In the small restaurant—a diner, I believe you call it?— near the railroad station."

"That's right across the street from Jack Lewis's office!" Gus said excitedly.

"I know that, Gus," Jasper said. To Hadji, "You got any witnesses who can corroborate that?"

"Witnesses!" Hadji was the epitome of wounded honor. "Why on earth should I need witnesses? What is going on here?"

"As if you don't know," Harriet said darkly.

Hadji turned to her. "Madam, I have no intention of—"
His eyes went wide with shock when he saw the empty
sarcophagus. "Where is the mummy? What has happened to
the mummy?" He rushed at Jasper and grabbed him by the
collar. "What has happened?!"

Jasper dislodged him easily and pushed him back a few
steps. "You keep your hands to yourself, my friend. You're in
enough trouble right now without adding to it."

*"What has happened?"* Hadji shouted.

"You tell us," Jasper said. "Tell us what happened to the
mummy. Tell us what happened to Jack Lewis."

"Jack Lewis! Who is Jack Lewis?"

Jasper looked at him closely, suspiciously, but doubting his
own suspicions. "There's been a murder. And a theft."

"Not the mummy! Oh, God, not the mummy! It has been
stolen?" Jasper nodded slowly, never moving his eyes from
Hadji's face. Hadji leaned dramatically against the wall and
shook his head. He covered his eyes with his hands, and when
he removed them tears were running down his cheeks. "You
stupid fools! I knew something like this would happen! You
can't keep exhibits of such value in a broken down barn like
this!"

"Who do you think took the exhibit, Mr. Hadji?" Jasper
asked.

"A rival museum, of course. Who else—" Hadji's eyes
shone forth with sudden understanding. "You suspect me?!
You think that I would so lower myself as to—" His face grew
red with indignation. "I shall report this to my embassy! I shall
formally complain to your State Department! How dare you
make such a loathsome accusation!"

"You can complain all you want to whoever you want.
Don't make no difference to me. I got a murder and burglary,
and you look good for both of them."

Hadji became suddenly, icily calm. "Am I to assume that I
am under arrest, as your fool assistant put it?"

"We'll see," Jasper said. "First I want to know if you have
any witnesses."

"Ah, witnesses," Hadji said slowly. "May I ask you what
evidence you have discovered linking me to these crimes?"

"We'll find some soon enough," Gus said heatedly, "just
you wait!"

"Gus, will you shut up?!" Jasper bellowed. Nothing like

letting a suspect know when you don't have any hard proof, he thought angrily.

"So there is nothing," Hadji said. "Am I to assume that the mere fact that I am a foreigner is sufficient cause for my detention?"

"Don't get wise with me, Hadji," Jasper spat. "I've got enough on you right now to lock you up."

"Come now, sir. I know enough about Anglo-Saxon jurisprudence to be well aware of the fact that you do not. Tell me, was this murder committed here, in conjunction with the theft?"

"You tell me."

Hadji laughed. "Such clever dissembling! I assume that the murder was committed elsewhere. What connection have you discovered between the murder and the theft?"

"He can't question you, Jasper!" Gus whined.

"Gus, will you shut up?!" Jasper repeated.

"Gentlemen, we are wasting time," Hadji said with exaggerated weariness. "You obviously have no concrete grounds upon which to suspect me, other than the fact that I have a legitimate claim to possession of the antiquities which you are apparently unable to protect. I have come here once more to reason with you. If you do not turn the remaining exhibits over to me, I shall initiate official protest and legal proceedings. I assure you that you will indeed lose possession of these exhibits, and you will find the process of losing very expensive and extremely unpleasant."

"That may be," Jasper said, "but in the meantime I'm gonna lock you up."

Hadji emitted a sound halfway between a sigh and a yawn as he reached into his pocket and withdrew a square orange booklet. He tossed it to Jasper, saying, "I think not."

Jasper opened the booklet and examined it. "Goddamn it! Shit!" escaped from his lips.

"What is it, Jasper?" Harriet asked.

"It's a goddamn diplomatic passport!"

"Exactly," Hadji said. "And as I am certain you know, sir, international agreements prohibit you from doing anything other than holding my passport in anticipation of a State Department ruling of persona non grata status. If indeed such a ruling would be forthcoming, which it is not."

"Yeah, yeah, I know the law, you son of a bitch," Jasper replied. "And I'm gonna do just that. I'm holding on to this goddamn thing and calling Washington."

"That is of course your prerogative." He turned to Harriet and Sam Goldhaber. "Can I assume that you persist in your refusal to relinquish possession of the remaining mummies?" He emphasized the word "remaining."

"We do," Sam said with finality.

"Very well. I shall proceed through official channels." He turned and began to walk out of the room.

"Wait!" Suzanne shouted. Hadji stopped and turned as she said to Jasper, "You can't just let him walk out of here! It's obvious that he stole the exhibit!"

"I'm sorry, Miss Melendez, but there's nothing I can do." Jasper seemed to be infuriated by his own admission.

"I don't want to have to report to my employers that the suspect was in your presence and you just let him waltz away!"

"You report whatever you goddamn want to! My hands are tied. I can't lock him up, and only the State Department can throw him out. It ain't my choice. I only enforce the law, and that, Miss Melendez, is the law."

"Precisely," Hadji said contentedly. "You know where I am staying, sir. I shall await your response to my embassy's actions." He turned on his heel and walked out.

"Son of a bitch!" Jasper said.

"This is incredible!" Sawhill exclaimed. "Do you mean to tell me that he can do whatever he wants, and we can't do a damn thing about it?"

"Pert' near," Jasper nodded. "That little bastard could commit murder in the sight of a dozen witnesses, and the worst thing that could happen to him is that he'd be sent back to Egypt."

"I don't believe this," Harriet said desperately. "He has my exhibit. I know he does!"

"Of course he does," Jasper agreed. "I'll search his room at the motor inn, but I doubt I'll find anything. He's a smart little prick."

"But we have to do something!" she cried. "We can't just sit around doing nothing."

"I know, ma'am. I'm sorry, but right now all I can do is finish up looking around in here and then take your statements." He shook his head. "Diplomatic immunity. Shit!" He paused. "Gus. Come here . . ."

Outside the museum, Ahmed Hadji was standing motionless, staring at Will Foster. Will was sitting beneath an elm tree, worriedly stroking his right cheek. His right arm hung stiffly from his side, and his right leg was thrust forward from his body as if the knee would not bend. And now, Hadji thought, to the purpose of my visit to this ramshackle barn these idiots laughingly call a museum.

Hadji watched Will Foster for a few more moments, making careful note of his condition. Then he walked over to him and said, "Good morning. Or is it afternoon?"

Will looked up at him quizzically, and then recognized him. He began to shout, "Jasper! Jasper! That Arab guy—"

"Calm yourself, my friend," Hadji said quickly. "I have already spoken with your policeman friend. Everything has been straightened out."

Jasper Rudd leaned out of the doorway of the museum and saw Hadji standing near Will. "What the hell's going on out here?"

"Nothing, sir," Hadji replied. "I was merely attempting to extend my apologies to this good fellow for having angered him so yesterday." He turned back to Will. "I was very angry at you for hitting me. But I realize that my behavior was offensive, to say the least. Please accept my regrets." He extended his hand toward Will. Seeing this, Jasper withdrew back into the museum.

Will looked at Hadji suspiciously. "You apologize to Professor Langly? It was her you insulted."

"Of course I have," Hadji lied. "That's why I am here right now. I behaved abominably yesterday, and I wish to make amends." He thrust his hand closer to Will, knowing that he could not shake it. Will could not move his right arm. He reached over with his left hand and grasped Hadji's hand. Putting on an expression of concern, Hadji asked, "Whatever is wrong with you, my good fellow? Are you ill?"

"It's nothin'," Will muttered, not wishing to discuss his ailment with a stranger.

"Oh, but it looks serious. Wait—wait—did you by any chance—yes, yes, I remember. You touched the mummy, did you not?"

"Yeah. So?"

"Why, you poor fellow! You have contracted the holachmay bacterium."

"The what? The hol—the what?"

"Yes, it is quite common, and easily treated. Have you seen a doctor?"

"Yeah, sure, Dr. Sawhill, just a little while ago. He says I may have scleropia, or something. I have to go to the hospital tonight for tests."

"Oh, nonsense, nonsense. This condition does not require hospitalization. It is quite common in the Mideast."

Will's eyes went wide with hope and relief. "No shit? It isn't serious?"

Hadji had gauged him perfectly. He had assumed that Foster would be confused and terrified by what was happening to him, this horrible degeneration without warning or explanation. He knew also that whatever help he sought would be unable to discover the cause. He knew that drowning men clutch at straws, and he began to throw some to Will Foster. "No, no, not serious at all. Of course, it isn't to be expected that an American physician would be able to recognize the symptoms. The holachmay bacterium thrives in the rotting linen on mummies. It can be a serious source of infection, but prompt treatment always effects a total cure."

Will tried to get to his feet, but unaided was not able to do so. "I gotta tell Dr. Sawhill. He's gotta find out how to cure it."

Hadji generously extended his hand again and helped Will to his feet. "No need to bother the doctor. He doesn't have access to the salve required anyway. He's busy with the policeman inside, and it would be unwise to disturb them."

"But—"

"And unnecessary as well. I have an ample supply of the salve back in my hotel room. I always carry it with me when I am engaged in work involving antiquities. Just a precaution."

"You mean you have the medicine I need?" Will seemed still a bit dubious, but he was becoming filled with desperate hope, hope that all the frightening things he had been contemplating—hospitals, chemotherapy, injections—would all be unnecessary.

"Oh, yes, indeed. As I said, I always bring an ample supply with me."

"Have you ever gotten this yourself? I mean, you say that you do this archeological stuff a lot."

"Yes, yes, a dozen times. It is no more dangerous or uncommon in my country than—what is it called—poison shrubbery—"

"Poison ivy?"

"Ah, yes, poison ivy. No more serious than that, when treated promptly. When did you first notice a problem?"

"Yesterday, I guess, when—" His eyes opened wide. "Hey,

right after I touched that mummy. Holy shit, that's right! Right after I touched that mummy!"

"Yes, of course. It is obvious." Hadji placed his hand amicably upon Will's shoulder. "Why don't you come with me to get the salve? Proper application will return you to health in two days, three days at the very most."

There was still a residue of suspicion. "Well, I don't know. Dr. Sawhill—"

Hadji silenced him with a wave of his hand. "Please. Allow me to do this for you to make up for my deplorable behavior of yesterday. The good doctor can do nothing for you because he is unfamiliar with the disease. I have been dealing with it for years."

"Well—"

"Please allow me to do this one service for you, allow me to restore the dignity I have lost."

Will Foster surrendered to his hopes and fears. "Okay, sure. You say it's a salve?"

"Yes," Hadji replied, leading Foster in the direction of the parking lot, "an ointment with an antibiotic base, mixed with certain other substances. I can't be terribly specific, because I am not a pharmacologist, but I can personally attest to its effectiveness."

"This is incredible. Thank God you're around, Mr. Hadji. I was gonna go into the hospital tonight."

"Yes, it is fortunate that we happened to meet again. The physicians at the hospital would eventually have discovered the nature of your malady, but not before permanent damage had been done. Another day and you would have been permanently scarred."

"But now there's no problem, right? I mean, now I can be completely cured, right?"

"Yes, yes, it is still early in the progress of the infection," Hadji said, smiling as he held open the door of his rented car for Will. As Will climbed awkwardly into the passenger seat, he added, "The salve may sting a bit, but I can assure you that the discomfort will be minimal."

"Jesus, that's great," Will sighed. "That's great."

Hadji started the car and began to drive slowly out of the parking lot and out onto the street. He smiled reassuringly at Will. "Just relax, my friend. Soon all your troubles will be over." Will returned his smile, looking pathetically like a dog which had just been tossed a steak.

Stupid idiot, Hadji thought as he began to drive down the main street of Greenfield. Ignorant ass. Praise be to the gods that they have not presented me with adversaries possessing more intelligence. They are so easy to fool, so easy to trick, so easy to—

Hadji's arrogant self-satisfaction dissipated when he noticed the police car in the rearview mirror. Damnation! he thought to himself. They are keeping me under surveillance. I should have realized that they would keep their prime suspect under their watchful eyes. He looked over at Will Foster, who was absently stroking his numb right cheek with his left hand. I must not allow anything to interfere with this day's task, Hadji thought. I must lose this fool of a policeman.

A few car lengths back, close enough to Hadji to indicate that no effort was being made to be inconspicuous, Gus Rudd peered through the car windshield at the subject of his surveillance. He took a cigarette from his pocket and pushed the lighter in on the dashboard. I wonder who Hadji has in there with him? he thought. Looked a little like Will from a distance, but it couldn't be Will. Ridiculous idea! Whoever that is up there looks like an old cripple.

Gus's chest had swelled with importance when Jasper told him to tail Hadji. Gus was constantly trying to live up to the expectations which his older brother had of him, and he usually failed. Not this time, he thought with determination. Not this time, Jas. I'll stick to this Arab guy like flypaper.

The two cars drove down the streets of Greenfield at a slow and steady rate of speed. Hadji was making no attempt to engage in a heated car chase, for he had insufficient confidence in his driving abilities. He also dared not risk the life of Will Foster, nor his own, until such time as the odds were more in his favor. That would be very soon, if all went as planned.

He pulled into the parking lot of the motor inn and drove as far to the rear of the lot as possible. He turned to Will and said, "I must make a quick stop here to confer with one of my associates."

"Oh. You got a friend here with you?"

"Not a friend," Hadji smiled amicably. "A local antique dealer I know is staying here at the moment. I shan't be long. Please wait and be patient."

"Yeah, yeah, sure. Hurry up, though, okay?"

Hadji patted Foster's left hand comfortingly. "Of course I shall." He got out of the car and was half-way to the parking lot entrance when Gus Rudd turned in to the entrance way. Hadji walked quickly over to the police car, hoping to prevent the policeman from driving close enough to his own car to see who was in it. *If he doesn't know already,* Hadji thought glumly. *If this occidental ass has recognized his friend, I must eliminate him before he can report this to the other policeman. Complications, complications,* Hadji thought. *If only I had been able to get to England before—*

"Hello again, officer," Hadji said to Gus. His voice was proper, but no one would have read any cooperative friendliness into his tone. "May I ask why you have been following me?"

Gus Rudd alighted from the car and attempted to swagger in the same way his brother did. "You know why, Mr. Hadji. Don't bother to try to get smart. Where's that mummy you stole?"

Hadji folded his arms and allowed annoyance to fill his tone. "I believe I've already discussed this with your superior. Am I to assume that you intend to subject me to harassment of this sort for the duration of my stay here?"

"Ain't no law against keeping an eye on a murder suspect, Mr. Hadji. And you can't call that harassment." Gus squinted down the parking lot at Hadji's car. "Who you got in there?"

*He didn't get a good enough look at him to recognize him!* Hadji thought with relief. He said, "Who? Oh, Khalid! That's my secretary."

"Secretary! Looked like an old cripple to me."

"Khalid is elderly, and he has arthritis. Is that illegal in this country?"

"Don't be smart, Mr. Hadji. I think I'd better have a word or two with him."

Thinking fast, Hadji said, "Before or after you search my rooms?"

"I know the law, Mr. Hadji. We'll search your rooms, but we're gonna get a search warrant first. Jasper's probably calling Judge McCormick right now."

Hadji waved his hand as if irritated at the thought. "Listen, my friend, I wish to dispense with these formalities and get all of us back to our proper tasks, which I hope will lead us to the stolen exhibit. I have to help my old secretary out of the car and bring him back to our rooms. I'll meet you in the lobby of this—this so-called hotel. You have my permission to search my dwelling, even without a warrant."

"But—"

"Please, officer, we are all wasting time! Meet me in the lobby, we'll go upstairs, you can question Khalid and conduct your search. All right?"

Gus nodded. "Yeah, yeah, okay. That'll save time." Make me look good to Jasper, too, he thought.

A few moments later, Gus Rudd was standing in the hotel lobby, watching with anger and shock as he saw Ahmed Hadji's car speeding out of the parking lot. "Goddamn it!" he shouted, running outside to his own car. He started the engine and tried to screech off in hot pursuit, but the wobbly flapping he heard told him that Hadji had let the air out of his tires. He repressed an urge to cry. Jasper's gonna kill me, he thought.

The patrol car radio came alive with a burst of static and Jasper's voice boomed out, "Gus? You there?"

Oh, well, here we go, Gus thought dejectedly. He pulled the radio microphone free from its holder and pressed in the button on the side. "I'm here, Jasper."

"How's it going?"

"I followed him to the motor inn, but"—oh, shit—"then he gave me the slip."

"He what!? Goddamn it, Gus!"

"I'm sorry, Jasper, honest to God I am. The son of a bitch tricked me, said he was gonna let me search his room without a warrant, and—"

"Never mind, never mind. You can tell me about it later. Damn it all, Gus! How the hell could you lose somebody in a town this size!"

"Jeeze, Jasper, I'm sorry."

"Hold on." The radio went dead for a moment, and then Gus heard Jasper's voice say, "I got Doc Sawhill here. He seems to have lost Will."

"Huh?"

"Will was with the doc, and he seems to have wandered off. You seen him anywhere?"

"No, not since last night. Why?"

"Doc says he's sick. Gotta go to the hospital. You didn't see him outside when I told you to go follow Hadji?"

"No, nobody was there when I went outside. Of course, I was watching Hadji pretty close. He was getting into his car by the time I got out there."

"Yeah, you were watching him pretty close, I'm sure,"

Jasper spat. "Get your ass back here, on the double." Gus stared at the now silent radio and sighed. Then he got out of the car and began to change the tire.

On the other side of town, Ahmed Hadji repressed an urge to laugh. *Praise the gods that they have given me the good fortune of having to deal with fools.* He grinned with satisfaction at the effectiveness of his actions thus far. He had known that no clues would be found connecting him to the theft of the body of the Lord Sekhemib, or with the murders of the ass of a British lawyer and the obsequious cretin at the real estate office. He had covered his tracks well, renting a room at the motor inn, renting this car, making it safe for him to appear at the museum today. His well-rehearsed shock at the disappearance of the mummy was convincing enough for his purposes, and by the time the local police discovered that his diplomatic passport had been forged, he would be long gone. Only being followed right now would have been a problem, but fortune had provided an idiot for a pursuer.

He glanced over at Will Foster and smiled. He almost pitied him. Almost, but not quite.

They soon pulled into the driveway of Mrs. March's house. "Wait, let me assist you," he said to Will as he got out of the car and ran around to the passenger side. He opened the door and helped Will out of the car. "Now, let us go in and attend to your problem."

"Great," Will said. "Hey, what was Gus doing at that motor inn?"

"Eh? Oh—oh, he wished to speak to my business associate about the antiquities which were stolen."

"Oh, sure. That makes sense." Will straightened up painfully beside the car. "Hey, isn't this old lady March's house? You're staying here?"

"Yes, I am renting a room for a week or so, just until this unpleasantness can be resolved."

"You mean about who owns those mummies? Well, no offense, Mr. Hadji, but you better not get your hopes up. I got to tell you, Professor Langly ain't gonna give them up without a fight."

"Yes, yes, well we can allow your courts to make that decision. I only regret that I was so impolite to the lady yesterday." He helped Will mount the three steps leading to the front door and then unlocked it and led him inside. He pushed the door shut and locked it quickly. Hadji felt a surge of anticipatory excitement well up in him. "My luggage is downstairs in the basement. Can you make it down the steps, my good fellow?"

Will was dismayed. "Can't you bring the medicine up? My legs ain't working too good."

"I'd rather not," Hadji said apologetically. "Exposure to sunlight reduces the potency of the ointment. We certainly don't want to take any chances with your recovery, do we?"

"Hell no!" Will exclaimed. "Anything you say, man! You know about this fuckin' disease, not me."

"Fine, fine. Follow me." Hadji led him to the basement door. "I'll go down first. You follow at your own pace, but take your time, be careful."

"Okay. I think I can manage it, Mr. Hadji."

"Very good." Hadji bounded down the steps to the basement and Will followed, slowly and hesitantly. Hadji stood waiting at the base of the steps, holding out a helping hand and largely blocking Will's view of the interior of the basement. "Here, please sit down in this chair."

"It's kinda dark down here, ain't it? Ain't there no lights?"

"Oh, my goodness, of course there are! Let's just sit you down in this chair and then I'll get the lights." Will saw a chair in front of him, dim in the darkness, and he managed to turn himself around and drop into it. "Excellent!" Hadji said happily. With a quick motion he snapped the handcuff shut upon Will's left hand. The other end of the cuff had already been affixed to the arm of the chair.

"Wha—what the hell are you doing?"

Hadji did not reply. Instead he reached around behind the chair and drew forth one end of a rope, which he pulled across Will's stomach and then tied to the back of the chair. He stood back and smiled contentedly. Then he said, "What am I doing? What do you think I am doing?"

"Where's the ointment? My condition—"

Hadji laughed. "You are so incredibly stupid, you empty-headed idiot. Did you seriously believe that I intended to help cure you? Do you actually think that there is an ointment or a holachmay bacterium?" Hadji giggled idiotically. "Such a fool! Such a fool!"

The realization that he had been tricked infuriated Will. He struggled against his bonds, but with only one half of his body able to move his struggle was futile. "I'll kill you, you son of a bitch!" he shouted. "I'll tear your fuckin' head off!"

"Oh, will you now?" Hadji asked pleasantly. "We'll see about that." He reached out and snapped on the light.

Will looked in front of him and saw the mummy of Sekhemib lying on the floor upon a small rug. "You took it! You took Professor Langly's exhibit!"

"Of course I did. That would be obvious to anyone. Even your thickheaded policeman suspects me. It was something of a risk for me to return to—the scene of the crime, shall we say? But I had to find you, and I had no other way to track you down. It was a stroke of fortune for me that you happened to be there just now. You've saved me from quite a troublesome search."

"You had to find me! What the hell for?"

"Why, for this, of course," Hadji replied. "You are singularly honored, my friend. You are about to perform a great service." Hadji laughed and walked over to the mummy. He reached down and slipped the chain with the medallion over the mummy's head, carefully and reverently lifting the stiff body slightly to allow the chain to move past the skull. "Allow me to prepare you," he said to Will. Hadji turned to Will and placed the chain over his head so that the medallion rested upon his chest.

"You let me go," Will shouted. "Help! Help!"

"Yes indeed, shout for help. No one can hear you in this basement. And very soon you won't be able to shout."

Will's anger was being replaced by fear. "Look, man, I'm sorry I slugged you in the mouth, okay? I didn't mean it. I'm really sorry, okay?"

"Certainly," Hadji smiled. "I accept your apology. Now please be quiet." Will continued to struggle and plead, but Hadji ignored him. He struck a match and held it to what looked like a saucer, and the oil in the primitive lamp began to burn, casting flickering shadows upon the walls of the basement. The flickering became all the more pronounced when Hadji switched off the electric lights.

"Let me go!" Will yelled. Tears began to stream down his cheeks, but still Ahmed Hadji ignored him.

Hadji knelt before the mummy of Sekhemib and bowed, his arms crossed upon his chest. Then he lowered his head and raised his arms outward with the palms facing away from him and the fingers pointing up. "*Anet hrauthen neteru*," he chanted. "*Anet hrauthen 'Anpu.*" Homage to thee, O gods. Homage to thee, Anubis. "*Anet hrak Sekhemib, ab 'Anpuf, neter khen ua 'amth abu.*" Homage to thee, Sekhemib, priest of Anubis, prophet of the priests.

"Let me go," Will wept softly.

"*Anet hrak Sekhemib. Aua Ahmed Hadji abu Tekhutif rexkuak, rexkua renk.*" Homage to thee, Sekhemib. I, Ahmed Hadji, priest of Thoth, know thy name. "*Tekenu enti khenak. Iuk enn tem sekhauk, iuk em arauk.*" The tekenu is with thee. Come thou to us without memories of evil, come thou to us in thy form. "*Auk er khekh en khekh, akha khekh.*" Thou shalt live for millions of years, a life of millions of years.

Will Foster felt a sudden stabbing pain in his chest. The medallion which dangled from the chain around his neck seemed to be growing warm. A slow but steady vibration began to arise from the golden circle, and Will became aware of what felt like gentle electric shocks coursing from the medallion to his body. He tried to pull his left hand free from the handcuff but found that it was now as immobile as his right. He tried to move his left leg. It was useless. The same numbing cold which he had first noticed the day before, which had afflicted first his right hand, then his right arm, then his right leg, was spreading over his entire body. He felt his heart pounding wildly and the tremors of fear which shook his frame still imparted sensation, but there was no surface feeling whatsoever. It was as if his entire body was covered with a thick layer of dead skin.

"*Anet hrak Sekhemib,*" Hadji repeated in his high, chanting voice. "*Aua Ahmed Hadji abu Tekhutif rexkuak, rexkua renk.*"

Will was whimpering through his tears. No words escaped his lips, only pathetic little cries. He blinked his eyes repeatedly as they filled with the warm, salty liquid, trying to maintain his focus on the room which had begun to blur and spin around him. He could not be certain of what he saw, but there appeared to be a steadily growing band of light pulsating somewhere in the room. He tried to shake his head, but was able merely to effect a slow, almost languid motion. It was sufficient to clear his vision temporarily, and he saw that the band of light, which fluctuated between a faint luminescence and an almost dazzling brilliance, which glowed dull red as it faded and bright yellow as it intensified, seemed to be stretching from the head of the mummy on the floor to the center of the medallion which dangled from the chain around Will's neck.

"*Tekenu enti khenak. Iuk enn tem sekhauk, iuk em arauk,*" Hadji continued his trancelike chant. *The tekenu is with thee. Come thou to us without memories of evil, come thou in thy form.*

Will tried once again to clear his vision by shaking his head, but his skin had become so stiff that he felt as if his body had been encased in plaster. He tensed his muscles and forced his head to move, but the motion caused the skin on his throat to blister and split with an abrupt, audible crack. As the blood began to stream out of the open slits, he saw the flesh shriveling and splitting open on his arms, and felt the same thing happening on his chest, his back, his legs, his face. His heart began beating erratically. It was becoming difficult to draw air into his decaying lungs.

*"Auk er khekh en khekh, akha khekh . . ."*

The pungent odor of urine and feces assaulted Will's bleeding nostrils at the same instant that a searing pain seemed to shoot through his midsection. As his bowels ruptured, green and brown fluids began to stream out of him in all directions, spurting at first and then flowing, mingling with the red blood which was accumulating at his feet. Pieces of dry, leathery skin were flaking off his fragmenting body as it shook in violent tremors of agony. The gray flakes drifted gently down and floated upon the rapidly spreading puddle of putrid fluids.

*"Iuk enn tem sekhauk, Sekhemib! Iuk em arauk, Sekhemib! Iuk em arauk, Sekhemib!"* Hadji was swaying back and forth in time with the cadence of the chant. The pulsations of the band of light caused an insane glow to reflect from his open, ecstatic eyes.

A final, silent, inaudible scream struggled to break free from Will's rotting mouth. He strained to draw in air, and his lungs collapsed. As wave after wave of pain washed over him, he sank into shock only to be roused by the searing agony as it swept upon him anew. The flow of liquid ceased, and what seemed to be dust burst out through the cracked and putrifying leather which encased his disintegrating body.

*"Anet hrauthen 'Anpu! Anet hrauthen 'Anpu! Anet hrauthen 'Anpu!"*

Will Foster saw the mummy of Sekhemib rise slowly and unsteadily to its feet.

And then, mercifully, he died.

# CHAPTER 8

▲ Thomas Sawhill gazed with irritation and some concern out over the campus quad. "Where the hell could he have gone?" he wondered aloud.

Harriet was standing beside him. "Does he realize the importance of the tests in the hospital?"

"He certainly should. I tried to impress upon him the seriousness of the situation." Sawhill shook his head. "I just don't understand this. I know he's afraid of hospitals, but I can't imagine him just wandering off. I mean, good God, the man can barely walk!"

"Maybe you should ask Jasper or Gus to try to find him?" she suggested.

"Oh, sure, as if they don't have enough to do!" He sighed. "I'm going to have to look for him myself."

Roderick Fowles walk out of the museum and approached them. "Professor Langly? May I have a word?"

"Oh, yes, Your Lordship. I'm sorry, but with all the excitement we've been rather ignoring you."

"Please don't give it a second thought. I'm terribly sorry for all the trouble you seem to be having, but if it wouldn't be too much trouble, I'd like to sign the transfer documents so that I can proceed on my own itinerary." He grinned boyishly. "I'm rather eager to get to Disney World, actually."

Harriet thought for a moment before speaking. "Well, sir, I am willing to accept receipt of the six exhibits we still possess. But as for the one which was stolen—well, I don't know."

"It was insured, after all, was it not?" he said. "I'm quite certain that Miss Melendez would not object to the filing of a claim on your behalf."

"Hold it," Suzanne said as she too walked out of the museum onto the grassy quadrangle. "The insurance covers shipment. That was the limit of the policy. As of this moment, there's no insurance on any of the exhibits."

"But we haven't taken possession yet, Suzie," Harriet objected. "Surely that means that technically they are still covered under the shipping insurance."

Suzanne smiled kindly at her friend. "Sorry, hon, it doesn't work that way. Can you imagine me trying to explain to my boss that the crates were all unloaded and stored on the grounds of their insured destination but were still in transit at the same time?" She shook her head. "I'm sorry, but at this stage of the game no one can file a claim on the one that was stolen."

"Damn!" Roderick muttered. "That's bloody inconvenient. What do you suggest we do?" It was typical of Roderick that he chose to act as if this were a problem common to them all rather than an issue between contending parties.

"Well, this is how it looks to me. I'm sorry to say that, unless the stolen exhibit is recovered, you're both just going to have to accept the fact that it's gone for good. I would be willing to write a policy on the remaining six—"

"We have blanket policy on all the contents of the museum," Sam Goldhaber said, walking over from behind them.

"How much is it for?"

He grinned sheepishly. "Not for too much, I'm afraid."

"Well, you should increase it. If you have an insurance company which you customarily work with, then contact them as soon as possible." She smiled. "I mean, I'm not trying to drum up business. Harriet, accept receipt of the six exhibits, sign the papers, and get them insured as soon as possible. I'm afraid," she turned to Roderick, "that you'll have to absorb the loss of the other exhibit, Your Lordship."

Damn, I wish Pearson were here, Roderick thought. I don't know anything about such matters. He shrugged, saying, "Well, I suppose that's all we can do."

"I really would like to make certain that the other crates contain what they're supposed to contain," Harriet said hesitantly.

"Oh, sure, of course," Suzanne said. "Are you satisfied with the authenticity of the mummies you've already seen?"

"Well, there are problems," she admitted. "No evisceration, for example. There are problems with the hieroglyphs—"

"Harriet, we shouldn't be talking about scholarly stuff. Are they real mummies, or aren't they?"

"Oh, yes, there's no doubt about that."

"Well, that really should be enough, shouldn't it? I mean, any sort of scientific research on the exhibits really has nothing to do with concluding the purchase, right?"

Harriet nodded reluctantly. "I suppose that's true."

"You sure, Harriet?" Sam asked.

"Yes," she said with a certainty she did not feel. "Yes. In any event, if the other mummies are in the same perfect state of preservation as the first three, then I don't want to lose them. Besides," she grinned, "half a dozen is better than none."

"Good," Suzanne said. "Before we left London, Mr. Pearson—" she paused, "poor Mr. Pearson gave me a box filled with documents about the shipment. Why don't we all go back to our hotel and take care of everything there?"

"Documents!" Harriet exclaimed. "Why didn't you tell me about this?"

Suzanne shrugged. "I didn't see any need to. I figured that they're just ownership certificates or something like that. Why?"

"Have you examined the documents?"

"Of course not! They're in a sealed box. All I know is what Mr. Pearson told me, that they're connected to the Selwyn collection. Hey, what's the big deal, anyway?"

"Nothing," Harriet said uncertainly. "Oh, nothing, nothing. I just had a—nothing. Forget it." She seemed to be attempting to bring herself out of a reverie. "Let's go look in the other four crates, and if everything's okay we can go and sign the papers."

"Why don't we go and get the documents and bring them back here?" Suzanne asked, glancing at Roderick. He smiled amiably, always ready to follow any suggestion.

Harriet smiled. "Good idea. It'd probably save time." And give you a chance to get His Lordship alone, she thought with amusement.

"Hiya," Gus Rudd said as he ambled hesitantly into the room.

Jasper drew himself up to his full height and fixed an angry glare at his younger brother. "What the hell happened?"

Gus spread his hands apart at his sides and shrugged. "I'm really sorry, Jasper, honest I am. I really tried, and I was doin' good, too, but he pulled a fast one on me."

Jasper nodded unsympathetically. "That doesn't seem too hard to do."

"Excuse me a minute," Sawhill broke in. "Gus, you didn't see Will anywhere in town on your way back here, did you?"

"No, I didn't, sorry. Is Will in trouble or something?"

"Could be," Sawhill muttered. "He's ill, very ill. He's supposed to check into the hospital this evening."

"No shit!" Gus said. "He seemed okay last night. I mean, sure, his hand was botherin' him, but—"

"Whatever was wrong with his hand has spread to his arm and leg. He can barely walk, and I don't really know what's wrong with him."

"Gee, that's terrible." Gus frowned.

Jasper shook his head. "Damndest thing," he said. "No idea what it is?"

"Well," Sawhill replied, "it could be scleroderma, a degenerative tissue disease, but I really can't tell without the tests he's supposed to take tonight."

A glimmer of realization flashed into Gus Rudd's mind, but he almost immediately snuffed it out. The man with Hadji, the cripple—could it have been? . . . No. No, that's ridiculous. Couldn't have been. Stupid idea, stupid.

"Well," Sawhill said tiredly, "if it's okay with everybody, I'm going to go out and look for Will."

"You want some help, Doc?" Gus asked.

"Not from you!" Jasper snapped. "With you helping him, he'd never find him." Jasper ignored Gus's crestfallen look. "You stay here and give me a hand."

As Sawhill, Suzanne, and Roderick left, Harriet turned to Jasper. "Can I borrow Gus for a few minutes? I want to get those other crates open to check out the contents before we sign the papers."

"Yeah, okay," Jasper muttered. "Just hurry it up, you understand?"

"Sure, Jasper, okay," Gus said. "I'll just pry off the lids." He turned to Harriet. "That'll be enough this time, right?" Gus seemed to think that being helpful now would somehow compensate for losing Hadji.

"Sure, Gus. I don't need to examine the sarcophagi. Just get the lids off the four crates and off the sarcophagi inside, and that'll be all I need. I just have to make sure there are mummies in there."

"Okeydokey," Gus said. "I'll go over to the grounds building."

"Good. I'll meet you there." She turned to the others. "You want to join me, or do you have other things to do?"

"Well," Suzanne replied, "I have to go back to the hotel to get the papers. You want to come along, Your Lordship?"

"Oh, yes, of course," Roderick said. "I'd rather like to get this all over with, actually."

"Well, I'll stay and help," Sam said. "I'd be interested in seeing the condition of the other exhibits before I give the final okay to the purchase. I'm the one who has to sign the papers, you know."

"Curators aren't trusted by administrators," Harriet explained wryly. "They're afraid we'll buy anything and everything."

Suzanne laughed. "Probably right. Well, we'll be back in a few minutes."

"Okay. See you." Harriet turned back to Sam. "Let's go see how Gus is doing."

They walked over to the grounds building quietly. Harriet had not reconciled herself to the loss of the first mummy, and Sam's attempts at light conversation did not interest her. She was certain—they were all certain—that Ahmed Hadji was the thief, but it seemed clear that Jasper's hands were tied. Son of a bitch, she thought to herself in reference to Hadji. Mummies in every museum in the world, and he has to come here and hassle me. Son of a bitch!

They entered the grounds building to find that Gus had already pried two of the crates open and was working on the third. "Piece of cake," he smiled. "These crates are so old that the nails pull out like—ouch!"

"What's the matter?"

Gus was shaking his hand back and forth. "Jeeze! I must have pulled a muscle or something. Ouch!" he repeated.

"Hey, are you all right?" Harriet asked.

Gus rubbed his right hand with his left. "Yeah, yeah, sure. Must be a muscle spasm or something." He returned his attention to the third of the four crates.

Harriet watched Gus with concern for a moment, and then walked over to one of the crates. "Sam, help me with the coffin lid, will you?" She took one end of the lid and he the other.

They lifted it easily from the sarcophagus and placed it on the floor. Harriet looked in at the fourth perfectly preserved mummy, obviously another woman. She looked down at the lid. "Khumara, priestess of Bast," she read. "Same hieroglyphs, same prayers, same medallion."

"Isn't that what you expected?" Sam asked.

"More or less," she agreed. They moved to the next crate and removed the coffin lid, again placing it on the floor beside the crate. "Another one, in a perfect state of preservation. This one is—" she looked carefully at the lid. "Senmut, priest of Ra."

Another crate was opened, another lid removed, another mummy revealed. "Herihor, priest of Horus," she read.

And yet another. "Wenet, priest of Thoth."

Harriet, Sam, and Gus stood looking at the four open coffins. She shook her head. "Sam, I'm sorry. I'm not trying to be a pain in the ass, but this just doesn't make sense."

"I know, you told us about the hieroglyphs."

"It's not just that. What are all of these people doing together? The Selwyns didn't just happen by coincidence to obtain them from different sources. These bodies are all buried in identical wooden coffins. They wear identical medallions. I haven't examined these four yet, but I'd bet my life that none of them have been eviscerated. And they are all priests, but of different gods, by virtue of which they should not have been buried together." Harriet frowned. "Sam, it just doesn't make any sense. There is nothing in my knowledge of Egyptian funerary practice which could account for this."

"Harriet," Sam said gently, "don't you think you're letting your academic imagination run away with you? There must be a simple explanation for all these things."

"Yeah," she conceded unwillingly. "It's just that I'll be damned if I can think of what it is." She shook her head again. "Well, I might as well put the time to good use while we're waiting for Suzie and the Earl to come back. I'm going to do some transcriptions of the hieroglyphs on the lids. But I'm sure they'll all be the same as the others, mistakes and all. What are you going to do?"

Goldhaber smiled. "Nothing. It's one of the prerogatives of academic administrators to be able to relax and watch their underlings labor."

"Nice, Sam. Real nice." She shot him a look of mock irritation tinged with affection, and then knelt beside one of the lids and, taking pencil and paper in hand, began to copy the hieroglyphs. Sam went outside and lolled about, enjoying the fresh air. There was a distinct odor of dust and age in the grounds building because of its recent boarders, and the cool green air outside was very pleasant.

Still rubbing his hand, Gus Rudd walked out and passed Sam Goldhaber. "See you later, Professor."

"Thanks for your help, Gus."

"My pleasure." As Gus walked back toward the museum where his brother awaited him impatiently, he continued to rub and poke his hand. Damn it, Gus thought. And it's my pistol hand, too! I got to be more careful moving things.

A half hour later Suzanne and Roderick drove into the parking lot near the museum, and Sam watched as they got out of the car and approached him. Roderick was carrying a small wooden box, about one foot long and wide, about six inches high, upon which were engraved geometric designs of uncertain origin. He seemed slightly miffed at having to carry the box himself. Sam smiled slightly. It must be tough to have to do without a butler, a chauffeur, and all the other servants. Poor guy, Sam thought with absolutely no sympathy whatsoever.

"Hi, Sam," Suzanne said as they approached. "Where's Harriet?"

"She's inside," he replied, gesturing behind him over his shoulder. "We opened the other four crates, just to check the contents."

"Everything okay?"

"Everything looks fine to me. Four more mummies."

"Good. The papers Mr. Pearson sent along with the shipment are in this box. Let's get to work and complete the transfer." She entered the grounds building with Sam and Roderick in her wake.

Harriet was still kneeling on the floor as they entered, bending over the last of the four coffin lids. She looked up at them and smiled perfunctorily. "That was quick."

"Yeah," Suzanne said, and added sotto voce, "unfortunately." Harriet laughed. Suzanne's campaign of seduction against the Earl of Selwyn was making no progress. "His Lordship has the papers in this box. Isn't it beautiful?"

Harriet moved her hand over the shining wood appreciatively. "It certainly is. Teakwood, isn't it, Your Lordship?"

"I suppose so," Roderick replied. "Uncle told me that

there were papers relating to the collection in a teakwood box, so I assume that this is it." He did not add that he couldn't tell teak from oak if his life depended on it.

"Do you think it's from India?" Suzanne asked. "That's where teak comes from, doesn't it?"

"Yeah, but this isn't Indian," Harriet said, still examining the designs on the box. "More likely from an Islamic country, maybe Pakistan. Moslems developed intricate geometric designs for decorations because of the prohibition against representing human or animal forms. Graven images, and all that." She paused. "Of course, Pakistan was part of Imperial British India. Could be. Suzie, have you examined the contents? Are there ownership papers or anything in it?"

"No, I figured I'd better wait until we got here with it so there would be witnesses. It's sealed. See?" She pointed to a small wire encased in red wax which had been looped through the clasp on the box.

"Oh, I hadn't noticed," Harriet said. "Well, put it down on that work table over there, Your Lordship, if you'd be so kind."

"I trust there are no further impediments to concluding the sale?" he asked hopefully. "I really would like to prepare to go to Florida as soon as possible."

"No, no, we'll accept the six mummies and make payment, according to the schedule agreed upon with your representative," Sam said. He looked at Harriet. "Right, boss?"

"Yeah, right," she replied. "I have to say that there are some disturbing things about these exhibits. But I'm convinced that they are genuine Egyptian relics, so I guess that's all that matters for now, anyway."

"Good," Suzanne said. "Your Lordship, if you'll do the honors?"

"I beg your pardon?"

"If you will break the seal? Open the box?"

"Oh, yes, yes, indeed." Roderick did not quite know how a seal was supposed to be broken, but the wax crumbled as soon as he grasped it, so that he was saved from any embarrassment. "Well, that's easy enough," he said, grinning. He began to tug on the twisted wire, which resolutely refused to come loose.

"Allow me, sir," Suzanne said, deftly unwrapping the wire

and pulling it free from the lock. Reaching into her purse she removed a key and fitted it into the key hole. "Mr. Pearson gave me this in London," she explained.

"Had he looked through the papers in the box?" Harriet asked.

"No. I don't believe anyone has. You haven't, have you, Your Lordship?"

"No, not I. As I said, Uncle mentioned it to me, but with all the excitement of his death and the trip to America and so forth—well, I rather forgot about it." He paused thoughtfully. "He seemed rather insistent that I read the materials in the box, actually. Of course, he was on the brink of death at the time."

Harriet failed to see what that had to do with anything, but she did not say so. "Let's see what we have here." She pushed up the small lid of the teakwood box and reached inside. Harriet drew forth a yellowed envelope and a small rolled papyrus scroll. She tossed the envelope back into the box and with an eagerness born of an unexpected bounty, she unrolled the scroll.

Suzanne looked at the scroll which, even upside down as she viewed it, was obviously not written in the English language. "What is it?"

"I'm not sure," Harriet replied.

"Egyptian, possibly?" Roderick asked.

"No, absolutely not," she said firmly. "It isn't hieroglyphic, hieratic, demotic, or Coptic. There are no other forms of Egyptian writing prior to the language's displacement by Arabic. And it doesn't look to me like Arabic." She turned to Sam Goldhaber. "Sam, you want to take a look at this?"

Sam Goldhaber took the scroll gently in his hands and examined it carefully. After a few minutes he said, "I'm not certain, but I think it's Proto-Sinaitic. Possibly Old Phoenician or Punic."

Suzanne stared at him blankly. "How could you possibly know that?"

Harriet laughed. "Sam wasn't always a college administrator, you know. He used to be a professor of Semitic languages at UCLA."

"Briefly, just briefly," Sam said with typical self-deprecation.

"Don't be so modest," Harriet said. She turned to Suzanne. "Whenever he says things like 'If I remember my

Hebrew' or 'When I was a child back in Hebrew school' and stuff like that, you can be sure he's about to talk about something he's studied for years."

"No shit!" Suzanne was surprised to learn of Sam's erudition. Accustomed as she was to the world of business, she had assumed that his administrative post had been achieved without relation to any scholarly ability. "So what did you say it was? What language?"

"I'm really not certain," he repeated. "It looks like Proto-Sinaitic, the language spoken and written by the nomads from the fringes of the Nile Delta north and east to the Jordan valley about four thousand years ago. Or it could be Phoenician or Punic from a later date. I can't tell without reference to my books. The scripts are very similar." He looked up. "But you're right, Harriet. This isn't Egyptian, not unless the Egyptians wrote and spoke a form of primitive Hebrew."

"You mean to say that this is a form of Hebrew?" Suzanne asked.

"Not exactly. Proto-Sinaitic is related to Hebrew in much the same way as Latin is related to French or Rumanian."

"Can you translate it?" Harriet asked hopefully. "If it's in here with any other documents relating to the exhibits, it may shed some light on the problems I have with them."

"It may do more than that," he said. "There aren't too many Proto-Sinaitic texts. This may be priceless." He looked up at Roderick. "This isn't technically part of this purchase. If you don't mind, I'd like to take this to my office and work on it for a while. If it's as valuable as I think it may be, I'd like to negotiate its purchase from you."

"Oh, yes, certainly," Roderick replied, pounds and pence dancing once again before his eyes. "By all means."

"Good," Sam said. "Harriet, I'll be in my office if you need me." He wandered off distractedly, studying the fragile papyrus.

"Well, that's a surprise, isn't it?" Suzanne said. "You're going to end up with quite a little museum here, my dear."

"Looks that way," she grinned. "What else is in the box? What about the envelope?"

"Let's see." Suzanne took the envelope out once again and opened it carefully. "There's a letter in here, a rather long one, from the looks of it." She unfolded the sheets of yellowed paper and began to read it. Then she looked at Roderick. "Your Lordship, I think this is addressed to you."

"To me! Whomever from?"

"Well, it's apparently a letter from one of your ancestors, addressed to his heirs and descendants." She handed it to him. "I think you should read it, not me."

"Oh, there's no need for that," he said, refusing to take the pages from her. "Just read it aloud. I don't mind a bit."

She shrugged. "As you wish." She cleared her throat and began to read:

To my heirs and descendants, from Arthur Fowles, ninth Earl of Selwyn, written in the year of our Lord 1836, in the sixth year of the reign of our dread sovereign William IV.

I am writing this for you, my dear son Henry, with the hopes that you will pass the information contained herein on to your heirs after you. There is a grave danger to me, and to you and our entire family. I bear the responsibility for visiting this misfortune upon our heads, and I do not desire to evade it. But it is a matter of vital importance that you know the whole truth, and not judge me too harshly.

To begin at the beginning: after Bonaparte's Egyptian campaign of the end of the last century, it became evident to His Majesty's ministers that the security of the trade route to India depended in no small measure upon the establishment of a British influence in Egypt. I was sent to that unhappy land with a contingent of His Majesty's soldiers in November of 1827, shortly after the Egyptian and Turkish fleets were destroyed in the Battle of Navarino, during the Greek revolt against the Ottomans. Given the fact that their military strength was negligible and their government in disarray, the Egyptians were in no position to refuse the establishment of a permanent British consulate in Cairo. I had the honor to be appointed chargé d'affaires to His Majesty's Consul, Sir Leopold Ramsey.

Allow me to review for you the recent history of that region. The empire of the Ottoman Turks, encompassing as it does the major part of the Mohammedan world, entered into a period of corrupt decline during the century just past. The several local rulers of the provinces of the empire have been increasingly behaving as if they were sovereign rulers rather than gover-

nors dependent upon the sultan's wishes. Thus it is
that Mehemet Ali Pasha, a scurrilous and totally un-
trustworthy Albanian adventurer, has been able both
to establish his control over the disgracefully Byzantine
bureaucracy in Cairo and to behave as if the foreign
policy of Egypt were independent of the foreign policy
of his master in Constantinople.

   I have had the unpleasant experience of having to
deal with Mehemet Ali on a number of occasions, and
I must say that no more extreme example of oriental
duplicity exists. I shall not burden you with examples
of his immoral mentality, my son; but I mention this
because Mehemet Ali is responsible for the difficulties
with which I am currently beset and which, I blush to
say, I must soon pass on to you.

   Suzanne looked up from the page. "Have you heard of this
guy?" she asked Harriet.
   "Oh, yes, certainly," she replied. "Mehemet Ali was
something of a fly in the nineteenth century diplomatic
ointment. He founded the ruling dynasty which ended when
Nasser and the other soldiers overthrew King Farouk in 1952.
From all accounts, Mehemet Ali was an unscrupulous
Machiavellian. Of course, the racist tone of the letter reflects
the prejudices of the day." She laughed. "Oriental duplicity!
This from a man whose nation produced Oliver Cromwell and
Lord Palmerston!"
   "And they were?"
   "Never mind. It isn't important." Harriet turned to
Roderick. "I meant no offense, Your Lordship."
   "Oh, none taken, none taken," he replied genially. Who
the hell was Lord Palmerston? he wondered. He had heard of
Cromwell, but he could not quite place the name.
   "Go on, Suzie," Harriet urged. "This is interesting."
Suzanne resumed reading aloud.

   In 1831 Mehemet Ali and his mercenary army rose in
open revolt against the sultan, and he sent his son
Ibrahim with a portion of his army north to attack and
occupy Palestine and Syria. This led the sultan to conclude a treaty of alliance with the Russian tsar, which
led His Majesty's government reluctantly to support the
Egyptians. This war, which was unwanted by all the

powers, was resolved by diplomatic activities in which we and the tsar were joined by the Austrian and Prussian representatives. The result, as you may know, was a reaffirmation of the Ottoman government and the withdrawal of Mehemet's Ali's troops from Palestine and Syria.

The significance of these facts for my difficulty rests in the antiquities which Ibrahim brought back to Egypt with him from Palestine. Ibrahim is cut from a different cloth than his father had been. While equally ambitious and violent, he has an interest in the past which is beyond his father's limited ken. Ibrahim returned to Egypt at the conclusion of the war against the sultan, carrying with him the contents of a subterranean vault his troops stumbled upon (or should I say, stumbled into when its roof collapsed under their weight) in Shechem, some twenty miles north of Jerusalem. In addition to numerous pieces of armor and vessels, he brought with him seven mummies.

"Wait a minute," Harriet said testily. "Are we supposed to believe that these relics originated in Palestine? That's ridiculous! I know there are quite a few unanswered questions here, but I know an Egyptian mummy when I see one!"

"Is it possible that other peoples of the period used the same methods?" Suzanne asked.

Harriet shook her head. "Absolutely not. In later years mummification was practiced according to the Egyptian method in Nubia and Cush, but they were to the south of Egypt, not the northeast."

"Are you saying this letter is a fabrication?" Roderick asked.

"No, I'm not saying anything of the sort. But there must be an error here somewhere. These are definitely *not* Syrian funerary relics."

"I thought Palestine—" Suzanne began.

"In ancient times Palestine was regarded as part of Syria. There are quite a few contemporary Syrians who still feel that way." She laughed grimly.

"I don't understand—" Suzanne began.

"Wait, wait," Harriet interrupted her. "Read the rest of the letter before we start arguing about anything."

Suzanne seemed miffed. "I wasn't arguing. You were arguing."

"Sorry, Suzie, sorry. Please go on, okay?"

Suzanne continued reading:

Ibrahim was aware of my interest in the antiquities of the region, and I spent many pleasant hours in his company discussing with him our mutual interests in the study of the distant past. I made the mistake of expressing to him my good-natured envy at his acquisition. He apparently mentioned this to his father, who proceeded to appeal to my worst instincts to his own advantage.

In 1833 a group of Saint-Simonians arrived in Egypt. Their expressed purpose was to westernize and modernize the country, an important element of which would be the construction of a canal connecting the Mediterranean with the Gulf of Suez. Such a canal would be both a great advantage to British trade as well as a potential hostage to hostile foreign powers. We Britons in Egypt and His Majesty's ministers in London debated the merits and dangers of the proposed canal, and we decided secretly to work to the frustration of the Saint-Simonian design.

Mehemet Ali and Ibrahim were unaware of this decision, however, and they took steps to suborn the British representatives in Cairo. Mehemet Ali feared that the construction of the canal would in the end make Egypt the site of a major European conflict. He also feared that any attempt to alter the traditional lives of his people would result in internal strife. He incorrectly assumed that His Majesty's ministers would wholeheartedly support the project. Thus, Mehemet Ali's attempts to bring financial inducements into our considerations, to turn our minds against the project, provided my colleagues and myself with the opportunity to enrich ourselves by presenting to the pasha a decision which had already been made.

"So much for honor," Roderick muttered. "Uncle used to speak of the family honor endlessly. Good Lord!"

"Don't be too harsh in your judgment, Your Lordship," Harriet said. "The niceties of ethical behavior did not extend to dealings with non-Europeans in those days."

"Oh, I'm not judging the ninth Earl harshly at all,"

Roderick explained. "It just annoys me that Uncle was always criticizing me for my behavior when I'm descended—no, when *we're* descended from a diplomat who took bribes."

"It can't technically be considered a bribe if it had nothing to do with the decision about the canal," Suzanne pointed out. "Only a fool would refuse to accept money in exchange for doing nothing!"

"But it wasn't money," Harriet said. "Don't you see? This is how the Selwyns ended up with the mummies. They were the bribe!"

"Wait a minute—wait a minute," Suzanne said. "They *did* build the Suez Canal. This must be wrong."

"No it isn't. The Suez Canal was built in 1869, with very deep British involvement. This document is talking about an abortive non-British plan in the 1830s. Everything we've heard so far is consistent with historical fact."

"Let's hear the rest," Roderick said. "It's nice to find out that I'm not the only black sheep in the family tree."

Rather than comment on the rather bizarre image Roderick had just conjured up, Suzanne cleared her throat and went back to the letter.

Some of my colleagues accepted gold and women, but I wanted nothing less than the artifacts which Ibrahim had brought back with him from Palestine. This was a matter of no moment to Mehemet Ali, though it angered Ibrahim greatly. I arranged to have the artifacts shipped to my home at Chudley, an arrangement done in secret for a number of reasons. It would have been unwise to allow my connection with the pasha to become known to my superiors in London, and I was uncertain as to the projected length of Mehemet Ali's reign in Egypt. He was both unstable and hated by the sultan. I was certain that the moment his father was dead Ibrahim would take steps to repossess his discovery. Thus it was that last year I had the antiquities returned to England. There was a general cry of complaint which rose from the Egyptian upper classes about the supposed theft of their antiquities, but I was able to keep my name from entering into the outcry by judiciously distributed gold.

"Taking bribes and now paying bribes," Roderick said.
"Shush!" Harriet ordered. Suzanne continued:

In addition to the mummies and the other artifacts, the
assortment contained a papyrus scroll, which I shall
place in the teak box along with a translation and this
letter. I shudder to think that only a few years more
would have prevented me from taking the accursed coffins out of Egypt. Had MacDougal been able to complete his studies earlier, I might have had the scroll
translated while in Egypt, thus saving myself from the
problem which I now face.

I cannot bring myself to outline for you the horror I
have brought back to England, my son. Read the translation of the scroll and you will understand. Heed my
words, and heed my warning, and be certain that your
heirs heed them, and your heirs' heirs. Do not touch
the mummies on any part of their bodies, especially not
the skull. Do not allow them to leave your guardian-
ship, lest they fall into the hands of the foul cult spoken of in the scroll. Do not burn them, lest a curse
fall upon you. If for any reason you can no longer keep
them secreted away in the attic at Chudley, then bury
them privately, with no fanfare. And speak of their existence to no one, not to your dearest friend, not to
the wife of your bosom.

And forgive me for bringing them to England. I
knew not what I had done.

"It's just signed 'Selwyn,'" Suzanne said.
"Whatever can he be talking about?" Roderick wondered.
"You know, Uncle said almost the exact same words to me
shortly before he died."
"But then why did you sell the mummies?" Harriet asked.
"Not that I'm complaining, you understand—"
"You must try to appreciate the fact that my uncle and I saw
eye to eye on absolutely nothing," Roderick explained. "I
never paid any attention to his advice before, and I saw no
reason to begin to do so. I'm sure that you, as a scholar, have an
interest in these things, but they are of no interest to me apart
from their value in the marketplace."
"Well, I suppose that makes sense," Harriet muttered,
masking her inability to comprehend how anyone could not be
interested in the past.

"Harriet?" Suzanne was peering down into the opened teakwood box. "Look. There's no translation of anything in here. In fact, there are no other papers at all in here."

"Perhaps he forgot to put the translation in there with the letter and the scroll?" Roderick volunteered.

"Not likely," Harriet said. "It seemed too important to him. Perhaps one of your ancestors opened the box and removed it. It's been a long time since this letter was written, well over a century and a half. Any number of things could have happened to a translation of the scroll."

"Shit!" Suzanne spat. "I'm dying to know what it says that upset the old fellow so much."

"Let's go up to Sam's office and see if he's made any headway with it. He never discusses it, but he's quite an expert with the Semitic languages." Harriet glanced around the room. "Will you two help me get the lids back on the sarcophagi before we leave? I don't want to risk any damage to the bodies before we get them into their glass cases."

"Sure," Suzanne said as she bent over to lift one of the lids. It was indeed rather light, as Will and Gus had remarked previously. As she and Harriet replaced two of the lids, both women noticed that Roderick was making no effort to assist them. Probably thinks it's beneath him, Harriet thought. Thank God for the American Revolution.

As Suzanne rested a lid on the edge of a crate before sliding it down upon a coffin, the edge of the lid dislodged a large splinter of wood which fell inward and landed upon the face of the mummy of Yuya. She reached down and brushed it off, stroking his face with her hand inadvertently. Feels like plaster, she thought absently, and then dropped the lid in place.

Harriet and Suzanne replaced the other two lids, and then they left the grounds building. After locking and checking the door, they began the walk to the administrative offices in the faculty tower. It was not a tower at all, of course: being the only building on the campus more than three stories in height, it had been laughingly dubbed a tower years before, and the label had stuck.

As they approached the charming Georgian building, Suzanne said, "Harriet, do you mind if I ask you a few questions?"

She laughed. "Suzie, I'm a teacher. I get paid to answer questions."

"Okay. First of all, who was this MacDougal he mentions in the letter?"

"I'm not certain, but I'm pretty sure he's referring to Sir James MacDougal, one of the early proponents of what is sometimes called higher criticism."

"Which is? Don't forget, you're talking to a business-woman, not another archeologist."

"Sorry. It's the subjection of the Bible to the same kind of critical analysis to which we subject other ancient documents, such as the *Iliad* and the *Gilgamesh Epic*. It's really a form of linguistic and historical dissection."

"Okay," Suzanne said, not fully understanding the explanation. "So what's this MacDougal got to do with the mummies?"

"Probably nothing. But if he did his work in the first half of the nineteenth century, and I think he did, then he may very well have done some work into the Proto-Sinaitic script which Sam thinks is on that scroll."

"I get it." Suzanne nodded as they mounted the wooden steps to the front door of the faculty building. "So the ninth Earl couldn't have the scroll translated until long after he had left Egypt."

"Right. MacDougal hadn't published his research."

"Okay. Second question: Who were the Saint-Simonians?"

"I have no idea. There was a French socialist philosopher of the eighteenth century named Saint-Simon, but I have no idea if they were connected to him."

"Hey," Suzanne jested, "you're supposed to know every-thing."

"Sorry." She laughed. Harriet opened the door and led Suzanne and Roderick into the main corridor of the first floor. They began to mount the first flight of stairs which would lead them to the third floor and Sam's office.

"One more question," Suzanne said.

"Shoot."

"What the hell was the ninth Earl so upset about? You'd think he brought the bubonic plague back with him, from the way he wrote about the antiquities."

"Beats me." She shrugged as they rounded the first landing. "I hope that Sam can shed some light on it for us. Whatever upset him so much is on that scroll."

"Did your late uncle ever say anything to you about them, Your Lordship?" Suzanne asked.

"Not a bloody word. In fact, I discovered them by accident when I was going through the collection in the attic. He didn't discuss them with me until the day he died, and even then . . ." Roderick paused, frowning. "It's funny, now that I think back on it. He seemed positively apoplectic when he found out that I was planning to sell the mummies. And there's the strangest story the butler told me . . ."

Roderick gave Harriet and Suzanne a brief synopsis of the odd tale of the bombing of Chudley during the Second World War and the fourteenth Earl's strange behavior. "Peculiar, isn't it?" he concluded.

"More than peculiar," Harriet said. "Apparently he knew something which we don't know."

"Yes, but what?" Suzanne asked. "If there was a translation of the scroll which he read, then what did he do with it?"

"Who knows? I doubt we'll ever know, and I also don't really think it matters too much. We know a good deal more about the ancient Semitic languages today than they knew a hundred and fifty years ago. Any translation Sam can make will be a hell of a lot better than one made in the 1830s." She noticed Suzanne scratching her hand. "What's the matter?"

"I dunno. Bug bite, probably."

Harriet led them to the door to Sam's office and she knocked on the door. There was no response from within, so she knocked again. "Sam?" she called. No answer. She opened the door hesitantly and peeked in. Sam Goldhaber sat behind an incredibly messy desk which was piled high with books. He was referring to two of them which were lying open before him. To his right lay the unrolled scroll, the ends kept from curling up by the weight of a stapler and a tape dispenser. He was writing furiously in a notebook. "Sam?" Harriet said again.

"Shut up!" he snapped. Then he looked up and blushed slightly. "I'm sorry. Come in and take a seat. But be quiet. I'm halfway done with this. Wait a few minutes."

"Sam, we've read—"

"Harriet, sit down and don't bother me! Let me finish translating this."

"Is it of any importance?" she asked.

"Harriet," he said threateningly.

"Sorry." She sat down on a wooden chair which stood beside the door and motioned for Suzanne and Roderick to do the same. Roderick took out a cigarette and explained with a few gestures that he would be outside in the hall.

A half hour passed. Harriet and Suzanne sat and watched Sam expectantly. Soon Roderick returned and wandered around the office, examining the artwork on the walls with thinly veiled disinterest. For all the attention Sam paid to them, he might as well have been alone in the room.

At last he tossed his pen down on the desk and leaned back in his swivel chair. "Unbelievable," he said. "Unbelievable."

"Well?" Harriet asked. "Could you put together a translation?"

"Yes," Sam replied, lifting his thick glasses from the bridge of his nose and rubbing his eyes.

"And?"

Sam shook his head. "Unbelievable," he repeated.

"Sam, come on. What's it say?"

"Okay. Let me begin with the language itself. It is definitely Proto-Sinaitic, and I'll swear that it's an original document. It must be over three thousand five hundred years old. Minimum."

Harriet whistled. "That's old, even by Egyptian standards."

"It's also much older than any complete document in any ancient Semitic tongue," Sam said. "And if what I suspect is correct, it is a document of priceless historical value. I mean really priceless!"

"Why? What's it say?" Harriet rose to her feet and walked around the desk to Goldhaber's side. "Read it to us."

"Okay, Professor, if you will resume your seat." He grinned. Harriet did so reluctantly. "Listen carefully to the way it opens." He put his glasses back on and began to read his own translation.

The words of Ousha Zaphenath-paneah, servant of the
great lord Dudimosh, ruler of the black lands and the
red lands, the destroyer of foreign gods, who nurtures
his people. I, Ousha Zaphenath-paneah, the servant
of the great god Xepheraxepher, write this with my
own hand, in the tenth year of the reign of the great
lord Dudimosh, in the one hundred and eleventh year
since the Hyksos overthrew the sons of Mizrim and
established their rule over the red lands and the black
lands. I am the mouth and the eyes of the great lord
Dudimosh. My words are true. I know the name of the
god.

Sam Goldhaber sat back once again and smiled at the three faces before him. Suzanne and Roderick were staring at him with looks of utter incomprehension. Harriet alone of the three understood the significance of what she had just heard. "God!" she whispered. "Sam, are you sure about this translation?"

"Absolutely. No doubt whatsoever. And," he added, "there's something else about this that even you may not have caught, Harriet."

"Well, I haven't caught any of it," Suzanne said. "Will somebody please let me in on it?"

"The Hyksos," Harriet began to explain, "were a group of Asiatics who conquered Egypt during the seventeenth century B.C. Records from the period are very sparse, because the Egyptians tried to eradicate as much memory of the conquest as possible. The Hyksos were overthrown about 1570, and the historical evidence for the preceding two centuries is meager. This scroll, apparently, is a record of something written by what we today would call the prime minister of one of the Hyksos kings. The name of the king was what, again, Sam?"

"Dudimosh," he said, glancing at the notebook.

"Dudimosh. Or Dudimose, as Manetho's history calls him. He was the Hyksos leader who extended Hyksos rule from the Nile delta to the entire span of Egypt." She turned to Sam. "This is fantastic! What does the rest of it say?"

"Hold on, boss. There's something else. I knew you'd miss it."

"What?"

"Your Lordship, will you please take down that Bible from the shelf behind you?" Roderick did as he was asked. "Please look up Genesis forty-one, verses forty-one through forty-five. Read them please."

Roderick fumbled through the Bible looking for a table of contents. "It's the first book," Suzanne prompted gently. Roderick smiled in appreciation and managed after a few moments to find the chapter and verse.

"Read it, please," Sam repeated.

Roderick cleared his throat and read from the book. "And Pharaoh said to Joseph, 'Behold, I have set you over all the land of Egypt.' Then Pharaoh took the signet ring from his hand and put it on Joseph's hand, and arrayed him in garments of fine linen, and put a gold chain around his neck; and he made him to ride in the second chariot; and they cried before him, 'Bow the knee!' Thus he set him over all the land of Egypt. Moreover Pharaoh said to Joseph, 'I am Pharaoh, and without your consent no man shall lift up hand or foot in all the land of Egypt.' And Pharaoh called Joseph's name Zaphenath-paneah."

"What?! Sam, are you serious?" Harriet asked.

"Don't look at me, boss. I'm just the bureaucrat making the translation. *Zaphenath-paneah* means 'he who furnishes the land with sustenance.' Remember the story of Joseph's dreams about the famine in Egypt, which led the Egyptians to stockpile food?"

"This is—this is—" Harriet stammered.

"Incredible, just like I said."

"Ousha," Harriet mused. "Similar enough to Yoshef, given a thousand years between the events and the writing of Genesis."

"Certainly," Sam agreed. "Ousha is most definitely a primitive form of Yoshef. And the title is exactly the same, as if it were special enough to be remembered and preserved."

"I'm sorry I'm so obtuse," Suzanne broke in, "but what's so important about this? I mean, this is in the Bible, right? So it isn't anything new, right?"

Harriet and Sam exchanged amused glances. Harriet struggled not to sound too condescending as she said, "Suzie, there are no external references to any Old Testament character before the time of King Solomon. Most modern scholars believe that the patriarchs—Abraham, Isaac, Jacob, and Joseph—are legendary. We have proof here that at least one of them was real."

"It goes beyond that," Sam added. "Have you read the Bible?"

"Sure, when I was a kid."

Sam shook his head disapprovingly. "It's when you're an adult that you need to read it. But be that as it may, do you remember the story of Joseph and Moses and Israel in Egypt?"

Suzanne did not like his tone. "Remind me of it," she said.

"The biblical account tells us that Joseph's brothers sold him into slavery in Egypt, and by means of accurate prophecies he rose to be the right-hand man of the king. He brought his whole family to Egypt, where presumably they flourished. The book of Exodus says that 'there arose a new

King over Egypt who knew not Joseph,' and who enslaved his descendants. They remained in slavery until Moses led them out of Egypt."

"Okay, that's familiar enough. So?"

"So this has always been dismissed by scholars as myth, or distorted ethnic memory at best. But what do we have here?"

"The Hyksos," Harriet said. "A Semitic people who conquered Egypt. And a clear statement that Joseph, or Ousha, call him what you will, was a government official under one of the Hyksos kings."

"Don't you see?" Sam asked. "The whole biblical account receives substantiation. The Hyksos are overthrown, and the newly reestablished native Egyptian dynasty enslaves their erstwhile allies, the Hebrews. And then, later, they escape from Egypt. And that's the Exodus."

The importance of the document began to dawn upon Suzanne. "So this is really of quite a bit of historical value."

"You've heard of the Dead Sea Scrolls?"

"Sure. What about them?"

"This makes them look as important as yesterday's newspaper." He paused and then laughed. "Of course, yesterday's newspaper may be pretty damned important in four thousand years. Your Lordship, I must own this document. I'll give you whatever you want for it. I'll sell my house, I'll sell my children, I'll rob Fort Knox, but I must have this document to study and research."

"Well, of course," Roderick stammered. "I'll have to have my solicitor . . ." He paused. "When I engage a new solicitor, I'll have him work out the details with you. Agreed?"

"Agreed." Sam held his hand out toward Roderick, who instinctively reached out and shook it. Sam smiled at Harriet. A handshake was a contract, and he knew it, even if Roderick didn't.

"What about the rest of the scroll, Sam?" Harriet asked.

"Oh, that. A lot of superstitious narration. It will be of great value to the religion and mythology people. This god of his, Xepheraxepher—never heard of him. Name doesn't even sound Semitic. More Iranian than anything else. Indo-European of some sort. But it—"

"Sam," Harriet said, "what does the rest of the scroll say? Does it give us any information about the mummies?"

"Yes, but I'd hardly call it information. You know how the ancients reasoned, Harriet. Everything, even the simplest things, had some sort of supernatural, religious foundation. It's filled with that sort of thing."

"Well, read it to us. Listen, Sam, the letter in the teakwood box was written by the ninth Earl of Selwyn, the one who brought the mummies back to England. He said that something in that scroll of yours was so terrible that he couldn't even bring himself to explain it in his letter. Well, you've read the scroll. What is it?"

Sam laughed heartily. "Good grief! I can't believe that an educated nineteenth-century Englishman would take this seriously! It's so ridiculous!"

"Okay, it's ridiculous. What the hell is it?" She was growing impatient with him. "Will you read the goddamn translation?"

"Okay, okay, relax." Sam looked back down at his notebook. "Okay, here's where I stopped." He read aloud.

My words are true. I know the name of the god. ("Oh, I read that already.") Know ye, whoever reads these my words, that the name of the god is Xepheraxepher. The name is the power of Xepheraxepher for his children who call upon his name.

Sam looked up. "An ancient perspective," he explained. "They believed that words held power, and knowing a god's name made one able to call upon his power in times of need." He looked back at his notebook and continued.

In the third year of the reign of the great lord Dudimosh, the dwellers in the temples of the red lands rose up against the great lord Dudimosh, and he smote them bitterly. Their leader was the priest Sekhemib of the false god Anubis ("Sekhemib!" Harriet cried. "That's one of the mummies!"), and his followers were the forty-eight other priests who drank the souls of the people. The great lord Dudimosh bound Sekhemib and the forty-eight priests of the abomination and cast them into the deepest of pits. He heaped fire upon them, yet they died not. He smote them with the sword, yet they died not. He buried them alive and uncovered them from their burial, yet they died not. He hanged them by their necks, yet they died not. Under great torture the people of the red lands told the lord Dudimosh that Sekhemib and his priests drank the souls of the people, and could not perish by human hands until the end of their days. When the end of their days drew nigh they were not gathered to their fathers after the manner of the people, but they drank the souls of the people and lived yet another lifetime. The priests of Sekhemib had lived since beyond memory, from generation to generation, and they died not.

Sam paused. "I wish old Ousha could see Sekhemib now. He didn't look too lively the last time I saw him."

"Sam, just keep reading," Harriet said. She took the past too seriously to find it an appropriate subject of flippancy.

I told the great lord Dudimosh of the power of Sekhemib (Sam continued), and he said unto me, "Bind him with chains and keep him until the end of his appointed days. Then shall we embalm him after the manner of his people and keep his body from the evil thing which it serves." So I bound the forty-nine priests, Sekhemib and his followers, and as the years passed they began to die after the manner of men. They begged for the tekenues to be brought unto them, that they might drink their souls and live; for the tekenu is he whose soul is consumed by the power of Anubis. But I did obey the word of the great lord Dudimosh, and I called upon the name of Xepheraxepher when Sekhemib called upon the name of Anubis. Anubis enabled Sekhemib to make my hands to move and my feet to walk as he willed, but I called upon the name of Xepheraxepher and kept Sekhemib and his followers bound in chains until the end of his days. When he died I ordered that he be embalmed after the manner of his people, but the embalmer's knife would not pierce his flesh. And so the forty-nine priests were embalmed at the end of their appointed days, and the great lord Dudimosh commanded me, saying, "Place them in coffins of wood, for stone would do too great an honor to their uncleanliness. Take the golden medallions which they wear and put them in the coffins with them, that no one might be defiled by the unclean gold. Take the bodies of the priests and hide them, that their people may not bring the tekenu nigh unto them." And I did as my lord commanded me.

I charge you, whoever reads these words, to guard
the bodies of Sekhemib and his followers. Know that
of the forty-nine, only Sekhemib and six others have
the power to command the arms and legs and tongue,
for these seven have served the god Anubis since before the dawn of time; and the other forty-two are mortal men and not high priests, chosen to serve the seven
chosen ones of the god Anubis. Only these seven are
hidden and must remain hidden, even unto the end
of the world. Touch not their bodies, lest they drink
your soul. Place not their gold upon your neck, neither
take unto yourself their riches, lest they drink your
soul. Know that the burning of the body of the tekenu
gives them a possession unto eternity, but the killing of
the priest releases the soul and gives the tekenu back
his days.

"What the hell does that mean?" Suzanne asked.

"Shhh!" Harriet snapped.

Sam looked up from the notebook. "Harriet, what do you
know about Egyptian numerology?"

"As much as anyone in my position, I suppose," she
shrugged. "Why?"

"Any significance to the numbers here? I mean, forty-two
priests serving seven other priests?"

She shook her head. "The significance is obvious, but it
isn't numerological. There are forty-two gods in the Egyptian
pantheon, seven of which are chief deities. It's sort of like the
Greeks with their dozens of gods, twelve of whom they called
Olympians. From what you've been reading us, it sounds like
there were forty-two priests, one for each of the gods, and
seven high priests, one for each of the chief gods. I would
assume that Sekhemib was the high priest of Anubis, and that
one of the other people was simply a priest of Anubis."

Sam nodded. "Makes sense."

"Makes sense!" Suzanne laughed. "Are you kidding?!
None of this makes the slightest sense to me!"

Harriet ignored her. "Is there more, Sam?" she asked.

"Yeah," he replied and returned his attention to the
notebook.

Know that the burning of the bodies of the priests
gives the tekenues back their souls, but he who burns

the body of the priest brings down upon himself the wrath of Anubis, who will destroy him utterly and his children after him into all the generations of the world.

I charge you to place the bodies of the seven with my body when I am gathered to my fathers, and to keep them with me, for I know the name of Xepherax-epher, and through his power I can restrain Sekhemib and the drinkers of the souls of the people, even in death. But neither you nor anyone else shall place his hand upon the body of Sekhemib or the six others, neither shall you wear their gold, neither shall you burn their bodies, lest the wrath of the god Anubis fall upon you. These are the words of Ousha Zaphenath-paneah, the servant of the great lord Dudimosh, the servant of the great god Xepheraxepher. My words are true. I know the name of the god.

Sam looked up. "There's more. In the margin of the scroll there's a gloss—"

"A what?" Suzanne asked.

"A gloss, a notation in the margin made by someone years after the scroll was written. If you think the scroll is interesting, listen to this." He began to read his translation, but stopped before the first word and added, "It isn't in Proto-Sinaitic, incidentally. It's in biblical Hebrew."

"Hebrew!" Harriet exclaimed. "But that's from a totally different time period!"

"So, apparently, is the gloss: some thousand years later than the scroll. Listen:"

The words of Hilkiah, scribe of the Temple of God which was in Jerusalem. Know that in the eleventh year of the reign of King Zedekiah did Nebuchad-rezzar the King of the Chaldeans come against us for our sins, and did slay the young men of Judah and burn the Temple of God. The forty-two follow-ers of the dead priest Sekhemib did follow in the path of Nebuchadrezzar and did seek to possess the bodies given into my keeping, as they had been given into the keeping of my fathers before me since the days when Israel sojourned in Egypt. But I, Hilkiah, scribe of the Temple, did remove the seven bodies and did bury them at Shechem. Thus have I obeyed the charge of our father Joseph, who though he worshipped foreign gods was beloved of the Lord. Thus do I charge all who come after me to obey the command of our father, for though the years have passed in great number, yet do the followers of Sekhemib remain from generation to generation, each generation seeking to find the seven priests of the idol that they may escape death. Do thou my son and my son after me preserve the land from the evil of the followers of the idol.

Sam sat back and grinned. "Incredible, isn't it? I mean, very fanciful, but fascinating."

Harriet shook her head in wonder. "Unbelievable. Unbe-fuckinglievable." She was so infrequently heard to utter vulgarities of that sort that both Suzanne and Sam realized how deeply she had been impressed.

"I feel embarrassed to show my ignorance again," Suzanne said, "but what's the importance of the gloss? Is there new information?"

"Not per se," Sam replied, "but Hebrew documents of this period, outside of biblical texts, of course, are a bit sparse."

"And what is the period?"

"Well, he mentions Zedekiah. He was king of Judah until the Babylonian conquest, which occurred in 586 B.C. So we're talking about a period of time some one thousand years after the scroll itself was written."

"Interesting references to religion," Harriet observed. "Ousha—or Joseph—seems to speak of Anubis as a real deity, while Hilkiah calls him an idol. Clear transition from henotheism to monotheism."

"Yes, yes, that's a good point," Sam said. "Also, we have a written admission from the biblical period, in no uncertain terms, that the patriarchs did not worship the Lord God, at least not exclusively."

"So much for the covenant with Abraham!"

"Not necessarily," Sam objected. "The covenant is not incompatible with henotheism. It's just our preconceptions which make them seem to be mutually exclusive."

"I'd ask you what you're talking about again," Suzanne said with irritation, "but I feel stupid enough already."

Sam and Harriet laughed. "Just a few issues in the study of religious development," Sam explained. "Only of interest to eggheads like the two of us."

"It's one hell of a find, Sam," Harriet said seriously, "one hell of a find."

"Yeah, it is that!" he agreed, dropping his notebook down upon the desk. "Its historical value is largely corroborative, but the mythologists will have a field day with it."

"Largely corroborative!" Harriet exclaimed. "Are you kidding? For one thing, it explains how the mummies ended up in Palestine."

Sam was momentarily nonplussed. "You mean they really were in Palestine? How do you know?"

"That's what the ninth Earl of Selwyn said in his letter. They were found there by Ibrahim, the son of Mehemet Ali Pasha, when he invaded Syria in 1831."

"Really! And that's where the English found them, in Syria?"

"In Shechem, just like the gloss says. It's fantastic! Genesis tells us that Joseph died and was buried in Egypt. Exodus tells us that when Moses led the Hebrews out of Egypt they took Joseph's body with them. They must have taken the seven mummies also!"

"And they were hidden in Shechem by Hilkiah, transferred from Jerusalem when the Babylonians attacked. Fantastic!" Sam shook his head wonderingly.

"Wait a minute," Suzanne said. "I still don't understand what any of this has to do with the attitude of the ninth Earl. I mean, he was very upset about the mummies, judging from his letter. Do you think that cult was still around in the 1800s? Was he afraid of the curse? Were Karloff or Lugosi involved?"

This suggestion was greeted with quiet laughter by Roderick and Sam. Harriet did not respond to the jest. Indeed, sitting there with her brow furrowed in thought, she seemed not even to have heard it.

"I'm sorry," Suzanne laughed. "I'm not making fun of this old story or anything. It's just so—well, so silly. I mean, people who don't die, 'soul drinking,' secret names of gods—it's all so grade B melodrama. You know?" She turned to Roderick for agreement. Ever the amiable gentleman, he agreed with a smile.

"I know, I know," Sam added, still chuckling. "It's all superstitious nonsense, as I've already said.."

"You think it's nonsense?" Harriet asked sharply.

Sam looked at her kindly. "Look, Harriet, I'm not ridiculing—"

"No, no, I just want to make a point. You think the idea of a holy name for a deity, a sacred name not to be spoken lightly, is nonsense?"

Sam Goldhaber knew exactly where she was heading. "It's not quite the same thing, Harriet."

"What's not quite the same thing?" Suzanne asked.

Harriet and Sam ignored her. There was a sudden infusion of tension in the air as Harriet snapped, "Okay, then, say the name."

"Cut it out, Harriet," Sam said testily.

"Why? What's the matter? Bast got your tongue?" She grinned, a hint of malice quivering upon her lips.

"What are you two talking about?" Suzanne demanded. "Did you follow that?" she asked Roderick. He smiled and shrugged.

"It's very simple," Harriet said. "Sam is making fun of this old belief, calling it superstitious, when he and his coreligionists hold the same belief."

"Harriet," he said with a thinly veiled impatience, "please don't misrepresent things. There is an enormous difference, and you know it."

Their eyes locked for a long moment of tension, and then she looked down. "I'm sorry, Sam. I didn't mean to be rude. I just hate to hear the ancients spoken of so disrespectfully."

He reached over and took her hand, all barriers between them suddenly lowered. "I know, boss. I'm sorry if I treated the old beliefs lightly."

"What the hell are you two talking about?!" Suzanne said angrily. "You want to let us in on this too?"

"Sorry," Harriet said. "I was trying to make an unfair analogy."

"Okay, fine," she snapped. "So what was the analogy?"

"Devout Jews do not speak the name of God," Sam explained.

Suzanne looked at him as if she doubted his sanity. "Of course they do. You're Jewish, right?"

"Yes," he nodded.

"Well, you just said God's name, didn't you?"

"No," he replied, shaking his head. He laughed at the look she gave him, and he continued. "You don't understand. The ancient Hebrews took quite seriously the injunction handed down to Moses on Sinai not to take God's name in vain. As a result of this, they soon stopped saying the name altogether."

"But you just—"

"No," he interrupted her. "The four Hebrew consonants which are written down as God's name are YHWH. Hebrew had no vowels until about two thousand years ago."

"The name was pronounced 'Yahweh,' according to most modern scholars," Harriet added. "No offense, Sam."

"None taken. You spoke the name as a scholar." He turned back to Suzanne. "Instead of saying the name of God, the ancient Jews began to say the word *adonai* whenever they came upon YHWH in reading the Torah. *Adonai* means 'lord,' or 'master.'"

"That's why we speak of God as the Lord," Harriet said. "We have perpetuated the ancient Hebrew caution."

"Precisely," Sam agreed. "During the Middle Ages some well-meaning but not overly intelligent monks combined the vowels from *adonai* with the consonants from YHWH and came up with the atrocious hybrid, *Jehovah*. That name is totally nonbiblical, of course."

"But it's not the same as from the scroll?" Suzanne asked.

"Oh, no. It was a matter of obedience and respect, not harnessing the power of God. Totally different thing." Sam turned to Harriet and smiled. "Right?"

"Right," she grinned. "Sorry." Sam squeezed her hand again.

"So is this—what is the god on the scroll?"

Sam glanced at his notebook. "Xepheraxepher?"

"Yeah, him. That's what they used to call the Lord? I mean, the Hebrew god?"

Sam and Harriet laughed. "Heavens, no!" Sam said. "Scholars are generally agreed that Hebrew monotheism was a much later development than the Bible indicates. Joseph—Ousha—and his ancestors worshipped a great variety of gods, and this Xepheraxepher was one of them, apparently. No connection with the god of Moses or later Judaism."

"But if this was Joseph, and he—"

"Suzie, it isn't that simple," Harriet broke in. "Xepheraxepher was probably a Hyksos god, or a Syrian one. Sam's right. No connection with the god of the Jews, the Christians, and the Moslems."

Suzanne frowned. "Then I don't understand why the ninth Earl wrote such an emotionally charged letter. I would think that he believed in God—I mean, our God—I mean, I don't believe in Him, but—you know what I mean—"

"Sure, sure, I know what you mean," Harriet said. "What's your point?"

"Well, what the hell was he afraid of? I mean, he sounded really terrified of something. If it's not a curse, which he couldn't have believed in, or some supernatural bullshit about the mummies, or the involvement of the god he believed in—well, then, what's the big deal? Why didn't he just think, 'Well, I've got a couple of mummies. Jolly good!' You know?"

Sam shrugged. "Beats me. I haven't read his letter, but from what you folks have told me about it, I have no idea what he was upset about. Do you, Harriet?"

She did not reply. She was staring out the window, lost in thought.

# CHAPTER 9

His heart was beating so loudly that its sound seemed to drown out everything, including the voice speaking to him. His eyes were tightly shut and he feared to open them, feared that it all might not be real. He remained motionless upon his knees, his left hand raised palm outward in the ancient gesture of supplication, his right hand grasping tightly the hand which he pressed to his forehead in the ancient gesture of submission. He forced himself to listen to the voice, strained to hear over the thunderous pounding of his heart.

Ahmed Hadji opened his eyes and raised them. Sekhemib stood towering above him, glaring down at him with eyes which burned with power and anger and perhaps a slight hint of apprehension. Sekhemib spoke to him in the long dead tongue which had been for Hadji merely a ritual language. He had studied it long and hard through the years of his novitiate, yet it sounded somehow alien, strange. He struggled to understand.

"Thou hast said that thou art a priest of Thoth," Sekhemib said. "Thou hast said thy name, but it falls strangely upon mine ears. Who art thou, in truth and upon thy life?"

"I have told you the truth," Hadji replied, using, of course, the polite form of the pronoun. It was only to be expected that the lord Sekhemib would not address him in the same manner, employing instead the familiar form appropriate for use with inferiors. "My name is indeed called Ahmed Hadji, and I have served the god Thoth for all my life."

"If thou speakest falsely, I will take from thee thy life."

"I speak no falsehood, my lord. We have been seeking to

find you and the others for many years, and I was sent here to this foreign land to rescue you from the hands of those who know not who you are, who worship not the gods."

Sekhemib looked down at his enshrouded body. He took his hand for Hadji's forehead and slowly pulled a strip of rotten linen from his chest. It seemed to crumble to his touch and he watched as dusty wisps floated to the floor. He looked down once again at Hadji. "Do Dudimose or his people still rule in the land of Egypt? Thy name comes to mine ear as a Hyksos name. Art thou a Hyksos, a traitor to thy people?"

"Dudimose has been dust for many years, my lord," he replied.

"How many years?"

How should I explain this? Hadji thought. The lord Sekhemib's yesterday was our ancient times. "My lord," he began hesitantly, "we have been taught that the Hyksos allowed you to die and withheld the tekenu from you. Your body has been lost to us, and we have sought it through the long years."

"How many years!" Sekhemib repeated firmly.

Hadji licked his lips. "Three thousand five hundred and forty-five years, my lord."

Sekhemib stared at him coldly. Believe me, Hadji thought, believe me. Sekhemib looked once again at the decaying shroud which he wore, and he nodded slowly. Hadji released the breath which he had been holding in. Sekhemib said, "Art thou Hyksos? Answer me truly, upon thy life!"

"No, my lord, I am Egyptian. But much has happened in our land since last you saw the light of day. The tongue in which we speak has not been spoken by living men in many years. Our land has known invasion and conquest, foreign rulers and foreign gods, and much tribulation."

"Who is the king in Egypt?" Sekhemib asked.

"There is no king, my lord." Sekhemib's expression bespoke disbelief, so Hadji added quickly, "The thousands of years have seen too many changes for me to explain them all to you so quickly."

Sekhemib continued to stare at him disbelievingly. They stood motionless, a tableau of silence and fear, for a few long moments. Then Sekhemib looked around the room slowly, as if he were examining each and every minute aspect of his environment. "Where is this place?"

"We are in the vault of a dwelling, my lord, in a land far from our own."

"How far? Is this Syria, or Cush? I have seen no dwelling like unto this one, and I have seen the whole world."

"This land. lies far from Syria and Cush, my lord. In your time, the existence of this land was not known to the wise ones or the priests. Far beyond the Great Sea lies an even greater sea, and far beyond that is this land."

Sekhemib grasped Hadji by the throat and pulled him to his feet. Hadji felt a vise close upon his windpipe as Sekhemib said angrily, "Dost thou make sport with me, Hyksos? Doth Dudimose treat my power as a jest, that he might make sport with me? There is no land beyond the Great Sea! And the priests have all knowledge!"

"I speak the truth to you, my lord," Hadji sputtered. "My life is forfeit if I lie to you."

"Thy life is mine to do with what I will, whether thou liest or not," Sekhemib said bitterly. "I am Sekhemib, the first servant of the god Anubis. I will not be mocked."

"I mock you not, my lord," Hadji said weakly. The grip on his throat had not abated and the room was swimming before his eyes. "Mount the stairs and gaze upon the world, my lord. Believe the testimony of your own eyes, if you believe not my words."

Sekhemib considered this for another long moment, and then relaxed his grip. Hadji drew air into his lungs spasmodically and tried to bring his vision into focus. "But my lord, I beg you not to leave the dwelling. We are both in danger here, and enemies abound."

Sekhemib did not deign to answer him. Instead he grabbed Hadji by the wrist and dragged him behind him as he walked toward the basement steps. He paused by the foot of the steps and looked down at the rotted, decayed corpse which seemed to be hanging from a shackle on a seat against the wall. He looked at Hadji blankly. "Your tekenu, my lord," Hadji said.

Sekhemib returned his gaze to the remains of Will Foster and a slightly inhuman smile passed briefly across his lips. Then he mounted the steps and climbed to the main floor of the house, his hand still clasped tightly around Hadji's wrist. He stood for a moment in the doorway of the basement entrance, looking from the kitchen to the living room in utter incomprehension. He walked into the living room and hesitantly pulled the closed drape aside. Hadji thought he heard a gasp escape from Sekhemib. A few people were walking down the street. A car and then a truck drove by. The approaching dusk had been greeted by the streetlights being turned on. The distant roar of an airplane caught Sekhemib's attention, and he gazed up in wonder at the silver ship gliding through the cloudy sky. Sekhemib released Hadji's wrist and stood in open-mouthed wonder. Then he allowed the drape to fall closed and he dropped to his knees. Raising his hands upward and lowering his head, he cried out, "Homage to you, my father Anubis. Honor to you, gods of Egypt. You have brought me through the veil of darkness into life in this strange world. I have been your slave, my father Anubis, I serve you still. You have heard my prayer from the darkness of the grave. Homage to you, homage to you." Tears welled up in Sekhemib's eyes and began to run down his cheeks, dusty tears filled with particles of rotten linen. "Homage to you, Osiris, lord of life. Homage to you Isis, mistress of rebirth. Homage to you Ra, lord of the heavens. Homage to you Bast, mistress of the pleasures of the flesh. Homage to you Set, lord of the high places. Homage to you Thoth, master of all wisdom. Homage to you Nephthys, mistress of the dead . . ." Hadji knelt beside Sekhemib silently and bowed his head as the high priest of Anubis gave heartfelt thanks to forty-two gods of the Hall of Judgment.

Sekhemib raised his head and looked at Hadji. Hadji's heart seemed to stop beating as he awaited the words of the high priest. "Thou hast served the gods faithfully, Ahmed Hadji. Their blessings shall follow thee all the days of thy life, and beyond that unto the days beyond life, until the days wherein thou shalt drink the souls of the tekenues with the company of the children of the gods."

Hadji fell on his face before Sekhemib and placed his forehead on the ground. "I thank you, my lord. I thank the gods that I have been of service. Homage to Anubis. Homage to the gods."

Sekhemib rose to his feet, saying, "Get me a knife and a bowl of water, that I may strip from myself the linen of the grave and wash from my flesh the dust of the centuries. And get me fresh raiment."

"Immediately, my lord," Hadji said, springing to his feet, his heart overflowing with joy. I shall not die! he cried within himself, I shall not die! Millions of years, a life of millions of years! He ran into the kitchen and searched through a drawer beside the sink, finding at last an extremely sharp slicing knife. He ran back to Sekhemib and extended the knife to him, handle first, and then ran upstairs to the bathroom. He stopped up the bathtub and began to run water of moderate heat. He then went into the room which Mrs. March's son occupied when he was at home and chose some clothes from the bureau and the closet. He pulled out underwear, socks, a plain white shirt, and a pair of cotton slacks. He took a pair of beach sandals from the floor of the closet, knowing that shoes were not only unknown to Sekhemib—indeed, all of these clothes would be alien to him—but would doubtless make him extremely uncomfortable.

Hadji ran back down the stairs and came to a shocked halt at the sight which confronted him. Sekhemib was peeling the rotten linen from his body in large clumps. He drew the shroud from his face as if it were a clinging mask which conformed to his features but had not been affixed to them. The burial cloth had rotted onto his mummified body so long ago that he did not need the knife which he had requested, merely needing to tug on the crumbling cloth for it to come free and drop in dusty swatches onto the floor.

What shocked Hadji was the man was being revealed to him. The skin was smooth and pink as a baby's, unwrinkled, unlined, almost tender looking, as if the entire surface of flesh had just been drawn from the womb. Sekhemib's eyes were deep and piercing, but his face was that of a young man, not more than twenty-five years of age. His hair was pitch black without a trace of gray or white, and it cascaded in flowing waves down around his face and neck. His hawklike nose rested beneath an unfurrowed brow, and his face, which had been shrunken and wizened such a short time before, was full, fleshy, radiating youth and health. Hadji had dreamed for years of the rebirth of life, but he had never dared to imagine what it would be like. He had assumed that the avoidance of death did not include the avoidance of the appearance of age, but the sight of the young, robust man standing before him filled him with even more wonder than he had felt when he saw the life drain from Will Foster and animate the dead body of Sekhemib a short while ago. A day of wonders, Hadji thought. Wonder after wonder. Praise the gods!

Sekhemib looked at Hadji as the last bits of linen fell from his naked body. "Where is the water?"

"Please follow me, my lord," Hadji said, bowing slightly.

"It awaits you in another room, at the end of these steps." He motioned Sekhemib up the stairs with a manner of obsequious deference, and Sekhemib proceeded to mount the stairs. Hadji followed behind him, and gestured toward the bathroom. "A large vessel is in this room, and I am filling it with warm water. In it you may immerse yourself. Allow me." Hadji preceded him into the bathroom and reached down to turn off the tap. "My lord?" he invited.

Sekhemib stepped carefully into the tub, gazing at it and the dripping tap with undisguised amazement. The water was hot, but not unpleasantly so, and he lowered himself slowly into it. Sekhemib smiled and sank up to his neck in the soothing warmth, very softly voicing a contented sigh. Dust which had been embedded in his leathery flesh for centuries now drifted easily upward from his smooth, pink skin and floated upon the surface of the water. He looked at Hadji and said, "Tell me of Egypt."

Hadji thought for a moment, trying to formulate a comprehensible summary of thousands of years of history. "My lord, I have said that our land has known foreign rule and great change. We were brought under the rule of the Persians and the Medes some one thousand years after your death"—after your death! he thought with amazement!—"and then the Greeks, whom you knew as the Achaeans, conquered us, led by their great king Alexander. After the Achaeans came the Romans, who claimed descent from the people of the city of Troy, and ruled our land." Sekhemib nodded. He knew of Achaea and Troy. Barbarians, all of them. "While the Romans ruled us, a new religion displaced the worship of the gods, a religion borne to us by the Jews, whom you knew as the Habiru—"

"Habiru!" Sekhemib exclaimed. "Allies of the Hyksos! They overthrew the temples of the gods?!"

"I weep to say the words, my lord, but it is true. A teacher from the Habiru named Yeshua was killed by the Romans, and his followers claimed that he rose from the dead. The people of Egypt knew not of the tekenu or the power of the gods, for you had been dead for one thousand five hundred years, and they turned to the followers of Yeshua in the hope of defeating death."

Sekhemib laughed. "The fools. Anubis is the master of life and death, not a Habiru barbarian."

"Yes, my lord. After a few centuries, another wave of

conquest swept over our land. The Arabs, whom you knew as the Aamu, brought with them another form of the Habiru worship, and they displaced both the followers of Yeshua and our ancient tongue. My name is strange to thee because it is an Aamu name. All of Egypt today speaks the Aamu tongue."

"And yet thou speakest the language of Egypt," Sekhemib observed. "How is this?"

"A small community of old believers has persisted throughout the millennia, my lord, adopting new members to replace the old when death overtakes them. We have preserved the knowledge of the old ways and we study the old tongue, though we speak the language of the Aamu as our native language. It is difficult to speak to you in the old tongue, for we use it only in ritual and worship."

"Yet thou speakest it well, though thine accent is peculiar. Continue. The Aamu rule now in Egypt?"

"Yes, Egypt is an Aamu nation. Our people even think of themselves as Aamu. But there have been other conquerors, peoples unheard of in the days before your death: Turks, Frenchmen, Englishmen. Our land no longer fills the hearts of foreigners with dread of our power. Other nations, so large that Egypt would be less than a province within them, guide the destinies of the world."

Sekhemib shook his head as he rubbed his arms languidly. "The destinies of the world are guided by the gods. Their power is undiminished. My presence testifies to their strength."

"As you say, my lord."

"Where are the others?"

"My lord?"

"My companions, Yuya, Herihor, the others?"

"Oh, they are nearby, my lord, still sleeping in death as you were until I brought the tekenu unto you."

"They are embalmed, as I was? They are whole and intact?"

"To the best of my knowledge, my lord, yes. There is a building here which is dedicated to the remnants of the past. They, and you, my lord, were to be placed on display for the people of this age to gaze upon." He saw Sekhemib's face flush with anger. "I have saved you from this disgrace, my lord, and I shall save the others as well. I speak the truth."

"I know thou speakest truth, Ahmed Hadji. We must bear their bodies hence, to Egypt."

"Yes, my lord, but we must prepare carefully. Movement from land to land is not as simple as it once was. I myself am a foreigner in this land."

"Thou art alone here? Thou hast no servants or confederates?"

"No, my lord. Only enemies."

Sekhemib cupped his hands and brought water to his face. He poured it slowly onto his forehead and gently rubbed his cheeks and eyes. "Thou knowest this world, Ahmed Hadji. Thou must decide what we shall do. Would a slave from this land help us to escape back to our land?"

Hadji did not quite know how to respond. "There are no slaves in this land, my lord."

"Would a slave be of use to us?"

He shrugged. "Yes, of course. But—"

"Then we shall have one. The practices of the people of this land are of no importance. Is there anyone here who knows the ancient tongue as thou dost?"

Hadji thought for a moment. "Yes, my lord, I believe so. A woman who planned to display your body to the eyes of the curious. She is a student of our land. I know that she can read the ancient writing. She may therefore know the ancient tongue." He paused, choosing his words delicately. "But she is an enemy, my lord. She will not help us escape from this land."

"Thou must learn the ancient ways, Ahmed Hadji. Thou must learn to think the ancient thoughts. We enslave our enemies, we do not run from them."

"But she will oppose us, my lord. She will—" He stopped as Sekhemib turned and stared at him. Hadji felt sensation drain from his limbs as Sekhemib's eyes bore into him. He felt his mind being disconnected from his body, and he heard the voice of Sekhemib speak to him, but his ears did not hear the words. The voice was in his thoughts. Sekhemib's lips did not move, and yet in his mind he heard the high priest say, "Come forward and kneel." Hadji's legs moved without his own effort. He walked to the edge of the bathtub and sank slowly to his knees. "Raise thy hands as if in supplication." Hadji felt his arms rise above his head, his palms facing away from him, his fingertips pointing upward. "Bow thy head," the voice in his mind commanded, and Hadji felt his head moving downward.

Then, in an instant, his body was his own again and there was no voice in his mind. He panted for breath. "My lord!"

Sekhemib laughed gently. "I am the beloved of Anubis,

Ahmed Hadji. I can make the limbs to move, I can make the tongue to speak. I enslave whom I will, I possess the mind by the power of Anubis, even as I drink the soul by the power of Anubis. This woman of whom thou speakest will not oppose us. She will do our bidding. She will be our slave."

Hadji was dumbfounded. He had read and studied and discussed with his teachers all the knowledge which had survived, all that was known about the seven lords, but he had never heard of this power. "My lord is more powerful than any of us had dreamed!" He was still on his knees, and he bowed his head once again, voluntarily. "I am weak with awe in your presence, my lord. My heart leaps with joy at the presence of the beloved of the gods."

Sekhemib smiled and nodded slightly, accepting the homage. "Now, thou must act quickly for my safety."

"Command me, my lord." He remained bowed on his knees.

"Take the remains of the tekenu. Burn them. As long as the remains exist, they threaten me."

"May I ask how, my lord? So much knowledge has been lost over the centuries that I fear my ignorance will endanger my mission."

Sekhemib nodded again. "Thy devotion and concern please me greatly, Ahmed Hadji. Tell me what thou knowest of the tekenu, and I shall tell thee those things thou knowest not."

Hadji lifted his head. "Yes, my lord. We have been taught that the tekenu, when chosen, must touch the body of the beloved of the gods. As soon as their flesh touches, the soul of the tekenu is linked to the body of the beloved of the gods."

"He who drinks the soul is called the axem. The word means 'holy image.'"

Hadji bowed thankfully for the correction. "The axem begins to drink the soul of the tekenu as soon as their bodies touch. Left thus it takes days for the soul to be consumed. Even though great distance is involved, the axem will still be able to drink the soul of the tekenu. If the sacred medallion is placed upon the tekenu and he is brought close to the axem, the soul will be drunk quickly. It is in this manner that I brought the tekenu to you, my lord." Sekhemib nodded, swishing the palms of his hands through the water and sending small waves against his legs. Hadji waited for a comment, but none was forthcoming. He continued. "We have been taught that once the axem has drunk the soul of the tekenu, he lives out the life of the tekenu, immune from all weapons and disease. This we have been taught."

"There is more," Sekhemib said after a moment. "Once the axem has consumed the soul, he lives again, but he is not invulnerable as long as the bones of the tekenu remain intact. That is why thou must burn them, reduce them to dust. At this moment if a sword pierced my flesh, I would die, and the tekenu would reclaim his soul. Only when the soul has no home to which to return is my life free from common dangers, free from injury and disease."

Hadji absorbed this. "My lord is saying that if you were injured now—"

"If I were injured to the point of death, I would be unable to contain the soul of the tekenu. His soul would return to him and he would live again. A connection remains between the tekenu and his soul. It can be severed only if the tekenu is burned."

"I understand my lord, and I obey. I shall remove the remains from this place and consign them to the flames." He rose to his feet.

"Anubis protect thee," Sekhemib muttered. "Where is the raiment for my limbs?"

"Beside you, my lord, on the—" He paused. There was no word for toilet bowl. "On the seat. I shall go with haste and return with haste."

"Ahmed Hadji. One question before thou goest to thy task."

"Yes, my lord?"

"The Hyksos god Xepheraxepher. Is his worship still known in this world?"

"I think not, my lord. I have heard of no such god, and only we of the old ways worship the gods. No other people of this age worship old gods, in any land. The Hyksos are but dust and memory, and there is no worship of this god of whom you speak. May I ask why this is of interest to you?"

Sekhemib stretched his arms out and seemed about to yawn, but did not. "The Hyksos had a powerful god. They defeated the armies of Egypt by virtue of his power. A man named Ousha knew the name of Xepheraxepher, and resisted my will by his power. I am pleased that he is forgotten, for even a god dies when no one calls upon his name. Xepheraxepher is a dead god, and thus no danger to me." He smiled. "I am pleased."

"Your pleasure gives me great joy, my lord." Hadji bowed. "I shall go now and dispose of the remains." Sekhemib dismissed him with a wave of his hand and closed his eyes, settling back contentedly into the warm water.

Hadji ran down to the basement and picked up the corpse of Will Foster. It was very light and delicate, yet seemed somehow cohesive, belying the appearance of a dusty bundle which a slight breeze could dissipate. Hadji smiled contentedly at the ghastly death's-head which grinned sardonically at him. He had been so excited by the resurrection of the lord Sekhemib that he had almost forgotten to gloat over the horrible death of the man who had assaulted him. Ignorant fool, he thought as he gazed at the leathery skull. I told you that you would pay. He walked back up the stairs.

Tossing the body casually onto the sofa in the living room, he searched through the closets for something in which to wrap the remains of Will Foster. Hadji found a large laundry bag in the pantry, and he found that by bending the body into a fetal position he could fit it into the bag. He tightened the cord at the mouth of the bag, and then went to the window.

The streets were largely deserted. The sun was nearing the horizon, and Hadji reasoned that most of the small minded idiots who dwelt in this pesthole of a town were at home for their evening meal. There was a risk in leaving the house with the body before dark, but what did he have to fear? The lord Sekhemib wielded a power which would protect them both.

Hadji moved stealthily out the door of the house and quickly opened the door of his rented car. He tossed the body into the front seat and then ran into the garage, looking for some sort of combustible material. He had hoped that the old woman or her son would have kept a can of gasoline for emergencies, but to his chagrin he found none. He saw a small portable barbecue grill in the corner of the garage, and upon lifting its lid he smiled at the can of lighter fluid which rested upon the grates. He thrust the can into his pocket and ran back out to the car.

Make haste, he thought as he turned the key in the ignition. You told the lord Sekhemib you would make haste. Make haste.

Hadji backed the car out of the driveway and drove aimlessly away from the house. He did not know the area, but he knew that a wooded rural area was what he needed for the immolation. As he drove out of town and the number of houses lining the road grew fewer and fewer, he glanced at the laundry bag lying motionless on the seat beside him. He will catch fire and burn like dried wood, like paper, he thought. He smiled.

In a very short time Hadji decided that he was in an area sufficiently isolated for his purposes. He pulled to the side of the road, and after looking around to make certain of his privacy, he pulled the laundry bag from the seat beside him and carried it into the woods. He found a small clearing without any low overhanging branches and took a few minutes to clear away the dead, dry leaves. Satisfied that nothing remained to spread the fire he planned to set, he opened the laundry bag and dumped the body unceremoniously onto the brown earth. Hadji drew the lighter fluid can from his pocket and doused the body generously with the clear, pungent liquid. He took a pack of matches from his other pocket, struck it on the matchbook cover, and tossed it onto the corpse.

The explosion of flame and smoke startled him and threw him backward a few feet. He had expected the body to catch fire easily and burn quickly, but the suddenly huge, brilliant fire which confronted him was a matter of concerned surprise. The flames rose so high that they licked the branches of the trees which reached out far from the ground, and he watched with dismay as they began to smoulder and smoke.

Hadji panicked. He ran back to the car and leaped into the front seat. He started the engine and pulled back onto the road in a rush, sending billows of dust into the air. He made a quick and ungraceful U-turn and sped back toward Greenfield. He looked in the rearview mirror and saw the orange glow of the incipient forest fire growing steadily stronger. Damnation! he thought.

As he drew closer to the town he calmed himself. There is no danger, he assured himself. The fire will certainly eliminate all traces of the body, and there is nothing to connect me with the blaze. All is well. All is well.

Still, it had not transpired as he had planned. He resolved not to mention to the lord Sekhemib that his disposal of the remains had not gone as cleanly as he had planned. It makes no difference, Hadji thought. The remains of the tekenu are destroyed. Sekhemib's power is secure.

Hadji presently pulled back into the driveway and ran back into the house. He found Sekhemib, dressed in the clothing he had procured for him, walking slowly about the living room examining every object with obvious curiosity. Sekhemib looked up at him as Hadji entered. He stood stonily, questioning Hadji with the expression on his face.

Hadji was out of breath. "The remains of the tekenu are no more," he panted.

Sekhemib smiled with satisfaction. "Excellent, excellent. Now we must go to the others, to Yuya, Meret, Herihor, and the others. Then we shall find the slave, and then we shall leave for Egypt."

Hadji paused and licked his lips. How could he explain to the lord Sekhemib things like passports, visas, airplane tickets, the complexities of shipping six crates containing Egyptian mummies? "My lord," he began carefully, "we cannot do this alone."

"We will have the slave," Sekhemib said casually.

"I beg your indulgence, my lord, but we must have help from our friends in our own land. There is a man named Haleel Haftoori. He is the current priest of Anubis, the leader of our small number." He saw Sekhemib's eyes begin to glower and he added quickly, "In your absence, of course. He is your servant, as I am. It is he who sent me to this land to find you and bring you back to Egypt."

Sekhemib considered this. "And what service can he provide which is needed to depart from here?"

"We need documents which will disguise our identities. We need to arrange transportation, and we cannot do it all from here."

"How far are we from Egypt?"

Hadji thought carefully. He did not know the manner of distance measurement from the ancient times, for such learning was of no importance and had never been taught to him. He made a very quick and highly inaccurate estimate and said, "We stand now thirty times the distance from Thebes to Nubia." He was pleased to see Sekhemib's eyes grow wide. He had impressed the priest. "You can see that the journey will be long and complicated. Arrangements must be made both by us and for us. The service of the woman will not be sufficient."

Sekhemib frowned, disturbed by this revelation. "I must rely upon thee, Ahmed Hadji, for it seems that we must sojourn in this land for a long time. How long will it take for a messenger to reach he whom thou saist sent thee here?"

Hadji blinked, and then realized what Sekhemib was thinking. "Oh, no, my lord. We have devices today which enable us to communicate, speak to other people over long distances. I can contact my master Haftoori in Egypt without leaving this dwelling." Sekhemib looked at him disbelievingly, and Hadji added, "Please allow me to give you proof. Please come with me." He led Sekhemib to the telephone which hung from the kitchen wall. He picked up the receiver and said, "This is connected to many other similar devices all around the world. By speaking to a series of people, relaying the identity of the person with whom I wish to speak, I can quickly make contact with that person and speak to him and hear him through this device." Sekhemib stared at him, not knowing what to make of Hadji's outlandish tale. "Allow me to demonstrate, my lord." Sekhemib nodded his wary assent. Hadji dialed for the operator and waited for a moment.

When the tinny voice said "Operator," he said, "Hello?" and quickly placed the receiver near Sekhemib's ear. "Operator. Your call please." Sekhemib leaped back away from the phone.

"It is a power from the gods!" he gasped.

"Not so, my lord. A device of men." He spoke into the phone. "Operator, I would like to place a person-to-person call to Mr. Haleel Haftoori in Cairo, Egypt. The number is 46–687–5344." As the connections began to be made, he said to Sekhemib, "My master has devoted his life to the gods and the search for you. He will wish to speak to you. Is that agreeable to you, my lord?"

Sekhemib gazed skeptically at the telephone. "From this I shall hear a voice from Egypt?"

"Yes, my lord. My master Haleel Haftoori speaks the old tongue as I do. I beg you, my lord, grace the old man's ears with your words."

"National Institute of Reclamation," he heard from the earpiece. "Mr. Haftoori is on the line."

Hadji waited for a moment and then heard the soft voice of the old man say in Arabic, "Yes?"

"This is Hadji," he replied in the same tongue.

"Greetings, my son. What is the status of your mission?"

Hadji decided to indulge his flair for the dramatic. "I have someone here who wishes to speak to you." He held the phone out to Sekhemib, saying, "Please greet my master in the tongue of Egypt. He is speaking the Aamu tongue as I was just doing."

Sekhemib took the receiver carefully from Hadji's hands and placed it very slowly against his ear and mouth as he had seen Hadji do. "I am Sekhimib, voices from the device."

Hadji could hear the cry of joy which burst from Haftoori's lips. He heard the old man's voice speaking loudly and rapidly in the ancient tongue, and Sekhemib threw the receiver away, backing off from what to him was a strange magic. Hadji picked up the receiver and said, "He lives, my master." He spoke in the ancient tongue so as to reassure Sekhemib.

"The gods will bless you through all eternity, Ahmed Hadji." The old man was weeping. "Homage to the gods!"

"Homage to the gods," Hadji repeated. "Master, we need help in returning to our land. I am suspected by the local authorities, and—"

"I began to make all necessary arrangements after you called me the other day," the old man broke in, speaking in Arabic. "Will you be able to bring the lord Sekhemib and the others to the city of New York?"

"Yes, master. I see no reason why that would present a problem." He also spoke Arabic, and he said to Sekhemib, "I ask your pardon, my lord. We must speak in the Aamu tongue to make plans." Sekhemib nodded his assent, and Hadji returned to his phone call. "Yes, master, we can reach New York."

"Good. Go to the Egyptian Consulate there and ask to speak with Fatima Razheed. All arrangements have been made through her. She will provide you with passports and shipping documents. You will not be going directly to Egypt. We have charted a course for you which will inhibit anyone trying to follow you."

"Where will we go, master?"

"From New York by train to Washington, and from there by plane to Hamburg. A ship will be waiting there. You will then set sail for Alexandria, sailing around Europe and past Gibraltar."

Hadji smiled. "Yes, good. I fear I may be followed. Such a route will increase our security."

"That is the intention. You must make the lord Sekhemib understand the need for his identity to be kept secret. Remember, Ahmed, he is a man accustomed to ruling. You must strive to make him understand the dangers which confront us in this present age."

"I shall do all I can."

"Good. Will he speak to me again?"

Hadji looked at Sekhemib, who was standing nearby, his

face bearing an expression of suspicion and anger. "I think not, master. He grows annoyed at our conversation. I must go."

"The gods speed you, Ahmed, my son." The phone clicked off and Hadji replaced the receiver in its holder.

Before he could speak a word, Sekhemib said, "Thou wert long in a strange tongue, Ahmed Hadji." He was clearly irritated.

"I regret that, my lord," he said, bowing. "As I told you, the Aamu conquered our land many centuries ago, and we still speak their tongue today, even those of us who worship the gods and maintain the ancient rituals. The plans for our return to Egypt are so important that I had to speak in the language which is natural to me."

Sekhemib seemed slightly, but not entirely, mollified. "And what are these plans?"

"We will take a long and complicated journey. But we will be home before long, before one cycle of the moon has passed."

Sekhemib nodded, satisfied. "I must trust thy knowledge of this new age. I know not how so long a journey, thirty times the distance from Thebes to Nubia, can be made in so short a time. But I must trust thee, and so I shall trust thee." He had spoken these last few words pensively, gazing off into space. Now he turned his eyes to Hadji and said, "Let us now go and retrieve the bodies of my companions, lest they be defiled."

"Yes, my lord," Hadji replied. "There are chariots in this age which need no horses. We shall travel in one of them to the building wherein the other lords rest in death."

"I saw such chariots moving along the pathway before this dwelling," Sekhemib said. "This is an age of great wonder and magic."

Hadji shook his head. "All these wonders are merely devices. In your day, devices were simpler—waterwheels, forges, and the like. All the wonders you have seen—and you will see many more—are like unto them, devices fashioned by the hands of men, nothing more. You have the great power, my lord. The great wonder is in you."

Sekhemib accepted this wordlessly. Hadji opened the door of the house and led him out to the automobile which was parked in the driveway. He opened the door for Sekhemib, who climbed awkwardly into the front seat and appreciatively stroked the upholstery. He started slightly when Hadji turned the key in the ignition, but showed no other reaction. What confidence, Hadji thought, what self-possession. He is fearless, as well he should be. If a man need not fear death, what can disturb his tranquillity?

Hadji drove directly to the college, allowing Sekhemib to observe without comment all of the strange and alien sights which confronted him in the small town. He turned off the headlights as he drove slowly to the side of the grounds building and parked the car on the grass. "This is where they rest, my lord." Hadji led Sekhemib from the car to the front door of the building. He took a hammer and a crowbar from the trunk of the car. In the company of Sekhemib, Hadji felt no fear of detection, no need to sneak through windows. He had switched off the headlights as a simple precaution, but he intended to smash the padlock from the door regardless of the noise it made.

He succeeded merely in making a loud clamor and nearly shattering his wrist. Hadji was a man of many talents and great dedication to his cause, but he was not particularly agile. He tried once more to break the padlock, positioning the crowbar tensely between the loops of the lock and bringing the hammer crashing down upon it, but the hammerhead glanced off the smooth metal shaft and pounded loudly but uselessly upon the door of the building. Hadji looked shamefacedly at Sekhemib, who returned his look with one of his own, a look of impatience and irritation. He pushed Hadji roughly aside and grasped the padlock in his hand. He closed his eyes and stood motionless for a moment. Then he ripped the lock from the door.

Hadji's mouth fell open in astonishment as Sekhemib tossed the shattered metal casually onto the grass and pushed open the door. He muttered to Hadji, "I trust my need of thee is not beyond thine abilities."

"How—how—" Hadji stammered.

"Didst thou believe that the powers of the gods which flow in my veins travel only to my mind and not to mine arms?" Sekhemib shook his head sadly. "So much of the knowledge of the priesthood has been lost during my long rest. It sorrows me greatly." He walked past Hadji and into the darkness of the grounds building. Hadji followed sheepishly behind him.

Once inside, Hadji felt with his hand on the wall beside the door and switched on the lights. The sudden flooding illumination startled Sekhemib, and he gazed upward at the lightbulbs which lined the ceiling. "It is but another device fashioned by the hands of men, my lord."

"Does it burn?" Sekhemib asked wonderingly.

"No. Well, yes, but—" Hadji frowned. Electricity. How to make this comprehensible? "It is like unto lightning—" Then he remembered that except for a narrow strip along the Mediterranean coast it neither rained nor thundered in Egypt. "My lord—"

"Enough, enough. We will have much time for thee to explain all these wonders to me. But for now, let us gather up the bodies of my companions and—"

"Hold it right there!" an angry voice shouted in English. Hadji spun around to find Gus Rudd standing in the doorway, his pistol drawn and leveled at him. "One move from you or your friend and I'll blow you both away!"

Hadji cowered instinctively from the revolver, but Sekhemib regarded Gus with amusement and curiosity. "Tell me, Ahmed Hadji, what device he holds."

"What'd you say?" Gus asked. "What are you talking about? That Arab talk?"

"It is like unto a bow, my lord, but more deadly. It shoots pieces of molten metal at a great speed."

"Interesting," Sekhemib said and began to walk slowly toward Gus.

"I said hold it. I ain't kidding," Gus warned.

"How does it operate?" Sekhemib asked, drawing ever closer to Gus and the barrel of the gun.

"There is a lever of release. His finger grasps it even now."

"And it can kill?"

"It can kill." Hadji gulped.

"Good," Sekhemib smiled. "Let us see this wondrous thing."

Gus cried, "Halt!" once more. Sekhemib was less than a yard away from him when he squeezed the trigger. Sekhemib rebounded slightly from the impact of the bullet, but he did not fall, he did not bleed. Gus fired again and yet again, and then his eyes registered fear. Sekhemib was standing uninjured before him. He was so drawn into the amused serpentine eyes that it was a moment before he realized that he was positioning the barrel of the revolver in the direction of his temple. He tried to stop, tried to force his hand away, tried to cast the gun from his grip, but it seemed as if his body was not his own. He felt the hot lip of the barrel press gently against his head, felt his finger beginning to depress the trigger. Then he froze.

Sekhemib had noticed the condition of his hand. "Ahmed Hadji," he said softly, "this is a tekenu."

Hadji was taken aback. "Are you certain, my lord?"

"Behold, his flesh withers. It is as always when the axem begins to drink the soul." He waved his hand and Gus fell senseless to the floor. "Where are the others?"

Hadji looked quickly around the large room and saw the four crates and the two uncrated sarcophagi. "Here, my lord." He ran over to them and pulled the lid from one of the sarcophagi.

Sekhemib shook his head angrily as he walked slowly toward his ancient compatriots. "Such coffins! Paupers' graves. The Hyksos are barbaric. *Were* barbaric," he corrected himself. He stood over the first open sarcophagus and looked down. "Yuya," he whispered. "Yuya, my friend." He looked at Hadji. "He is dust and decay. Was I thus before thou settest the tekenu beside me?"

"Yes, my lord."

"And yet I live. And thou shalt live, my friend, Yuya, beloved of Set." He reached down and placed his fingers gently upon the temple of the mummy. "He drinks," Sekhemib whispered. He looked up as if feeling something in the air, something disturbing. Sekhemib walked to the second sarcophagus and flipped the wooden lid easily from it onto the floor. He smiled. "Meret, child of Isis." He touched her temple also and said, "She drinks. He"—and he pointed at the unconscious policeman behind him—"is her tekenu."

"But then who is the other?" Hadji asked. "There is no way for me to learn! I have not been able to keep watch on the other lords. Anyone might have touched the lord Yuya! And if the tekenu begins to lose its life unguarded——" Hadji seemed to be beginning to panic. "This could be our undoing," he whimpered. "I saw you touched by your tekenu, my lord, and so I knew for whom I had to search. But this!" He cast a despairing look at the mummy of Yuya. "What can we do? What can we do?"

"Ahmed Hadji!" Sekhemib snapped. "Thy weakness shameth thee and maketh me wroth! Art thou in truth a priest of Thoth, or art thou a timid old slave with dung between thy toes? Command thyself before thou seekest to command others!"

Hadji bowed his head. "I beg forgiveness, my lord. I grew fearful, for I know not how to seek out the tekenu of the lord Yuya."

"We shall not seek out the tekenu," Sekhemib said. "The tekenu shall do my bidding and shall come to us." Sekhemib closed his eyes and concentrated, sending a command through the mummy of Yuya out to the stranger who had dared to touch the face of the priest of Set.

At that moment a few miles away, Suzanne Melendez began to have the strangest dream.

# CHAPTER 10

▲ The bedroom was still and dark, illuminated only by the tip of her cigarette, which glowed briefly brighter as she inhaled. She had smoked constantly in her years of graduate work, but the pristine atmosphere of the small country town had been an inducement for her to break the habit. She had, almost but not totally successfully. That one cigarette after making love was the one she could not, or would not, give up, and it had a calming and soothing effect upon her even when the lovemaking had been perfunctory, as it had been tonight. Too many thoughts and apprehensions were rushing around in her mind for any hint of erotic interest to intrude upon them, and she had accepted his overtures, not unwillingly, but with a lack of enthusiasm offset only by her love for him and her desire to please him. He had not known of her feelings tonight, had not known that their lovemaking had been for her a submission rather than a sharing. And she had not known that for him it had been done tonight out of a sense of obligation, for he was as distracted and preoccupied as she.

She snuffed out the cigarette in the plastic ashtray and rolled over to embrace him, resting her head upon his chest. His arms enveloped her. He drew meaningless little circles upon her back. "I love you, honey," he said.

"I love you too, Tommy," she whispered. They lay there in silence for a long while, each lost in thought, each in a sense absent from the other even as they lay in an embrace. At last she said, "It's possible, isn't it? Anything's possible."

He sighed, not wanting a repeat performance of their

conversation of a few hours ago. "Almost anything's possible, Harriet. But not that. That is not possible."

"It would explain a lot," she insisted.

"It wouldn't explain anything. Look, honey, you bought some antiquities which obviously somebody else wanted to buy first, and he stole one of them. That's all, that's the whole story."

"Yeah, but the letter from the ninth Earl, and the way that the old man—His Lordship's uncle, I mean—was so obsessed with keeping the mummies protected—"

"Come on, Harriet. A doddering, senile old man makes a lot of strange comments on his deathbed, another guy who lived a century and a half ago has all these morbid, superstitious fantasies . . ." He shook his head. "You can't take any of this seriously. It's absurd!"

She refused to be dissuaded. "It's fantastic. It isn't absurd."

He sat up slightly in bed and faced her in the darkness. "Do you seriously believe that Hadji stole that mummy so that he could pour somebody else's soul into it? I mean, walking dead men? Do you think Karloff got off the noon train at Greenfield?" He laughed.

"It isn't funny, Tom," she snapped. "It's scary."

"It's stupid," he corrected her. "If you want to worry about something, why don't you worry about Will? Nobody has seen him since this afternoon. He never showed up at the hospital. I have a seriously ill patient, suffering from a disease the nature of which I can only guess at, wandering around somewhere, probably dying. And if what he has is infectious . . ." He laughed again, this time without humor. "If you want a horror to think about, think about that!"

"I'm worried about Will too, Tom," she said. "But I'm not so close-minded that I'm ready to dismiss as impossible any sort of—"

"Walking dead?" he finished for her sarcastically.

"No," she said, the anger rising in her voice. "I don't believe in resurrected mummies any more than you do. But what if Hadji does? Wouldn't he steal, even kill for his belief? What if there *is* some sort of pagan cult which wants the mummies we bought? Aren't we all in danger from them? Look what happened to poor Mr. Pearson. And poor Mr. Lewis."

"Harriet," he yawned, "people get killed. It's a sad truth, but it's still a truth. People do get killed. Just because that English lawyer was killed, three thousand miles away, doesn't mean that we are in any danger. And as for Lewis, we don't even know if there's a connection between his death and the theft of your mummy." He slid back down in the bed and pulled the covers over them both. "Let's try to get some sleep, okay? Everything will work itself out. I wouldn't be surprised if tomorrow Will comes in and tells me that he crawled into a bottle of bourbon tonight, Jasper catches the burglar who killed Lewis, and the state police show up with your mummy and Hadji. Okay?"

"No, it isn't okay," she sniffed. "Besides, I'm not sleepy." She reached over to the pack of cigarettes on her night table and took one out. She was about to strike a match when she stopped and put the cigarette back into the pack. No smoking when you're tense, she told herself. That's how you start again. "Just think for a minute, Tommy," she said. "Just for a moment try to use your imagination, try not to be so empirical."

"We're both scientists," he muttered sleepily. "We're supposed to be empirical."

"Well, just for a minute or two, let's try to remember that most people aren't as empirical as we are, okay?" He murmured his assent, and she continued. "You and I are both religious skeptics. You were raised as a Lutheran, I was raised as a Roman Catholic, and neither of us has any connection with our churches; we think religion is self-delusion and superstition. But not everybody thinks that way. I mean, I don't believe in walking mummies any more than I believe in a resurrected Christ or a Great Flood or a thundering Jehovah on Sinai. But there are people who believe all of that stuff, so why shouldn't there be people who believe in Anubis and resurrected mummies? There are cults all over the place, Tommy, and they believe all sorts of weird things. Why shouldn't we accept the possibility that there's a group in Egypt which maintains some strange old beliefs, and are willing to steal and murder for them? Religious beliefs have power over the minds of people all over the world, make people do all sorts of bizarre things. Look at Iran, Ireland, the Middle East. It's possible, Tommy." There was no reply. "Tommy?" He began to snore softly.

"Shit," she muttered. Harriet grabbed the cigarette pack again, paused again, and then said, "Oh, what the hell," and took one out and lighted it. She inhaled deeply and lay back down upon the pillow. It always irritated her that he could fall asleep so easily and so quickly while she so often spent hours tossing and turning in an insomnial funk. How can he sleep tonight? she wondered, annoyance mixing with envy. With all the things that have happened since yesterday, how the hell can he sleep? She took another drag from the cigarette and then put it out. If he can sleep, I can sleep, she thought with resolution. But she knew that she could not. As she lay in the dark silence of the bedroom, words and ideas kept drifting in and out of her thoughts. Sekhemib . . . Ousha . . . Hyksos . . . tekenu . . . Anubis . . . Xepheraxepher . . . Hadji . . . Selwyn . . .

Harriet got wearily out of bed and went out to the kitchen. She poured some milk into a saucepan and placed it on the stove. Some warm milk, maybe, she thought. That'll help. She turned on the burner to a low flame and sat down at the table to watch it from a distance. There's something, she thought. There's something that will make sense of all this, but I don't know what it is. If only I could talk to Tom, bounce ideas back and forth. There's something, some connecting thread, to make sense of all this.

She looked at the clock which whirred in mute electronic service upon the wall. Three in the morning. I wonder if Suzie is awake? She dismissed the thought. If she was awake, she was screwing the Englishman. If I disturbed that, she'd kill me. But I have to talk to somebody. Sam? she thought. No, he is even more of a skeptic than Tom.

It's funny, she thought. All those centuries of Catholic-Protestant animosity and anti-Semitism, all eradicated by a few decades of rejection of religion. Sad, somehow, to live in a world without absolutes. Probably healthy, in the final analysis. But still, somehow sad, unpoetic.

The milk was beginning to froth slightly, and she rose from her seat, took the pan by the handle, and poured the warm liquid into a glass. She stared at it for a moment, and then poured it into the sink. I hate warm milk, she thought.

She went back into the bedroom and switched on the lamp which stood upon the dresser beside the door. The light did not awaken Thomas Sawhill. Nothing short of a police siren would awaken him, as she well knew. Harriet pulled on her underpants and then her bra, and took a sweater and a pair of dungarees from the closet. Maybe a short walk will tire me out, calm me down, she thought. She would never have ventured out onto the streets at three in the morning back in Manhattan or Chicago, but the only danger at night in Greenfield was the mosquitoes and the occasional misdirected raccoon which wandered in from the woods. She pulled the sweater over her head and the dungarees up from her feet and then sat down on the edge of the bed. She put on a pair of sneakers, laced them up, tied them, and then left the room, switching off the lamp before closing the door.

She took her keys from the hook on the living room wall and walked out into the hallway. She locked the door of her apartment more out of habit than necessity and walked out onto the street.

The air was cool but not unpleasantly so, and the only sounds were the ubiquitous crickets and the muffled roar of a truck on the thruway a few miles away. This was a good idea, she thought as she began to walk down the deserted street, as a sense of peace and tranquillity began to seep into her osmotically from the surrounding calm. She noticed that she was strolling, and she forced herself to adopt a quicker pace. Strolls don't tire you out, she thought. Got to walk briskly.

She was walking in the general direction of the college, and she reflected upon how differently things looked at night and how much you miss by driving everywhere. She had never noticed the carefully painted curlicues which formed a border of the movie marquee on Main Street, glowing red against the white and blue, or so it seemed in the dim light of the streetlamp near the theater. She passed the alley beside the diner and saw a few foraging cats pause tensely as she passed before returning their attention to the garbage cans which stood against the brick wall. She walked past the old Dutch Reformed church which the Huguenots had built centuries ago out of stone and mortar as firm and rigid as their faith. She paused before it and gazed up at the steeple and the cross which capped it. Faith, she mused. Such an anachronism. All we have faith in today is science, which asks more questions than it answers and causes more problems than it solves.

No, that's not quite true, she thought as she continued down the street. Science has given us longer life spans, medicine, transportation, communication, a million other things so commonplace today that we don't even think about them anymore. We all tend to idealize the past—I certainly do, anyway—but I sure wouldn't want to live in a world without antibiotics, birth control, television, washing machines, or a shot of novocaine in the dentist's chair.

She reached a street corner and looked needlessly to the right and left. There were no cars, of course. The good burghers of Greenfield were all safely tucked away between their clean white sheets. A motion in the dim distance caught her eye, and she peered myopically down the street. A person, some two blocks away, was slowly approaching her, and a brief wave of vestigial urban panic washed over her, but it dissipated almost immediately. She continued to watch the slowly moving figure and was able to conclude quickly enough that it was another woman. Odd, she thought. The woman seemed to be wearing a nightgown. The woman drew closer, crossed the street a block away from Harriet, and began to assume a familiar appearance. Harriet squinted at her, trying to discern her features, and then gasped slightly. "Suzie!" she whispered.

Suzanne Melendez walked toward her, barefoot and clad only in a sheer white nightgown. Her tousled hair fell haphazardly about the face which bore no trace of cosmetics, and her brown nipples showed clearly through the flimsy cloth. What the hell's the matter with her? Harriet thought. She shouldn't be walking around like this, dressed like this. Is she nuts?!

Harriet walked down the street toward Suzanne and called out to her, making an attempt at levity. "Hiya, Suzie. If you're out looking for men, you're in the wrong town. You'd be better off back . . ." Suzanne walked past her somnambulistically, her gaze never wavering or registering any acknowledgment, her gait never changing, her face frozen in a blank impassiveness. "Suzie?" Harriet said. "Suzie? Is something wrong?" She stood motionless for a moment as her friend continued her slow progress away from her, and then Harriet ran to catch up with her. "Suzie? What are you doing? Suzanne?" My God, Harriet thought, she's sleepwalking! She must be sleepwalking. Concern for her friend mingled with fascination as Harriet kept pace with her, eyes glued to Suzanne's face. You're not supposed to awaken a sleepwalker, she remembered. So what the hell *are* you supposed to do? Just stay with her, I guess, so you'll be there when she wakes up.

She walked along beside Suzanne, never taking her eyes off her, and stumbled over a gnarled tree root which had thrust its way up through the sidewalk. She fell forward and sprawled out on the pavement, skinning the palms of her hands. Ignoring the discomfort, Harriet got back to her feet and caught up again with Suzanne, who had neither turned nor stopped when Harriet fell. This is so creepy, Harriet thought. She and Suzanne had lived with each other at college for years, and never had Harriet seen one episode of sleepwalking. This must be a recent development. They say that tension and frustration causes people to walk in their sleep. Poor Suzie. She must have a lot of things bothering her that she never talks about. I wonder if it's because there's no one special in her life? Maybe she's frustrated in her career?

Harriet walked along beside Suzanne for what seemed to be nearly an hour. Suzanne walked with what appeared to be a slow but steady determination, as if her sleepwalk was following a particular path to a particular destination. There was nothing erratic about her progress, no hint of random direction, no indication on her blank face or in her immobile arms that she was dreaming. She walked as if in a trance, but purposefully. Harriet looked into her eyes every few moments, hoping to see some spark of wakefulness. There was none.

They walked past the statue of Montgomery Winthrop, and Harriet reflected that the eyes and face of the statue were as lifeless as those of her friend. She tried unsuccessfully to repress a shudder, and she crossed her arms, suddenly very cold.

Why is she going onto the campus? Harriet wondered. Foolish question! She's just walking. She doesn't know where she's going. This is coincidental, not intentional. Maybe I can steer her a bit, get her to turn, change directions, head back in the direction she came from. Maybe I can even get her back to the hotel and back into bed. I know I'm not supposed to wake her, but maybe just a little pressure on her hand, a little guidance, might not disturb her. Poor Suzie.

Keeping pace with Suzanne, Harriet carefully reached out and very gently touched her hand with the intention of trying to push her slightly, of trying to alter her direction. She recoiled with a start and hopped back a few feet from Suzanne. What's wrong with her hand? she wondered. She had not noticed it before, but her friend's right hand seemed unusually cold, hard, almost leathery. Could she have eczema or psoriasis? She had never suffered from either affliction before. God! Could it be whatever Will Foster had? Even Tom didn't know what Will was suffering from, or even where Will was. Could it have been something contagious, something Suzie picked up from him. I just took her hand in mine. Could I have just gotten a disease from my best friend? Harriet began to examine her hand closely in the dim light of the half moon and the lampposts along the pathway through the college campus. Don't let your imagination run away with you, she told herself. You can't get a skin disease that easily. Calm down.

Suzanne continued on up the path and then turned toward the grounds building. Harriet followed her cautiously, careful not to touch her again and feeling simultaneously guilty and foolish. They were drawing near to the building before Harriet noticed Gus Rudd carrying something awkwardly from the door to an automobile which was parked nearby. Thank God Gus is here, she thought. He can help . . .

Then she recognized what Gus was carrying. One of her mummies! All thought of Suzanne vanished immediately along with her fears and worries as anger surged up in her. Gus was stealing one of the exhibits. Why, that son of a bitch had probably helped Hadji steal the first one! Probably took a bribe! "GUS!" she shouted. "You stop right there!" Gus Rudd ignored her. He slowly opened the rear door of the car and slid the mummy into the back seat. He then slowly closed the door, turned, and walked back into the grounds building in a measured, somehow distracted manner. "Gus, goddamn it! Come back here!" Harriet ran past Suzanne and entered the grounds building angrily. "Gus, you son of—"

Her words were cut off abruptly by a hand which clamped down upon her mouth as another hand reached around her waist and pulled her tightly to the body of her captor. "Good morning, Dr. Langly," Ahmed Hadji said vindictively. "It's so good to see you again."

Harriet struggled against him, stamping on his foot and dragging his hand away from her mouth. "Hadji, you bastard, you goddamn thief! Get your filthy hands off me, you goddamn son of a bitch!"

"Please, please, madam, your manners! There is someone here whom I know you would like to meet, especially considering your line of work." He pointed to the left with the hand she had just pulled away from her mouth.

Harriet looked in the direction Hadji was pointing and saw a rather handsome young man standing casually beside an empty crate. His black hair shone in the light of the bulbs which burned above them, and his penetrating eyes rested above a thin, aristocratic nose and a fine-lipped mouth which was at the moment turning upward in an amused, somehow disquieting smile. "Who the hell are you?" she demanded, her anger diminishing and fear replacing it.

"Don't you recognize my friend?" Hadji asked smoothly. "Look carefully. Look closely." He kept her gripped tightly to him.

Harriet studied the man's face. He was familiar, but she could not quite place him. His shoulders were broad and his waist narrow. His skin was a pinkish white, but the hue seemed inconsistent with his features. He was a Mediterranean type, and a skin color more closely approximating Hadji's olive complexion would have seemed more appropriate. He walked closer to her, still smiling, and she felt her knees weaken as his eyes bore deeply into her own. She gazed weakly as his eyes seemed to draw her into him and blinked only when he turned to Hadji. When he spoke, her ears registered the sounds, but her mind refused to accept what she heard.

His voice was rich, melodious, and strong—masculine but possessing a subtle delicacy the like of which she had never heard. But it was not his voice which startled her. It was the words which he spoke in a tone filled with equal parts of amusement, confidence, and command.

"*Uat en sat nefer khra,*" he said to Hadji.

Ancient Egyptian! she thought with wonder. *A woman beautiful of face*, he had said. But why in ancient Egyptian? No one actually spoke the language. Like all dead languages it was studied to be read, not spoken, as she had studied it for so many years. Yet this man spoke it naturally, without any air of pretension or effort. Hadji emitted a brusque laugh. He must have understood him, Harriet realized. But why? Why would either of these men be able to speak ancient Egyptian? What could possibly be the purpose of learning to speak a dead language?

"*Ten kebten, neba,*" Hadji said cheerfully. "*Netem er aut retus.*"

The man glared at him suddenly. "*Rexk tesk, abu Tekhutif?*" Hadji did not reply. Harriet felt his grip loosen as he mumbled unintelligibly in a voice which dripped with embarrassment and apology.

This is impossible! I couldn't possibly have heard the words I just heard. This is just simply impossible! Her mind translated: *This is your slave, my lord*, Hadji had said. *It is pleasant between her legs.* The other man's angry response was to ask, *You know this yourself, priests of Thoth?*

Harriet's thoughts rushed back and forth between the implications of Hadji's comment and the implications of the other man's response. Both filled her with overwhelming fear, fear of rape and fear of . . .

Fear of . . .

She looked at the face of the man who had spoken to Hadji. He had called him the priest of Thoth. But that's ridiculous. There's no priesthood of Thoth! There hasn't been for over sixteen hundred years! Unless, of course, it had survived secretly, underground. Unless it had a reason to persist. Unless . . .

She looked closely at the face of the young man. Her conscious mind fought to keep the recognition from forcing itself out from the recesses of her memory, but it burst out nonetheless. It can't be him, she thought frantically. It just can't be him. It's absurd. It's ridiculous. It's horrible.

"Dost thou understand my words?" he asked her. She did not reply. She was staring into his face with shock. "Dost thou understand my words? Answer me, woman!"

Harriet shuddered. Ancient Egyptian! The young man was addressing her in ancient Egyptian. She thought hard, trying to pick out the correct words of response from the vast reservoir of linguistic knowledge she possessed of a language which she had never spoken, only read, and never heard until this moment. "I understand thy words," she finally said haltingly.

He ignored the use of the familiar pronoun. Her broken response told him that her mastery of his language was far from perfect, and he chose not to grow angry at her impertinence. "Dost thou know who I am?"

Another pause as Harriet arranged her thoughts. "Thou canst not be he who I think thou art."

He laughed grimly. "Then thou knowest me, woman. Be thou certain. I am Sekhemib, the servant of the god Anubis, the lord of the winds."

Harriet shook her head. Her body was trembling from head to foot, and only Hadji's unrelenting grip kept her from collapsing upon her rubbery legs. "Thou art not," she whispered. "This thing cannot be."

"Guard thy tongue, woman," he snapped. "Cast no doubt upon the word of the beloved of Anubis!" He turned toward the door as Suzanne walked slowly in. "This is the tekenu of Yuya," he said to Hadji. He closed his eyes for a moment and Suzanne stopped moving. She stood beside Gus, who was as immobile as she. Both of their faces were empty, devoid of expression.

Harriet looked at them both and then turned to Sekhemib. "What is wrong with my friends? What has been done to them?"

"They serve me," he explained simply. "But they serve me only for a little time, and then they shall serve my compatriots. Thou too shalt serve me, but for a longer time."

"I do not understand," she said weakly. "Thy words are strange to me. How do we serve? What do we do for thee?"

"Thou shalt assist me in my return to the land of my birth. I have a thirst which only Nile water will quench. They shall serve me now by helping to restore to me that which was mine long ago, mine for thousands of years, my friend Yuya and my beloved Meret."

"But—" she began in English, and then, remembering, began again in Egyptian, "The names thou saist are known to me. They are dead bodies, they are mummies."

"Now, thou speakest truly, woman. They are dead, embalmed bodies, even as I was a short time ago. But now I live, I walk again, after a sleep of three thousand five hundred years—"

"Since the Hyksos?" she asked weakly.

Sekhemib's eyes went wide in impressed surprise. "Thou knowest much, woman! Yes, since the Hyksos king Dudimose imprisoned me in my own mortal flesh. But now I live, and soon they shall live, and then we all—we three of the old times, the four who sleep still, Ahmed Hadji, and thou—shall begin our journey back to the land of my birth. Thou shalt aid me and serve me." He paused and studied her face for a moment. "What is thy name?"

"Harriet," she whispered.

"Heret," he repeated, mispronouncing her name perhaps intentionally to make it sound more familiar to his ear. "Thou shalt come with us to Egypt, Heret, and thy knowledge of this world shall serve as a help to us in our journey. Thou shalt be my voice in this land and beyond it, until we come to Upper Egypt, where I shall be safe with my people."

She did not respond. Her mind was a maelstrom of confusion and shock. At last she asked weakly, "And then?"

"Then thou shalt serve one of my compatriots, as thy friends shall serve Meret and Yuya this night."

Somewhere inside she knew fully what he meant, but she refused to allow herself to understand. "What is this service? I do not understand."

Sekhemib smiled cruelly, delighting in informing her of her fate. "This night, Meret and Yuya shall drink of the souls of thy friends, and they shall live again, even as I live again. And when thy day comes, then shalt thy soul be given as a draught of life to one other who shall join the company of the immortals, who die not."

Harriet fainted. Hadji held her limp form in his arms, grinning at the vicarious revenge he was feeling at her condition. "Shall I take her to the chariot, my lord?"

"In a moment," Sekhemib replied. He turned his eyes upon Gus, who promptly bent over and lifted the second mummy in his arms. As he carried it outside, Suzanne turned and followed behind him. "Carry her out, Hadji," he commanded. "I shall keep my friends company in the rear. Thou and the tekenues shall seat yourselves in the fore, with Heret."

That will make a very crowded front seat, Hadji thought; but he decided against pointing out the fact. Instead he bowed slightly and said, "Yes, my lord," and carried Harriet out of the grounds building.

It took a few minutes of manipulation and effort to fit Harriet, Gus, Suzanne, Sekhemib, and the two mummies into the automobile, but when it at last had been accomplished, Hadji took his position behind the steering wheel and pulled the door shut. He found to his chagrin that he was barely able to move his left arm because it was wedged so tightly against the inside of the door, and he found himself sitting slightly to the left of the center of the wheel. Well, he thought with resignation, it is a short drive, and traffic is not likely to be heavy. He started the car and, keeping the headlights off, drove slowly toward the exit from the college campus.

Suzanne Melendez and Gus Rudd were still sitting stone-like, and Harriet, whose head was slumped down upon her breast, was still unconscious. Hadji glanced in the rearview mirror and saw Sekhemib whispering quietly to the mummy of Meret, whose hand he touched and gently stroked. 'My beloved Meret,' Sekhemib had called her. Beloved! Hadji had known the pleasures of women—his friend Fatima Razheed, currently priestess of Hathor, came immediately to mind—but he realized for the first time that the idea of an eternal love, a truly eternal love, was not necessarily poetic hyperbole. How long had Sekhemib loved this woman whose body was now a withered and woodlike shell encased in rotten cloth? Thousands of years? Tens of thousands of years?

Would he want Fatima Razheed for the next thousand years? No, not Fatima, he thought. Khadija Hassam, perhaps, the nubile and enthusiastic priestess of Bast, perhaps. That would be interesting. He looked once more into the rearview mirror. Was that a tear he saw upon Sekhemib's cheek? No, it must be a trick of the moonlight.

When he reached the street where the March house stood, he again switched off the headlights. It was nearing dawn and the local residents might be beginning to stir. Of course, they could do nothing to harm Sekhemib, and Hadji felt still safe under the protective wing of the beloved of Anubis, but he also saw no reason to invite difficulty.

He rolled the car quietly into the driveway and then climbed out of the front seat. A quick survey of the surrounding houses told him that the townspeople slept still in blissful ignorance. He ran up the steps to the door of the house and opened it wide, making certain that it would remain open until they were all safe inside. He went back to the car and asked, "Shall I carry the slave inside, my lord?"

"Yes," Sekhemib replied, and then closed his eyes for a moment. Responding to the command he had just issued in dreadful silence, Gus and Suzanne stepped out of the car one at a time and walked around to the opposite side, from whence Sekhemib had already exited. Gus reached in mutely and pulled out the mummy of Yuya and began to walk toward the door of the house. Suzanne grasped the mummy of Meret and followed him. Hadji, already holding Harriet's limp form in his arms, had preceded them. Sekhemib followed, and once the others were inside, he pulled shut the door of the house.

Harriet's head was throbbing and she felt nauseous. My God, she thought weakly, what the hell did Tommy and I drink tonight? I feel like I'm coming down from one hell of a drunk. I haven't felt this bad since . . .

Memory assaulted her. She looked around her, trying desperately to fight down the surge of hysteria which she felt rising in her. Over against the wall . . . the wall of what? she asked herself. Where am I? It looks like a basement . . .

cold, damp, dark but for the flickering candles . . . no, not candles . . . it looks like bowls of . . . of oil, perhaps? Animal fat, from the smell. The scent struck her nostrils, and the pungency elicited a cough from her. The smell seemed not to bother Gus or Suzanne, who were . . . yes, over against the wall were her old friend and the deputy policeman, sitting calmly. How can they be so much at ease when . . .

Memories continued to assault her. Suzanne's bizarre behavior of a short while before . . . a trance? Some sort of hypnotism? But they always say that you never do anything under hypnotism that you wouldn't do normally . . . but what do I know about hypnotism? she asked herself? And who are 'they,' anyway?

Harriet looked to the right of the chair in which she . . . what am I doing in this chair? she wondered. I don't remember . . . yes, yes, I do remember, I remember Hadji's hands and arms, I remember being lifted, I remember being deposited not too gently upon this chair, I remember . . .

She tried to lift her hand, but could not. She was bound, hand and foot, to the chair. She looked to her right and saw Hadji and Sekhemib . . . Sekhemib! Good God, it's true, it's true! . . . kneeling in front of the burning pot of oil. The two mummies were lying on the floor beside them, and in the flickering light Harriet could see a small statuette of . . . Anubis. My God, it's Anubis! They're praying to . . . no, wait. Are they praying? What are they saying? She strained to hear the words of the soft chant:

"*Anet hrak, Yuya, anet hrath Meret,*" they chanted. Homage to you, Yuya, homage to you, Meret. "*Aua Sekhemib abu 'Anpuf, aua Ahmed Hadji, abu Tekhutif, rexkuak, rexkuak, rexkua renk, rexkua renk.*" I, Sekhemib, priest of Anubis, I, Ahmed Hadji, priest of Thoth, I know thy name, I know thy name.

What the hell are they talking about? Harriet wondered. Of course they know the names of the mummies. Of course they . . .

Names! The ancients believed there was a power in names. What was the name of the god whom Ousha worshipped? Xepheru . . . Xephera . . . no, it was Xephera-xepher, Xepheraxepher—

A sudden cry of pain escaped from Suzanne, and an identical cry issued forth from Gus a fraction of a second later. They were both suddenly conscious, and their bodies shook with shock and bewildered terror. They each made spasmodic movements with their arms and legs, and they fell onto their sides and began to flop about like beached fish. It was then that Harriet noticed that they were bound as well, their wrists behind their backs and their ankles together. A white froth appeared around Suzanne's mouth. Gus rolled from side to side, shrieking in agony. The golden medallions they wore were vibrating.

"*Tekenu enti khenak, Yuya. Tekenu enti knenath, Meret. Iuk enn tem sekhauk, iuk em arauk,*" they chanted, a dirgelike song in a minor key. The tekenu is with thee, Yuya; the tekenu is with thee, Meret. Come thou to us without memories of evil, come thou in thy form. "*Auk er khekh en khekh, aha khekh.*" Thou shalt live for millions of years, a life of millions of years.

The chanting was momentarily eclipsed by the screams from Suzanne and Gus, whose bodies were writhing in the most rending anguish. As Harriet watched them their cheeks seemed to draw inward tightly against their jaws, and their teeth began to cut outlines in their gray and brittle facial skin. Blood seemed to seep through their pores and began to drop thickly onto the cold stone floor. Harriet's eyes connected with Suzanne's, and she felt her heart leap to her throat at the look on her friend's face. Suzanne said, "Harriet . . . help me . . . help . . . ," but it was not a voice which spoke, it was an inhuman rasp, a liquid gurgle which oozed from the split green lips in the company of slime and blood.

Help! Harriet thought. How in God's name can I help?

In God's name . . . ! Or in *a* god's name . . . ! That's it! she thought. If the story on the scroll is true, then the Hyksos god . . .

But there's no Hyksos god, she reasoned. There are no Egyptian gods, either. Hadji and Sekhemib are worshipping a piece of stone, an idol. The gods do not exist. They never existed.

But Sekhemib is here, he is alive!

If Anubis has power . . . if Anubis exists . . .

Xepheraxepher—

Gus Rudd screamed horribly as he rolled about the floor, kicking his legs impotently like a trussed animal. A large fragment of flesh detached itself from his face and fell onto the cold stone floor with a loud slap and then lay there in the midst of a puddle of putrescent, sanguine liquid.

"*Anet hrak, Yuya, anet hrath, Meret, aua Sekhemib abu 'Anpuf, aua Ahmed Hadji, abu Tekhutif, rexkuak, rexkuak, rexkua renk, rexkua renk—*

"Xepheraxepher!" Harriet cried out. "Xepheraxepher!"

Sekhemib ceased his chanting and turned to her quizzically. Hadji continued the chant for a few moments and then he too ceased and gave Harriet his attention.

"I call upon the god Xepheraxepher," Harriet said loudly. "I ask the help of Xepheraxepher." Then she shouted, "Xepheraxepher, help me, help us all, protect us from the followers of Anubis." Sekhemib rose from his knees and slowly approached Harriet. In Egyptian, she thought wildly, it must be in Egyptian. What are the words . . . what are the words . . .

*"Nekhemkua, Xepheraxepher, nekhemkua ma aputat sexeperiu aterit! Nekhemkua, Xepheraxepher, ma aputat sexerperiu aterit!"* Deliver me, Xepheraxepher, she cried, deliver me from those who make to arise calamities. She looked directly into Sekhemib's eyes and shouted defiantly, *"Xepheraxepher, rexkua renk! Xepheraxepher, nekhemkua, nekhemkua, nekhemkua! . . ."* I know your name, Xepheraxepher, deliver me, deliver me, deliver me.

Sekhemib laughed, not grimly, but lacing his laughter with sarcasm. He laughed loud, deep, long. "Xepheraxepher!" he laughed. "Do you confront me with the power of a dead god, woman? Shall I tremble and fall upon my face and weep at the power of a dead Hyksos god?" He grabbed her chin in his hand and squeezed it hard, lifting her face upward toward his. "Pray to the Hyksos god Xepheraxepher, Heret," he laughed. "Pray until your voice grows weak and your throat grows dry. Pray to a dead god. I live! I live! Three thousand five hundred years ago that unwashed god of an unwashed people fought the god Anubis and triumphed for but a little time. Now Xepheraxepher is nothing, the Hyksos are dust, and I live, and Anubis lives!" He turned from her toward the small statue of the ancient Egyptian god of the grave and cried, *"Anet hrak 'Anpu! Anet hrak 'Anpu!"*

*"Anet hrak 'Anpu!"* Hadji echoed ecstatically. *"Anet hrak 'Anpu neb nest! Anet neb nifu!"* Homage to Anubis, Lord of Thrones, Lord of the Winds!

"Yuya, Meret!" Sekhemib cried, "Come forth to us in your forms! Come forth to us without memories of evil! Yuya, my old friend, Meret, my love of ancient times, come forth in your forms. *Anet hrak, 'Anpu!"*

A low, mournful moan crept from Suzanne's mouth and

shortly died as her face contorted in mute agony. Every muscle in her body seemed to tense and flakes of dry, leathery flesh broke free from her body and spun wildly out as she writhed in her convulsions. Gus ceased to thrash about and lay upon his stomach, his disintegrating body twitching horribly.

"*Anet hrak 'Anpu!*" Sekhemib cried. "*Anet hrauthen neteru!*"

The small basement was suddenly filled with the stench of rotten meat. Harriet felt her stomach straining to expel its contents, and she struggled to master it, but failed. She vomited painfully onto the floor but felt no relief of her discomfort. The smell emanated from Suzanne and Gus. She looked at them and saw their bodies streaming reddish-green liquids, saw their flesh cracking, splitting, withering before her eyes.

Suzanne emitted a terrible cry dripping with pain and anguish. Gus shrieked. And then they lay still but for the particles of flesh which even now dropped thickly from the light gray bones.

Harriet heard a series of labored, almost frenzied inhalations. She found her attention captured by an unexpected movement on the other side of the room.

Impossible. Impossible! Impossible!!

The mummy of Yuya was moving. His mouth seemed to be open beneath the decaying veneer of linen, and he drew long, painful gulps of air into his lungs. His hands seemed to be flexing. His eyes were open. Beside him, Meret also struggled to force air into her lungs. She raised her left hand upward in a gesture of supplication, and Sekhemib leaned over and grabbed it. "Meret, my sister," he whispered, using the ancient term of endearment. "Thou livest, beloved! Fear not, for I live, and thou livest, and all is well."

"D—D—" Harriet heard the thin, weak voice mutter. "Du—"

"Dudimose?" Sekhemib asked. "He is dead. He is dust. We are safe from him, from his god, from his powers. They are all dust, and we live again." Sekhemib rose to his feet and extended his hand toward her. "Come to me, my beloved. Rise up upon thy feet and make welcome this new day and this new age!"

The mummy of Meret, priestess of Isis, rolled over onto her side and tried to push herself up onto her knees. She seemed to falter, and Sekhemib quickly reached out to steady her. She took his hand eagerly, and with his aid rose up to her knees and then slowly stretched upward until she stood, wavering but erect, upon her feet. She reached up to her face and peeled away the layers of decayed bandages which covered her mouth. "Sekhemib," she whispered. "Brother—"

Sekhemib grabbed her in his arms and squeezed her hard against him, weeping softly. "Meret, my sister, beloved, Meret, Meret!"

"Where are we, my love?"

Sekhemib smiled and shook his head. "Shall I measure the thousands of miles or the thousands of years, my sister? We are far, far from all we knew, far from all we loved."

Harriet sat mesmerized as she watched the mummy continue to strip away the rotten linen. "Not so far from all we loved, my joy and my love," Meret said. "Are we alone of our company? Do we alone live?"

"No, beloved, for behold Yuya!" The other mummy had sat up and was busily engaged in stripping away the linen. "And the others—Herihor, Wenet, Senmut, Khumara—they are near but still sleep. Soon we shall return to the land of our birth, my love, my love."

Harriet's senses reached the point of overload. She fainted once again. But her swoon was of a shorter duration than the previous one; for when her eyes opened and focused, nothing in the room had changed.

Nothing had changed! All the definitions of truth and sanity had changed! Before her stood a handsome young man and an exquisitely beautiful young woman, whose decaying linen raiment was being peeled away to reveal a body of fresh, smooth pinkish skin. Beside them, another young man was removing his own funeral dress, uncovering his own unlined, unwrinkled, taut, fresh flesh.

They are beautiful! Harriet thought. Beautiful beyond description!

And Gus and Suzanne, or rather what was left of Gus and Suzanne—the rotting husks, the decaying shells, the reptilian remnants of leathery skin and cracking bones of Gus and Suzanne—lay in pathetic stillness upon the floor.

Why am I not crying? Harriet wondered. Why am I just sitting here as if I were calm and untroubled? "Suzie," she whispered, and the mere act of speaking the name aloud seemed to unpen the floodgates of her tears. She wept loudly and her head fell forward upon her breast.

Ahmed Hadji walked over to her. "I told you, didn't I? I told you that you would pay, and you shall, even as they have paid."

"Hadji," Sekhemib said in the ancient tongue. "Gather up the bones of the tekenues and dispose of them as I instructed you earlier. Make haste, for we must make ready to leave this place and begin our long journey."

"Yes, my lord." Hadji ran upstairs and looked in vain for more laundry bags. He found none, and realized that he would have to carry the bodies out in his bare hands, a prospect which did not please him.

When he returned to the basement he found Sekhemib and Meret still embracing, even as they and Yuya spoke cheerfully to each other, laughing and jabbering away in the ancient tongue much too quickly for Hadji to follow their conversation. Harriet was still weeping, her body trembling and shaking. Hadji ignored her even as he was being ignored by the three ancient ones. He picked up the body of Gus Rudd and placed it atop the body of Suzanne Melendez, noting as before with Will Foster how light they were, how oddly cohesive in their state of decay, and he carried them up the stairs and out into the gray light of early dawn. Make haste, he told himself. Make haste.

He tossed them unceremoniously into the back seat of the car and started the engine. A middle-aged man was walking his dog down the street, and Hadji casually (he hoped) covered the side of his face with his hand as he passed by him, and then accelerated as he turned the corner and headed once again out of town.

He glanced up nervously at the reddish orb of the sun which was creeping inexorably up over the horizon. Damnation! he thought. The risk of capture increased with every passing moment. He sped past the You Are Now Leaving Greenfield sign and turned onto a small road which bore the title Route 51. After a few moments he came to the foot of a small bridge of the cantilever type which stretched over a body of moving water too small to be called a river but too large to be called a stream.

Hadji stopped the car and got out. He leaned over the railing and looking at the rushing water. I must destroy the bodies of the tekenues, he thought, but that does not mean they must be burned. If I bind them to rocks and throw them in the river, the fish will eat whatever is edible and the current will reduce them to nothing in a short time. He looked up again at the sun. I cannot be seen, I must not be seen outside of that house until we are prepared to depart. To start another fire now would be foolish, dangerous; it would jeopardize my whole mission. If I throw them in the river, it will serve the same purpose. Sekhemib would approve, he would understand, he would see the logic of my actions.

Sekhemib need never know.

He got back into the car and drove off the road onto the narrow shoulder just before the bridge. He opened the trunk and removed the coil of rope which he had seen there earlier, when he had removed the hammer and crowbar, and tossed it to the ground. He then dragged the remains of the two tekenues from the back seat and tied the end of the rope to their ankles, binding them together. A few moments of searching provided him with a rock, large enough to hold them on the bottom of the river but small enough for him to handle. He swiftly and securely wrapped the rope around the rock, tying it numerous times at appropriate places around the irregular shape, and then, holding the rock in his arms, carried it onto the bridge, the tekenues dragging behind him. When he reached the middle of the bridge, he placed the rock carefully on the flat surface of the steel railing and, steadying it with one hand, pulled the light bodies up and draped them over the railing beside the rock. Then he pushed everything over the edge.

Hadji watched with satisfaction as the rock pulled the bodies downward, as they hit the water with a resounding slap, as they sank from sight beneath the surface. He waited for a few moments, searching the surface with his eyes for any hint of their presence, and then, smiling, climbed back into the car, made a U-turn, and drove back toward Greenfield.

He should have waited a little longer. He should have tied better knots.

Not five minutes later the grinning death's-head of Gus Rudd bobbed playfully to the surface of the river, and the current carried him downstream. All that was left of Suzanne Melendez followed almost immediately. The two withered, leathery corpses floated downstream for a half hour before the current deposited them upon a sand bar which thrust outward from the bank. They lay there in the sun, upon their backs, looking for all the world as if they had abandoned their graves and gone to the water side to get a tan.

# CHAPTER 11

▲ At first, Thomas Sawhill was unable to discover the cause of his feeling of frustration because his mind was generally incapable of reason as it climbed slowly from sleep to wakefulness. Some people awaken quickly, their eyes springing open, their mental faculties instantly alert and functioning clearly, but Sawhill was not such a person. It took him a few minutes of head shaking, eye rubbing, and arm stretching to restore himself to the condition of mental clarity necessary for any degree of analytical thought.

Thus it was that when he rolled over in his half sleep to embrace Harriet and found her gone, he at first felt confused disappointment without understanding the cause. He sat up in bed and proceeded very slowly to rouse himself to full wakefulness. Scratching his scalp through tousled hair, he looked blearily around the bedroom. Where is she? he wondered. Breakfast, he thought, smiling. She must be making breakfast. Do I smell coffee brewing?

No, I don't, he realized after a few moments. I don't smell bacon either. Sawhill pulled on the pajama bottoms which he had discarded the previous evening and stumbled out into the kitchen. It was uninhabited. "Harriet?" he called out into the empty apartment. "Honey, are you here?" He checked the bathroom, finding it likewise free of human presence.

He looked a bit foolish as he stood, almost but not quite awake, in the middle of the living room, gazing about him with a look of helplessness upon his face. "I wonder where she went?" he muttered aloud to no one in particular. "Store, maybe."

He decided that she would return soon. He had no reason to believe this, but he chose to believe it because it made him feel good. Sawhill went back into the kitchen and began to make some coffee, but then stopped and thought. She wouldn't have just left without leaving a note or waking me up. Besides, where would she go? She had no classes to teach between terms. There was no—

Wait! She must have gone to the museum to examine the other mummies! Sawhill smiled and shook his head, embarrassed at his own lack of clarity. She still had four crates to unload, and Lord knows what other curatorial work to do over there. He glanced up at the clock. Eight in the morning. Harriet always was an early riser, and she knew that he wasn't, so leaving without disturbing him was an act of courtesy, nothing more. He resumed preparing the coffee.

As the coffee began to perk he went over to Harriet's address book beside the telephone in the bedroom and looked up the museum's number. He rehearsed an opening quip in his mind as he waited for her to answer the phone. She did not. He leafed through the address book until he found the central switchboard for the college and dialed the number. A few rings later it was answered.

"Hello, Winthrop College."

"Hello, this is Dr. Sawhill. Could you please connect me with the grounds building?"

"I'm sorry, sir, but the switchboard isn't open."

He paused for a moment and fought down his sarcasm. "Then who am I speaking to?"

"This is Cindy Abrams. I'm the emergency operator between terms, but I'm not allowed to—"

"Well, this is an emergency," he cut in. "This is *Doctor* Sawhill. Please connect me with the grounds building."

A pause, and then, "Oh, okay. Wait a minute." He waited as the student operator made the appropriate connection, and then waited some more as the phone rang. "I'm sorry, sir, there's no answer."

He frowned, perplexed. "Okay, thank you." He hung up and stood there for a few moments, tapping his fingers on the night table in annoyance. Then he picked up the phone and dialed information. He asked for the number of the Huguenot

Hotel, where he knew Suzanne and Roderick were staying, and asked to be connected to Ms. Melendez's room. There was no answer. He called the desk once more and asked to be connected to Lord Selwyn's room.

He waited as the phone rang once again. After a few moments he heard Roderick's voice say thickly, "Hello? Are you there?"

"Your Lordship? This is Thomas Sawhill."

"What? Oh, er, yes, hello." A long, protracted yawn issued forth from the receiver. "What time is it? Am I supposed to be doing something?"

Sawhill repressed a laugh. "No, no, Your Lordship. I'm sorry to bother you so early, but I'm trying to find Harriet or Suzanne. I don't wish to be indelicate, but might Suzanne be with you?"

Roderick laughed. "Oh, certainly not!"

"Well, I just thought I'd check. Thanks any—"

"I haven't seen Ms. Melendez since—oh, last evening, I suppose. Why? Is there something wrong?"

"No, I just don't seem to be able to find Harriet. I thought she and Suzanne might have—well, I don't know, gone out to breakfast or something."

"Have you called the college, or Professor Goldhaber?"

"Not yet. I'll try Sam next. I have called the college, but she isn't there. Really, I'm sorry I woke you up."

"Perfectly all right, old fellow. I had to get up to answer the phone anyway."

Roderick hung up before Sawhill could think of an appropriately absurd response to this parting statement. He replaced the receiver in its holder and picked up Harriet's address book, intending to look up Sam Goldhaber's number. An instant later the phone rang, and Sawhill smiled. Mystery solved, he thought. She's probably calling to tell me she's somewhere with Suzanne. He picked up the receiver and said, "Hello?" in a drawn out, somewhat whimsical manner.

The voice he heard was neither whimsical nor Harriet's. "Who the hell is this?" Jasper Rudd said darkly. Sawhill could tell by the sound of Jasper's voice that something was wrong. He sounded hoarse, tremulous, angry.

"Jasper? This is Tom Sawhill. What's—"

"Good. Glad you're there. Been tryin' to find you. I want you here as soon as possible."

"Where are you?"

"At the hospital. In the morgue."

Sawhill's stomach froze. "Another murder?"

"That's what I want to know. Is Miss Langly there?"

"No," Sawhill said, silently relieved. If Jasper could ask that question, then Harriet was not the subject of his phone call. "I've been trying to find her. I thought I'd—"

"You'll do nothing but get over here!" Jasper snapped. "I'll send somebody out to find Miss Langly. Just get here!" Jasper hung up without another word.

Sawhill stared numbly at the phone for a moment and then tossed it down into its holder. He pulled his clothes on hurriedly and rushed out the door.

He hopped into his car and sped to the hospital, running two traffic lights and breaking every town driving ordinance. A freight train was crawling slowly along the tracks which bisected the town and lay between him and the hospital. He pounded his fist in frustration upon the steering wheel as one half of his mind counted the procession of freight cars and the other half preoccupied itself with morbid fantasies of what awaited him. After what seemed an eternity the last car rumbled loudly past, and the striped wooden gate slowly lifted. Sawhill gunned the engine and virtually leaped across the tracks.

He screeched to a halt in front of the hospital and jumped from the car. He nearly knocked Sam Goldhaber over before he saw him. "Sam! I'm sorry. What are you doing here?"

"I got a call from Jasper Rudd," Sam explained. "He asked me to pick up the Earl on my way over." He jerked his thumb over his shoulder toward Roderick, who was stumbling, disheveled, unshaven, and just barely awake, toward them.

"Have you heard from Harriet or Suzanne?" Sawhill asked.

"No. Why?"

Sawhill shrugged. "Can't seem to find either of them."

"That's funny," Sam said, frowning. "What does Jasper want, anyway? All he told me was that I should come to the hospital."

Sawhill shook his head. "I don't know, but he told me that he'd be in the morgue."

"The morgue! This hospital has a morgue?! A little place like this?"

Sawhill laughed grimly. "Every hospital has a morgue, Sam. People do die in hospitals, you know. The bodies have to be stored somewhere."

"Yes, but—" Sam Goldhaber really had no response. He simply continued speaking. "I mean, a morgue!"

"I say," Roderick broke in, "who's died?"

"I'm as much in the dark as you are, Your Lordship," Sawhill muttered as he began to climb up the steps of the hospital. "I know one thing, though: Jasper sounded pretty strange on the phone."

"Yes, I noticed that too," Sam said. "He sounded like he was about to scream, like he was struggling to hold himself in."

"Yeah?" Sawhill said. "I didn't get that kind of impression. He sounded to me like he was on the verge of tears." He and Sam smiled at the ludicrousness of the image, Jasper Rudd crying.

"Mornin', Doctor." The young nurse smiled as the three men walked past the reception desk just beyond the entrance way. "Are you looking for the chief?"

"Yes, Marcy. He's expecting us. Is he . . ." Sawhill nodded toward the stairway.

"Yes. He's been down there all by himself for over an hour." She added a bit melodramatically, "Just between you and me, he doesn't look too well."

"Do you know who the deceased is?"

She shook her head. "Nope. He and Dr. Harrison brought the bodies in before I—"

"Bodies?" Sawhill exclaimed. "More than one?"

"Two, I'm afraid," she said. "Dr. Harrison said he was going to have to perform an autopsy after you had examined the bodies."

"Me?! Doug Harrison doesn't need my input into something like this. He's the county medical examiner."

The young nurse shrugged. "All I know is what I heard, Doctor. And that's what I heard." She returned to the papers on her desk.

"Damned peculiar," Sawhill said. He began to walk toward the stairs and then, almost as an afterthought, he turned to Sam and Roderick and said, "It's this way, down in the basement."

"Colder down there?" Sam asked.

"Not really," he answered as he pushed open the door and began to descend the steps. "Oh, I guess a long time ago, last century, morgues were always located in basements because it was colder down under, but that isn't the case in modern buildings. I think we just tend to put morgues downstairs nowadays out of tradition."

"Eh, gentlemen," Roderick broke in, "I do hate to be troublesome, but do you think I might wait for you upstairs? I'm not particularly eager to visit with the deceased."

"Suit yourself, Your Lordship," Sawhill said, "but Jasper asked Sam to bring you along, so he must want you for something."

"That's right," Sam agreed. "And from the way Jasper sounded on the phone, he isn't in the mood to be crossed." Sam followed Sawhill down the steps, and Roderick, heaving a sigh, followed Sam.

The basement of the hospital was strangely quiet, as only those places dedicated to death can be. Hospitals are places devoted to life, to its preservation and improvement, and despite the sterility and ominous atmosphere which hospitals occasionally exude, the underlying current of hope and possibility seems always present. But the section of a hospital where the bodies of the dead are stored pending final disposition partakes of no such feeling. The cold stone walls reflect the fluorescent light starkly, and the soothing colors painted in hopes of dispelling the gloom fail in their purpose.

Sawhill and Sam made a few desultory comments as they approached the door to the morgue. Roderick made no attempt at conversation whatsoever. The repository for the bodies of the deceased was not demarcated in any special way; rather, the simple identification B5 stood out in black against the cream-colored door. Sawhill pushed the door open and leaned into the room. He saw Jasper sitting beside the desk in the morgue anteroom, bent over, his head resting in his hands. "Jasper?" Sawhill said softly. "Are you all right?"

Jasper's head snapped up. He stared hard at Sawhill through narrow, bloodshot eyes. "Sam and the Earl with you?"

"Yes," Sawhill replied, entering the room. Sam Goldhaber and Roderick Fowles walked in behind him. "Are Harriet and Suzanne here?"

"Can't find Miss Langly," Jasper said. He rose to his feet. "Come with me. I have something to show you." He led them back into the cadaver storage room which the orderlies referred to rather irreverently as the meat locker. The room was constructed in the standard manner of all morgues: rectangular drawer cases on rollers, recessed into the walls on three sides of the room.

Jasper walked over to one of the drawer cases and grasped the handle. Sawhill thought he saw Jasper take a deep breath and squeeze his eyes shut quickly before pulling on the handle. The drawer slid out silently on the rubber wheels. Jasper pulled it out all the way, instead of the three feet customary for simple identification of the deceased. He reached down and swept back the sheet which covered the cadaver.

Sawhill and Sam walked forward and peered into the compartment. Roderick maintained a discreet distance, not wishing to view the body, but straining his neck to see out of an irrepressible curiosity. Sawhill's mouth dropped open.

"It's Gus," Jasper said brokenly as tears began to stream down his cheeks.

Sawhill shook his head numbly. "It can't be Gus."

"It's Gus. His clothes, his wallet. And I even recognize him, even though he's—like this." Jasper's hand made a jerky, involuntary movement in the direction of the corpse's head as if he meant to stroke his brow.

"That's impossible!" Sawhill said. "I'm sorry, Jasper, but this just can't be your brother."

Jasper Rudd walked to another drawer and wordlessly pulled it out from the wall. He lifted the sheet and said, "Suzanne Melendez." The three other men crowded around the drawer and stared down at the corpse. Then Roderick muttered, "I'll be damned!"

"Jasper, are you sure about this?" Sawhill asked. "These people have been dead for—well, Jesus, I don't know! They look like . . ." He paused.

"Yeah, I know what they look like!" Jasper suddenly shouted. "They look like those goddamn mummies!"

"Jasper—"

"This is Miss Melendez," he said loudly. "And that's my little brother over there, and they're both dead and I want to know how and why!"

"Jasper, an autopsy—"

"Yeah, I already talked to Harrison. There's gonna be an autopsy. But I want some information from you first, Doc."

"From me! Jasper, I don't know—"

"You know what was wrong with Will Foster, don't you? Didn't you tell us that he had some kind of rot disease?"

"I don't recall saying anything about—"

"Back when we was investigating the theft, back at the college. You said you'd scheduled him for a whole lot of tests because of some disease he had, and then he just upped and disappeared. Remember? Well, what's the disease?"

Sawhill closed his eyes for a moment. "Jasper, I know what you're thinking, but it's absolutely impossible that—"

"Don't tell me you know what I'm thinking," Jasper shouted. "You got no goddamn idea what I'm thinking! Just answer my question."

"Jasper, you've got to calm down," Sawhill began. "It won't do any of us any—"

"Listen, Doc, I'm investigating a couple of unexplained deaths here," he bellowed. "Just answer the goddamn question!"

The last thing he needed to deal with just then was a hysterical and hostile policeman, so Sawhill decided to humor him. "I made a very tentative diagnosis of scleroderma, but—"

"What? What? Scler—what?"

"Scleroderma," he repeated, "a degenerative tissue disease. But listen to me, Jasper. I can't be sure until I find Will and run those tests. His blood and urine tests were negative. And even if he does have scleroderma, you have to realize that it isn't a contagious disease. And even if it were, there is no degenerative tissue disease, none at all, which could have done this to these two people in so short a period of time." He looked down again at the grinning skull of Suzanne Melendez, her still shiny long black hair flowing incongruously from the taut, withered leather which was pulled tight around her skull. "I can't think of anything—"

"Well, I can!" Jasper shouted. "Some goddamn Asiatic disease you people"—and he shot a look at Sam—"brought over here with those goddamn mummies! I know enough about corpses to know that they can carry disease, and God knows what germs those things have running around in them!"

Sawhill tried not to smile at the absurdity of Jasper's conclusions. "Jasper, those mummies have been dead for thousands of years! They're no more germ-ridden than an old vase or dinosaur fossil!"

"Okay, then you explain it! You got three people with the same disease—"

"Jasper, this is not the result of a disease!"

"—and all three of them had contact with those goddamn mummies," Jasper continued, ignoring Sawhill. "Isn't it obvious—"

"Damn it, Jasper, will you listen to me?" Sawhill shouted. "It is impossible, I repeat, *impossible* for any disease known to medical science to have done this to Gus and Suzanne in one day. It is absolutely impossible! We don't know what Will Foster has—we don't even know where the hell he is. And, look, just because these bodies are wearing clothes and have identifications which lead you to think that they're Gus and Suzanne doesn't mean that they are! From the looks of them, they could be almost anybody."

Jasper stared at him, long and coldly. Then he said softly, "I know my little brother, Doc. And if you don't recognize that pretty girl's hair, you ain't got much of an eye for women. This is Miss Melendez, and that's Gus over there." He put his hands on his hips and leaned forward. "Now, what the hell happened to them?"

Sawhill shook his head. "You'll have to wait for the autopsy results. When is Doug going to do them?"

"In about an hour. Look, Doc—"

"Jasper, don't try to connect the mummies with whatever the hell this is. They do *not* carry disease. They're dried up leather, like belts and shoes, that's all."

Jasper turned slowly from Sawhill to the open drawer in which Gus Rudd's remains lay. He burst out in tears and sobbed, "My brother! My little brother!" Sawhill placed his hand on Jasper's shoulder and squeezed it supportively.

"Jasper, why don't you wait upstairs, go get a cup of coffee or something? You're just upsetting yourself by staying here."

He shook his head. "Gus's the only family I got. I'm staying here."

"You shouldn't be here during the autopsies, Jasper. You know that as well as I do. It isn't—"

"Doc, if you want to stay here and help out, that's fine. But I'd rather you go out and try to find Foster." He wiped a tear from his cheek. "If he's still alive, I mean."

"Of course he's still alive." Sawhill could not think of anything to say. Even with his own patients, he fell mute in the face of death. Finally he turned to Sam and Roderick. "I think I'll go and check out some of Will's hangouts. You want to come along?"

"I'd just as soon go back to bed, if it's all the same," Roderick said, a hint of petulence creeping into his voice.

How the hell can you go back to sleep after all this? Sawhill thought, but he said, "Fine. We can drop you off. Sam?"

"Yeah, I'll go with you. Let me drop my car off at the college, and we can cruise around in yours." He turned to Jasper, who was still standing over the remains of his brother. "You gonna be okay, Jasper?"

"Yeah, sure," the policeman muttered. "Terrific."

The three men stood awkwardly for a moment, each feeling that something more needed to be said but none of them able to find the appropriate words. Then, silently, they left the room and passed through the anteroom to the hallway. Once back in the corridor, Roderick said, "Horrible thing, actually."

"I can't understand it," Sawhill said, shaking his head. "I've never seen of or heard of anything like this."

"They do rather look like mummies, don't they?" Sam mused. "Say, Tom, you don't think that there might be some sort of disease—"

"Sam, don't be ridiculous! Mummies carrying a virus that turns people into mummies? Come on!"

"Yeah, I guess it's a silly notion." He frowned. "But what happened to them? What could have done that to them? They look like they were dried up by some incredible heat, dry heat."

"I know," Sawhill agreed as he opened the stairway door and began to mount the steps with the other two men behind him. "But what sort of heating process could do that without burning the flesh?" He sighed. "It's beyond me. I just don't understand it."

They walked up the rest of the way without speaking. As Sawhill opened the stairway door and walked out into the corridor of the main floor, he saw Dr. Douglas Harrison walking toward them. "Doug!" he called out. "Got a minute?"

"Just a minute," Harrison said. "I have a hell of a schedule today."

"I've just seen the bodies down there, the ones that Jasper brought in. He's convinced that they're his brother and a friend of ours."

"Yes, I know," Harrison nodded. "He may be right. I don't know if we can get any fingerprints from them, their fingers are so withered. We'll try to get a set of prints before I start the examination."

"Who found the bodies?" Sam asked.

Harrison stared at him for a moment and then nodded in recognition. "Professor Goldman, isn't it? From the college?"

"Goldhaber," he corrected him, "Sam Goldhaber. And this is His Lordship, the Earl of Selwyn."

Roderick smiled impatiently and extended his hand. "How do you do?"

As Harrison shook his hand, it was clear from the expression on the doctor's face that he was rather skeptical of the identification of the unwashed, slovenly young fellow. Harrison turned back to Sam and answered his question. "Two boys were fishing down by the Walkill and found them lying on a sand bank. They were pretty shaken up."

"Sure," Sam nodded. "It would shake me up, that's for sure."

"You have any ideas about them?" Sawhill asked.

Harrison shook his head. "Not a one. Jasper was hoping that you might be able to shed some light on the situation. You have any ideas?"

"No, of course not. Jasper has this crazy notion that they contracted a disease from some mummies the College museum just purchased."

"That's absurd!"

"Course it is. But Jasper's not thinking straight just now."

"Can't blame him. Well, I'd better get down there and get to it. I have a full day ahead of me. Take it easy."

"'Bye." As Harrison opened the stairway door, Sawhill called after him, "Oh, Doug."

"Yeah?"

"One of my patients, Will Foster, was supposed to come in here last night for some tests. Have you seen him or heard anything about him?"

"Sorry. Don't know the guy." He disappeared behind the closing door.

"Shit," Sawhill muttered. A loud and pointed yawn from Roderick brought him out of the reverie he was beginning, and he said, "Well, let's get His Lordship home and then go look for Will."

"Sure," Sam said. "Where are we going to look for him?"

Sawhill shrugged. "I know a few bars where he hangs around. We can start there."

The three men left the hospital and got into their respective automobiles, with Roderick joining Sam in his. Sam started his car and pulled out from the curb and Sawhill followed in his own vehicle close behind him.

I know I should spend the morning looking for Will, Sawhill thought as he drove along, but it's Harriet I'm concerned about. Maybe she's at the college. Maybe when I called there before she was en route. Yeah, sure, she's probably there right now, working on her exhibits. We can stop in when we drop off Sam's car.

Sawhill was still busily engaged in convincing himself that she was all right when they pulled into the main parking lot near the faculty tower. He waited as Sam and Roderick left Sam's car and walked toward him, Sam's obvious attempts at conversation apparently eliciting nothing from Roderick other than a few irritable grunts. Sawhill rolled down the window as they approached him, saying, "Hey, Sam, if you don't mind I'd like to take a spin over to the museum and see if Harriet's there, okay?"

"Sure. But weren't the two of you together last night? I mean, I'm not trying to get personal, but—"

"Yes we were," he said matter-of-factly, "but she was gone when I woke up this morning. I called the museum earlier, but there was no answer."

"Probably called before she got there. You mind a little detour, Your Lordship?" he asked Roderick.

"Oh, no, of course not," he replied untruthfully. What am I doing here? he thought to himself. Why can't we just sign the bloody papers and be done with it so I can get to Florida? Then he remembered that the person who was to have supervised the transfer of ownership was lying in the morgue.

"Good," Sawhill said. "Hop in." Sam opened the rear door and climbed in, allowing Roderick to sit up front. As they pulled out of the parking lot onto the main road through the campus, Sawhill said, "This has been one hell of a week. Murders, burglaries, deaths—" He shook his head. "Not your customary Greenfield experience."

"I know. But this business with Gus and Suzanne—if it really is them, I mean—this is the most bizarre thing yet." Sam leaned back in the seat and sighed. "I'm starting to reconsider my plans to retire here."

Sawhill laughed. "Don't jump the gun, Sam. It still beats Manhattan. If all this stuff happened in New York City, nobody would notice it." He decided to try to draw Roderick into the conversation. Sawhill was growing annoyed at the vacuous presence of the young nobleman and decided that anything Roderick said that was not a complaint, a request, or an expression of strained politeness would be an improvement.

"How's the crime rate in London, Your Lordship. As bad as American cities?"

Roderick sniffed and yawned. "I can't say, actually. I spend most of my time in the country. Dirty place, London."

"I guess the English countryside is as quiet as ours, right?" He shrugged. "I suppose." Sawhill gave up.

As they rounded the turn which would take them to that side of the quad where the museum stood, Sawhill slowed down and peered intently out the window. "I don't see her car anywhere."

"Does she have a van?" Sam asked.

"No. Why?"

"Well, there's a van over there by the grounds building. I don't recognize it. Could it be Will's?"

"No, he doesn't drive a van. He—" Sawhill stopped the car. "Hey! Isn't that Hadji?"

Sam leaned forward from the back seat. "I believe it is. Who's that with him?"

"I don't know," Sawhill replied. "I've never—wait a minute! Look at that!"

"Son of a bitch!" Sam muttered. "In broad daylight! What gall!" Ahmed Hadji and Yuya were carefully carrying a mummy out of the grounds building. Hadji was holding the mummy by the shoulders and he gently placed it head first into the back of the open van. Yuya then slid the body in the rest of the way, and they both turned and walked back into the grounds building.

"That's unbelievable!" Sawhill said as he began to drive toward the building. "As if he has every right in the world!" He grew suddenly concerned. "Harriet! She might be in there!"

"I doubt it," Sam said. "If she were here, her car would be here too, and it isn't. Don't worry about that, Tom. She must be elsewhere."

"Well, I'm going to give that stupid son of a—"

"Hold it, wait. I think we should pull back. Stop the car, Tom, now! Please!"

Sawhill did as he was requested, but the look he then gave Sam Goldhaber was not one of agreement. "Pull back! Are you nuts?"

"Listen to me. There's been at least one murder, not including the bodies in the morgue. Who knows what happened to them. But it's obvious that we're dealing with some dangerous people here. I think we should wait, let them leave, follow them, and then, when we can, call Jasper or the state police."

"Look, Sam, there's three of us and only two of them. We can—"

"We can get ourselves killed if we aren't careful. I'm not a young man, Tom, and the Earl here—pardon me for saying this, Your Lordship—isn't exactly a pugilist. Let's watch them and follow them and then call the police. Pull back, away from here. Please, Tom!"

Sam's arguments made unwelcome sense, and Sawhill threw the car into reverse and backed away onto the road. They sat quietly and watched as Hadji and his companion brought another mummy out of the building and placed it into the back of the van, and then another, and yet another. As Hadji and Yuya shut the rear doors of the van and climbed into the front seat, Sam muttered, "That seems to be all of 'em." The van began slowly to move onto the main campus road and Sawhill began to follow the other vehicle. Hadji drove away from the quad toward the campus exit and Sawhill followed at a discreet distance.

"Not too close," Sam said. "We don't want him to see us."

"He won't," Sawhill said, biting his lower lip. "He's probably so nervous he won't even look in the rearview mirror."

"Don't count on it. He'll probably look just because he *is* nervous. When we get out onto Main Street, see if you can let another car come between us and him for a while."

Sawhill frowned. "You want to drive?" he spat, and then regretted his remark and his tone. "Sorry, Sam. I'm just a little—"

"I know, Tom, I know." Sam patted him on the shoulder from behind. "Let's all just calm down a bit." He glanced over at Roderick to get his agreement. Roderick seemed to be sleeping.

They followed the van as it wound its way slowly through the back roads of the small town before coming to a stop on a narrow residential street. Hadji and Yuya left the van and went up the few steps to the door of a house, the street address of which neither Sam nor Sawhill could make out from their position at the end of the street.

"They don't seem to have seen us," Sam said.

"No. Can you find a phone? You call Jasper at the hospital and I'll go over and see if I can see anything."

"Sure I can find a phone. Dick Staudt from the chemistry department lives a few doors down from here. But you should stay in the car, Tom. Don't take any chances with these people. Except for Hadji, we don't know who's involved in this or what they may be willing to do. Stay in the car."

"I appreciate your concern, Sam, but I'm still going to go and peek into those windows." He opened the car door and got out.

"Tom, I'm not just concerned about you," Sam said as he followed him out onto the sidewalk. "If they see you they might bolt, and that would be the end of any chance we have of getting back the exhibits. And if they're involved in all the other stuff that's been going on around here, we might never be able to figure out the connections."

"I'll be careful," Sawhill insisted. "You just go and call Jasper. The hospital's number is 269–6000. I'm just going to scout around a little and then come back to the car." He grinned. "Don't worry. I'm not the heroic type. I won't break in on them or anything."

Sam shrugged resignedly. "Okay. But don't dawdle. Take your peek and then get back here. I'll go call Jasper. 269–6000, you said?"

"That's it." Sawhill turned and walked briskly down the street towards the house. Sam watched him, worry written on his face, and then began to jog in the other direction. Roderick roused himself long enough to watch them both go, and then closed his eyes again and leaned back in the seat.

Sawhill stepped onto the lawn of the house before the one into which Hadji and his companion had disappeared, and he moved close to the front wall of the dwelling. He moved as quietly and as unobtrusively as he could along the wall and then ran carefully across the driveway. He reached the corner of the house and stood still, breathing heavily. He heard no one and saw no one. He was about to hoist himself up onto the ledge of one of the windows near the edge when he heard, or thought he heard, voices speaking softly. He froze, suddenly frightened, wishing he had remained in the car. He stood perfectly still, only his eyes moving from side to side in a search for the location of the voices. They seemed to be coming from beneath his feet. He looked down and saw that a series of small casement windows ran at intervals along the side of the house a few inches above the surface of the driveway.

"In the basement," he whispered to himself. He quickly lay down prone on his stomach and very slowly, very carefully pulled himself up to the side of one of the basement windows. He peered into the dimly lighted basement, and felt a sudden rush of instinctive fury rise in him. He fought to control it.

Harriet Langly was sitting in a chair against the basement wall, her hands bound to the chair arms. Beside her stood Ahmed Hadji, and in front of her another man whom Sawhill did not know. He heard other people moving around in the basement, but he did not see them. Hadji was cutting her bonds with a long, nasty looking knife as the other man and Harriet spoke. He could not make out their words, but what they were saying did not strike his ear familiarly. That isn't English, he thought to himself. He waved his hand rapidly, hoping to catch her eye while Hadji was intent upon his task and the other man's back was to the window, but she did not see him.

Sawhill pushed his way carefully away from the edge of the window and then, getting to his feet, began to run madly back to the car. When he reached it, he flung open the door and jumped in. He reached into the back seat and grabbed Roderick roughly by the collar and shook him, demanding, "Where did Professor Goldhaber go? What house did he go into?"

"I beg your pardon?" Roderick said, confused.

"I said, where did Sam go!" he shouted. "What house? Tell me, goddamn it!"

"Sorry, I was, eh, that is to say I didn't really pay any—"

Sawhill thrust him backward in anger and disgust and jumped out of the car. He began to run up the street, screaming, "Sam! Sam!" as loudly as possible. Venetian blinds were raised and curtains slightly parted on all sides as the residents, unaccustomed to the commotion, indulged their curiosity and looked out their windows. Sam Goldhaber opened the door of one of the houses and bounded down the steps. "Sam!" Sawhill said frantically.

"Tom, what's the matter? Why are you—"

"They've got Harriet in that house, Hadji and some other people! They've got Harriet!"

"Damn!" he spat. "I called Jasper. He's coming right over. Oh, and they were able to make a more positive identification. It is Gus in there, and most probably Suzanne also. The autopsy just got—"

"The hell with the autopsy! They've got Harriet in there! We have to—"

Sam grabbed him by the shoulders and shook him. "Damn it, Tom, will you get hold of yourself? We have to wait here for Jasper. We don't even have a gun, for Christ's sake. What the hell can we do by ourselves?"

"But Harriet—"

"We'll get her out of this, don't worry. Jasper—"

"Look!" Sawhill pointed down the street. In the distance Sam could see figures walking out of the house and opening the door of the van. "Harriet!" he shouted and began to run. Sam Goldhaber followed as quickly as his aging legs could carry him.

Ahmed Hadji was holding Harriet Langly tightly as he led her out of the door of the house and down the front steps. As Sawhill drew closer his mind vaguely registered the impression that Harriet was not struggling at all but rather was walking numbly down the steps with Hadji guiding rather than restraining her. Harriet and Hadji reached the paved walkway which stretched out from the front steps just as Sawhill reached the edge of the lawn at a dead run and flung himself wildly at them. He brought them both down with him, and he tried to grab Hadji around the neck, all the while shouting, "Run, Harriet! Run!" She lay, limp and motionless, staring with open eyes up at the clouds.

Hadji began to battle Sawhill viciously, kicking and biting against the pummeling fists which rained blows down upon him. He managed to wedge his left foot against Sawhill's stomach and pushed outward forcefully, sending Sawhill sprawling backward. Hadji jumped to his feet and reached into his coat pocket. He drew out his dagger and clasped it in his right hand, blade downward.

Sawhill rolled out of the way as Hadji leaped at him, and the knife sliced deeply into the short-clipped grass. Sawhill placed a hard kick in Hadji's side and then brought his fist crashing down on the back of the Arab's neck. As Hadji lay there stunned, Sawhill grabbed the dagger and pulled it out of the ground. He raised his arm and prepared to bring the blade down into Hadji's back.

"*An khem! Ster!*" the other man said in a tone of command. Withdraw, Sekhemib had said. Sleep.

Thomas Sawhill fought to retain control of his body, but he fell weakly back upon the ground as the world swam before him. The dagger fell harmlessly upon the grass with an almost inaudible thud, and he lost his grip on consciousness.

Sekhemib looked at Harriet and released her from the power of his psychic fetters. Her eyes closed briefly and her lungs drew in a massive, trembling breath. Then, too frightened to rise to her feet, she lay there and looked up at Sekhemib. "Who is this fool?" he asked angrily.

"He is my—" her mind searched for the proper term for "lover" in the ancient language, "he is my brother in joy."

Sekhemib nodded, understanding the expression. "He is brave, though foolish." He turned to Hadji, who was rising uneasily to his feet. With one hand he held the back of his neck while Sekhemib grasped him by the other to assist him. "Art thou injured?"

Hadji's eyes blazed with anger when he saw Sawhill lying insensible before him. "You son of a whore!" he spat between clenched teeth. He ran over and picked up his dagger, murder in his eyes, but Sekhemib stepped between him and Sawhill and stopped Hadji with one imperious look.

"He thinks to save his lady, Ahmed Hadji. Is that not an honorable impulse, even in this world?"

"But he—"

"Priest of Thoth, learn proper views. Seekest thou vengeance on a mortal man, when immortality shall be thine inheritance?"

"But I want to see him dead! He attacked me!"

"And he has been defeated. Were we in need of a tekenu at this moment, I would give his soul to Senmut; but we must not return more of my company to this life before we stand again in the holy place. And dost thou wish to see him dead? Then return here years hence, when he dies."

Hadji was angry and confused. "But what matter? Why may I not kill him? Why do you stop me?"

"To kill out of passion pollutes the mind, Ahmed Hadji. I have killed ten times ten thousand, and yet my mind was ever cold and my blood rushed not. Pity the mortals, and use them even as they pity and use the dumb beasts of the field. But to kill a mortal man in anger is like unto killing the beast in anger. It is degrading, and unworthy of your oath." Hadji cast one more angry look at the unconscious form and then went in a huff to the van.

Sekhemib's will roused Sawhill from his stupor. He coughed and tried to move his still numb body but found that he was in the grip of a paralysis from his neck downward. He looked desperately from Harriet to Sekhemib. The priest looked down at Harriet and said softly, "The bravery of a fool amuses me and makes me remember events of the past, for men have always fought for women. I give you a gift, Heret, out of my triumph. Bid farewell to your brother, for you shall not see him again this side of the tomb."

Harriet looked up at Sekhemib, and then slowly turned her eyes to Thomas Sawhill. "I love you, Tommy," she said weakly, miserably.

"Harriet," he rasped, "who—who—"

"The scroll was true, Tommy, all of it. That's Sekhemib, the Egyptian priest. He drank Will's soul. They killed Gus and Suzanne too, took their souls."

"Can't be," he whispered softly. "It just can't—"

"It is, Tommy. He's taking me—"

"Enough," Sekhemib said, softly but in a tone which invited no debate. "Come, Heret." Harriet felt her body moving against her will, and she rose to her feet. She moved mechanically toward the van and climbed into the passenger seat. Sekhemib and Sawhill watched her until she pulled the door shut, and then the priest caused her to fall asleep. He turned back to Sawhill and smiled coldly, saying words which Sawhill could not understand. He then turned and joined Hadji, Meret, Yuya, Harriet, and the four ancient dead in the van. Hadji turned the key in the ignition and backed the van down the driveway onto the street. The sound of a police siren and the glimpse out of the corner of his eye of flashing red and yellow lights caused Hadji to lean out the window and look behind him. "Damnation!" he spat.

"What is amiss, Ahmed Hadji?" Sekhemib asked calmly.

"An official of the rulers pursues us, my lord."

He smiled. "And you fear?" Hadji did not answer, and Sekhemib smiled, shaking his head sadly.

As the van rounded the corner, Jasper Rudd's patrol car screeched to a halt in front of the house. Thomas Sawhill was still lying on his back, the feeling slowly returning to his arms and legs. Jasper jumped out of the car and ran over to him. "You okay, Doc?"

"Jasper," he said hoarsely, "in the van—that van . . ."

Jasper looked down the street and saw the red rear lights disappearing around the corner. "Hadji's in there, right? Professor Goldhaber said you saw him stealing—"

"They have Harriet in there—they're kidnapping her." He reached up and grabbed Jasper's sleeve. "They killed Will. They killed Gus and Suzanne too. It's a cult—a cult . . ."

Jasper's eyes clouded over with red and went wide and he looked down the street. "Son of a bitch," he muttered darkly. "Goddamn fuckin' son of a bitch!" He jumped back into the patrol car and gunned the engine, sending wisps of burned rubber into the air as he sped after the van.

Sawhill sat up painfully, feeling as if every nerve in his body had been overloaded. Sam's car pulled up, a bit more slowly than Jasper's had done, and Sam and Roderick came over to him. They took him by the arms, one man on either side, and helped him to his feet. "Can you walk?" Sam asked hurriedly.

"I—I think so," Sawhill replied. "But we have to follow them, have to follow Jasper."

"Yes, yes, I know. Are you sure we don't need to go to the hospital?"

"Yes, damn it! Get back in the car. We have to catch up with them. Quick, Sam, goddamn it!"

He practically shoved Sam Goldhaber away from him as he stumbled to the car. Roderick, moving with an alacrity for which no one who knew him would have given him credit, hopped into the back seat seconds before Sam positioned himself behind the steering wheel and drove off in pursuit of the patrol car.

It was fortunate for them that Jasper had his siren blaring and his flashing lights switched on, else they would never have been able to remain in the chase. Sam sped down Main Street and caught a glimpse of the flashing lights turning in the direction of the entrance to the thruway. "Hold tight," he warned. "I doubt Hadji or Jasper are going to stop to get a toll ticket, and we aren't going to either." They drove through the toll gate without any reduction in speed, and Sawhill took a quickly passing look at the astounded expression on the toll collector.

Sam followed the distant glow of the flashing lights and saw that both other vehicles had entered the southbound side of the road. His old car was not as fast as Jasper's patrol car, but he felt confident that they could outrun the van and thus, of course, catch up with Jasper. In a few short minutes they drew up behind the policeman, who was at that moment drawing close to the rear of the van. "How fast are they going, Sam?" Sawhill asked.

Sam looked quickly at the speedometer. "We're doing eighty."

"Dr. Sawhill?" Roderick asked, a bit meekly.

"Yes, Your Lordship? What is it?" If you ask us to take you home, so help me God I'll slug you in the mouth.

"What the devil is going on? Who are these people?"

It was only then that Sawhill realized that he had not explained to Sam or Roderick any of what Harriet had told him. "Brace yourselves. You remember the story on the scroll?"

"Of course. How do you know about it?" Sam asked.

"Harriet told me the whole story last night. Well, apparently it's true. Harriet said so. She said that one of those people up there, one of those alive and well people, is the mummy that was stolen the other night."

Sam Goldhaber did not respond at first. When he did, he simply said, "She was hysterical."

"She wasn't hysterical, Sam," Sawhill said pointedly. "She seemed scared and sad, but she wasn't raving."

"Oh, come on! Do you seriously think——" He stopped speaking when the road curved and his car began to skid frighteningly toward the shoulder before righting itself. *"Gott im Himmel,"* he muttered.

"Listen, Sam, I know it's crazy. I'm not even sure that I believe it myself. But . . ."

The sound of gunfire distracted him. Up ahead, Jasper Rudd had drawn his service revolver and was firing wildly at the van. "Jesus Christ!" Sawhill said. "He's going to kill somebody like that!"

"That may very well be his intention," Sam replied.

"But Harriet's in there!"

Sam nodded slowly. "I know. But so are the people who killed Gus."

Ahmed Hadji ducked instinctively as a bullet crashed through the window of one of the rear doors of the van. "My lord!" he gasped. "These projectiles can kill mortal men, and I am still a mortal man. They are dangerous."

"Fascinating weaponry, Ahmed Hadji," Sekhemib said. "How does the weapon impel the projectile toward the target?"

Not now, by the gods! he thought, but said, "By rapidly expanding heated air, my lord." Another bullet crashed into the rear door of the van, and Hadji ducked again. "If one of them hits our wheels, our vehicle might be destroyed. Please, my lord!"

Sekhemib looked behind him at Yuya and Meret. "My friends, let us dispose of the insect. Turn his weapon back upon himself."

Yuya and Meret were a bit unnerved by the speed at which they were moving, but they rose from their seated positions against the wall of the van and moved unsteadily back toward the shattered window. Meret looked out at the patrol car which was racing not fifteen feet behind them, and Yuya stood behind her, looking over her shoulder.

It was a perfect shot. Before either of them could bring their long unused mental powers to bear, Jasper took as careful aim as he could under the circumstances and sent a bullet directly into Meret's throat. It passed through her and hit Yuya squarely in the chest. Meret fell to the floor of the van and Yuya stumbled back, shocked and confused by the searing pain. "Sekhemib," he cried, and then fell.

Sekhemib looked back, turning his head with a casual, languid motion, but his expression turned to astonishment and anger when he saw his two ancient compatriots lying on the floor. Blood was pouring from Meret's mouth and Yuya was clutching his chest as if attempting to stem the sanguine tide which issued forth from it.

Sekhemib's eyes, filled now with fury, turned on Hadji. "Thou didst not burn the tekenues!"

"But I did, my lord," Hadji said frantically. "I swear by the gods, by my ka, by Anubis."

"Blasphemer!" Sekhemib grabbed him by the throat. "Thou hast not done that which I commanded thee!"

"I swear, my lord, I swear!" he said, choking. "Perhaps the powers have weakened after all the centuries. Perhaps the powers of the gods are less potent so far from Egypt." He felt the deathlike grip relax slightly. He was trying to steer the van, maintain the rate of speed, and save his life all at once. "Perhaps they are not seriously injured. They are but newly restored to life. Perhaps the tekenues themselves were weak. Perhaps . . ." Sekhemib released him and jumped over the seat into the rear of the van. Hadji wiped the sweat from his brow and concentrated on the road.

In the rear of the van Sekhemib knelt down and cradled Meret in his arms. He called her name softly. She opened her eyes and sought his face in the darkness, darkness engendered both by the interior of the vehicle and her rapidly ebbing life.

She tried to say his name, but was able only to gurgle through the blood. "Be at ease, my love," he whispered. "Thou diest. But thou shalt rise in due time, and we shall again dance upon the Nile banks and drink wine through reeds." He watched as the spark of life flickered and then went out in her eyes. He turned to Yuya, and saw that he was already dead.

Sekhemib stood up and looked out the back of the van. Jasper Rudd had reloaded his revolver and was firing at him. He felt a bullet strike his shoulder, but it did not penetrate, and he ignored it. He stared at Jasper.

"Get you now, you son of a bitch!" Jasper shouted, taking aim, but for some inexplicable reason he felt his right hand turning the steering wheel far to the left. He struggled to control his hand, but it continued to turn the wheel, and a few seconds later the patrol car drove off the thruway and careened wildly into the wooded expanse of land which formed the highway divider. He reduced his speed only slightly by depressing the brake, and came to a stop only when the car crashed headlong into a tree. Jasper was thrown forward into the windshield, which cracked and splintered from the impact with his forehead. He fell heavily back into the seat, bleeding freely from the lacerations he had suffered.

"Sam, pull over," Sawhill said when he saw the patrol car come to a stop in a tangled heap before a now broken tree.

"But Harriet's—" Sam began.

"Harriet's alive. Jasper's probably injured. Now pull over!"

Sam Goldhaber had never really thought about the seriousness with which some physicians took their oath before. Impressed, but still worried about Harriet, he pulled off the road and watched as Sawhill got out and ran over to the wreck.

Sekhemib watched with grim satisfaction as his pursuers abandoned the chase. He returned to the front of the van and said, "Thou need not fear, Ahmed Hadji. We are safe."

Hadji closed his eyes and breathed heavily. "*Anet hrauthen, 'Anpu,*" he muttered. "The lord Yuya and the lady Meret?"

"They are dead, for the time being. But that will pass." Hadji nodded and smiled slightly. He was paying careful attention to the road as he reduced his speed. He did not see Sekhemib's furious eyes glaring at him.

Fifteen miles away, in the morgue at Harrison Hospital, the son of the hospital's founder was unaware of the events which had been transpiring on the thruway. Dr. Douglas Harrison, the county medical examiner, was in the midst of the autopsy of the woman tentatively identified as Suzanne Melendez. He had already opened the chest cavity and removed the lungs and heart for measurement and weighing. Next would come the brain.

This is the strangest thing I've ever seen, Harrison was thinking. The heart was almost hard to the touch, reminding him of coral. The lungs were similarly ossified, but small bits of them fell crumbling into the chest cavity as they were removed. Cutting through the leathery skin had been as difficult as slicing an overcooked steak of atrocious quality. Damndest thing!

He heard a sound.

Harrison turned around and stared over the rims of his bifocals. The corpse which had been positively identified as Gus Rudd was quivering on the slab. His arms and legs were vibrating and his open mouth was opening and closing spasmodically.

The medical examiner gazed at the trembling cadaver with open-mouthed wonder. He left the body of Suzanne Melendez and walked over to Gus. Harrison leaned over and stared into the face of the corpse.

"Jesus Mary and Joseph!" he muttered. Gus Rudd's eyes were open and were darting insanely back and forth. Harrison doubted the reliability of his own vision as he noticed the leathery skin beginning to smooth out and grow full, as the prunelike face of the dead man began to expand away from the skull and assume a human visage, as the fingers began to flex and the softening lungs began to struggle to draw air into themselves. When, a few minutes later, Gus Rudd sat up on the slab and started to scream, Harrison fainted.

He was fortunate. The county medical examiner lay unconscious upon the cold floor of the morgue, unable to hear the frenzied cries issuing forth from the deranged mind of the police deputy. But more importantly, and more fortunately for his own subsequent mental health, he was unable to look back at the autopsy slab where the gutted body of Suzanne Melendez was coming briefly, but horribly, to life.

# CHAPTER 12

▲ It was late, very late, nearly three in the morning. The three men sat silently around the table in the office of the police chief, three glasses before them, a depleted bottle of bourbon in the middle of the table. None of them spoke. None of them moved. The only sounds were the incessant chirping of the crickets outside the window and the slow, steady ticking of the clock on the wall.

The phone rang. Thomas Sawhill reached over and picked up the receiver and said in a depressed monotone, "Police station." He paused. "Yes, this is Dr. Sawhill. Have you . . ." He paused again, a long pause as he listened to the voice on the other end and nodded periodically. Roderick Fowles watched him intently. Samuel Goldhaber took the glass of bourbon from the table before him and raised it to his lips. They both waited, hoping for the best and expecting the worst. At last Sawhill muttered, "Yes. Thank you," and hung up the phone.

He sat back wearily in the chair and said, "Nothing."

"That was the state police?" Sam asked.

He nodded. "Nothing. No sighting of the van we described, no shipments of antiquities out of the country, no one fitting the descriptions we gave them trying to leave the country on any flight bound for Egypt. Nothing." He began to weep, and Sam pushed the glass of bourbon toward him.

Roderick shook his head. "I can't believe this. All those years those things were in our attic. All those years."

"I can't believe it either," Sawhill said, wiping the tears from his eyes. "But I have to believe it. I tried to speak to Gus before he was sedated. I saw what was left of Suzanne on the floor after it had crawled off the table in the autopsy room. It can't be true, but it must be true."

"But how?" Roderick asked, pleading for some sense to be made out of it all. "It's impossible!"

"Everything's impossible, until it happens," Sam said thickly. "Ancient gods!" He shook his head.

"Did you ever read *Dracula?*" Sawhill asked. "Harriet loves that kind of book. She got me to read it."

"What about it?" Roderick asked.

"There's a character in that book who said something like, a vampire's greatest power is our refusal to believe he exists." Sawhill sighed. "That's what has happened here." He took a swig of bourbon and then stared pensively into the empty glass. Then he threw it angrily at the floor. It shattered loudly, but the other two men sat motionless, as if their senses had been dulled by the shocks of the day's events. "Damn it all!" Sawhill shouted. "We knew the whole story, we knew all the facts! It was all staring at us, all along, but we wouldn't even give it a thought. Blind, blind!" He trembled violently and then convulsed in weeping.

Roderick reached over and placed his hand on Sawhill's forearm. "It was all just too fantastic. Don't blame yourself, old fellow."

"Of course not," Sam agreed. "You can't be expected to accept as true ideas that run contrary to everything you've ever been taught. This is the twentieth century, after all! Walking dead! Living mummies!" He laughed humorlessly. "It's ridiculous!"

"But it's true," Sawhill muttered, wiping a tear from his cheek.

Sam Goldhaber nodded grimly. "That's the catch. It's true. Ancient priests of ancient gods who drink human souls and live forever, and an age-old cult which has been trying to find their mummies for nearly four thousand years. All true." He sighed. "God help us, it's all true."

They were silent for a while. Roderick picked up the bottle and poured some bourbon into Sawhill's empty glass. Then he asked, "How is Chief Rudd?"

"Jasper?" Sawhill responded weakly. "Broken neck, multiple lacerations, skull fracture. He's in bad shape, but at least he didn't sever his spinal cord. He should recover. It'll take a while, though."

"And his brother?"

Sawhill shrugged, and Sam said, "He's in the hospital too,

under heavy sedation. I spoke with—what's his name, Tom? Harrison's intern?"

"Markowsky," Sawhill muttered. "Jake Markowsky."

"Right. He said that they're going to arrange to have Gus sent to Kings Park State Hospital."

"Is that a lunatic asylum?" Roderick asked.

Sam smiled. "They're called psychiatric hospitals nowadays. Yes, it is. Poor Gus. He has no idea what's happened to him. He didn't stop screaming until they knocked him out." Sam shook his head sadly. "The poor kid."

The morose silence descended upon the three men once again. Only the ticking of the wall clock and the sobs which burst occasionally from Thomas Sawhill disturbed it. At last Roderick whispered, "But why Pearson?"

"Hmmm?" Sam asked.

"Pearson, my solicitor. Why did Hadji kill him?"

Sam considered this for a moment. "There are a number of possible explanations, I think," he said. "It was from Pearson or from his records that Hadji learned where the mummies had been shipped. Perhaps he didn't want Pearson to call you and warn you about him. Or maybe it was a cultic thing, a human sacrifice. Remember what Jasper told us, about the murder looking like a ritual murder?"

"They practice human sacrifice?!" Sawhill asked, aghast at the thought. "Then Harriet—maybe Harriet—"

"No, Tom, no," Sam said firmly. "That isn't rational. They seem to have gone to a good deal of trouble to take her with them. They wouldn't do that if all they wanted was someone to kill. They want her as a hostage, perhaps."

"But they aren't rational," Roderick objected. "They're madmen."

Sam shook his head. "I'm sorry, Your Lordship, but I disagree. They're murderers, religious fanatics, evil, to be sure. But they are as rational as you and I. Everything they've done so far has had a logical purpose."

The silence returned, a silence born of impotence and sorrow. Then a heavy sigh broke forth from Sawhill's throat and he rasped, "Harriet!" in a voice filled with mourning and loss.

"We'll do something, Tom," Sam said. "There must be something we can do."

"What the hell can we do?" Sawhill asked desperately. "We don't even know where she is! She may be dead already!" His weeping overwhelmed him again, and Sam and Roderick watched him uneasily, unable to give meaningless comfort, speechless, numb.

The phone rang again. Sawhill reached for it, hoping that the state police might be calling with encouraging news. "Hello?" he said eagerly.

"Hello? To whom am I speaking?" The voice seemed somehow familiar, though muted by the apparent distance of the phone call.

"This is Dr. Thomas Sawhill, at the Greenfield police station. Who is this?"

"Oh, yes, Dr. Sawhill! How nice to speak to you!"

"Who is this?!"

"This is your friend, Ahmed Hadji. I trust you are well?"

Sawhill sprang to his feet. "Hadji, you son of a bitch! Where the hell is Harriet?"

An evil chuckle came across the line. "Oh, Professor Langly is quite well. For the moment, at least. Your concern is touching, I must say."

"Let me talk to her!"

"No, no, sorry, that's quite impossible. She is, ah, preoccupied with matters of our transit."

Sawhill struggled to control himself. "Listen, Hadji, I'll pay you, I'll give you money, any amount you want, I'll raise it somehow—"

"Money?!" he said with mock resentment. "What need have I for money? Listen to me, my friend. Do you know why I have called you?" He waited for a response, but Sawhill stood silent and tense at the other end of the call. "I have called to tell you that I have beaten you all! I have won!"

"Hadji, you have to listen to reason—"

"No, you listen. We shall go to the holy place and there I, or someone else—it doesn't really matter—will drink the soul of your lady friend. And I shall spit on her grave, do you hear me? And I shall wait a few decades, and then I shall spit on your grave." He laughed joyfully. "You shall die, you shall all die, and I shall live forever, millions of years, millions of years!" He was still laughing as he slammed down the phone.

"Hadji!" Sawhill screamed. "Hadji! Hadji! HADJI!" He ripped the phone cord from the wall as he hurled the phone against the door of the office. "You BASTARD!" he shouted. "You miserable bastard!" He began to pound the table top with his fists, weeping hysterically. "You bastard!" he repeated as he sank weakly to his knees. "You miserable bastard!"

"Tom!" Sam said sharply. "Was that Hadji? Did I hear you call him Hadji? Was that Ahmed Hadji?"

"That animal!" Sawhill wept. "He was gloating! He was gloating!"

"What did he say?" Roderick asked. "It may be important. It may give us a clue, something to follow. What did he say?"

"He said he was . . ." Sawhill's body was trembling so violently that his knees gave way and he fell onto the floor. "He said—he was going to drink her soul . . ."

Sam Goldhaber put his hands under Sawhill's arms and lifted him to his feet. "Listen, Tom, the Earl is right. Did he say anything, anything at all which might serve as a lead for us? Think!"

Sawhill struggled to control himself, to stop his body from shaking. "He said something about a holy place—a holy place—"

"Then it's Egypt," Sam said with grim satisfaction. "I was thinking that they could have gone anywhere in the world—Brazil, Burma, anywhere. But if there's a holy place, it must be in Egypt." He looked Sawhill in the eye. "We're going to Egypt."

"Egypt's not a little country, Sam—"

"It's a fifty-mile-wide strip of land running along either side of one river. I'm not saying it will be easy, but it narrows down our search. Look, Tom, if they're going to Egypt, they must be arranging it somehow through that institute or that company Hadji partly owns. We have to go there and start snooping around, seeing what we can turn up."

"Shouldn't we get official assistance?" Roderick asked.

"It would be great, but who would believe us?" Sam replied. "We're not talking about a normal kidnapping here. We're talking about the resurrected corpses of ancient pagan priests. The State Department would kick us out of their office!"

"Your Lordship," Sawhill said slowly, "this is the second time you've said 'we.' Are you going to help us? I didn't think—"

"I know, you assumed I'd bid you a cheery farewell and be off. But I feel responsible for this whole unpleasant business." He leaned forward and looked at the other two men earnestly. "You must try to understand, my friends, that I've never felt responsible for anything before in my life. Lord, I've never had to be responsible for anything! But I've been thinking quite a bit about the things my late uncle kept telling me over the years, the family honor and all that. It was my family that brought these creatures to England, and it was I who brought them here. I can't just walk away as if it were none of my concern."

Sam and Sawhill were quiet for a few moments. Roderick seemed to blush slightly, as if embarrassed by his own words, and his blush deepened when Sawhill grasped his hand and began to shake it. "I've misjudged you, Your Lordship."

"No you haven't, actually," he stammered. "And please, call me Roderick." He was uncomfortable with the sudden amiability, and he coughed, straightened his shoulders, and tried to be businesslike. "Well! What's the plan? How shall we begin?"

"We begin by getting airplane tickets to Cairo," Sam said, reaching for the phone. Then, remembering that Sawhill had torn its wire out of the wall, he sat back in his chair. "We can go to your place, Tom, and make arrangements from there. Do you have a passport?"

"Somewhere," Sawhill replied. "I don't know if it's still good. It may have expired."

"Well, we'll check. Mine is still good, as is His Lordship's, obviously."

"Roderick," the Earl said.

"Yes, of course," Sam smiled. "I'm not certain, but I think we'll need to be inoculated. We may need visas in addition to the passports."

"I have lots of credit cards," Roderick said helpfully.

"No, Roderick, a visa is a special document you need to enter certain countries. But we will need a good deal of money—"

"I shall provide it, of course," Roderick said grandly. "I shall wire my bank in London in the morning."

"Great," Sam said. He picked up his glass, the only one with any bourbon left in it, and poured some of the liquor into the empty bottle and into Roderick's glass. He handed his glass to Sawhill and then raised the bottle into the air. "A toast, gentlemen, to the success of our journey." They each raised the bourbon to their lips and drank. Sam poured a few drops from the bottle onto the floor.

"Why did you do that?" Roderick asked.

"An ancient Greek custom," Sam explained. "Pouring a libation to the gods."

His action might have been amusing under other circumstances. As it was, none of them laughed.

# III

# XEPHERAXEPHER

▲

I have divided the heavens, I
have cleft the horizon. I have
traversed the Earth and conquered
the mighty spirit-souls. Mine
enemy hath been given to me, and
he shall not be delivered from
me. I have come forth from the
horizon against mine enemy, and
he shall not escape my wrath.
>      —*The Egyptian Book of*
>           *the Dead*, XLIX

# CHAPTER 13

▲ Harriet Langly could not swim. Having lived her entire life in urban areas such as New York and Chicago before coming to the little rural town of Greenfield, swimming was one of many skills which she had never acquired. She could not sail, she could not water-ski, she could not ride a horse, she could not mark a trail, she could not swim. She had never seen any need to learn any of these things. But then she had never envisioned a time in her future when she would want to jump from the stern of a ship into the frigid waters of the North Sea.

She glanced over her shoulder at Ahmed Hadji, who was as always keeping a close watch on her. He smiled politely at her and inclined his head slightly, but the smile and the bow bore no element of courtesy or civility. His smile was bitter, vindictive, smug. "It is a beautiful day, is it not, Miss Langly?" he asked amicably.

Harriet tried to ignore him. She disliked everything about him—his looks, his manner, his attitude, and of course his actions. She was particularly unnerved by the leering way he allowed his narrow eyes to drift up and down over her, fixing them frequently upon her breasts and buttocks and belly. She was still wearing the sweater and dungarees she had donned in her room a week before, and she regretted being so attired. It was not merely that her clothing was filthy and redolent of perspiration and grime. In that regard her clothing differed only slightly from the flesh it covered, for she had not been given the opportunity to bathe or even wash her face. Her hair was greasy and matted, her fingernails black with dirt, her skin covered with a film of soiled sweat. Her body was no cleaner than her clothes.

What bothered her about her attire was that the sweater and dungarees were, after the fashion of casual dress, quite tight, quite form fitting. The sweater hugged her large breasts and the dungarees were stretched tight around her legs and buttocks. Hadji's constant staring caused her instinctively to attempt to draw her collar and lapels closed across her throat and bosom, but the sweater of course had no collar, no lapels. Fully clothed, she felt naked and exposed to the leering eyes.

Harriet looked out at the rolling waves of the North Sea. If I jump, I'll drown, she thought. If I don't jump, then God knows what will happen to me; God knows what they'll do to me before they kill me. And of course, they will finally kill me. They feed on death, all of them. Vultures, vultures . . . !

She raised her left foot very slightly off the deck, as she had done so many times before over the past three days, and then put it down again. She lacked the courage for suicide. So many people seem to think that suicide is the coward's way out, a way to run from reality rather than face it. They are wrong. It takes courage to kill yourself when reality presents as the only alternative the sort of fate to which she seemed condemned. Harriet lacked the courage to accept reality's choices. As long as there was hope, she lacked the courage to pursue the only logical course of action.

She closed her eyes and bowed her head. Hope! What hope?! Hope that Thomas Sawhill was following them? Ridiculous. With her unwilling help, she, Hadji, Sekhemib and the six bodies of the priests had gone from Manhattan to Washington by train and had then flown to Hamburg. How could Sawhill follow so irrational, so circuitous a trail to Egypt? How could he possibly deduce such an itinerary? They had boarded the ship in Hamburg a few days ago and were now sailing leisurely around the northern reaches of the continent of Europe, heading west, to Brest in France, to Lisbon in Portugal, to Tunis in Tunisia, and then to Alexandria in Egypt. Hadji had explained their route to her in some detail. Why should he not? No one could follow them. This old freighter with Liberian registry had been purchased by Hadji's people in Egypt, had been fitted with a crew imported from Singapore, had been cleared in advance at each port of call by means of judiciously distributed bribes. She was totally isolated. The captain and the crew were Chinese; whenever they drew near a port, she was locked in her cabin; the ship had no radio. She could speak to no one other than Hadji in English and

Sekhemib in the ancient tongue. None of the crew spoke English, and of course neither did they speak ancient Egyptian.

No way out. No way out.

She looked again at the white-crested blue waves. That's the only way out, she thought. And I just can't bring myself to do it.

"Thou thinkest on foolishness, Heret," Sekhemib said from behind her. "To take one's own life out of a fear of death is the reasoning of a madman."

She spun around when she heard his voice, and recoiled slightly at the sight of him. It was not his appearance which caused her to shrink back: indeed, he was rather pleasant looking. His skin had darkened over the past few days, and he now looked radiantly healthy. Why shouldn't he? she thought. He's living Will Foster's life. Sekhemib had abandoned the (to him) bizarre and uncomfortable clothing which he had worn in Greenfield and was now clad in a simple white kaftan with a waist sash of purple linen. No, it was not his appearance which caused her stomach to turn. It was the knowledge that she was talking to a dead man, or at least a man who should be dead, should have been reduced to dust thousands of years ago, a man who had shed more blood than she could imagine, a vampire, worse than a vampire, a leech, worse than a leech. She turned away from him and stared out to sea at the dim gray distant mass which was the coast of Normandy. "You don't know what I'm thinking," she muttered. "You can't read minds."

"No, I cannot read thy thoughts, Heret," he said, coming forward and leaning against the railing, "but I can read thy face, and thy face speaks of death."

"And what is my fate to be at your hands, if not death?"

"Have thy people no gods, no beliefs, to comfort thee? Art thou like unto the Achaeans, who take their own lives in desperate times, or like unto the people of Tyre? If now thou livest and next month thou are to die, why does this make this month less sweet? Is it not possible that thou mayest die today or tomorrow in accordance with the nature of things?"

"This is an easy thing for you to say, Sekhemib." She refused to call him by any of his titles, though she had been forced by Hadji's threats of violence to employ the polite form of the pronoun. "It is easy to speak of death when you can defeat death. Health is not prized by the healthy, but by the ill."

"No, Heret, thou dost not understand. I have died, a thousand times I have died, if but for an instant while I drank the souls of the tekenues. I know death better than any man."

Her curiosity was pricked by this. "I know that you died when you were defeated by Ousha and his god—"

"They did not defeat me, Heret, for I live, and Ousha is dust, and Dudimose is dust, and Xepheraxepher is a dead god, an empty word, a name without power. They did not defeat me, they did nothing more than interfere with me for a little time."

"A little time! Three thousand five hundred years!"

Sekhemib shrugged. "But a moment in the life of the world. It is of no matter."

Harriet felt the scholar in her, so long repressed by the horrors of her situation, slowly reasserting itself. "How old are you, Sekhemib?"

He shook his head. "I do not know. Anubis came to me in a vision long, long ago, in the dim time, before there was an Egypt, before men had learned to build or smelt or fashion."

Predynastic period, probably, she thought. "We have learned that a king named Namar or Menes united Egypt nearly five thousand years ago. Do you mean that you were born before that?"

He laughed. "I knew Namar well. He served me well for the years of his power. No, Heret, I was ancient in the days of Namar. The years pass and the memory fades, but in my youth I was not as I am now, for each time I drink a human soul I take some of that mortal's visage and some portion of his shape, and I change. I remember that during the dim time I was small and hair covered. I ate raw meat and lived with the beasts on the plains, far to the south of the land of Egypt. Meret was with me, and Yuya and the others, Herihor, Senmut, all the others, but they too were not as they are now. We all changed over the thousands of years as we drank the souls of the people."

Harriet's mouth was hanging open in shock. Prehumans!? Hominids on the plains of Africa? "Are you trying to tell me that you are hundreds of thousands of years old? That's impossible!" She realized that she had said this in English, and she quickly repeated it in the ancient tongue.

Sekhemib smiled. "Anubis is an ancient god, older than Amon, older even than Osiris. I have served him since before men spoke and gave their thoughts in language. I have served him since the beginning of the world, and I shall serve him until the end of the world." He bowed his head reverently. *"Anet hrak 'Anpu."*

Harriet shook her head. "I cannot understand this, Sekhemib. There are no gods. They do not exist, they have never existed. This all cannot be!"

"Art thou blind, woman? Do I live? Do my limbs move, does my eye see, does my mouth speak?"

"But the gods, all religions, are just wishful thinking, just ways of comforting ourselves, just—

"And thou hast no gods, nor thy people?"

"Oh, there are religions, but intelligent, educated people don't take them seriously. They just aren't true. They're fables."

Sekhemib nodded in agreement. "Thou speakest rightly, for if thy people do not worship Anubis and Isis and Set and the other ancient gods, then they worship false gods indeed."

"That's not what I mean," she said tiredly. "There is some way in which you have been able to prolong and restore life, that's obvious. But there must be a scientific explanation for it. All religions are fables, all the gods are myths."

"I pity thee, Heret," Sekhemib said sadly. "Dost thou believe that nothing exists beyond thyself, that no life exists beyond this life?"

"Well, if you don't believe that, then why are you so determined to stay in this life? I mean, if you believe in an afterlife or in some form of existence beyond death, why are you so obsessed with staying alive?"

"Oh, Heret, thou art so simple. Hast thou never asked thyself why Anubis has blessed me with this gift, why he has given me my powers with which to protect myself?"

She shrugged and looked back out to sea. "I assumed it was part of a deal. You worship me, I'll bless you, like Abraham and God."

"Who is this man?"

"An ancestor of the—of the Habiru. It doesn't matter." She sighed. Depression was once again blanketing curiosity.

"Ah, the Habiru. Allies of the Hyksos. Ousha was a Habiru, but he worshipped no god with the name God."

"*God* is an English word," she said tiredly. "It's a general term like the Egyptian word *neter.*

"And this god had no name?"

"Look, why are you asking me all this? What do you care about the Hebrews and their religion? Why don't you just leave me alone? Why don't you just kill me and be done with it?" She started to cry.

"Compose thyself, Heret," Sekhemib commanded. "I speak with thee for my pleasure, for Ahmed Hadji is a fool and no companion. But I have no wish to listen to weeping and gnashing of teeth."

She was sufficiently frightened of him to force herself to stop weeping. "I'm sorry," she said, and then thought, Why on earth am I apologizing to this creature?

"Thou are forgiven," he said seriously. "Answer me. This god had no name?"

"He had a name, but the Hebrews were not allowed to say it."

Sekhemib laughed heartily. "Such idiocy! How can you use the power of a god if you cannot speak his name?"

She shrugged. "Your concept of the relationship between man and God is somewhat primitive." She was instantly regretful that she had made the statement. She did not want to anger this man, because he was correct in saying that the certainty of death did not make the presence of life any less sweet. Quickly, she added, "But you did not make a pact with Anubis?"

Sekhemib had heard and understood her criticism, but he chose to ignore it. Why should he be offended at the ignorance and ill manners of a mortal woman whose life lay in his hands? "Yes, a pact, but not made in words, for I had no words during the dim time. Anubis has no need of my worship. I worship him because I am his servant, because I want to worship him."

Harriet frowned. "Then why? . . . I mean, I don't understand."

Sekhemib smiled. "I drink the souls of the tekenues. And I am the tekenu of the god. Through me, he drinks the souls of men, and he lives, even as I live."

She stared at him skeptically. "You are a tekenu? You?!"

"Yes. A god who has no servants, whose name is never called upon, is a god who dies, even as the god of Ousha, Xepheraxepher, is a dead god. Anubis would live forever, so he chose seven of us from the mud of the dim time to live forever. And as we drink the souls of the tekenues, he drinks our souls and lives."

"I don't follow this," she said. "Do you mean that Anubis lives, that gods live, only so long as they have worshippers?"

"No. A god needs no worship. He needs his name only. But Anubis is a wise god and an ancient god, and he went beyond the power of the other gods and made them his servants. The ancients worshipped all the gods, but exalted Amon above the rest. They knew not that Amon, and Osiris and Ra and all the others, serve Anubis."

He was digressing, and she wanted to understand what he had said. "But what does this have to do with soul drinking? Why does this make you tekenu of some sort?"

Sekhemib shook his head. "You people of this age are so far from the gods that the simplest truths are hidden from you. You have no gods, and so you understand nothing. We seven— I, Meret, Yuya, Herihor, Senmut, Wenet, and Khumara—we seven *are* Anubis. When we meet once each full moon for the ceremony, we give our souls to the god and we become one, we become the god. He lives because we live, he assumes physical form by the power of the souls we command. Once each full moon he drinks the souls we possess and he lives."

Her mind was simultaneously reeling and rejecting what she was hearing. "And you? What happens to you when Anubis takes your soul? I mean, the soul you are living on?"

He shrugged. "I die for a brief time. When the ceremony ends, the god returns the soul to me and to the others, and we live again until the next full moon. When we grow old and the appointed days of the souls we have taken come to an end, Anubis takes the souls and we in turn drink the souls of other tekenues." He smiled at her. "You see, Heret, that is why I say that I know death better than any man. Thou knowest that I live forever, and that is true; but I die for a time each full moon. I know death very well."

"I'm sorry," she said. "None of this makes any sense to me. You say that Anubis is the seven of you, that he exists separately from you, you talk about gods actually coming to life—I mean, actually being visible in physical form—none of this makes any sense." She shook her head in depressed bewilderment. "Very soon I shall awaken, Sekhemib, and I shall be in my own bed in my own home, and all of this will have been a dream, a nightmare. None of this is true. None of this is real."

"What men believe is what is real, Heret." Sekhemib was speaking to her as if she were a particularly slow child. "You people of this age believe only in that which can be measured and seen, and therefore that is all which exists."

"Ridiculous," she muttered in English. In Egyptian she

said, "What is real is what is real. It makes no difference whether you believe it or not." She turned back to Sekhemib. "For thousands of years men believed that the world was flat, but that didn't make it flat."

"The world *is* flat," Sekhemib said simply.

Sighing, she returned her gaze to the North Sea. "Forget it."

Hadji had been leaning back against the cabin door behind them during this exchange, out of earshot. Now he approached them and said, "My lord, behold the city in the distance. That is Brest, of the country called France. We will stop there for a few hours to pick up supplies."

"Yes, Hadji, very good. Take thou the woman and lock her away." To Harriet he said, "Think thou on my words, Heret, for it is not good to die in ignorance." He turned and walked away from them, walking along the deck in a cheerful and sprightly manner.

"Come, woman," Hadji said in English, taking her by the arm. She allowed him to lead her through the cabin door without resistance. What purpose would it serve to resist? she thought. No way out. No way out.

Hadji led her through the stateroom into a small bedroom connected to it. He pushed her roughly down upon the bed and removed a length of rope from the dresser beside the bed. He then bound her ankles together and tied her wrists to the bedpost. He stood back and smiled. "Behave," he admonished, wagging his finger at her, and then left the room, closing and locking the door behind him.

Harriet was too depressed even to struggle against the rope. She lay there, quiet and still in the darkness of the unlighted cabin, as a few stray tears trickled down from her eyes and plopped onto the mattress. "Tommy," she whispered sadly. "Please help me, please . . ." The tears began to flow freely, and she moved instinctively to bring her hand to her face to wipe them away, forgetting about the rope which bound her to the bedpost. She was reminded of her bonds when her arms came to a stop with a sudden jerk.

But wait. Had there been a give in the rope?

She strained her neck to turn and look above her. She tried again to pull her arms away from the bedpost and saw that the ropes were securely tied, but that there was a slight give in the post itself. She pulled again, harder this time, and one of the rails of the headboard snapped free from its position. The old bed, which had in all likelihood been on the decrepit old freighter since its maiden voyage, was rusted and cracked. She pulled again, and another rail moved slightly forward. Again, and the two rails to which she was tied fell forward, striking her on the head.

Her forehead felt bruised, but the pain was eclipsed by the thrill of sudden hope which sprang up in her. Eyeing the locked door nervously, she began to twist her hands around in the knotted ropes until she was able to get her fingers on the knots themselves. Untying them was a long, frustrating process. Minutes passed . . . fifteen minutes . . . a half hour. She pulled the first knot free just as the old freighter slowly moved into its slip in the docking area of the French port. Harriet reached down and began frantically to work on the ropes around her ankles. She untied them in a much shorter time, and then crept quietly across the cabin to the porthole.

Harriet looked out and smiled with relief through her fear and anxiety. There were people out there, real people, not enemies, not murderers, dockworkers shouting and carrying and running to and fro along the wooden walkways. She lifted a trembling hand to the latch of the porthole and moved it to the left. It opened easily, and she pulled the window toward her. It was a small opening, but Harriet would be able to fit through it.

I have to fit, she thought. I *have* to!

She stretched both her arms out before her and pushed them through the porthole. Her shoulders were too wide to fit through, but she pushed and wiggled and wiggled and pushed. Her shoulders eased slowly through, and the steel porthole rim scraped painfully against her breasts. Harriet looked down and saw that there was a six or seven foot expanse of water separating the hull of the freighter from the thick wooden piles which formed the side of the slip. Good, she thought. I'm sure I can make it a few feet in the water to those big logs, even if I can't swim. She pushed against the outside of the ship, trying to throw her weight forward by lifting her legs, which were still inside the cabin, up higher than her torso. She slipped quickly forward as her breasts cleared the rim and then came to a sudden stop as her hips slapped against the circular opening. Damn! she thought.

Harriet continued to wiggle and press, continued to throw her weight forward, and thus made slow and painful progress inch by inch. At last she felt her hips and rump clear the rim and her elation turned into fear as she then plummeted headfirst out of the porthole. She fell for what seemed only a fraction of a second before hitting the icy water.

Harriet lacked the presence of mind to hold her breath. Indeed, her emotional condition was so shaky at the moment that any attempt at holding her breath would have failed. She struggled underwater to climb back up to the surface as she coughed and inhaled the filthy water alternately. When her head broke the surface she was nearly passing out, but desperation gave her a strength which she would not otherwise have possessed, and she flailed her arms and legs desperately in an attempt to draw closer to the wharf. She felt herself failing, however, felt her legs growing numb from the bitter cold, felt her consciousness fading as water and mucus streamed from her mouth and nostrils. Her lungs gulped air and water both as her head bobbed in and out of the water. She tried to cry for help, but no words came forth from her mouth, only more water, more mucus.

Harriet's vision was becoming blurry when she felt a hand grasp her by the arm. Hadji! she cried to herself and tried to focus her eyes on the face before her. She laughed aloud at the bearded Gallic face which was smiling at her and speaking soothingly in French. The man had lowered himself down on a rope and he was holding her arm tightly with one hand as he held on to the rope with the other. In a few moments she felt a tug and looked up to see a group of men leaning over the edge of the slip and watching them as the stevedores began to pull on the rope and hoist Harriet and her rescuer upward.

A multitude of hands grasped her by the arms and waist and lifted her up onto the dock. Their voices blended into a cacophony of concern and cheer, and she wished that she knew enough French to be able to thank them.

Her joy dissipated instantly when she looked at the ship and saw Hadji standing at the rail, screaming at her. She realized that she was not safe, nowhere near safe, as long as either Hadji or Sekhemib knew where she was. She broke free of the supporting hands and ran wildly away from the dock, knowing not where she was running but knowing that she had to put as much distance between her and the ship as possible, as soon as possible. She ran into a few people, knocking them down but not stopping, not speaking, just running madly.

She left the wharf area and entered the industrial morass which was the coastal district of the coastal city. She ignored the angry shouts and jeers which followed her as she ran. Harriet came to a corner and turned, running down the narrow street, plowing through the crowd like the bow of a ship through waves, sending people and possessions sprawling. A hand grabbed her firmly on the shoulder and she fell as her legs continued to move while her upper body was held immobile.

She hit the ground hard and a sharp pain shot up her left side. She looked up into the face of the policeman, who was glowering at her angrily and yelling in French. "I need help, protection," she screamed back at him. "Do you speak English? I need protection." An idea flashed into her mind and she started yelling, "American consulate! Where is the American consulate? Le consul de États-Unis," she said, dredging up words from her high-school French class and forgetting the grammar. "Le consu—la consul—Oh, Christ, American consulate! American consulate!"

The policeman seemed either not to understand her or not to care. He continued to yell at her, shaking her by the shoulders. She tried to pull free from his grip but he tightened his hold on her.

Ahmed Hadji came running up behind her and began screaming at the policeman in what sounded like heavily accented French. Hadji tried to grab Harriet by the arm but the policeman struck his hand away and began to outshout him. Harriet kept pulling, but her strength was not adequate. Then she felt the policeman's grip suddenly loosen and then drop from her shoulders. She was elated until she tried to turn and run and found that she could not move. She looked down, hoping to find the impediment to her motion. There was none.

Sekhemib, she thought with despair.

The priest of Anubis approached them through the crowd, which parted before him, whether by his will or their own volition. He walked over to Harriet, his eyes blazing with anger, and said in the ancient tongue, "Some slaves prove to be more troublesome than others, but any slave can be broken. Thou hast been a trouble to me this day, Heret, and thou shalt be punished." She felt her legs moving and beginning to take her back toward the docks. The policeman stood staring at them, bewildered and angry, and Hadji began to speak to him, saying anything which came into his mind, anything which would end the altercation there and then. Harriet walked beside Sekhemib silently, trying to force her voice to cry out, trying to stop her legs from moving, and failing, failing.

No way out, she thought miserably. Doomed. No way out.

They reached the ship in a few minutes and walked with a silent dignity past the crowd of dockworkers who had just effected her rescue. They yelled and babbled as she and Sekhemib passed, but she could not help but ignore them. Her limbs, her voice, her mind were not her own. They mounted the gangplank and boarded the ship, just as Hadji, panting heavily, ran up behind them. "My lord," he began.

Sekhemib turned on him viciously and struck him across the face. "Did I not command thee to bind the woman? Are even the simplest tasks beyond thine abilities?"

Hadji dropped to his knees and bowed his head. A few drops of blood were oozing from the corner of his lip as he said, "I implore you to forgive me, my lord. I beg my lord's forgiveness."

Sekhemib placed his balled fists on his hips and said, "Take her and bind her, Ahmed Hadji. Fail again, and this life shall be thy last!" Sekhemib turned angrily on his heel and strode quickly away from them. Hadji watched him go with a manner of tremulous obsequiousness.

He rose to his feet and grabbed Harriet around the waist. He kicked open a cabin door and threw her into the cabin, sending her onto the floor with a resounding thud. "You bitch!" he shrieked at her. "I ought to kill you right now!"

"Well, why don't you!" she screamed back at him, her tears beginning to flow afresh. "Don't do me any favors, you greasy son of a bitch!" She got to her feet and swung her fist at him. He deflected the blow with ease and then struck her in the face with a closed fist. Harriet lost consciousness under the impact of the blow, and she awakened shortly thereafter with a terrible throbbing pain at the left hinge of her jaw. Hadji was busily engaged in binding her once again, this time to a heavy wooden table. He had wrapped rope around her ankles, her calves, and her thighs, tying her legs to together from foot to buttocks. He proceeded to tie her wrists behind her back, connect the bonds of her wrists to those of her ankles, and then connect the entire length of rope to the leg of the heavy table.

Hadji stood back and glared at her. "Now listen to me, woman, and listen well. I have devoted my life to the gods in the hopes of defeating death. I have been successful in rescuing Sekhemib and the other immortals from your silly little museum, and soon we will be safe at home in Egypt, where I will receive my reward for my faithful service."

"Congratulations," she spat.

"Shut up! I am warning you, if you do anything else to make my master angry at me, I will make you pay, pay so dearly that death will come as a welcome relief!" He began to pace the room as he yelled at her. "I told him that we had no need of you once we had left your country, I told him that we would be safer if we disposed of you then, but he would not agree. He wants you to be a tekenu, the gods alone know why! And so you still live." He dropped to his knees beside her. "But mark me, woman! If you cause me any further embarrassment, I will present you as a tekenu at the holy place without eyes or tongue, without arms or legs, do you understand me?" He rose swiftly and left her lying on her side. The door slammed loudly behind him.

I was so close, she thought mournfully, so close.

Hours passed and Harriet lay weeping softly. She listened to the sounds of the crew carrying things onto the ship, heard the loud voices calling back and forth in the singsong language of China, broken on occasion by distant sounds of French from the wharf. She was not aware of any sensation of movement when the ship sailed out of the harbor, but the vibrating strain of the engines, which she felt clearly through the wooden floor upon which she was lying, told her of their departure. She waited for Hadji or Sekhemib to come up and release her, but time continued to pass and she was left alone in the dark cabin.

The sun had been down for a long while when she heard the door open and looked up to see Sekhemib enter, followed by Hadji. The latter was carrying a tray which he placed on the table before kneeling down to cut her bonds. When the last of the ropes had been removed, Harriet moved painfully up onto her knees. Her entire body ached and her joints were sore. She gently touched the painful swelling on her jaw and winced as the featherlike touch of her forefinger sent a jolt of pain shooting across her face. She reached up and placed her hand flat upon the tabletop and slowly pushed herself up onto her feet. Then she looked defiantly at Sekhemib.

He pointed at the tray which Hadji had placed on the table. "Eat," he commanded her. Then he turned and walked out with Hadji in tow. The door slammed behind them.

Harriet looked at the door wistfully for a moment and then turned her attention to the food upon the table. Rice and fish and a bottle of some nondescript asian beer. The beer was warm. The rice and fish were cold. She ate and drank anyway.

When she was done she walked over to the door and tried the knob. To her surprise, it had not been locked from outside. She opened it and walked out onto the deck, pulling the collar of her blouse closed against the chilly night air. She heard the gulls crying in the distance and saw the lights of Brest fading far beyond the stern of the ship.

Sekhemib approached her slowly, seeming to appear gradually out of the darkness. He had wrapped a woolen robe around himself and looked for all the world like a bedouin. He walked up to her and stared at her. She felt her knees grow weak and her heart flutter under his penetrating gaze. My God, she thought, he terrifies me! All the foolish hopes of escape and freedom had left her, replaced only by fear and trepidation, fear so intense that it drowned out even her deep depression.

He stared at her long and hard for a few minutes and then abruptly turned to look out to sea. He leaned his forearms against the railing and put his weight on them, bending the knee of one leg and lounging forward casually. "Thou hast angered me," he said, but he did not sound angry.

"I know," she replied in a monotone. "What do you expect from me, that I should go smiling to my death?"

He shook his head slowly from side to side. "No, Heret, no. Thou strivest to live, and that is what all things which live strive to do." His voice carried a hint of something, regret perhaps, or sorrow.

She looked at his face and thought she saw him frown slightly, but it was not an angry frown, it was a sad one. "Must you kill?" she asked softly. "All those innocent people, all those innocent lives snuffed out. Can you not give up your life so that others might live?"

He glanced at her impatiently. "Art thou willing to give up thy life so that Meret might live? Thou speakest foolishness, Heret."

"No, for it is my life, not hers. Do I not have a right to my own life? Do not we all have the right to live?"

Sekhemib did not answer. He stared intently out at the black undulations of the waves and the winds. At last he said in a soft, dreamy voice, "When Zoser ruled in Egypt in the days before the pyramids were built, Meret and I lived in a small daub and wattle hut near the Nile, not far from the village which would later become Thebes. We had grown weary of opulence, bored with the purposeless and uninteresting pursuit of pleasure, tired of being served. So we decided to go down unto the common people and live in their manner for a while." He smiled. "It was all a game, a form of play."

"Marie Antoinette's sheep," she muttered.

"What?"

"A queen of—of the country we just left," she explained wearily. "She liked to play at being a simple peasant girl as a diversion."

"Precisely. A diverson. Yuya and Senmut thought we were mad, but they just laughed as we went our ways. We always returned for the ceremonies, of course, but we lived out many years in happy peacefulness in the hut. I fished in the Nile and Meret ground the grain into flour, and we laughed at the naked children playing on the bank of the river."

He turned and faced her. "But we had to leave, we had to return to the temple and the palace in the wilderness. We must treat the people—the mortals, the tekenues—as animals awaiting slaughter, Heret, or else we would weaken and die forever. Life feeds on death. It has always been so, from the lion devouring the gazelle to the human devouring the lamb. He cannot love the lamb, the lion cannot love the gazelle. The beloved of Anubis cannot feel the pain of the tekenu. It must be so."

Harriet began to weep again, but forced herself to restrain her tears. "But I want to live, Sekhemib. I want to live! I am not an animal, I am a human being."

"Thou are a mortal," he said firmly, "I feel some affection for thee, Heret, but it is the affection one feels for a pet. It would be easier if thou wert a dumb beast, not knowing what awaited thee, but thou art not."

"Then why are you taking me with you? You can find your damned tekenues in Egypt. Why not kill me now, or let me go?"

He closed his eyes for a moment and then said, "I have told thee that we partake of some aspect of the mortals whose souls we drink. I want my Meret to drink thy soul when we come unto the holy place in Egypt." He turned back toward the sea and leaned over the railing, crossing his right leg over his left. "Women were not like unto thee in old times. I wish thy soul to nourish my Meret."

Harriet looked at Sekhemib's position. He had put all of his weight on his left leg and was leaning far over the railing. A mad impulse seized her, impelling her to an act of desperation. She dropped quickly to her knees and grabbed Sekhemib firmly around the knees. He was momentarily startled, but that moment was all she needed to push herself up onto her feet, causing him to fall forward over the railing.

Sekhemib cried, "Hadji! Hadji!" as he fought to retain the

grip his right hand had on the railing. Harriet began to pound his hand with her fists, but he was able to wrap his left hand around the railing also. She raised her fist to strike at him, but he was once again in control. Her hand stopped moving in midair and she stood frozen.

Sekhemib climbed back up over the railing as Hadji came running up to him. "My lord!" he asked breathlessly. "What—"

"Assemble the crew!" Sekhemib shouted between clenched teeth. "Now!" As Hadji scampered away, Sekhemib released Harriet from her paralysis. His eyes seemed to glow with fury. "I had forgiven thee for thine attempt to flee, but for this thou shalt not be forgiven. Stiff-necked slave!" He struck her hard across the mouth, sending her sprawling onto the deck, waves of pain radiating from her already injured jaw. "Rise up!" he hissed. She struggled against his will, but in the end she complied, and she walked unsteadily in the direction his mind caused her feet to follow. They walked down the steps to the cargo loading area of the ship, which was at the moment devoid of all cargo save the crates of supplies which had been loaded at Brest. The Chinese crew had been summoned by the captain at Hadji's request, and they were come in ones and twos from all over the ship. They milled about, confused and cold.

Harriet felt herself walking forward even after Sekhemib stopped. She moved, trancelike, into the middle of the cargo deck and then stopped abruptly. She heard Sekhemib's voice whispering in her mind. "A slave must be punished in order to be taught, Heret. It is yet a long way to Egypt. Learn well thy lesson!"

Harriet fought to control her limbs, but the will of the ancient priest was so much more powerful than her own that her efforts did not in the slightest impede the directions he was sending to her arms and hands. She clenched her eyes shut as her fingers moved beneath the bottom of her sweater and slowly pulled it up over her head. The sweater was tossed away, and then she felt her fingers move to her back. She unhooked her bra and then pulled the straps down from her shoulders. The bra fell to the deck, and a murmur of delight and appreciation arose from the assembled crew as her pendulous breasts came into view. She struggled all the while to prevent her hands from following the commands of Sekhemib, but she was able to offer absolutely no effective resistance. Her nipples contracted painfully as the cold sea wind smote them. She tried to will herself into unconsciousness, tried to sever her mind and sensations and awareness from what she was doing, or rather from what she was being forced to do. But this too was of no avail. Though her eyes were closed, she remained miserably aware of each and every movement of her limbs.

She felt her hands reach up and cup her breasts in a horrid parody of seductive manipulation, felt them squeeze and knead the soft flesh, felt them tweak and pull on the light brown nipples. She fought to restrain the tears which were gathering beneath her eyelids as the sounds of laughter and vulgar appraisal reached her ears from the dozens of unwashed men who surrounded her. She failed in this as well, and the salty liquid began to pour freely from her eyes.

Her hands pulled open the snap on the front of her dungarees and then pulled down the zipper. She bent over as she pulled the dungarees down around her ankles and then stepped out of them. She felt her hands pulling down her underpants, felt her right foot step out of them, felt her left foot kick them away. She stood naked upon the deck in the midst of the crew, and she heard the lewd cackle of Ahmed Hadji's laughter above the excited chuckles which came from all around her.

Still her eyes were shut, still she attempted to remove herself mentally from the situation, still she failed. She fell backward onto the deck and her soft flesh slapped noisily upon the cold wood. She felt her legs bend at the knees and then move upward, spreading widely apart as they moved. She felt her hands caress her vulva, felt them pulling her labial petals deftly apart, felt them move up and down within the moist entrance to her womb. Then she felt her hands fall numbly to her sides as she lay motionless and exposed.

God, she thought, God, God . . .

Sekhemib lifted his arm slowly and pointed down at the pitiful creature which lay motionless upon her back, motionless but for the terrified trembling which racked her frame. "Take her!" he commanded loudly in the ancient language.

The crew did not understand the words, but the gesture and the condition of the woman made clear the meaning. They pounced on her like a pack of wolves falling upon a wounded fawn.

# CHAPTER 14

▲ It was difficult to say which form of life was the dominant one on the streets of Cairo, human or insect. They both seemed to buzz about ubiquitously, incessantly, in numbers so vast as to startle even the most worldly-wise urbanite. There are times in any large metropolis when the streets are filled with people and other times when the city streets are relatively quiet, but not so in Cairo. One can stroll down Wall Street in New York City early in the morning and revel in the quiet seclusion amid the towering buildings; a stroll along the Strand in London in the wee hours of Sunday morning affords a peaceful respite from the hustle and bustle of the city; when the cafés of the left bank area of Paris finally close their doors and shutters to keep out the rays of the rising sun, there is peace; even that street of permanent carnival, the Kurfürstendamm in Berlin, slumbers at last as the first solar rays touch the broken steeple of the Kaiser Wilhelm Church; but Cairo never rests, Cairo never sleeps. As if from some vast subterranean hold, the city vomits forth people and insects and dogs and cats and birds incessantly, hour after hour, day after day, an endless line of humanity surrounded by an endless array of animal life, constantly moving and shouting and buzzing and filling the narrow medieval streets with the crowded boisterousness of permanent activity.

By any standard but that of Egypt, Cairo is an old city. When it was founded in A.D. 969 by the Fatimid general Juahar, London and Paris were mud holes, nomads still fished in the Moskva River, and the Manahatta Indians still hunted wild turkeys along the banks of the Hudson. When the world's most important Moslem university was founded three years later in the great mosque of El Azhar, Berlin was still a collection of wooden huts, Vienna was a border town and the illiterate Scandinavians were still trying to decide if Odin or Christ was the more powerful deity. When the great citadel of Saladin—the great tower which still affords a commanding view of the sprawling metropolis—was built in 1179, most of Holland was still under water, and the rulers of England were still French-speaking vikings.

By the standards of general humanity, Cairo is old; but by the standards of Egypt, it is a parvenu, a recent arrival, a possibly temporary place of congregation for Egypt's teeming millions. Just south of Cairo are the ruins of the ancient capital of Memphis, which was old when the first alphabet was imported to Europe; just north of Cairo are the ruins of On, which the Greeks called Heliopolis, which was old when Memphis was young; just west of Cairo are the great pyramids of Giza, which were old before the Europeans had the wheel. The ruins of the ancient past surround Cairo, reminding the Cairenes that their city is young in the annals of mankind.

Like all Middle Eastern cities, Cairo grew erratically and irrationally. There is no city center per se, though the area around the palaces of the defunct dynasty of Mehemet Ali Pasha serve as a central reference point. A few Western-inspired skyscrapers thrust up oddly from the midst of the squat nineteeth-century buildings which house businesses, government offices, hashish houses, whore houses, and millions of people. The address numbers and street names follow no logical sequence, and a foreigner in Cairo for the first time is hard pressed to find anything for which he is looking without paying the exorbitant fees charged by the cab drivers and street urchins who derive so large a portion of their livelihoods from the confusion and chaos which is Cairo.

Of course, the amount of money that was sufficient to feed an Egyptian family for a week was merely pocket money for the Earl of Selwyn. He, Thomas Sawhill, and Samuel Goldhaber had not even finished unpacking their bags at the Cairo Hilton when Roderick had begun to make inquiries as to the location of the offices of the National Institute of Reclamation. Neither the desk clerk nor the bellboy had ever heard of it, but that was not surprising. Given the true nature and purpose of the organization, it was not to be expected that its activities would be highly publicized.

As Roderick and Thomas Sawhill sat in their hotel suite trying to work out a course of action, Sam went out and enlisted the assistance of a sun-baked, half-naked, lice-ridden ragamuffin whose sole appellation seemed to be the given name Faz. Sam had no difficulty finding this local assistant, for he had not walked ten feet outside the hotel before he was surrounded by a throng of begging children. Faz was the loudest and the most aggressive, and Sam decided that he would serve the purpose well.

He took Faz into the outdoor café beside the hotel and bought him a bowl of soup and a soft drink. He smiled kindly at the boy, feeling a bit sad at the type of life the child must be living. Faz was obviously part of the vast underclass of Egyptian society, and the grinning, bright-eyed boy was, Sam knew, destined to a life of poverty, hard labor, malnourishment, disease, and early death. He forced himself to remember that this was the fate of the overwhelming bulk of the human race and quickly squelched any urges to take the child permanently under his wing.

He waited until the boy had finished eating before beginning to explain what he wanted, knowing that the boy's attention would be riveted on the food anyway. When the last drop of soup had been licked from the bowl and the last bit of Coca-Cola had been consumed, Faz sat back contentedly and said in his gutter Arabic, "Effendi is kind and generous. Allah will bless him."

"That is my hope," Sam replied. His knowledge of Arabic was deep, but like most scholars, his familiarity was restricted to its classic form, and he knew that he sounded as strange to the boy as the boy sounded to him. But language is but a medium for expression, and as long as each understood the other the differences were of no importance. "But now you must assist me, and for your assistance you shall be well paid."

"I am your servant, effendi," the boy said eagerly, his eyes lighting up at the thought of payment. This will probably be the best job the boy will ever have, Sam thought sadly.

"Faz, I need for you to locate an address for me and possibly to watch the people who come and go at that address, but you must do this without anyone knowing that you are doing it. It is very important that no one sees you or suspects you. Can you manage to do this?"

"Of course, effendi!" he replied proudly. "I have lived by my wits all my life. I once picked the pocket of a policeman as he was arresting me for picking pockets, and I bribed him with his own money!"

Sam repressed a chuckle. "Good. My friends and I are seeking the National Institute of Reclamation, which is said to be somewhere on the street of the potters, but we cannot find this street." He reached into his pocket and took out some of the large, tissuey paper money of the country. He peeled off five bills and handed them to Faz. "Here is five pounds. When you bring me the information I need, when you lead my friends and me to this institute, I will give you another five pounds, and if we need you to spy for us you will be paid yet again. Agreed?"

Faz was almost salivating over the money. Five Egyptian pounds translated into only $3.75 in American currency, but it was a small fortune to a child in a land where the per capita income was only $600 per year. "Allah has truly looked down with kindness upon this miserable servant," the child cackled gleefully. "May Allah bless effendi in all his generations."

Sam smiled at the poetry in the mouths of even the most uneducated in this part of the world. "Now listen carefully, Faz. You must find the National Institute of Reclamation on the street of the potters and then return here. Tell the man at the desk that you have information for a man named Selwyn."

"Al-sewin," he repeated imperfectly.

"Close enough. I will tell him to call me when you return. Now be off, and go quickly." He had not yet finished his sentence when the boy leaped from his chair and scurried off into the human sea which thronged the street before the café.

Sam tossed a few coins onto the tabletop to pay for the boy's meal and then returned to the hotel, forcing himself to ignore the legion of children who followed him. It would be unwise to become known as an easy touch, for clandestine operation would be made rather difficult if he were followed everywhere by a crowd of beggars. He entered the hotel lobby and walked over to the desk. The desk clerk smiled at him. "Back so soon, Mister Goldhaber?"

"Yes. Listen, sometime today a little boy, a street boy, will come with information for the Earl of Selwyn. Please admit him and call us immediately."

"My pleasure, sir," the clerk said, forcing a smile. The prospect of an unwashed urchin in the lobby of his precious hotel was not a pleasant one; but the fees and gratuities which would be provided by a British nobleman outweighed the distaste the desk clerk felt for his social inferiors. "I shall call your suite immediately when the child arrives."

"Thank you," Sam said, and went over to the elevator. As he waited for the doors to swish open he reflected briefly upon the incredible economic inequity of the so-called developing countries. The world which he knew, even the luxurious/world of this hotel building, was as far from the imagination of a child like Faz as was possible.

He told the elevator boy his floor number after he entered the elevator and stood quietly as they began the slow ascent. He exited the elevator and walked quickly to the door to their room, entering to find Roderick on the phone to room service and Sawhill pacing nervously back and forth in front of the window. Sawhill turned expectantly when he heard Sam enter. "Well?"

"I hired a spy," he said, smiling. "A street kid named Faz. He's off trying to find the institute right now, and I think he has enough savvy and street sense to do it without arousing any suspicion."

"Good, good," Sawhill said. He reached into his shirt pocket and took out a pack of cigarettes.

"I thought you gave them up years ago."

"I did," Sawhill muttered as he lighted one. "Ten years ago." He offered no explanation as to why he has resumed the habit, but Sam could guess.

"I've sent for some victuals," Roderick said. "This bloody hotel has no menus in the rooms, so I told the clerk to use his own judgment. God knows what we'll get." He walked to the window and looked out at the sprawling city. "Horrible place, Cairo. It's hard to believe that my ancestor the ninth Earl spent years here."

"It was probably worse then than it is now," Sam remarked. "We at least have air-conditioning and running water in this hotel."

"Yeah, yeah," Sawhill said impatiently. "What will we do when we find out where the institute is?" He was in no mood for small talk or casual conversation. He had been a nervous wreck for the past week, ever since Interpol had contacted them to inform them about the incident in the French port city of Brest. It had taken a very imaginative and thoughtful European police officer to make the connection between the Liberian freighter, the American woman, the diminutive Arab dispensing bribes right and left, and the urgent report sent to them by the Greenfield Town Council through the FBI about the kidnapping of Harriet Langly. Even now there was no certainty that she was the woman who had been involved in the strange altercation with the gendarme; but the sudden loss of control by the policeman over his own body was enough to convince Sawhill that Sekhemib had been there. The American knew from personal experience what it was like to have self-control wrenched away by the will of the ancient priest.

Sam did not reply to Sawhill's question immediately. Instead, he reached into his suitcase, which still lay open but unpacked upon one of the beds, and took out a pile of clothes. "The first thing we're going to do is dress differently. Here." He tossed one folded garment to Roderick and a second to Sawhill. "I picked these up at the airport tourist shop."

Roderick held the garment by the top and allowed it to unfold itself downward. "Oh, I say! Local clothing?"

"Yes," Sam said. "It's called a galabia. Local style of kaftan. We can't very well walk around in Western clothes and expect not to be noticed."

Roderick held the simple eggshell-colored galabia up against his body and appraised himself in the mirror which hung above the bureau. Noticing his fair hair, he shook his head. "I don't know if this will make much difference."

"Better than nothing," Sam pointed out.

"Okay, okay, so we wear kaftans. Then what? What will we do when we find out where the institute is?" Sawhill repeated tensely.

The search thus far had been a long series of frustrations and false trails. It had taken them days back in the United States to get the necessary visas, and Sawhill became almost hysterical when he found that his passport had lapsed the year before. Another day was wasted renewing it. Another day and a half was taken up by the flight from New York to Cairo, with everything from the traffic on the Major Deegan Expressway to the backed-up air traffic over Kennedy Airport seeming to conspire against them.

When they finally reached Cairo for the first time, they found that the official address for the institute was a warehouse near the wharves, empty, deserted, and apparently never really used. It had taken them more time to learn of the institute's location on the street of the potters, but they could then find no clue as to the location of that street. A false report to the

effect that the ship had docked at Port Said led them to leave
Cairo and travel north, where they were further diverted to
Alexandria by yet another false report. After thus wasting
precious time, they had returned to Cairo this morning,
realizing at last that in this world of baksheesh and circumben-
dibus a local guide and confederate was a necessity, not a
luxury. And so Sam had found Faz.

As Sawhill pulled the galabia over his head, he asked,
"Well?"

"What will we do?" Sam said. "We have a number of
courses of action open to us. We can try to work with the
authorities and get arrest warrants—"

"And get ourselves locked away as lunatics," Roderick
finished for him. "Next option?"

"We can use force, abduct someone of importance at the
institute and hold him as an exchange for Harriet."

"No, that's no good," Sawhill muttered. "We don't have
any weapons, and buying any here would be next to impossible. We'd land in jail, and I for one have no desire to see the
inside of a Middle Eastern prison. Besides, I don't think that
human life means very much to these people. We can't coerce
them by kidnapping one of them."

"And I doubt that any sort of force would be effective
against Sekhemib," Roderick added, "considering his rather
unusual mental abilities."

"You have a gift for understatement," Sam said. "I know.
I've been thinking about this and I've rejected both of these
options."

"So?" Sawhill asked. "What should we do? I know I should
have a plan of my own worked out, but I just can't think
straight."

"I know, Tom," Sam said kindly. "It's hard to keep the
mind working logically in the middle of all this insanity. But I
have an idea."

"Shoot," Sawhill said.

"Well, when Faz returns with the information, I think
Roderick should go there and pose as, say, an antique dealer
with antiquities he might be willing to sell to the institute."

"Fine with me," Roderick commented, "but what purpose
would that serve?"

"I'm not sure, really. But you might be able to pick up
something of use, some information which might help us
locate their real center of operation."

Sawhill frowned. "Sam, that isn't much of a plan!"

"That isn't all of it, either." He sat down in the large overstuffed chair which stood beside the table. "This little fellow is willing and able to spy for us. Interpol told Jasper that the institute's chairman is named—what was the name again?"

"Haftoori," Roderick said, consulting a small notebook which he pulled from his pocked. "Haleel Haftoori."

"Right, Haftoori. If we can locate Haftoori, we can eventually locate the others because he is the head honcho of this cult of theirs. We have Faz follow him and get word to us when he leaves Cairo. Then we follow him to Harriet."

"But what if he doesn't leave Cairo?" Sawhill asked plaintively. "What if this holy place Hadji talked about is right here someplace? We could be sitting in front of his home, waiting for him to leave, while he's killing Harriet in his living room!"

"No, Tom, it can't be like that. Hadji's holy place has to be somewhere old, a lot older than Cairo or Alexandria or any of the other major cities here. None of them go back to ancient times. All the ancient cities are in ruins, and if there is an ancient holy place, it must be either somewhere in the ruins or somewhere out in the desert. That's where he's going to have to go."

"And what if he already has?" Roderick asked. "What if his presence isn't necessary for the cult to do whatever the hell they do? What if he isn't even part of the cult, what if he's just an ignorant figurehead? There are a lot of ifs involved, Sam."

"I know," he nodded, "and if any of them are correct, then we've failed, and Harriet is lost."

There was a depressing and ominous finality about these last few words, and the three men were silent for a few moments. Roderick broke the quiet at last by saying, "Well, I suppose we have to operate under the assumption that none of the ifs are correct. But I must say that I can't see much purpose in my posing as an antique dealer. That is to say, we don't want to attract attention to ourselves, do we?"

"He's right there, Sam," Sawhill agreed. "Hadji has seen him. We can't let any of them know that we're here. And another thing: say that your little friend does lead us to Haftoori, and he in turn does lead us to Harriet. Then what?"

Sam was getting annoyed. "Look, if either of you has a better idea, I'm willing to listen to it."

"Well," Roderick said, "I'd have to say this: The plan is

good up until the point at which we locate Miss Langly, but Tom is correct in asking what we would do then. I think that if we're willing to take as many risks as we will be taking, we should be willing to risk being arrested for weapons possession as well."

"Roderick," Sam said patiently, "to buy a weapon in a country like this—"

"Sam, please listen. I don't claim to be conversant with the underworld in any way, but I've seen enough on the telly to know that if you have enough money, which we do, you can get anything you want in a city. In Cairo everything's for sale— drugs, women, everything." He leaned forward. "And that includes weapons."

"Yes, but guns don't have any effect on Sekhemib," Sam protested. "At least that's what the scroll indicates, and it's been right about everything else."

"But Sekhemib is only one of our problems. Hadji isn't invulnerable. Neither are the other people in this cult of his. If we find Miss Langly, it isn't likely that Sekhemib will be guarding her. With guns we have a chance."

"And how do you propose to get them?" Sam asked. "Walk around the streets trying to find the criminal element? Come on!"

"Sam, if Faz can find the institute, he can find weapons," Sawhill said. "Of course. Why didn't I think of this?" He slapped Roderick familiarly on the back. "Good idea, good idea. I'll bet that little kid knows enough about this city to get us anything we want. You asked him to find the institute, and he agreed. If you'd asked him to get us drugs or whores or guns, I'll bet he would've agreed just as readily."

"Listen, Tom, just because the kid knows his way around the streets of the city doesn't mean he knows how to procure weapons. I know my way around Manhattan pretty well, but I don't have the foggiest notion, I wouldn't even know how to *begin* to buy illegal weapons."

"No need to speculate," Roderick said. "When he comes back with the information, we can ask him. If we are all agreed about getting weapons, I mean."

"I think it's a great idea," Sawhill said. "Sam?"

He shrugged. "Okay, okay, I'll go along with it. But we may just wind up in prison."

A knock was heard on the door. "That must be the food," Roderick said eagerly, springing to his feet and going to the door. He opened it to admit the steward, who pushed a roll table before him into the room. Roderick stuffed a few bills into the delighted man's hands, in his ignorance giving him an astronomical tip, and quickly ushered him out of the room. He lifted the silver covers on the plates and trays and sniffed happily at the food. "Such a pleasant surprise!" he said cheerfully. "Roast beef, fried potatoes, vegetables, brandy, sweets—I was half expecting some exotically disgusting garbage."

"More food there than the average Egyptian sees in a week," Sam muttered, thinking of Faz.

"Come on, Sam," Sawhill said as he pulled a chair up to the table and unwrapped the napkin which had been folded around a fork and knife, "dig in. We're all going to need our strength."

Sam acquiesced grumpily. There was enough of the old unreconstructed political radical left in him from his college days all those decades ago to give him a pang of guilt at this largess while the teeming millions swarmed, underfed and undernourished, all around the hotel. He sat down with noticeable ill grace and began to pick at the food. Roderick, of course, needed no encouragement. He attacked his food as if he had not eaten for days.

After eating they sat about the room nervously, hoping that little Faz would contact them soon. Sawhill smoked cigarette after cigarette as he paced back and forth before the window. Roderick watched television, switching the channel selector around and around until he at last found something in English, an old *Beverly Hillbillies* being shown with Arabic subtitles. Sam did nothing but sit and gaze at the ceiling, occasionally closing his eyes as if in sleep, but never sleeping.

Hours passed before the phone rang. "Selwyn," Roderick said into the receiver. "Are you there?" He paused and then smiled. "Ah, good. Please escort him up to our suite. No, no, please just bring him up. Thank you." He hung up and turned to Sam. "The fellow at the desk didn't seem too eager to have your friend in his hotel."

"I think they're very class-conscious around here," Sam explained. "Most of the Egyptian middle class was part of the lower class not that long ago, and the division between classes means quite a bit to them. It probably bothers the desk clerk to think that his grandfather probably looked like that little kid when he was a child."

"Really!" Roderick said. "Remarkable."

"Not really, Roderick. You must remember that this whole area of the world, except for Israel, is just entering the twentieth century, and the process is creating a good deal of social disruption and social tension. The Shah of Iran, for example, found—"

A knock on the door stopped his lecture, and Thomas Sawhill was grateful. The last thing he felt like listening to was a declamation on modernization in the Third World.

Roderick opened the door to find a disgruntled bellhop standing beside an incredibly filthy little boy. The child was gazing around him with the wide-eyed, openmouthed wonder to which only the unsophistication of childhood allows full expression. Sam smiled at him and said in Arabic, "Faz, come in, come in." He looked at the bellhop. "Thank you. That will be all."

Faz walked hesitantly into the center of the room as the door closed behind him. "Effendi, you must be a king to live thus!" the boy gasped.

"You're close," Sam said. He pointed at Roderick. "This man is an English lord."

Faz stared at Roderick with awe, and Roderick, who of course did not understand the exchange, asked, "What the devil is he staring at, Sam?"

"You. I just told him you were a nobleman."

"Ask him, Sam!" Sawhill demanded. "Ask him!"

Sam returned to Arabic and said, "We have waited eagerly for you, Faz. Have you found the institute I told you to look for?"

"Oh, yes, effendi, that was easy. I can lead you there whenever you wish. It is not far from here, no more than two hours."

That would make it on the other side of the city, Sam thought. The boy has a peculiar concept of distance. "Good, Faz, very good." He turned to Sawhill and Roderick and said in English, "He's found it."

"Great!" Sawhill. "Now ask him about the guns."

"Tom, I don't know if—"

"Please, Sam," Roderick said. "We can't go against these people unarmed. Ask him, please."

Sam shrugged and turned back to the child. "Faz, I need more help from you. I am going to need you to spy on someone for me, as I said, but I also need to know if you can get us some things which the law says we may not have. We—"

"Very simple, effendi," the boy broke in, "very easy. You want hashish or opium?"

"No, no, Faz, you don't under—"

"Want girls? I can get you girls, very young, very pretty."

"Faz, be quiet and listen!" The boy, cowed, closed his mouth tightly and stared at Sam with a childish expression of rapt attention. Sam could not help but laugh as he said, "We need weapons, guns. Do you know of anyone who might be able to help us? I don't expect that you—"

"Guns? Guns? No problem, effendi. You want sarineet-shpeesuhl?" It took Sam a moment to realize that the boy was saying "Saturday night special," the term apparently having entered into the general vocabulary of the streets around the world. "You want maybe Kalishnikovs? Shotguns? Any gun you want, effendi, I can get for you."

"Well?" Sawhill asked impatiently. "What did he say?"

"He says he can get weapons for us," Sam said, "but I don't know if I believe him." In Arabic, he asked, "Tell me where you will get the guns."

Faz shrugged. "From my brother Khalid."

"Yes, okay, but where will he get them?"

"Oh, effendi, there are many places. Palestinians left much here when they left, and many people took rifles and bullets and hand grenades. Many other groups of people—the Copts, the mullah people—have secret stashes of weapons which I can steal or Khalid can steal. We can rob the police—"

"Faz, hold it! I don't want you to rob the police!"

"But why, effendi? I rob the police all the time. The army is easy to rob too. You want maybe bazookas?"

Sam bowed and shook his head. "And we sell this country armaments," he muttered.

"Can he do it?" Sawhill asked. "Do you think he's telling the truth?"

"Unfortunately, I think he is."

"But that's good, Sam," Roderick said. "Why does it seem to bother you?"

He sighed. "What kind of world is this where a little boy can get hold of guns and drugs and whores?"

Sawhill leaned forward. "It's the kind of world where dead men walk and innocent people are killed and kidnapped. Now tell him to get us guns!"

Sam's dislike of the situation did not blind him to the logic, and he shook his head sadly. To Faz he said, "Now, listen. We will need handguns and rifles and much ammunition. How much money will you need? You can include a fee for your help in the amount."

The child did some quick mental calculation. He could neither read nor write, but he knew the value of things on the enormous black market. "I think maybe fifty pounds for each weapon, another fifty pounds for the ammunition. Say four hundred pounds, effendi, to be safe?"

"Four hundred pounds—" he turned to Roderick and said in English, "He says four hundred Egyptian pounds, but that's only about three hundred bucks. You can't buy three rifles and three pistols for such a small amount of money."

"Maybe you can here," Sawhill said. "Don't forget, we're paying thirty dollars a day for a suite of rooms. Where will he get the weapons?"

Sam sighed. "Apparently he's going to steal them."

"Then he's getting them for free, and the fifty pounds is clear profit. It sounds good to me. How about you, Roderick?"

"As long as we get the guns, I don't care what they cost. Shall I give him the money now?"

"Give him half," Sam said. "I like the little guy, but we may never see him again." To Faz he said in Arabic, "We will give you two hundred pounds now, and the rest when we get the guns. Is that all right?"

Faz grinned happily. "Wonderful, effendi, wonderful. I will go to the river and find Khalid, and—"

"But first you must take us to the institute I asked you to find. After that you tell your brother to get the weapons, and then I want you to come back to the institute where we will wait for you. I will need you to keep a close watch on the people who come and go from the institute. You may need help, so get some friends. We will pay them, as well as we pay you."

"Yes, effendi! That will put them in my debt!" He smiled.

Yes, Sam thought, and doubtless make them willing to fork over to you that percentage of their fee which you intend to extort from them. The world is a sewer. "Come, let us go to the street of the potters."

"Immediately, effendi!" the boy chirped as he sprang to his feet.

Roderick heaved himself up from his chair and joined Sawhill, who was already pacing tensely in front of the door of the hotel room. They had not understood the last words spoken by Sam to the child, but when Faz bounded over to the door they both felt a surge of anticipation, as if all the days wasted in Egypt and in the U.S. were at last about to be followed by action. Harriet Langly's face, her smile, the smell of her hair, drifted constantly about in Sawhill's mind. He clenched and unclenched his fists obsessively.

Faz led the three men on what was almost a travel backward through time as they followed him deep into the labyrinthine streets of the oldest section of the city of Cairo. It was easy to imagine, walking down the narrow stone streets, that it was the tenth century still. The smell of excrement, sweat, and stagnation mingled oddly with the delicate aroma of burning incense, the scent of a hundred different spices making palatable the varieties of foods which were being cooked, the perfumes and essences which graced the carefully concealed flesh of the shrouded women who walked barefoot or sandaled along the cobblestones. This was the face of Cairo which was turned from the world, and from which in turn the world turned its face. Medieval Cairo, a city combining elements of charm and desperation, tradition and misery, simplicity most pristine and poverty most abject: old men struggling along on bandy legs; young women giggling to each other furtively from behind their veils; workers carrying heavy bundles borne upon muscles glistening with sweat; old women trudging on in slow, numb steps, their faces cracked and wrinkled with years, decades, a lifetime of unspoken sorrows and unrelenting labor; crowds of bitter and hostile young men who roamed about seeking whipping boys upon whom to vent their rage; beggars pleading for food and money; cripples lying helpless against old walls imploring alms for the love of Allah; the barking of undernourished dogs; the incessant buzzing of flies and gnats—old Cairo. Surveying the crooked streets and the sweltering mass of humanity, one could almost imagine that not far from there Saladin was making ready to ride north and engage Richard the Lion-Hearted in battle over the fate of Jerusalem.

Sam Goldhaber was filled with a sense of time, a sense of history, as he followed the little boy through the maze. Roderick Fowles held his nose expressively. Thomas Sawhill saw nothing but Harriet's face.

"It is here, effendi," Faz said happily, as they came to a stop in front of a basket shop and the boy pointed proudly down a narrow alley which terminated in a simple mud-brick building with a single door and no windows.

"That's it, apparently," Sam said to his companions.

"No wonder we couldn't find it ourselves," Roderick muttered. "It doesn't even have an address on it, or a sign of any kind."

"Course not," Sawhill said. "They're not going to advertise their location. The less anyone knows about them, the better off they are."

"Sure." Sam squinted his eyes and looked down the dark alley. "The only reason they're registered with the government at all is probably to avoid any sort of complications when the regimes change."

"What do you mean?" Roderick asked.

"Well, despite what our government tells us, Egypt is not a particularly stable country. Whenever a regime is overthrown in one of these countries, any person or group which is in any way suspicious is usually targeted for attack in the general free-for-all which follows. It's a perfect front for their cult. A nationalist organization devoted to the return of national art work stolen by the West over the years." He laughed grimly. "No regime, right wing or left wing, could do other than applaud their intentions. A perfect front."

"Well, Roderick coughed, his delicate nostrils still not accustomed to the powerful smell of the city, "now that we're here, what shall we do?"

"I still think that you should go in and see what's to be seen," Sam said.

"Sam, I hate to be so contrary, but I can't see what—"

"Wait!" Sawhill broke in. "Look. Someone's coming."

Sam grabbed Sawhill by the arm, saying, "We can't be seen here. We stick out like sore thumbs on this street."

"Into this shop, quickly!" Sawhill said, moving tensely into the small basket shop and pulling Roderick behind him. They stood motionless in the shadow afforded by the canopy which hung low over the piles of woven reed baskets which rested in lopsided heaps on either side of the door. The old man who tended the shop began to babble to them excitedly, pushing basket after basket in front of their faces. Roderick reached into his pocket and withdrew some paper money. He peeled off a bill and thrust it into the old man's hand and then gestured for him to be quiet. The old man flashed them a toothless grin and retired to the back of the shop.

They watched as a very old man hobbled slowly out of the shadows of the alley, his back slightly bent in what at first seemed to be an arthritic stoop but which they soon realized was an attempt at a permanent bow of obsequiousness in the direction of his companion. They watched as another man, tall and straight, emerged from the dim recesses of the alley.

"Sekhemib!" Sam whispered. "My God! It's unbelievable."

"I know it is. But it's true." Sawhill's body was tense and rigid, and only the knowledge that the ancient priest could paralyze him with a glance restrained him from springing forward upon him and beating him into a bloody pulp. "Why so surprised, Sam?" he asked between teeth clenched so tightly that his jaw began to ache. "You knew what we were here to find."

"Yes, but I'd never actually seen him, except for a glimpse of a face through the back window of that van of theirs." He shook his head as he watched a living, breathing proof of what for him had been until this moment an abstraction, as the bizarre, unreal situation ceased to be a belief or an idea and became a physical presence, a living danger, a monstrous reality. "Three thousand five hundred years old! And alive!"

"Older than that," Roderick commented, "in all likelihood."

"Can we follow them without being seen?" Sam asked.

"We have to follow them, whether they see us or not," Sawhill replied. "We may never have a chance to find that creature again, and he's the one who can lead us to Harriet."

Sam turned to the little boy who had been listening in curious incomprehension to the alien conversation, and said in Arabic, "Faz, these are the people we must follow, but we fear that we may lose them in the crowds or be seen by them. You must follow them also and continue to follow them even if we cannot. Do you understand?"

"Certainly, effendi! I shall cling to them like lice!"

Aptly phrased, Sam thought to himself, as the three men and the child began cautiously to follow behind the two Egyptians. Sekhemib was so much taller than the average man on the Cairo street that his head was clearly visible above the crowd, even from a distance, so that his four pursuers did not need to follow closely. They stayed well back of him, but kept him constantly in sight. They made no conversation as they fixed their attention with an obsessive intensity upon the back of the head of long, luxuriant black hair as it bobbed up and down through the human sea of Cairo's back streets.

They followed for over an hour at a slow pace, for the old man who walked beside Sekhemib seemed unable to walk as quickly as he would probably have liked. Sekhemib seemed to be strolling casually as the old man struggled to keep up with him. Through the very infrequent breaches in the crowd, the three Westerners could see the old man chattering away at Sekhemib cheerfully, while Sekhemib, his face fixed before him, seemed to be ignoring his companion.

They came at last to the wharves along the Nile. The wharves stretched for miles along the entire western boundary of the city, and continued on the opposite bank of the river off into the distance. Cairo had been built on the Nile's eastern bank, but the centuries of almost continuous urban growth had sent populations sprawling onto the land on the other side of the river as well. Like all dock areas of all cities situated beside bodies of water, the wharf district of Cairo was redolent of industry and humanity, mixing into an overwhelmingly unpleasant stench.

They watched as Sekhemib and the old man approached a low lying barge which was tied to a wooden post beside a narrow, decaying walkway of splintering planks. Six burly men lounged in front of the barge, baking their already blackened and overdeveloped muscles in the hot sun, but their air of relaxation turned into one of attentive respect as Sekhemib and the old man approached them. One of the six men, apparently the foreman of the watch crew, nodded politely to the old man and appeared to eye Sekhemib quizzically. The old man and the foreman spoke for a few moments, with the old man doing most of the talking and the foreman restricting his conversation to grunts, nods, and a few desultory words of agreement.

Sam, Roderick, and Sawhill positioned themselves partially beside and partially behind the end bale of a large shipment of cotton whick stood some fifty yards away from the barge. "Sam," Sawhill whispered, "look there, on the barge."

Sam squinted through his sweat-fogged glasses. "Are those the crates from the museum?"

"I don't think so," Sawhill muttered. "No, of course not. They just took the mummies, remember? They must have bought coffins for the four—I mean the six, after . . ." He did not finish the sentence. The sound of Gus Rudd's insane screams and the sight of Suzanne Melendez's still twitching, mangled body on the floor of the morgue was sufficiently fresh in all of their minds without any need for a reference to them.

"Yes," Sam agreed. He thought for a moment. "Look, if this is where the mummies are, then eventually they're going to have to move them somewhere less open, less conspicuous. We know at least part of what they intend to do—"

"Bring those things back to life," Roderick muttered, shaking his head.

"Yes, precisely. They won't do that here. I'll wager that they're going to sail this barge up the Nile, south toward Nubia—"

"Nubia?" Sawhill asked. "Where's Nubia?"

"Eh—sorry, I meant south toward the Sudan. I'll bet that if we follow the barge, we'll find Harriet being held wherever the barge docks."

Sawhill considered this and nodded. "Makes sense. Makes sense. Can we find out where it's going?"

Sam moved behind the cotton bale and pulled little Faz with him. He knelt down and, taking the child by the shoulders, said, "Faz, how are you at finding things out?"

"Effendi?" the boy replied, confused.

"You see that barge over there, with the men standing in front of it?"

He looked. "Yes, effendi."

"We have to know when that barge is leaving the wharf and where it is going, but we must not let anyone know that we wish to know. Can you go over there and listen to the conversation those men are having without letting them know you're listening?"

Faz smiled. "It is an easy thing, effendi." The child scampered off toward the barge.

The three Westerners watched from behind the cotton bale as the child ran over to the barge and grabbed a small melon from a pushcart which an old woman was laboriously moving along the wharfside. Her head was bent into her effort and she did not notice the theft. Faz tossed the melon up and caught it as if it were a ball, and then seated himself casually upon a mooring post some five feet away from the barge. Sekhemib glanced at him, and immediately dismissed his presence as irrelevant. Faz did not look at the men upon whom he was eavesdropping; rather, he sat quietly and happily devoured the melon.

A few minutes passed. Sam, Roderick, and Sawhill watched impatiently as the old man continued to speak, the foreman continued to nod, the little boy continued to eat, and Sekhemib gazed distractedly off at the horizon. At last they saw the foreman give what seemed to be a final bowing nod to the old man, and then he and Sekhemib turned and began to walk back in the direction from which they had come. Silently but in obvious haste, Sawhill moved to the far side of the cotton bale, followed quickly by Sam and Roderick. They waited until Sekhemib and the old man had passed by before walking back away from the river's edge. "Shouldn't we follow them?" Roderick asked.

"Not necessary," Sam replied. "We know where their precious cargo is. It's the mummies we have to keep close to, not them." He turned to see Faz running toward them, his bare, calloused feet seeming to click upon the hot wood. "Well?" Sam asked. "What did you hear?"

"The old one was giving the strong one instructions to pay his men for another day's guarding," the boy said breathlessly. "He said the men are to stay until sunrise, and then they can go."

"Did they speak of the destination of the barge?"

"No, effendi. I heard nothing else."

After Sam relayed the information to the others, Sawhill said, "Well, at least we know when they're going to move the barge."

"Yes," Roderick said. "Ask the boy when we can get the guns."

Sam turned back to Faz. "Tell me, little one, can we obtain the weapons tonight?"

"Oh, yes, effendi," he chirped. "No problem. I go see Khalid right now, okay?" His last word was in English, another apparent foreign adoption.

"Yes. We will be back in our hotel. You get word to us there as soon as possible."

"I shall, effendi," the boy said and then ran off with that mad enthusiasm which only children exhibit.

Sam grinned slightly as he watched the boy disappear into the crowd and then turned to his companions. "He says we can get the weapons tonight."

"Good," Sawhill said, biting his lower lip. "How do you suggest we follow the barge? Maybe we should follow it by land, along the side of the river. Those things move pretty slow, by the looks of them."

Sam shook his head. "No. We might not be able to keep them in sight while we're in urban areas, and if they sail far enough south to go past the settled parts of the country, they'd be able to spot us in a minute."

"Okay. So? What shall we do?"

Sam thought for a moment. "Roderick, how's our money supply?"

"You mean right here?"

"No, I mean generally."

"Oh, well, it's unlimited, to all intents and purposes. I can cash another draft in the bank back by the hotel. Why?"

"I think," he said slowly, "that we should rent a boat, an excursion ship of some sort, one which would arouse no suspicion on the river. Excursion boats sail up and down the Nile every day, so no one would think it unusual."

"That's good," Sawhill nodded. "Can you manage that, Sam? I mean, is your Arabic up to a business transaction?"

Sam laughed. "What do you think my conversations with Faz have been? It's all a matter of knowing the currency and making the terms clear. Sure, I can handle it."

"Okay, good." Sawhill sighed. "Now all I have to do is figure out how to wait until dawn without going crazy."

Neither Sam nor Roderick made a reply. Sam was impelled to this mission by a loyalty to his colleague Harriet Langly and a moral commitment to prevent the murderous cult from succeeding, thriving. Roderick was there because of an uncharacteristic sense of responsibility, something which surprised him more than anyone else. Had he not ignored his uncle, had he not wanted more than the croesus-like wealth he already had, the seven mummies might yet be gathering dust in the attic at Chudley. And so he had shouldered a burden which he could as easily have avoided.

But Thomas Sawhill had been driven to Egypt by love and despair. He had loved Harriet for quite a while, but he had never realized, until this tragic situation had descended upon them, how central she had become to his life, to his very existence. Were he not on the brink of emotional collapse, he might have speculated on the fact that for the first time he had come to realize that the old hyperbole about loving someone more than life was more than poetry. He was willing to die attempting to save Harriet Langly.

And he very well might.

# CHAPTER 15

No bride on the morning of her wedding day was as exuberant as was Ahmed Hadji as the ropes were cast off and the small rebuilt outboard motor began laboriously to push the barge against the current, up the Nile. The shouts of the dockworkers and the sound of the motors and the buzzing of the insects seemed to blend in his mind into a general background paean of praise and thanksgiving, and he hummed contentedly along with the musicless melody. The day had come! At last, the day had come! By this time tomorrow he would be like the Lord Sekhemib, he would be immortal, he would be invulnerable. Millions of years. A life of millions of years.

He was standing at the front end of the barge—to call it a bow would be a disservice to true boats—watching as the urban congestion of Cairo became increasingly more sparse. There were no truly unpopulated areas along the Nile River, not at least until one passed beyond the first cataract, but the incredible, oppressive concentration of people which was to be found in the northern part of the ancient land was not repeated in the southern. Once the barge passed the town of Bensi Hasan, a few miles north of the ruins of Akhetaton, the river banks would be bordered by villages, and the tension Hadji had felt for so long would begin to decline.

Hadji glanced behind him. There, sitting comfortably upon a folded rug, was his old benefactor Haleel Haftoori. It was Haftoori who had noticed him, had recruited him, had trained, taught, and cherished him. He owed the old man a debt so great that it could never be paid. When Hadji became

eternal this night, it would be because of the old man's choice
of him to head the priesthood of Thoth in their ancient faith. A
priesthood with but one priest, to be sure; but one was all that
was needed. As long as his name was spoken, Thoth lived.
There was power in the name of a god.

Sekhemib was standing beside Haftoori, ignoring the
ceaseless chatter which the old man was emitting. His long
black hair flowed in the wind as the barge trudged up the Nile,
and Sekhemib seemed to be almost oblivious to his surround-
ings. Hadji could well imagine the thoughts which were going
through the mind of the ancient priest. Tonight he would have
his love Meret back again, and his friends Yuya and Senmut,
Khumara, Herihor, and Wenet. Tonight these seven immortals, all of whom until oh so recently had been nothing more
than mummies mouldering in their coffins, would be once
again together, alive, powerful, together after three thousand
five hundred years of death. The four mummies still slept in
their rotted wrappings. Meret and Yuya, killed by the policeman far away, were decaying in the two boxes which he, Hadji,
had procured for them in New York City; but it was all
temporary, as Sekhemib said, a brief sleep, barely a single
heart beat in the long life of the universe.

Hadji licked his lips excitedly. And then, when all seven
stood together, the priests and priestesses of Anubis, Isis, Set,
Ra, Bast, Horus, and Thoth, then they would join as one to
become the great tekenu of the god, and Anubis would come
to them, and he, Ahmed Hadji, would bask in the radiance of
the divinity. He smiled and sighed. *"Anet hrauthen 'Anpu,"* he
whispered. Homage to you, Anubis.

He turned back to the river which stretched out before
them. The mother Nile, he thought, the bosom which has
suckled Egypt for six thousand years. And now our mother
bears us south to the ruins of our temple, to the presence of the
god, to life eternal. Millions of years, a life of millions of years.

Hadji took a quick circumspective look around. All was as
it should be, all was as planned. The bodies of the six holy
ones were resting in their temporary homes. The woman, the
American who was soon to be the tekenu of the lady Meret,
was bound and gagged and imprisoned in the large basket
which stood beside the crates. Sekhemib and Haftoori were
here. He, Ahmed Hadji, was here. Around them the people of
Egypt toiled and sweated in the hot sun, and the river was
filled with boats and barges: merchants moving goods, tourists

taking a pleasant excursion up the Nile, in boats such as the dahabeah which sailed along behind the barge. All was well. He looked back at the river before him, and began to whistle cheerfully.

Egypt had never developed a true maritime tradition. Though the Mediterranean Sea lay across her northern border, Egypt's shipping had always been largely up and down the river which bisected the land. Thus the dahabeah, the most common of the many boats which moved gracefully along the river surface, had been able to develop an elegance born of simplicity and an absence of concern over storms and waves. The dahabeah which sailed peacefully behind the barge was typical of such boats. It was a long, narrow craft which rested low in the water. Two masts thrust upward into the sky, supporting two triangular sails which billowed slightly in the gentle wind. From the stern of the boat a low-ceilinged cabin, little more than a wood and canvas canopy enclosing the deck, stretched forward half way to the bow. In that cabin Roderick Fowles was busily engaged in loading guns.

"Ever fired a pistol or a rifle?" he asked Samuel Goldhaber.

"I'm afraid not," was the reply. "I'm not a hunter, and I was too young for World War Two and too old for Korea." Sam put a match to the bowl of his pipe and watched the blue smoke hang in the air for a moment before it was swept away by the currents of air. "I wouldn't have thought that you knew much about guns either, Roderick."

"I don't, really. But we always go grouse hunting in the fall, and I've always enjoyed shooting skeet, so I have some small acquaintance with firearms." He smiled. "Of course, the servants always loaded the weapons for me. I've never actually seen a bullet before. Have you?"

"No," Sam replied. "But they seem to fit, so you must be doing it right."

"Hope so." He frowned. "I can't help but wish that your policeman friend were here with us."

"I know, but I doubt he would have come even if he'd been able to."

"What do you mean?" Roderick put down the pistol and picked up a rifle clip for one of the old M-14 automatics they had purchased. The rifles looked to be twenty years old, but still serviceable.

"I think the whole business with Gus left him too upset, too drained emotionally, to be of much use to anyone for a while. Don't misunderstand me. Jasper is a brave man. But nothing in his experience in war or in police work prepared him for anything like this." Sam looked out from the cabin toward the bow of the dahabeah where Thomas Sawhill stood, his eyes fixed on the barge which labored along in front of them, the folds of his kaftan fluttering about his calves. "Look at Tom," Sam said. "He's an emotional wreck, just like Jasper. But Jasper has his brother back, physically at least. Tom is still in the waiting and hoping stage."

Roderick continued to load the weapons. "What do you think will happen to the chief's brother? Do you think he'll ever recover?"

"Emotionally? I don't know. Perhaps, but I don't think so, not completely, anyway. I don't know if he'll ever be able even to understand it all."

Roderick laughed humorlessly. "He's not alone in that. I don't understand this myself."

Sam nodded, still watching Sawhill. "I don't either. I accept it as fact, but I can't say that I understand it. The whole thing runs contrary to everything I've ever known or believed. But we're on this boat on the trail of a walking dead man, and I saw what happened to Gus and Suzanne"—he shivered slightly at the memory—"so I can't just dismiss it. 'More things in heaven and earth . . .' and all that."

"Hmm?"

"'There are more things in heaven and earth than are dreamed of in your philosophy, Horatio.'"

Roderick frowned. "Who's Horatio?"

Sam laughed, astounded once again, as he had been so often, at the breadth of Roderick's ignorance. "It's a quote from *Hamlet*."

"Oh, yes, Shakespeare. I've seen a few of his plays."

Sam rose to his feet. "I'm going out to see how Tom's doing. You sure you don't need any help?"

"None at all. This helps pass the time." He began to push bullets into a clip for an M-14.

Sam walked forward in the boat toward the bow and placed his hand gently on Sawhill's shoulder. His friend spun around tensely and his eyes glared at Sam for a fraction of a second before relaxing into the weary, bloodshot visage which had been so characteristic of Sawhill for so many days. "Don't sneak up on me, Sam," he muttered.

He's like a coiled spring, Sam thought. He's ready to snap. "Any activity on the barge?"

"Not really. I can't see too well from this distance, but they don't seem to be doing much of anything." The dahabeah was trailing the barge at a distance of about a quarter of a mile, close enough to keep it in sight, far enough to be inconspicuous. "Damn it, Sam, we should have some binoculars."

"Yeah, I didn't think of that."

"Can't we pull closer to them, just for a while at least? I can't see if Harriet's on board."

Sam shook his head. "It wouldn't be wise, Tom. We shouldn't take any chances, not now."

Sawhill sighed and rubbed his eyes. "Sam, I think I'm losing my grip."

Sam patted him gently on the back. "Hold on, Tom. By tonight it will all be over." One way or the other, he thought, but did not say the words.

Through the long morning and afternoon into the early evening the barge chugged up the river with the dahabeah maintaining its distance. The ruined wonders of ancient Egypt drifted past them on all sides, but no one on the barge and no one on the dahabeah paid them much attention. Only Sekhemib seemed at all moved by the sight of the world he had known lying in shattered, fading heaps, but even he was too preoccupied with the coming events to give thought to the ruins.

The two boats sailed past Giza and the ruins of the ancient capital of Memphis. The three great pyramids stood at some distance from the river, but their massive forms were still clearly visible. As the barge and the dahabeah moved past the town of Beni Hasan, the ancient pillars of the tomb of Amenemhet greeted them with the same mute majesty with which they had greeted boats on the Nile for the past four thousand years. They sailed past the low ruins of the holy city of Akhetaton, where the heretic king, the madman Amenhotep IV, had relocated the Egyptian government a century before the Achaeans attacked Troy; past the fertile plain, the graceful minarets, the fruitful palm groves of the village of Asyūt; past the austere white square building which the British had built a century before to house their consuls in the same town; past the medieval tomb of Mourad Bey at Sohag, a tomb built thousands of years later than those of the ancients, but already a crumbling ruin.

The great temple of Seti I at Abydos drifted by, the carefully carved figures which covered the walls on either side of the entrance way to the hypostyle hall still bearing faint traces of the blue, red, and green pigments which had covered them in that ancient time. The boats passed Dendera, and only a careful examination of the mound of dust and rubble on the west bank could tell the observer that this was once the great temple of the goddess Hathor. Only one wall was at all visible, and even there the centuries seemed to have tried to erase the images of the long procession of crowned deities. The eastern gate of the wall which had once surrounded Dendera stood alone, thrusting up out of the red ground in isolated and incongruous majesty, connected to no walls, a doorway to nowhere.

Soon they drew close to Luxor, the ancient holy city, upon which pharaoh after pharaoh had lavished gold and labor. A cluster of contemporary houses of mud brick stood a stone's throw away from the great pylon of Rameses II, behind which the minarets of the mosque of Abn'l-Haqqay towered, as if to illustrate the triumph of Allah over the old god Ra. The broken, roofless colonnades of the temple of Amenhotep III, whom his people called the Magnificent, lined the hills beyond the river bank, and the Northern Gate of Ptolemy III, whose grandfather had snatched Egypt from the dying hands of Alexander the Great, stood near the river. In the distance behind the gate, far from the Nile, one could see the broken, shattered, but still majestic temple of the god Amon. This was the largest place of worship ever built by the human race. The cathedrals of Europe took centuries to build; the Great Temple of Amon took millennia. From the time of the Twelfth Dynasty, some four thousand years ago, until the end of the reign of the Ptolemys with the suicide of Cleopatra near the time of the birth of Christ, building and rebuilding, expansion and addition, was almost continuous. But the succeeding two thousand years of neglect had reduced the massive worship complex to a collection of mutilated, skeletal ruins, still majestic, to be sure, but pathetic as well in their mute testimony to the futility of human endeavor.

The first massive pylon of the temple thrust upward into the sky, now connected to nothing, standing alone at the outer boundary of the holy place. The gray and red rubble extended outward from the pylon's base and led to the remnants of the Great Hall, whose enormous columns thrust strongly upward to support the massive roof which had collapsed centuries ago. Past the Great Hall stood the obelisk of Thutmose I, dwarfed by the larger obelisk of Hatshepsut. A series of granite pillars erected by Thutmose III, the great conqueror of Syria and Palestine, stood before a series of sphinxes whose faces had been mutilated by time and wind and artillery practice.

This huge complex of temples and monuments sat facing the ruins of the great capital of Thebes, from which the great pharaohs of the empire ruled all the world as far south as Ethiopia, as far east as Babylon, and as far north as the borders of the land of the Hittites. This was once the capital of the world. It was now a dusty shamble of cracked walls and fading friezes, faceless statues and crumbling obelisks, roofless buildings and broken highways. Where once stood palaces which housed the masters of the world, there now stood decaying ruins which housed scorpions and lizards. Where once the walls of sanctuaries echoed with the voices of chanting priests, there now echoed only the voices of tourists and tour guides. Thebes, even more than Luxor, testified to time's unrelenting contempt for the Ozymandian arrogance of foolish men.

The barge and the dahabeah sailed south, ever south, through the long day and the long night, through the next morning and afternoon into the next evening, past Esna, past Edfu, past Kom Ombo, and drew nigh to the Aswan High Dam and the first cataract of the Nile. Three miles north of the dam, the barge docked at an irregular, solitary wooden wharf far from the normal docking areas. The dahabeah sailed past the barge, for the Egyptian sailors whom Roderick had hired along with their boat would not turn the bow to the shore and ground the dahabeah on the sand. But once past the barge they raised the sails halfway, thus reducing the driving power of the wind to a delicate balance with the current of the river so that the dahabeah rested motionless near the western bank, the conflicting forces of wind and water canceling each other out.

"Tell him to get us to shore," Sawhill demanded of Sam impatiently. "Those bastards are getting ready to unload."

Sam Goldhaber and the boat's pilot engaged in a heated exchange for a few moments, after which Sam turned to his two friends and said, "He won't beach his craft, but he can get close enough to shore for us to get over the side and wade."

"Wade!" Sawhill shouted. "Wade! We'll get our ammunition wet! And the guns—!"

"Not necessarily," Roderick said soothingly. "If the water really is shallow enough for us to wade ashore, we can hold everything over our heads. It will only be for a few feet, anyway. And we don't seem to have much choice."

"Okay, okay," Sawhill said in an angry, bitter tone, "then let's get going." The pilot was calling upon his sailors to tack the sails so as to move the dahabeah sideways, and when they were no more than twenty feet from the shore he called out to Sam that this was as far as they could safely manage.

"This is it," Sam said. He climbed awkwardly over the side of the dahabeah, intending to slip gracefully from the low-lying hull into the water, but he lost his grip on the railing. He fell backward, landing in the water with a loud splash.

Roderick leaned over and asked, "Are you all right, Sam?"

Sam Goldhaber stood up in the water and shook the water from his eyes and ears. "Yeah, yeah, I'm okay. Why don't you hand me some of our stuff?" The water came only up to his waist. The long, narrow dahabeah displaced even less water than he had supposed.

"Righto," Roderick said, and began to pass pistols and rifles to Sam. Thomas Sawhill hopped from the dahabeah into the Nile and took weapons and ammunition belts from the Englishman. Roderick held the two remaining rifles slightly aloft as he leaped from the boat. Faz had managed to get them two rifles and two pistols apiece and an ample supply of ammunition for each one.

They waded ashore as the dahabeah lowered its sails and turned the helm about, allowing the currents of the Nile to begin to carry it back toward Cairo, some three hundred miles to the north. Sam watched the boat drifting homeward as he stood on the shore, wringing the water out of the kaftan and the burnoose he, like the others, was wearing in an attempt to conceal his identity. Sawhill was slinging one rifle over his shoulder by its strap. He stuck his two pistols into his belt on either side of his body, and stood holding his second rifle, waiting impatiently for Sam and Roderick to imitate him. "Come on, come on, hurry up, will you?" he demanded.

"Okay, Tom, I'm hurrying, I'm hurrying," Sam said, trying to keep annoyance out of his tone. His affection for his friend, his sympathy for what he was going through, and his own worry about Harriet Langly did not serve to displace his own tension and growing feelings of fear. It had all seemed so obvious, so indisputably clear back in America, that they had to rescue the woman. But now, alone on the banks of the Nile, armed to the teeth, hurrying to engage in violent confrontation with a group of murdering fanatics, he was less objective and secure than he had been.

Roderick seemed strangely calm, as if his sheltered and pampered existence had bred into him an inability to even conceive of danger to his own person. Well, that's good, Sam thought. At least he'll probably be able to keep a cool head. I doubt that Tom will. And me? Sam shook his head. Calm down, he ordered himself. Calm down.

The three men began to walk along the Nile bank in the direction of the barge, which had docked some three hundred yards north. Sam noticed a motion in the distance and squinted to see it. "What's that?" he asked. "A caravan?"

The other two men looked at the moving line coming out of the desert toward the river, far beyond the position of the barge. "I can't tell," Roderick said. "There seem to be draft animals pulling something—wagons, perhaps?"

"Of course," Sawhill snapped his fingers. "Transportation for the coffins."

"Transportation where?" Roderick asked.

"To their holy place, most likely," Sam said. "Whatever they intend to do, they won't do it here on the riverbank with ships passing them constantly. They must have a place off there"—he pointed into the desert with his rifle barrel—"in the desert somewhere."

"Shit!" Sawhill muttered. "That will make it damned hard to follow them on foot without being seen." He glanced out at the flat expanse of sand which stretched off to the horizon.

"Then whatever we intend to do must be done here," Roderick said with finality.

"If we run into Sekhemib before we can get Harriet, we won't be able to do anything," Sam pointed out. "If she's here, I mean. I didn't see her on the barge."

"I could bloody well hardly see the barge!" Roderick said. "She might have been on it. We weren't that close."

They continued trudging through the sand, all the while watching as the caravan drew ever nearer to the barge. When they drew close enough to be able to see the people on the barge closely, they moved more carefully. The Nile banks just north of Aswan were not as fertile as the banks farther north, but palm trees enough grew to afford them occasional cover. A cluster of trees not fifty yards from the barge was sufficient to conceal all three of them, and they stood motionless, watching, waiting for an opportunity, their only plan being attack, their only tactic being surprise.

They watched as the caravan arrived. It was an odd

caravan, one which carried no goods. Three men rode at the head of the procession, rocking back and forth in keeping with the rhythm of the camels upon which they sat. Three riderless camels followed behind them, attached by rope from the bridle of one to the saddle of the other, and four mules pulling four carts followed behind the camels. The mules were being pulled forward by short ropes attached to their bridles, held by four men who were dressed, like Sekhemib, Hadji, and Haftoori, in plain kaftans of brilliant white girdled by richly colored sashes at the waist.

The human contingent of the caravan dismounted from camels and released ropes and came forward. They prostrated themselves at the feet of Sekhemib and remained for a long while with their faces pressed into the sand. He spoke to them in a firm, commanding voice which carried far enough for the three Westerners to hear him distinctly in the midst of the otherwise totally silent stretch of riverbank, but his words carried no meaning to them.

The people rose to their feet and began to unload the barge. The barge crew assisted them as they carefully moved the six crates one by one from the deck of the wagons, putting two of the recently purchased boxes into each of two wagons, reserving the other two for the remaining boxes which housed the decaying corpses of Meret and Yuya. Two of the barge crew took hold of the large straw basket which rested now alone upon the deck of the barge and lifted it upward. They carried it to the edge and passed it to two of the men on the shore. They in turn carried it away from the bank toward the wagons and set it down upon the sand. One of them lifted the lid and then overturned it.

Harriet Langly fell out onto the sand and then lay motionless. Her naked body was bruised and deathly pale, and her wrists and ankles were bound with thick lengths of rope.

Sam Goldhaber grabbed Thomas Sawhill by the arm and held him tightly, knowing even before the latter began to move that the sight would impel him into an irrational attack. "Wait, Tom, wait! Not now, not while Sekhemib is so close. We have to wait!"

Sawhill's attempted response issued forth as a strained, high-pitched cry of anger. His body was trembling so violently that Roderick felt compelled to take him firmly by the other arm. "Wait, Thomas, just a little while longer."

Sawhill was staring at the woman he loved, his face

contorted into a grimace of rage and pain. "Look at her!" he managed to say. "Look at what they've done to her! Those animals, those fucking bastards!"

"Tom, quiet down, *please*!" Sam said urgently. "We have to choose our own time. We can't let them hear us!" Sawhill shoved a knuckle into his mouth and bit down hard upon it. Blood began to ooze from the freshly inflicted wound.

They watched as one of the people of the caravan took a canteen and poured a stream of water onto the motionless woman. Her body twitched visibly when the liquid struck her parched skin, but she made no other movements. "At least she's alive," Sam whispered.

"They kept her in that basket all day, all the way up the river," Sawhill muttered, a hint of hysteria creeping into his shaking voice. "I'll kill them, I'll kill all of them!"

"Tom, be quiet!"

Sekhemib and the old man walked slowly away from the wagons and approached the camels. The grooms pulled down upon the bridles and the camels dropped to their knees with slow, ungainly movements, and then remained that way, grunting and spitting and chewing their cuds as first Sekhemib and then Haftoori mounted them. Sekhemib barked a few commands to the caravan boss, and then he and Haftoori began to slap the camels sharply on the sides of their long necks. The camels rose bellowing to their feet, and the two men turned their mounts toward the desert. They began slowly to ride away, leaving the barge crew and the caravan under Hadji's direction. The small man seemed to grow in height as he began issuing orders in all directions in a tone of haughty arrogance.

"Sekhemib's leaving!" Sam whispered. "That's great!"

"Shall we rush them?" Roderick asked. He seemed to be as eager and enthusiastic as he might have been before a Rugby match, if he had ever played Rugby, which he had not.

"Listen," Sam said, "this is what we should do. We'll attack as soon as Sekhemib is far enough away to give us a safety margin. We have to hit them fast, guns firing, and hope we can clear them off the barge. Tom, you grab Harriet and get her onto the barge. Roderick, you and I will keep up the fire while we cast off those ropes. We'll escape on the barge."

"What if we can't start the motor?" Roderick asked. "Have you ever had anything to do with motorboats? I know I haven't."

"We don't have to start the motor. The river current runs north from here, back toward Cairo. If we can get the motor started, fine and good, but even if we can't all we have to do is steer the barge, keep in the center of the river. I mean, anyone can use a tiller."

"Good," Roderick nodded. "That's good. But what about Sekhemib and the others?"

"One thing at a time," Sam said. "Let's just worry about getting Harriet and ourselves out of here in one piece. If we manage that, then we can plan a next step. Maybe she can even get the authorities to believe her, at least partially."

"Let's go, let's do it!" Sawhill spat. "I can't leave her lying there like that any longer."

Sam looked over at the figures of Sekhemib and Haftoori, which were growing increasingly small in the distance. "Just another few minutes, Tom, please. Let's wait until they're out of sight."

Tears of frustration began to roll down Sawhill's cheeks. "Harriet," he croaked, his hands squeezing the stock of his rifle so tightly that even the bleeding knuckle showed white against the brown wood.

Those few more minutes seemed to be an eternity to Thomas Sawhill. His eyes were fixed on Harriet Langly's motionless form and he fought to keep his mind from imagining what had been happening to her since her abduction. His heart was pounding and his legs were twitching with erratic spasms, as if he were an automobile in first gear with both the brake and the accelerator pushed down to the floor. He was so intent upon staring at her that he did not hear Sam at first when he gave the word to attack. He snapped to attention after a few moments as if awakened from a dream. The three men looked at each other, a gesture of silent encouragement and acceptance of whatever awaited them, and then ran from behind the cluster of palm trees, guns blazing.

At the sound of the gunfire the men on the barge leaped into the water, and those on the shore dropped to their bellies. No one returned the fire, for none of them was armed. Only Ahmed Hadji stood erect, his arms folded, a look of disturbing nonchalance upon his smirking face.

Sawhill ran directly at Hadji, firing the automatic rifle directly at him, but Hadji did not fall. Sawhill whipped the other rifle from his shoulder and emptied another clip into the Arab, but Hadji stood motionless, staring at him coldly. The

men who had fallen to the ground rose slowly to their feet as
the men in the river clambered onto the shore.

Pistols and rifles blazed in the hands of the three men, but
something was terribly wrong. No one was falling wounded,
there were no cries of pain, no streams of red upon the yellow
sand. They continued firing until the cylinders and clips were
empty and then stood in motionless bewilderment in the
sudden silence of the river bank. Hadji stood in the midst of
his underlings, some one dozen men, all looking at the three
Westerners blankly. No more than fifteen yards separated
Hadji from Sawhill, and the latter could see the grin on Hadji's
face spread slowly into a broad, friendly smile. "Hello, old
fellow!" Hadji said. "We've been waiting for you. And, by the
way, my nephew Faisal sends his regards and asks you to
forgive him for selling you blanks."

Sam and Roderick stood immobile from shock as the barge
crew and caravan crew grabbed hold of them. Only Sawhill, his
anger and frustration now well beyond the breaking point,
fought against his assailants, swinging the rifle in his hands as a
club, but his efforts were doomed to failure by the odds. Two
Arabs each were sufficient to bind Roderick and Sam, but it
took six attackers and ultimately a blow to his head with the
barrel of his own rifle to subdue Sawhill. He fell to the ground
unconscious beside Harriet, and the Arabs wrapped rope
around his wrists and arms.

Hadji walked casually over to Sam and Roderick and patted
them amiably on their shoulders. "You really have no idea how
pleased I am that you good fellows showed up so quickly. I was
afraid that you had some foolish notion about waiting until
dark. I much preferred that you attack us than that we had to
chase you down the river."

"Faz—" Sam muttered, "—he's your—your—"

"My nephew, yes," Hadji replied happily. "My sister
Ayesha's boy. Such a clever little child, don't you think? We
have high hopes for him. I had once hoped that I would be
able to initiate him into the priesthood at some point in the
future, when one of my colleagues passes away, but now that's
impossible of course."

"What—what do you mean?" Sam stammered.

"Why, none of my colleagues is ever going to pass away, my
dear friend! Do you still not understand what this is all about?
Sekhemib and his six compatriots are the immortals chosen by

Anubis, but they require servants, assistant priests, such as my friends and myself. Beginning tonight, when the rituals and sacrifices are done again as in the ancient days, they and we shall enter into the ranks of the beloved of Anubis." He feigned pensiveness as he scratched his chin. "I wonder which of your souls I shall drink tonight?"

"How did you know?" Roderick asked. His customarily impassive face was filled with fear as the true nature of his situation became clear to him. "How did you know?"

"How did we know? What, how did we know that you would be following us?" Hadji laughed. "My poor fellow, we have been watching you ever since you arrived in Egypt! Did you think that you could sneak up on the lord Sekhemib, that he could be kept in darkness as you pursued him? Foolish, foolish men! The lord Sekhemib has the wisdom and the cunning of hundreds of thousands of years! You have to die, you three and the policeman back in America, and our only problem was whether to go to the trouble and expense of having you murdered there or waiting for you to come to us. I am very, *very* pleased that you chose to simplify our task."

"But why?" Roderick asked desperately. "Why do we have to die? If we left right now, if we promised—"

"Don't be silly, Your Lordship, don't insult my intelligence. No promise you made right now would be worth even listening to. More importantly, you know about us, you know about the lord Sekhemib and the other immortals. Such knowledge alone condemns you to death." He smiled again. "But be of good cheer! Your lives will not have been wasted. Because of you, I or one of my associates will have our lives extended by decades! And then, of course, after living out your life spans, we shall honor some other equally cooperative people by drinking their souls as well." Hadji looked at the men who were finishing the task of securing the barge by pulling it up onto the sand. "It appears that we are ready to leave. I'm terribly sorry to ask you to accompany us on foot, but as you can see we are rather short of transport."

Hadji barked an order to one of the crew, and the crewman grabbed Roderick by the wrists and pulled him to the rear of one of the wagons. He fastened a long rope to the ropes around Roderick's wrists and then tied the other end of the rope to the bracing slat behind which rested the coffin of Yuya. He then walked over to Sam and, grabbing him in the same manner, repeated the process.

Sawhill was still lying senseless beside Harriet, who was moving very slightly, her bound hands slowly digging into the surface sand. Hadji issued another order, and two other crewmen dragged Sawhill by the legs over to another wagon. "Unfortunately," Hadji explained, "our friend does not seem able to walk. I'm afraid we shall have to drag him to our destination." He shrugged sadly and shook his head, as if resigned to a regrettable situation.

Sam and Roderick watched as the crewmen tied Sawhill's wrist bonds to the rear of the other wagon. "You can't do this to him!" Sam said in openmouthed astonishment. "It's inhuman!"

"Yes. Pity, isn't it?" Hadji smiled.

A few muffled laughs caught Sam's attention, and he turned to see two of the Arab crew carrying Harriet toward the wagons. They paused every few feet to squeeze and fondle her breasts and press their hands and fingers into the velvety recess between her legs. Thank God Tom can't see this, Sam thought. Poor girl. Poor, dear girl.

He turned to see Hadji standing close beside him, grinning at Sam's discomfort and sorrow. A surge of anger rose up in him, and unable to strike out at the leering smile, he spat in Hadji's face. The Arab blinked in surprise and stepped back a few feet. He wiped the saliva from his eyes and, growing red in the face, he struck Sam in the mouth with a closed fist. The older man staggered back into the side of the wagon and then slumped to his knees.

"Sam?" Roderick asked. "Are you all right?" The older man did not reply. "Sam? Sam!"

"Yes, Roderick, I'm okay, I'm okay." He shook his head in an attempt to clear it. Blood dripped from his mouth, and as he spit it out a few of his teeth followed it.

"What shall we do?" Roderick asked. "Do you have any ideas?"

Sam looked up at him. "I can't think of a goddamn thing. Can you?"

Roderick sighed. "No, unfortunately. Damn! It all seemed like such a good idea!"

Sam rose uneasily to his feet. "You can't win a game when the other fellow cheats." He shook his head. "Faz, of all people! I never even suspected!"

A sudden jerk took both of them unwares as the wagons began to move forward, and they were almost pulled off their feet. They ran a few steps to give themselves enough slack to get their balance, and then they walked slowly behind the slow moving wagons. Sawhill, still unconscious, was being dragged on his back along the hot sand. Ahmed Hadji led the procession atop a camel, and the rest of the caravan followed behind him in single file.

"Bloody wogs!" Roderick muttered.

The Nile River passed from sight as the sun set gently behind the red hills of Upper Egypt, and the silence of the desert night descended upon them. Only the grunting camels and the squeaking wagon wheels broke the stillness. Somewhere off in the distance a jackal howled at the starry, moonless sky.

"Do you hear that, my friends?" Hadji called back to them. "A jackal, the symbol of the god! Anubis is welcoming you!" He laughed madly.

The three captive men moved for hours through the black desert, two on foot and one on his back. At last in the distance they saw a slight flicker of lights, and as they drew closer the soft sounds of chanting reached their ears. They could not understand the words of the long-dead tongue, but the sounds sent thrills of terror up their spines.

"'*Anpu, nekhemkua ma ab!* '*Anpu, nekhemkua ma ab!*"

Anubis, deliver me from death.

# C H A P T E R  1 6

▲ The line of freshly carved hieroglyphs was the first thing she saw as she opened her eyes and tried, at first unsuccessfully, to focus them. She almost imagined that her eyelids squeaked audibly as she forced them open, but the sound of creaking joints as she slowly and painfully moved her legs and arms was not imagination. Her body seemed to be one long wound from head to foot, battered and sore. The cold stone floor upon which she lay scraped painfully upon her soiled skin

when she attempted to rise to a sitting position, and she could
not suppress a small, weak moan.

·Where am I? she thought, her mind confused and numb.
She looked up again at the line of hieroglyphs which had been
carved tall and deep upon the archway of the door which stood
at one end of the long subterranean vault. She squinted her
eyes, trying to bring the ideographs into clearer focus in the
flickering torchlight.

"'*Anpu anet hrak suten neteru,*'" she whispered as she ran her
vision across the carving, "*xeperu xer khat 'Anpu kheq tetta.*" She
read it again, silently, her scholar's mind fighting its way
upward through the miasma of pain and grief which radiated
without explanation from her subconscious. A few moments
passed, and then the meaning of the words arranged themselves in her mind, bringing with them memory of what had
happened, of what was happening now.

Anubis, praise to you, king of the gods, who came into
being in ancient times, Anubis, prince of eternity.

"No," she muttered weakly as the tears began to stream
from her cloudy eyes. "Oh, Jesus, no." She remembered
everything. She was sitting upon her folded legs, and she
rested her elbows upon the junction of her inner thighs as she
bent over slightly and drew her bound arms tightly to her
bosom in a pathetic attempt to hide the nakedness which had
been open to so many men for so many days.

"Harriet," she heard a voice say softly.

She looked up in the direction of the voice. Sam Goldhaber
sat against the wall beside her, his arms and legs tied in the
same fashion as hers, looking drawn and haggard, older than he
had ever seemed to look before. He was wearing a torn, dirty,
sweat-drenched kaftan, and his half-open eyes gazed at her
sorrowfully. "Sam?" she asked, only half believing what she
saw. "Sam? Is that you?"

He smiled sadly. "Who else should it be?" he muttered.

"What are you doing here?" She looked around. "And
where is here?" She had not noticed before that they were
seated on the stone floor of a large rectangular room whose
walls were covered with freshly carved and painted inscriptions
and friezes, illuminated by a series of torches which fitted at an
angle into holders attached to the walls. They were not alone.
People, dozens of people, male and female, sat along the sides
of the chamber and in its open midst, all of them bound hand
and foot. Occasional cries of anger and terror rose intermittent-
ly from the soft background noise of weeping and prayer. The

other captives seemed to be local people—Arabs—from the lowest stratum of society, judging by the worn and tattered rags which most of them wore.

Tekenues, Harriet realized. All of them. All of us.

She turned back to Sam. "Why are you here, Sam? What happened?"

He sighed. "We came to try to rescue you, Tom, the Earl, and I. We didn't succeed, obviously."

"Tommy?! He's here? Where?" Sam nodded his head and pointed with his vision to the huddled pile of filthy rags beside her, and she looked down at the still unconscious form of Thomas Sawhill. His face was pale and cadaverous, and there seemed to be traces of blood on the stone floor beneath him. She could see dried flecks and spots, the red turning to brown in the dry heat. Only the slow and regular rise and fall of his chest told her that he was still alive.

"He fought them when they took us," Sam explained weakly. "They knocked him out and dragged him here across the desert, tied to the back of a wagon."

Harriet found herself weeping freely as she reached out with her bound hands and touched the cold, fishlike skin of his cheek. "Oh, honey," she whispered sadly. She half fell and half bent over to rest her face upon his chest, her body racked with sobs.

He seemed to stir slightly as her shaking body imparted its motion to his, and his eyes opened half way. "Harriet?" he muttered. "Harriet?"

"Oh, Tommy, I love you, I love you—"

"I'm sorry, honey," he said thickly. "I tried, I tried—"

"I know, sweetheart," she wept. "I love you."

"I love you," he replied, and then fell back into unconsciousness.

Harriet lay weeping upon the motionless form for a long while. Sam Goldhaber looked at her, his tired face filled with pity and defeat, too weary to be angry, too exhausted to give expression to his own fears. After a few minutes Harriet looked up at him and asked, "The Earl is here?"

"Yes, Roderick's here, right next to me. He's sleeping."

"How can he be sleeping!"

Sam smiled weakly. "He's tired. He and I walked all the way here, tied behind a wagon just like Tom."

Harriet sat up again but kept her hands on Sawhill's chest, which she stroked absently. "Where are we, Sam? What is this place?"

"I don't know how far we walked, but we're somewhere in

Upper Egypt west of Aswan, out in the desert. I think we're in some sort of temple. It was hard to see too clearly in the dark outside—they just had a few torches lit when we got here—but I'm pretty sure that we're in the subchamber of an old mastaba."

"How long have we been here?"

He shook his head. "Not long. A few hours, maybe. These poor devils"—he nodded at the other people in the room—"seem to have been here longer. They were all here when we were brought down, and I've been able to catch a few bits of conversations. Some of them have been here for days."

"Tekenues," she muttered.

"What?"

"They're tekenues, all of them, just like us."

He shook his head. "This is madness. I just can't believe it."

"Believe it, Sam, believe it. I saw them kill Suzie and Gus. They just rotted away, shriveled up, while two of the mummies—" she shook her head, only partially believing it herself as she heard her own words, "while two of the mummies drank their souls."

"There must be an explanation of this," Sam said. "I can't accept all this talk about ancient gods and drinking souls."

"It doesn't matter what the explanation is," Harriet said, her voice expressionless, defeated, resigned. "Somehow or other, Sekhemib is alive. Somehow or other, he can control our minds and bodies. And they're going to kill us."

"There must be a way out of this," he whispered, more to himself than to Harriet. "There simply *must* be."

"There isn't, Sam," she replied. "I've tried to escape, but I couldn't. They—they punished me for trying."

His brow furrowed. "What do you mean? What did they do?"

Her voice broke. "They gave me to the crew of the ship."

Sam understood the reason for her nakedness. "Oh, Harriet. You poor thing." His lip trembled as a tear rolled down his cheek.

She shuddered and shook her head, fighting to retain what little composure she had left. "I tried to use the name of Ousha's god, but it didn't work."

"Ousha's god? What are you—oh, the scroll!"

"Yes. Ousha wrote that he could control Sekhemib by the power of Xepheraxepher, and I tried to use his name, but nothing happened." She smiled slightly, feeling a bit foolish. "I mean, of course nothing happened. I was desperate."

"I understand," Sam said soothingly. "I would have tried it myself."

Harriet looked around the room. "Maybe we should try to untie each other's bonds."

He shook his head. "Look over there, against the far wall."

She did as he suggested. Down at the end of the long room stood a large, burly man, dressed in a pure white robe. His hands rested upon the hilt of a deadly looking scimitar whose point was balanced upon the stone floor. His eyes moved continuously over the mass of huddled, weeping people.

"A little while ago, before you came to, a couple of these poor devils tried to untie each other's hands. That guard pulled them apart from each other and and then chopped their hands off."

Harriet trembled, feeling her stomach grow queasy. "Madmen. These people are insane."

"Ah, but no, my dear lady," Ahmed Hadji said from the doorway beneath the hieroglyphs. "We are merely eager to receive our reward for all the years of faithful service to the god."

Sam and Harriet turned their heads in the direction of the voice and watched as Hadji walked into the room and approached them. Sam felt a surge of anger and Harriet shrank away from him against the wall. "I trust you are comfortable?" he asked politely.

"You're the perfect host," Sam muttered. "You son of a bitch."

"Tch-tch-tch," Hadji said, clicking his tongue as he wagged a finger in remonstrance. "Please attempt to maintain some dignity. You are in a house of worship, and a service is going to be conducted upstairs. Listen!"

The faint echoes of a chant drifted down into the subterranean vault. *"Anet hrauthen neteru,"* the chorus of voice sang. Praise to you, O gods. *"Anet hrauthen 'Anpu."* Praise to you, Anubis.

Hadji smiled. "How do you like our choir?"

"Listen to me, Hadji," Sam said. "You can't get away with this. There are people who know we're in Egypt, who will come looking for us if we disappear."

He seemed sad in his mocking manner as he replied, "I'm terribly sorry, my friend, but I don't think so. And even if there are such people, they will present us with as little difficulty as you have. No," he sighed, "I'm afraid your fate is fixed. I'm terribly sorry."

"Do you want money?" Sam asked. "We can give you money, as much as you want if you'll let us go."

"Please, dear sir, don't insult me! I have more money than I know what to do with. I'm a wealthy man in my country, you know. All of us are. Why, we've been accumulating wealth for over three thousand years!" He shook his head. "No, I'm sorry. A bribe is out of the question. Unless . . ." He paused.

"Unless what?"

"Unless you can somehow arrange for me never to die. After all, that's my payment for services rendered to my companions." He paused again, as if waiting for a reply. "No? Well, then, I'm afraid we'll just have to leave things as they are." He laughed loudly and sat down beside Roderick, who was snoring. Hadji smiled at the innocent face of the young nobleman. "Ah, the English. Stiff upper lip, and all that. Remarkable people, what?"

Roderick's eyes opened slowly, his sleep disturbed by the conversation. "What—what—oh, I say!" He sat up, suddenly wide awake and frightened.

"Terribly sorry to disturb you, Your Lordship," Hadji said in a jovial, friendly manner. "We're going to begin soon, and I thought that you all might like to know what's going to happen upstairs." He shrugged apologetically. "Unfortunately, we don't have missals like the Catholics used to have, and our service is in an ancient language. I hope that doesn't detract from the beauty of the ceremony. I'm certain that scholars such as you, Dr. Goldhaber, and you, Dr. Langly, will enjoy the experience." He smiled. "For a while, at least."

"Please, Hadji," Harriet moaned, "please—"

"We begin with some ritual chanting—it has already begun, as you can hear—and then have a preliminary sacrifice. Similar to Christianity, as I understand the communion service, the crucifixion, and all that, except we aren't symbolic. We use real blood. You, my dear Dr. Goldhaber, are to be the sacrifice, or so my lord Sekhemib informs me. I'm sorry, but you are too old to be a tekenu. Your soul has too few years remaining to it for any of us to wish to drink it. I really am terribly sorry." Sam, his face deathly pale, did not respond to the goading. "Then the ceremony of the resurrection shall begin. I'm pleased to say that you, my dear lady, and our good friend the Earl of Selwyn, along with your boyfriend—oh, is he still asleep? Poor fellow. He's had an exhausting day—shall be honored by the immortals by serving as three of the six tekenues. We shall choose the other three from this motley assortment here." He waved his hand around the room.

Hadji seemed to warm to his subject as he continued. "And then comes the best part. You see, my friends—oh, Dr. Langly, you already know this, don't you?—once all seven of the immortals are with us again, they shall summon forth the god Anubis from the limbo of the ancient gods, and he shall come to us and grant us our reward. We shall drink these souls"—he waved his hand once again around the room—"and we shall become immune to disease, invulnerable, immortal ourselves, living out the lives of the tekenues and then drinking other souls, through the centuries." He smiled boyishly. "Isn't it exciting?"

"Hadji," Roderick said, "wait, listen, please. I'm a rich man. I can give you—"

"Forget it, Roderick," Sam said. "I already tried that."

"Quite," Hadji said. He cocked his ear toward the door. "Oh, dear, I think the ceremony is about to begin. We'd better take our places." Hadji walked to the door and shouted an order to the guards who stood outside, each armed as was the guard against the rear wall of the chamber. The two guards from without and the guard within began to pull the captives to their feet and drag them, many of them kicking and screaming, out of the room and up the steps toward the chanting voices. "I hope you will enjoy the temple," he said to Harriet. "It had fallen into a deplorable state of disrepair over the years, but I was delighted to find that my friends had made an effort to clean it up a bit during my absence. We even have a few new inscriptions, like this one"—he pointed to the hieroglyphs above the archway—"and we've given some of the older carvings a fresh coat of paint." As the guards pulled three of the Westerners to their feet, leaving Sawhill on the ground for the time being, Hadji continued, "Of course, once we have reestablished ourselves as in the old days, we shall arrange to have the whole area reconstructed as it once was. It should be quite a tourist attraction. We only need it one night each month, after all. Our current government will support anything which will bring in more Western currency, of course."

Hadji continued chattering away in his mocking, conversational manner as Sam, Roderick, and Harriet were dragged up the stairs and out into the courtyard of the holy place. The ancient mastaba had undergone some repair since last Ahmed Hadji had stood in its midst, but the roofless walls still opened to the starry, moonless sky. A new high place had been constructed of gray marble, and it stood at one end of the long, rectangular court. Upon it rested a new altar of white stone, with sacred texts carved vertically upon the front, and behind the altar a huge statue of Anubis overlooked the entire area. The statue, while obviously new, was nonetheless identical in form and design to the ancient statues of the god, from the jackal head to the human body, from the delicately carved robe which seemed to drape the muscular chest and arms to the ankh clasped in the human hands. Large oil lamps burned high on either side of the altar, casting flickering light upon it and upon the statue of Anubis, which seemed almost alive amid the shifting shadows.

Before the altar knelt Sekhemib in a position of supplication and praise. He rested on one knee, the other drawn upward to his chest as he bent forward at the waist, head bowed and arms stretching out before him, palms forward, fingers pointing up. He was dressed still in a robe of pure white linen, a purple sash tied at the waist; but now he was also draped in golden jewelry. The shiny yellow medallion which was the medium for the power of the god to enter the physical world hung from his neck along with other golden chains. Golden bracelets encircled his wrists. A headband of gold encircled his forehead, and a small cobra, also of fine gold, reared up and out of the headband. His sandals had golden thongs.

Six bodies lay on the ground before the raised platform upon which Sekhemib knelt before the altar, their heads resting a few inches from the gray marble, their feet extending outward toward the court. Four of them were mummies, and the other two were corpses in a state of putrefaction. The two rancid bodies were those of Meret and Yuya; the four mummies those of Wenet, Senmut, Herihor, and Khumara. All six were waiting motionless and insensate for other people's souls.

Haleel Haftoori rested upon his old, arthritic knees a few feet from the six bodies, and behind him forty other people, all in the same position of genuflection, fanned out in a triangular pattern which was made complete when Ahmed Hadji took his place in the ranks. Forty-two worshippers, one for each of the forty-two gods of the Hall of the Two Truths, where Isis, Osiris, and Thoth sat in judgment on the souls of the dead; forty-two worshippers and the seven immortals. So it was again as it had been in ancient times.

The guards, whose cooperation with the cult was caused by reasons known only to themselves, who had been seduced by promises of money, of women, of wealth, finished dragging the tekenues up from the vault and deposited them roughly upon the sandy stone at the rear of the courtyard opposite the altar and the statue of Anubis. Thomas Sawhill was the last one brought up and his eyes opened weakly as the guards dropped him with a jolt onto the ground. Harriet sat beside him, weeping softly. Sam sat beside her, and Roderick beside him. None of them spoke, but each uttered a few muffled, choaking sobs, thus joining in the soft, terrified desperation of the assembly of tekenues.

The rhythmic chanting stopped for a long moment. Then Sekhemib rose to his feet and turned to face the assembly. He spoke as always in the long dead tongue of the ancient land. Of the tekenues, only Harriet Langly could understand him, but she paid only scant attention to his words.

"Long have you watched and waited, beloved of the gods," he said to the still kneeling priests. "Tonight is the reward for your faithfulness. Tonight shall you partake of the blessing of Anubis, and from this day forth shall the eternal darkness of death be held from you."

A few frenzied cries of "*Anet hrauthen neteru*" broke from the assembly, and Sekhemib raised his hand to silence them. "Let us praise the gods, let us sacrifice to them and spill the sweet life-wine upon the altar of Anubis, let us each take the sacrificial blood upon our foreheads, and fill the air with words of praise to the Prince of Eternity." Sekhemib looked directly at Hadji, who stood up quickly when the ancient priest said, "Ahmed Hadji, priest of Thoth, rise and approach." Hadji tried in vain to repress the blushing smile which spread across his face. So I am to be especially honored, he thought, for my services to the lord Sekhemib! He will command me to initiate the sacrifice and pour the blood upon the altar, and I shall be the first to take the ritual blood upon my forehead!

Hadji bowed deeply to Sekhemib. "My master honors me beyond words!"

Sekhemib nodded at Hadji and then said to the assembly, "Ahmed Hadji, the priest of Thoth, traveled far through much danger to bring me and my companions home to Egypt. For this he merits our thanks and our praise." A muffled chorus of goodwill toward Hadji arose from the assembled priests.

Sekhemib's eyes went suddenly cold and he stared hard at

Hadji. "But I instructed him to burn the bodies of the tekenues of my beloved Meret and my brother Yuya, and he disobeyed me. They were subjected yet again to the pain of death because of his disobedience. For this, he merits death."

Hadji's face still held the remnants of a smile as the meaning of the words sank into his brain, as the two guards who stood on either side of the altar approached him and grabbed him firmly by the arms, as a third guard drew a ritual dagger from its sheath. Hadji looked at Sekhemib with disbelief. "My lord—my lord, this is—" The two guards pulled him to the altar and bent him over it so that his chin rested just beyond the blood gutter which had been carved into the altar top. They twisted his arms to the breaking point and held him motionless. "No, wait, my lord," he sputtered, "this is a mistake—I did burn the tekenues, I swear, I swear— my lord, please—I did as I was commanded, I swear, I swear . . ."

Sekhemib ignored him. Turning to Haftoori, he commanded, "Haleel, servant of Anubis, call forth the new priest of Thoth and stand him before me."

Haftoori said a few words in Arabic, and from the shadowy recesses of the corner of the mastaba courtyard, little Faz walked happily forward. He was clean and groomed and dressed like the others in a robe of pure white linen. He stood in front of Sekhemib and beamed up at him. Sekhemib smiled at the little boy. "Thou hast been of service to me and to the gods, my child," he said kindly, "and we shall reward thee with a gift which thou art yet too young to appreciate. But we shall teach thee and train thee and nurture thee, and thou shalt be a joy to us and a joy to the gods until the end of the world." He nodded at the third guard, who held the drawn dagger, and he reached over and removed the chain with the golden medallion from Ahmed Hadji's neck. He handed it to Sekhemib who lifted it high and cried out, "I now proclaim that Faisal, the son of Ali, is the new priest of the god Thoth. Let us honor him and honor his master."

"*Anet hrauthen Tekhuti!*" the priests cried in unison. Praise to you, O Thoth. Sekhemib placed the golden chain around the child's neck.

"My lord—" Hadji wept with trembling voice, "my lord . . ."

Still ignoring him, Sekhemib said to Faz, "Go now and stand with the old one, and do what he does." Faz understood not one word of what was spoken to him, but Haftoori translated for the child, who nodded and, still grinning impishly, hopped over to the old man. He knew that for some reason his uncle Ahmed was about to die, but it did not bother him. Life was cheap in the slums of Cairo, where little Faz had spent all of his brief life while his wealthy uncle lived in luxury and opulence. The prospect of seeing his uncle murdered did not disturb little Faz. He had seen many people murdered. And he had never really liked his uncle.

Sekhemib turned back to the altar and took the dagger from the guard, who bowed and stepped back off the gray marble platform. The ancient priest slowly placed the tip of the dagger upon the throbbing skin just above Hadji's carotid artery. Hadji cried out, "My lord, I rescued you from oblivion! I saved you from the darkness of death! My lord, I have served you well! Do I not deserve better than this? Do I not deserve thanks?"

Sekhemib's lips curled in a cold, inhuman smile. "I thank thee," he said, and then drove the blade home.

Pain and shock stretched Hadji's eyes wide as his blood burst from the wound, a sanguine fountain spurting out and drenching the altar, splashing loudly upon the stone. He tried to cry out, but only a rasping gurgle escaped from his lips amid the flow of blood. His body shook and jerked spasmodically as the light of awareness slowly faded from his eyes and then went out entirely. The guards held him over the altar until the blood ceased to spurt, and then dragged his body away, tossing it unceremoniously into the same corner in which Faz had been standing.

Sekhemib looked out over the assembly, whose faces registered shock, sorrow, and fear. "Be it known to all," he cried, "that the gods bless the obedient and destroy the disobedient." He took the dagger and dipped the blade into the red pool in the blood gutter. Holding the bloody knife aloft, he cried, *"Anet hrauthen neteru!"*

A brief, almost imperceptible moment of hesitation, and then the priests responded, *"Anet hrauthen neteru!"* Homage to you, O gods. Haleel Haftoori took little Faz by the hand and walked forward with him to the foot of the altar. He knelt and the boy imitated him. Sekhemib wiped the flat side of the dagger across the old man's forehead and said, *"Anet hrak Set."* He alone was privileged to address the gods in the familiar form.

"*Anet hrauten Set,*" the priests chanted in reply. Homage to you, Set.

Sekhemib wiped the dagger on the child's forehead. "*Anet hrak Tekhuti.*"

"*Anet hrauthen Tekhuti,*" came the response. Homage to you, Thoth. Sekhemib went through the list of the names of the gods in the ancient pantheon, and each priest of each god in turn came forward and received the sacrificial blood upon the forehead.

When at last each priest and priestess was back in position, the ancient high priest of Anubis turned to the altar and cried out, "*Au arina neterhetepu, perchkheru en khu!*" I have made offerings to the gods, I have sacrificed to the spirits!

"*Anet hrauthen neteru,*" came the response of the priests.

"'*Anpu kheq tetta, nekhemkua am aterit!*" Anubis, Prince of Eternity, deliver me from calamity.

"*Anet hrauthen neteru!*"

"'*Anpu neb nest, nekhemkua ma 'aputat utetiu themesu!*" Anubis, Lord of Thrones, deliver me from the messengers of evil.

"*Anet hrauthen neteru!*"

"'*Anpu ned Ut, 'Anpu chent neter het, 'Anpu neb nifu, nekhemkua ma ab.*" Anubis, Lord of the City of Embalming, Anubis, Dweller in the Tomb of the Gods, Anubis, Lord of the Winds, deliver me from death.

"'*Anpu, nekhemkua ma ab! Anet hrauthen neteru!*"

Sekhemib turned to the assembly and nodded to the guards. They took hold of the arms of Thomas Sawhill and dragged him forward, placing him beside the mummy of Senmut, high priest of the god Ra. The mummy wore its medallion upon a golden chain, and the guards slipped the chain over the mummy's head and placed it around Sawhill's neck. Then they retired to the area where the sobbing, terrified tekenues lay bound and weeping.

Sekhemib stepped down and walked to the foot of the mummy, turning then to face both the altar and the motionless form. "*Anet hrak, Senmut!*" he cried. "*Aua Sekhemib abu 'Anpuf rexkuak, rexkua renk!*" Homage to you, Senmut! I, Sekhemib, the priest of Anubis, I know your name. "*Tekenu enti khenak! Iuk enn tem sekhauk, iuk em arauk!*" The tekenu is with thee! Come to us without memories of evil, come to us in thy form. "*Auk er khekh en khekh, aha khekh!*" Thou shalt live for millions of years, a life of millions of years!

"*Anet hrak Senmut!*" the priests cried in unison. "*Anet hrauthen neteru!*"

A sudden wave of incredible pain swept over Thomas Sawhill, rousing him to sudden, horrid consciousness. His eyes stared wildly around and a scream of agony burst from his throat. He continued to scream as his flesh withered, as his heart and lungs began to grow hard and rigid, as the shrinking skin crackled and blistered all over his crumbling form, as blood and mucus began to gush forth from his pores, his mouth, his ears, his nose, his eyes. He screamed and screamed and then froze in mute pain as his chest collapsed inward, as the skin of his face drew tight against the bones of his skull, as the internal disintegration proceeded apace and the leathery form which had been a living man but a few moments before twitched and then lay still.

Harriet Langly watched with a strange detachment. She wept and felt sorrow, but she was not overwhelmed by the hysteria of grief which she felt she should have experienced. Something had died in her, some element of the spark of human feeling had been snuffed out by the endless succession of horrors. She looked sadly but with resignation as the crumbling corpse of the man she loved was picked up and carried to the rear of the temple and dropped like a bag of rubbish onto the sand just outside the door.

The mummy of Senmut, the high priest of Ra, rose slowly and stiffly to its feet. Two attendant priests quickly stripped away the linen shroud which had rotted onto his pink, fresh flesh, and then reverently washed him. When after a few minutes they had removed the dust of the long millennia, they slipped a white robe over his head. Senmut turned and smiled at Sekhemib, who smiled back at him. Then Senmut raised his hands and cried out, "'*Anpu, anet hrauthen, suten neteru, xepera xer khat, kheq tetta!*'"

Those are the words they carved above the doorway, Harriet thought distractedly. Anubis, praise to you, King of the Gods, who came into being in ancient times, Prince of Eternity. Then she thought, Oh, Tommy, my dear love, Tommy, Tommy. She wept afresh, quietly, as if she had not the strength to mourn.

Something was buzzing about in her mind, but it did not assume a comprehensible form. Something she had heard. Something.

Two guards grabbed Roderick and dragged him forward.

The young man was weeping, begging, pleading with them, but they silenced him with a blow to the mouth. They tossed him down beside the rotting body of Yuya and placed the golden medallion about his neck. He tried to rise, but they kicked him in the chest, knocking the wind from his lungs, and he lay there stunned.

"*Anet hrak, Yuya!*" Sekhemib began again. "*Aua Sekhemib abu 'Anpuf rexkuak, rexkua renk!*"

Sam and Harriet watched silently as the words of the ritual were spoken over the body of Yuya. They closed their eyes and tried not to listen to the frenzied screams of the young Earl as he felt his body disintegrate, as wave after wave of pain swept over him, as his life was sucked from him by the putrid corpse of the ancient high priest of Set. His screams grew fainter and fainter, weaker and weaker, and then ceased.

"Sam?" she muttered.

"Yeah, kiddo?"

"Thanks. Thanks for trying."

Sam sniffed back a tear. "We had to try, all of us." He paused and then added, "Tom really loved you, you know."

She smiled sadly. "I know. I loved him too, more than anything or anyone in the world."

They watched in numb attention as Yuya rose again from the dead and was ritually washed by the attendant priests. Two guards took Harriet by the arms and pulled her to her feet. "Goodbye, Sam," she wept.

"Goodbye, boss," he whispered as they took her forward and placed her beside the body of Meret. She did not resist, she made no effort to rise or run. She lay, resigned and softly weeping, as the golden chain was placed around her neck.

Yuya was facing the altar, and she turned her head and watched him as he cried, "'*Anpu, anet hrauthen, suten neteru, xepera xer khat, kheq tetta!*" Anubis, praise to you, King of the Gods, who came into being in ancient times, Prince of Eternity.

She gasped in shock as the buzzing in her thoughts became suddenly clear, as she realized what she had heard. "SAM!" she yelled, struggling to get up, blocking the kicks of the guards with her arms, "SAM! IT'S EGYPTIAN! XEPER MEANS TO BE OR TO BECOME IN EGYPTIAN!" A guard struck her across the face with the hilt of his scimitar, and she fell back upon the stones.

Sam Goldhaber had heard her cries, but they were

meaningless to him. Poor Harriet, he thought. On the edge of death, and all she can think of is some silly little scholarly question we raised back home. Xeper is Egyptian. Xephera-xepher is an Egyptian god. Well, he thought sadly, at least we've figured out one final point of etymology before we die. Scholars to the last, for all the good it does us.

Harriet Langly screamed horribly as the corpse of Meret sucked forth her life. Sam sighed and closed his eyes once again, trying to withdraw into himself, to separate himself from all that was happening around him. The chanting continued, the screams and cries of the tekenues one after the other reached his ears, the words of praise to Anubis were repeated over and over, but he felt strangely removed from the proceedings. It was true, as Hadji had said, that he was too old to be a tekenu for one of the seven immortals, but he felt certain that this fact bore with it no element of hope for his survival. They would use him for a tekenu of one of the other priests, the mortal priests, or they would just kill him outright or use him for another sacrifice, or something. He was a dead man, and he knew it.

Sam Goldhaber opened his tired eyes and looked toward the front of the temple. Seven people stood around the free-standing altar, all of them dressed in white linen, six of them pink-skinned and fleshy, and he did not have to look to know who they were. Sekhemib and Meret, Yuya and Senmut, Herihor and Khumara and Wenet, walking dead, living corpses, vampires from the dawn of history.

He watched as Sekhemib cried out, *"Anet hrak 'Anpu, urk er nebt neteru!"* Praise to thee, Anubis, greater than every other god!

*"Anet hrauthen 'Anpu!"* the priests chanted.

The seven immortals joined their hands as they stood in a circle around the altar and closed their eyes. Samuel Goldhaber could not understand the chant which arose from the priests who knelt before the seven immortals. As with one voice they sang, *"'Anpu xepera xer khat, iuk em arauk!"* Anubis, who came into being in ancient times, they chanted, come to us in thy form. *"'Anpu xepera xer khat, iuk em arauk! 'Anpu xepera xer khat, iuk em arauk!"*

Sam blinked and shook his head, thinking for a moment that he was beginning to succumb to the fatigue and the series of emotional shocks he had sustained, for there seemed to be spots before his eyes. But he realized almost immediately that it was not his vision with which something was amiss. There seemed to be a sparkling glow suffusing the air in the temple, a glow which appeared to grow increasingly bright as the chanting continued. The glow slowly circled the room like a languid whirlpool of charged air and began to coalesce in the area of the altar, slowly drawing together above the bloody marble block, in the midst of seven entranced ancients.

"*'Anpu xepera xer khat, iuk em arauk!*" the chant continued. "*'Anpu xepera xer khat, iuk em arauk! 'Anpu xepera xer khat, iuk em arauk!*"

The whirling glow continued to spin more and more rapidly as it drew together into a pillar of brilliant, radiant light upon the altar, a pillar stretching up above the heads of the assembly, illuminating the interior of the temple with a painful intensity. Soon the glowing whirlpool was moving so rapidly that the human eye could no longer detect its motion, and it seemed to solidify, seemed to begin to assume a form. It formed itself into what seemed to be the rudimentary shape of a torso, which glowed indistinctly as the blur slowly resolved itself down into clarity.

A bellowing cry, inhuman and terrible, a roar of hatred and anger and triumph and joy, smote the ears of the assembly, echoing with a deafening power from the trembling stone walls of the ancient mastaba. Sam's mouth hung open in an astonishment so profound that even his own danger was momentarily forgotten.

Its fist raised defiantly at the sky, the god Anubis stood upon the altar.

The creature was huge, at least fifteen feet high, muscular in the chest and arms and narrow-waisted. The muscles of its arms and legs and stomach rippled as it moved. Its phallus was huge and erect, throbbing eagerly as its inhuman voice bellowed insanely at the silent heavens. Its head was that of an animal, long-jawed, flat-nosed, covered with fur, bristling with fangs.

"This isn't real," Sam muttered to himself. "This can't be happening."

Anubis looked down at the seven holy tekenues who circled the altar, and a lascivious grin seemed to spread across the canine face and brighten the mad, staring eyes. A low but loud growl of joy and approval issued forth from the salivating jaw as it looked from one to the other, from Sekhemib to Meret, from Yuya to Senmut, from Wenet to Herihor to

Khumara. Then it raised its snout at the sky and raised both its fists and howled deafeningly.

One of the guards, almost paralyzed with fear, dragged a young Arab from the rear of the chamber and dropped him before the altar. Anubis watched with its irrational eyes as the guard scurried back to the rear of the room. Haleel Haftoori crawled forward on his stomach, and his voice trembled as he cried imploringly, "*'Anpu, urk er nebt neteru, ikua xerten! Terten tu neb aria ma ennu ari en ten en xu sefex apu, amiu ses en nebsen neb neteru!*" Anubis, he had prayed, I have come before you! Do away with all evil dwelling within me as you have done for those seven spirits who follow the king of the gods!

A pleased snarl escaped from the creature's jaw, and it stretched out its hand at Haftoori. A charge of brilliant light streamed forth from the creature's taloned but humanoid hand and engulfed Haftoori and the terrified tekenu. The stream of light, blinding all who did not avert their eyes, continued unabated for a few seconds, and then ceased suddenly.

Before the altar was a charred heap of ash and smouldering bone, all that remained of the tekenu. Beside it stood a young man of no more than twenty-five years, tall, straight, strong, his rich jet-black hair streaming in waves down his neck onto his muscular shoulders. It was Haleel Haftoori.

Haftoori turned to the assembly of priests and cried, "*Anet hrauthen 'Anpu! Anet hrauthen 'Anpu!*" His cries were echoed by the others, who wept and fell upon their faces and cried out words of praise and raised a cacophonous, frenzied din. The guards began to drag the tekenues forward one by one as the priests and priestesses, one by one, crawled on their stomachs toward the altar and the god. Anubis emitted howls and roars of triumph and pleasure as it engulfed each priest and each tekenu in the power of its blinding divinity, giving to its servants the souls of the people. It had slept in limbo for all these thousands of years, and its joy at resurrection caused it to howl and shriek and bellow. As the power flowed forth from the taloned hands and the thick, heavy saliva dripped from the grinning jaws, its phallus began to spew ejaculate freely. The priests and priestesses, male and female alike, rushed forward to cover themselves with the inhuman seed, to bathe in the potent, splendorous liquid which streamed forth from the enormous, throbbing fountain.

Samuel Goldhaber felt himself being lifted up from the floor of the temple by strong yet trembling hands. He did not look at the faces of the terrified guards, did not notice the frenzied, orgiastic priesthood which rolled about the floor amid cries of praise and terror. He was staring at the monster which stood upon the altar, its eyes blazing madly and sounds, too awful for the human ear to hear or the human mind to accept, bellowing forth from the moist, open maw from whence the long red tongue slavered obscenely over the pointed fangs.

"This can't be happening," Sam cried aloud as the guards dragged him forward from the rear of the temple. "This can't be happening!" This can't be happening, his mind repeated madly, this can't *be*, it just can't *be*, it just can't

be.

It can't
        be.
It can't . . .
            Be.
Be.
Be!

Samuel Goldhaber felt his body rock as if he had been struck by a bolt of lightning; but it was not the power of the monster Anubis which had struck him. He suddenly understood what Harriet Langly had been trying to tell him before her death, and the impact of the realization had dealt him an almost physical blow of shock.

"*Sam,*" she had cried, "*it's Egyptian! Xeper means to be or to become in Egyptian!*"

"Yes!! Yes!!" he screamed aloud. "He dictated it! He dictated it!" Ousha—Joseph—did not write the scroll with his own hand! He dictated it to a scribe! He spoke the ancient Semitic tongue which would one day evolve into Hebrew, and he dictated the scroll to a Hyksos scribe! Of course he did, of course he did! Samuel Goldhaber began to laugh insanely and struggled to maintain his wits even as the truth flooded in on him and filled him with a mad, desperate hope. Xepheraxepher! There never was a god named Xepheraxepher! When Ousha came to the name of the god he dared not speak it, so he translated it into Egyptian! Xepheraxepher! The Being Who Becomes, the Existence Which Exists, the Self-created One!

*Then Moses said to God, "If I come to the people of Israel and say to them, 'The God of your fathers has sent me to you,' and they shall ask me, 'What is his name?' what shall I say to them?" And God spoke from the burning bush and answered Moses, saying, "I AM*

*THAT I AM. Say this to the people of Israel, "I AM hath sent me."*

Xeper, to be! Sam thought. Egyptian!

Hayah, to be! Hebrew!

I am that I am, the Being Who Becomes, the Existence Which Exists, the Self-created One!

Xepheraxepher!

Yahweh!

The Lord God Almighty! The Lord of Hosts! The God of Abraham, of Isaac, and of Jacob.

And of Joseph! And of Joseph!

Sam felt the golden chain being slipped around his neck, felt himself being pushed down to the ground before the altar, saw the monster grinning insanely at him, saw the priest beside him crying in ecstatic supplication, saw the creature Anubis begin to raise its hand in his direction, and the ancient words of the psalms of David rushed from his memory to his tongue, and he cried them aloud in Hebrew, he cried out the name of the Lord, he cried out Yahweh, to the God of his fathers.

"OUT OF THE DEPTHS HAVE I CRIED UNTO THEE, O LORD! O LORD, HEAR MY VOICE!"

The monster seemed frozen as the sound of the word "Yahweh" reached its ears.

"IN THEE, O LORD, DO I TAKE REFUGE! MAKE HASTE TO HELP ME, O LORD! BE NOT FAR FROM ME, FROM THE VOICE OF MY SUPPLICATION! SAVE ME, O GOD, FROM THE EVILDOERS, PROTECT ME FROM THOSE WHO SEEK MY HURT!"

The words "Yahweh" and again "Yahweh" assailed the pointed ears of the creature which stood upon the altar, and it bellowed forth a scream of fury as the bolt of power shot from its hands and engulfed Sam and the priest who lay beside him. The heat of the energy surrounded them, and then—

Nothing.

Nothing happened.

The temple was suddenly silent. The priests ceased their frenzied cries. The tekenues ceased their terrified wails. Anubis stood motionless upon the altar, glaring at Samuel Goldhaber with undisguised dread.

Sam rose to his feet and returned the monster's stare. Then he shouted, "THERE IS NONE LIKE UNTO THEE

AMONG THE GODS, O LORD, NOR ARE ANY WORKS LIKE THINE! *FOR THOU ALONE ART GOD!*"

The ground began to tremble.

"BE THOU TO ME A ROCK OF REFUGE, A STRONG FORTRESS TO SAVE ME, FOR THOU ART MY ROCK AND MY FORTRESS, O LORD OF HOSTS!"

The trembling increased rapidly, the low rumble growing into a loud roar as the stones of the ancient mastaba began to shake and dislodge, casting dust into the air and bits of age-old mortar flying in all directions. Anubis lost its balance and tumbled from the altar, falling headfirst onto the ground in front of Sam. The monster looked up at him, no more than two feet away, and the howl which it cried out assaulted Sam's face with fetid, damp breath. It reached out and tried to swipe at Sam with its talons, but it could not, for some reason, make contact with the human's flesh. Anubis pounded the stone floor with its fist and bellowed hideously in overwhelming, furious, impotent wrath.

Sam's face seemed aglow with ecstacy as he cried, "O LORD, THOU GOD OF VENGEANCE, THOU GOD OF VENGEANCE SHINE FORTH! RISE UP, O JUDGE OF THE EARTH, AND RENDER TO THE PROUD THEIR PUNISHMENT!"

The rupturing earth began to sunder and a long fissure opened abruptly in front of Sam Goldhaber. He feared for a moment that it would draw him into it, but he found that the ground upon which he stood held firm. The stones of the floor of the temple split and tumbled into the fissure, and Anubis, caught unaware by the sudden split in the surface of the floor, fell feet first into the black gulf. Its talons clawed hopelessly at the edge of the fissure, and billows of flame shot up and enveloped the creature. The inhuman cry of pain and fury rang out as the god of the dead fell into the fire which issued forth from the bowels of the Earth.

Sam laughed and wept simultaneously as he heard the words of the prophet Isaiah spilling out of his mouth. "How art thou fallen from Heaven, O Lucifer, son of the morning! How art thou cut down, thou who didst lay low the nations! Thou art brought down to Hell, to the depths of the pit!"

With a painful cry of sudden and unexpected revival, Sekhemib and the six immortals fell back from the altar, their trembling hands grasping their heads. Pain shot through them, a wrenching pain of abrupt disconnection. Sekhemib looked out at the chaos in front of him and cried out, "What has happened? What has happened?" but no one answered him. The priests of the cult were running madly from the temple, screaming and crying in fear. Sekhemib saw Sam Goldhaber standing alone before him, a look of anger, of triumph, of hatred, of vengeance, of vindication beaming from his ecstatic face. He shouted joyfully, "WHO IS LIKE UNTO THEE O LORD, LORD OF HOSTS?"

Sekhemib recoiled from the sound of "Yahweh, Yahweh," and he shouted as loudly as he could, "Stop his mouth! Stop his mouth! Silence him at once!" but no priests remained in the holy place to answer his command. Sekhemib rushed forward from the altar and leaped at Sam, but a power which was horribly familiar to him, a force which he had known before, long ago, stopped him and sent him sprawling backward onto the hard, splintering stones.

Sam raised his eyes to the black sky and cried out, "THE LORD REIGNS! HE IS ROBED IN MAJESTY! THE LORD IS GIRDED WITH STRENGTH!" He stared directly at Sekhemib and shouted, "HE WILL BRING BACK UPON THEM THEIR INIQUITY AND WIPE THEM OUT FOR THEIR WICKEDNESS! LET THEM WITHER, O LORD, LIKE THE GRASS WHICH TAKES ROOT UPON THE ROOF! LET THEM FALL DOWN IN THEIR DESPAIR, O LORD! LET THE MIGHTY BE BROUGHT DOWN!" And then, softly and in his own words, not the words of the ancient King of Israel, he prayed, "And Lord, I beg you, let the souls they have stolen be freed."

The rumbling ceased abruptly, and a chilling silence descended upon the mastaba and the surrounding desert. Sekhemib drew himself up slowly from the cracked stones and stood erect before Sam Goldhaber, his livid face shaking in fury. "Thou miscreant!" he spat in the ancient tongue. "For thy blasphemy shalt thou pay dearly, in pain shalt thou slowly pay for this sacrilege!"

Sam understood not one word of the threat, but Sekhemib's tone and expression communicated it to him quite clearly. But the just shall live by faith, the prophet said. The just shall live by faith. He lifted his eyes once again to the dark vault of the heavens, and he cried out the name of God over and over and over. "YAHWEH! YAHWEH!"

"Servants of the gods!" Sekhemib shouted. "Return ye to

this place! I command you, in the name of Anubis! Return ye hither!"

The priests and priestesses heard the command of the high priest of Anubis and they began slowly and hesitantly to walk back to the mastaba. They entered the ruined holy place in timid groups of twos and threes, looking furtively about them, shamefacedly drawing closer to the altar. Sekhemib stood and glowered angrily, his balled fists resting upon his hips. "Cowards!" he spat. "Hope ye all to drink of the font of life, and yet tremble before the tricks of a Hyksos god? Know ye not that Anubis cannot be conquered, that Anubis cannot be defeated?"

"YAHWEH," Sam cried. "YAHWEH! YAHWEH! YAHWEH!"

A very, very soft and gentle sound seemed to arise from the patches of sand which were visible between the rubble of cracked and broken floor stones. The sand was shifting, moving, undulating to some unheard rhythm, sending feathery, rippling waves outward from the center of the mastaba. The waves swelled increasingly, and bits of sand flew outward in all directions. As the clumps of sand fell to the ground they did not dissipate, they did not merge back into the desert floor, they did not scatter into the myriad grains of which they were composed. They fell into patterns: long, narrow rows here, shorter narrow rows there, spherical piles in some spots, large rectangular piles in others. And regardless of the particular pattern of the individual sandpiles, they had one characteristic in common: they were moving.

Sekhemib struggled to keep his balance as the stone floor block upon which he was standing began to move violently from side to side. He jumped back onto the altar slab and watched dumbfounded as the long, narrow piles of sand and the short, narrow piles of sand sought out the large rectangular piles and attached themselves to the corners, as the spherical piles of sand seemed to waddle and roll to the rectangular piles in their turn. "'*Anpu*,'" Sekhemib muttered fearfully, "*nekhem-kua . . . nekhemkua . . .*" Deliver me, Anubis, deliver me.

Sam's mouth was hanging open in wonder as he watched the moving, shifting formations of sand. "O give thanks unto the Lord, for He is good, and His mercy endureth forever," he whispered as he slowly came to realize what exactly it was that he was seeing.

The long, narrow piles of sand slowly assumed the form of

human legs; the shorter narrow piles assumed the form of arms, all now attached to the rectangular patterns which were solidifying into human torsos even as the spherical sand concentrations formed themselves into faceless human heads. The sand creatures were forming themselves everywhere, in the mastaba and out on the desert beyond. One of them came to its final shape at the foot of the altar, and it stood to its feet. Moments later dozens, and then hundreds, of the humanoid beings stood up and began to move unsteadily upon stiff and fleshless limbs.

Sekhemib cried in sudden, horrible pain. A hand had grasped him by the wrist and was squeezing with an inhuman force so incredibly strong that he felt his bones cracking beneath the pressure. The floor stones of the ancient mastaba were thrust upward, dislodged from their ancient mortar, cast aside as the sand continued to give birth to the sand creatures, the pitiful images of human beings, the senseless, shuffling things whose eyes did not see and whose ears did not hear, but whose featureless faces radiated eternal wrath, unrelenting anger, a lust for vengeance, a murderous fury, a hatred older than the very sands of Egypt.

Sam had prayed for the freedom of the stolen souls. And now they were free.

Tekenues. They were the tekenues.

All the dust and all the ashes of all the murdered innocents of all the millennia were being reconstituted from the sand into which their remains had been cast by the murderous priests. Ten thousand years, a hundred thousand years, since before humanity was human, since before the dim mentalities of the prehuman creatures whose sons would build the pyramids could even conceive of deities, since before mankind existed, the remnants of the tekenues had been burned and buried in the area around this mastaba. And now they were all coming back, hundreds of thousands of years of victims, an army of tortured, stolen souls, rising from the trembling sand into the broken forms of embodied human hatred.

Sam Goldhaber lost consciousness as the multitude arose from the sand which stretched for miles in all directions, as the screams of agony burst forth from Sekhemib, from Meret, from Yuya and Senmut and Herihor and Khumara and Wenet, as thousands, tens of thousands, millions, of inhuman hands grasped them and tore them and ripped them and rent them asunder, casting bloody bits of severed flesh up into the air, turning the collapsing mastaba red with blood, the muffled laughter from each vengeful throat merging with the identical muffled laughter of each other identical epitome of hatred until the combination produced a massive, deafening thunder of screaming, murderous fury. Those mortal priests who had fled from the temple added their cries of terror and agony to the general din as hands thrust up from the sand beneath their feet everywhere outside the temple walls and held them, crushed them, tore them to pieces.

And then there was silence.

Sam Goldhaber did not know how much time had passed, but when he drifted back up to consciousness the silence was the first thing which he noticed. He was lying face down upon the ground, and particles of sand were in his mouth and eyes and nostrils. He tried to spit the sand from his mouth, tried to bring forth tears to clear his eyes, but found that he was too dehydrated to manage it easily. He blinked and blinked and blinked, and eventually produced enough liquid to free his eyes of the irritants. He sat up and looked around him.

The mastaba was gone, devoured by the now motionless expanse of desert. Not one stone remained of the ancient temple which had such a short time ago been the site of such unspeakable monstrosity. As the first rays of the morning sun crept over the hills to the east on the other side of the Nile, he could dimly see dozens of bodies lying motionless upon the sand all around him. No, not motionless, for their chests were rising and falling in living, breathing bodies, their own bodies, resurrected bodies with liberated souls. All the people who had been brought there the night before to serve as feed for the monster and his servants were alive and free.

Harriet Langly lay upon her side ten yards away, and near her was Thomas Sawhill. Far away from them both, Roderick Fowles was stiffly raising himself up on his left elbow. He looked over at Sam Goldhaber quizzically, and then, exhaustion and shock reasserting themselves, he fell back unconscious onto the sand.

Sam smiled softly as he sat silent upon the warm sand. As the sun rose into the clear blue Egyptian sky, the words of David's psalm drifted in and out of his mind.

"The fool hath said in his heart, 'There is no God.'"

# EPILOGUE

▲ The summer sky of rural New York State was already beginning to grow gray and dusky, and the first cool breaths of the impending autumn winds were slowly beginning to repaint the leaves. The air of Greenfield was already filling with the subtle aromas of apple pies and pumpkin pies, of traditional autumn cakes and roasts, of the last few ears of the season's corn harvest as they bobbed in steaming pots of bubbling water. Soon the brightly colored leaves would drift downward from the boughs and carpet the sidewalks, the streets, and the floor of the nearby forests with patches of red and yellow and brown, adorning the peaceful world with its annual coat of many colors.

Harriet Langly Sawhill lay in her husband's arms on the sofa in front of the fireplace, her gaze drifting lazily back and forth from the rustic panorama which stretched out before the long picture window to the comforting flames which licked the edge of the logs. Thursday was always a peaceful, restful day. Thomas Sawhill had no office hours and she had no classes. It was a day upon which they had decided that they should do absolutely nothing, and this intentional idleness was both regenerative and rejuvenating. Harriet's mind was not constructing coherent thoughts but rather was allowing itself to be washed by waves of contentment, peacefulness, security, and calm.

"My parents called today, while you were still asleep," she said softly.

"Yeah?" he replied, stretching his arms out like a contented cat. "What's new with them?"

"Not much."

They were silent for a long while as they sat upon the sofa and listened with uncomplicated ease to the crackling of the fire and the low moan of the October wind. They said nothing, for nothing needed to be said. Each knew the other's thoughts and shared the other's memories. Each knew that a merciful and benevolent Providence had granted to them an opportunity for a life together, a life which had seemed fated such a short time ago never to be.

"Have they accepted our compromise?" he asked.

"Hmmm?"

"Your parents. Have they gotten used to the idea of what we did?"

"Not really," she replied, "but give 'em time. They'll get accustomed to it eventually. After all, Tom, you're a Lutheran and I'm a Catholic. What else could we do but get married by an Episcopalian priest?"

"Made sense to me," he laughed. "Of course, we could have followed Sam's advice and become Jews."

"Oh, sure," she said, smiling. "That would have thrilled both families. Let's face it, neither of our families is particularly broad-minded."

He nodded. "I know. And none of them went through what we went through, either. After what happened, the differences between Protestants and Catholics don't really mean very much to me. It all seems so petty and silly, somehow."

"I know what you mean," she replied, nestling down slightly into the crook of his arm. "Who would have ever thought it? I mean, three old agnostics like us and Sam. We're going to an Episcopalian church and Sam's decided to become a rabbi."

He laughed softly. "Strange world, isn't it?"

She nodded. "Stranger than I'd ever imagined it could be." She was silent for a few moments. "Did it really happen, Tommy? It all seems like a dream."

"A bad dream," he agreed softly. "But it happened, Harriet. It happened. Maybe it'd be better if we did think of it as a dream."

"Maybe," she said pensively. "I don't think I'll ever really be able to understand what happened there, over in Egypt."

"It defies logic," he said. "I've decided not to attempt to try to analyze it rationally. It's a mystery, that's all. A mystery."

They became quiet again and looked out the window

as one unfortunate leaf was severed from a branch and drifted erratically down to the grass. Harriet muttered, "Xepheraxepher."

"Hmmm?"

"Nothing, honey. Nothing."

Harriet smiled into the flames which danced upon the logs. The world was beautiful, and life was fine.

Three hundred miles away, Professor Samuel Goldhaber sat patiently, amusement and a tinge of annoyance mingling in his expression as the old bespectacled man on the other side of the large desk paged slowly and thoughtfully through the folder of papers which he held in his hands. At last he looked up over his bifocals and smiled at Sam. "I'm very happy about this, Dr. Goldhaber, very happy indeed, but a bit surprised."

"How so, Rabbi?" Sam asked.

Rabbi Myron Schamis sat back in his chair. He preferred the title of Rabbi to those of Doctor or Professor, even though he was entitled to all three. "Well, you must admit, Dr. Goldhaber—"

"Sam, please. Call me Sam."

"Okay, Sam, fine. You must admit that applicants for admission to our university, or to any university, tend to be people of a less advanced age. Please don't be offended—"

Sam waved his hand in a gesture of dismissal, smiling. He had found that for the past year, ever since he had awakened on the quiet desert in the early dawn, he was neither upset nor disturbed by anything. "No offense taken, Rabbi. But please remember that I'm sixty years old, and that's twenty years younger than Moses was when God called him from the burning bush."

"Yes, yes, of course. It's just that . . ." Rabbi Schamis paused, trying to find the words to express his doubts without calling into question the motives or attitude of the man who sat before him. "Sam, the vocation of the rabbi is more than just a scholarly pursuit, more than a—an insurance policy with God, if you know what I mean." He paused and waited for Sam to respond, but the only response was a gentle smile, so he continued. "Your qualifications, academically, are of course quite impressive. In fact, I remember reading your monograph on the Semitic elements of the Sumerian language, back in—when was that article published?"

"In 1965," Sam replied, "when I was at the University of Toronto."

"Yes, yes. Fascinating article, erudite and informative."

"Rabbi," Sam said with the slightest hint of impatience, "may I ask what the problem is?"

"Sam, please don't be offended. It just strikes me as peculiar that a man who seems to have had no connection whatsoever with a synagogue of any kind for all of his adult life should suddenly decide in late middle age to study for the rabbinate. I hope you realize that the rabbi's responsibilities—"

"Rabbi," Sam sighed, "let me assure you of a few things. I am not just an old man, frightened of death, trying to make up for a lifetime of neglect. I am not frightened of death, not in the slightest. And I am not just an academician drawn to the rabbinate out of scholarly zeal. I'm already a scholar of some reknown, if I may be so immodest as to say so."

Rabbi Schamis shook his head. "There's no immodesty in speaking the truth, Sam."

"My feelings exactly," he smiled. "I have come to the realization that the things I used to regard as mythology are not mythological, that's all. When I was much younger, tending toward what I believed to be enlightened deism, I used to say that either the words of the Scriptures were true or they were false. If they were true, then nothing in life made more sense than to devote one's self to the service of God and man; and if they were not true, which is what I then believed, then any attention paid to religious activity was a waste of time." He leaned forward and his eyes seemed to glow with an intensity which Rabbi Schamis found a bit disquieting. "But I know now that they are true. All I wish to do is live up to my own injunction."

The rabbi nodded, agreeing but not satisfied. "I'm pleased to hear that, Sam, very pleased indeed. But you must understand—"

"Rabbi, listen to me." Sam's impatience was becoming apparent. "I am quite serious about my beliefs, and my desire is a selfless and sincere one. No man can read the heart of another, and I must ask you to accept my word. I mean"—and he laughed slightly—"I am well beyond the age of mercurial changes in attitude."

The rabbi nodded. "Yes, but you seem to have just made one, no?"

Sam considered this for a moment. "Yes, I suppose so. But

there are reasons, personal reasons, private reasons, which I would rather not go into just now."

Rabbi Schamis nodded again, and then smiled. "Well, Sam, I've never refused a student who wished to study for the rabbinate, and I don't propose to start now. At least we both know that the linguistic studies aren't going to discourage you."

They both laughed, the tension broken by the quip. "No, I don't think they will."

"Of course, we'll wave the language requirements. You know more about that curriculum than some of our teachers!"

"I know. I took the opportunity today to browse through your bookstore. Your Aramaic I course uses a text I wrote."

"Is that a fact! Well, why don't you come in tomorrow afternoon. We'll sit down with Professor Hirschfeld and work out some sort of course of study for you which will satisfy the rabbinical board, who will have to approve you for ordination. With all of the study and research you have done, I doubt that it will take too long." He rose and held his hand out to Sam.

"Fine. I'll see you tomorrow, Rabbi. It's been a pleasure meeting you." He shook the proffered hand.

"Same here, Sam, and I hope we get to know each other better." He smiled. "And I hope someday you'll tell me what it was that made this change in your attitudes."

Sam laughed. "Maybe someday."

Never, Sam thought as he walked down the yeshiva's steps and buttoned his coat against the brisk autumn wind which was racing down the Manhattan streets, carrying dust and paper refuse with it. Never. I'm too old and well respected to have my sanity questioned. He looked up at the tall buildings which stood out starkly against the gray sky. If man is God's special creation, then the city, like the heavens, declares the glory of God.

"Give thanks unto the Lord, for He is good," Sam muttered, "and His mercy endureth forever." You hit it right on the nose, King David, he thought, right on the nose. He began to walk toward his hotel, grinning and humming contentedly.

Fifty miles to the east, Jasper Rudd paced back and forth in the reception area of the Kings Park Psychiatric Hospital, glancing irritably at the wall clock. They told him to be there at noon, and it was already nearly one o'clock. Goddamn paper-pushing record keepers, he thought. Hell of a way to run a hospital.

His irritation dissipated as Gus and his doctor entered the room. Gus grinned broadly but nervously as he walked over to Jasper and hugged him. "Hiya, Jas," he said.

"Hi, Gus. You all ready to go?"

"Yeah. I can't wait."

A few desultory comments were exchanged between Jasper, Gus, and the doctor, but neither of the two brothers paid much attention to them. For Gus, it was sufficient to know that he was going home after a year of care and treatment. For Jasper, having his brother back was all he cared about.

They did not converse too much as they got into Jasper's car and began the long drive home. The damp chill in the air caused Jasper a twinge of pain in his neck. Damn thing's never gonna heal right, he thought. Probably gonna get arthritis there, too.

They drove through the bumper to bumper traffic on the Long Island Expressway, through the Queens-Midtown Tunnel, up the FDR Drive, around the northern tip of Manhattan and onto the New York State Thruway without saying a word to each other. They were speeding through Westchester before Gus asked, "Did you do it? What I wanted you to do? Did you do it?"

"Yeah, Gussie, I found the grave and put some flowers on it. That Calvary Cemetery is enormous. Took me an hour to find the goddamn stone."

Gus nodded. "Is it a nice stone?"

"Yeah, yeah," he said brusquely, wishing to change the subject, "real nice. I don't know why you wanted to buy it for her, though."

Gus shrugged. "She didn't have no family or nothin'. I felt—I dunno—might have been me. I mean—"

"Gus, cut it out. It's all over. Forget it."

Gus did not reply. He would never forget it. He could never forget it. And he kept thinking, if poor Miss Melendez had been second instead of first, if the autopsy had been—

No! he thought, Stop it! You're okay, you're okay, everything's okay. The brief surge of panic which had begun to rise receded. It's all over. Everything's okay.

"And listen, you little bastard," Jasper said gruffly, "I don't want no more trouble from you when we get home, you hear me?"

Gus smiled, recognizing the affection which lay beneath the gruffness. "I hear you, Jas. I hear you." Only the fact that they were speeding along the thruway at seventy miles an hour prevented Gus from throwing his arms around his brother. Instead he punched Jasper softly on the arm. Jasper reached down and squeezed Gus's knee quickly.

"We're invited over to dinner tonight at Miss Langly's—I mean, at the Sawhills'."

"Oh, great!" Gus said with genuine enthusiasm. "I haven't had a decent meal in God knows how long."

"Yeah, that's what she figured."

"What are we gonna have?"

Jasper gave him an annoyed glance. "How the hell do I know? I didn't ask her for a menu!"

"Well, I'm sure it'll be good. Gotta be better than the shit they feed you in hospitals."

Jasper smiled. "I know. I ate it for a month myself." He rubbbed his neck distractedly.

They drove on in silence, feeling no need for conversation. Everything was all right. Everything.

Twelve hundred miles away, the sun was setting over the bustling, growing metropolis of Orlando, Florida, and a few miles away the crowds were beginning to gather around Sleeping Beauty's Castle, eagerly anticipating the famous fireworks display at Walt Disney World. The multitude included people of all nationalities, of all ages and backgrounds, wearing every conceivable type of attire. But even in the midst of this cross section of humanity, a rather odd image was struck by the chubby Englishman with the helium-filled Donald Duck balloon floating from his wrist, the enormous pile of cotton candy in his other hand which left sticky traces upon his lips and cheeks as he tore chunks of it off the cardboard tube, and the undersized Mickey Mouse ears which were perched precariously upon his head.

Roderick Fowles, the fifteenth Earl of Selwyn, was madly in love with Disney World. He had called his new solicitor in London after his first day at the park to tell him to buy it, and Roderick was a bit miffed to hear that such an expenditure was beyond even his ample resources. When his subsequent suggestion that he be able at least to purchase Fantasyland was met with an impatient rejection and a rather tiresome and uninteresting explanation of why this was not possible, he decided both to forget the idea and find another solicitor. Old Pearson could have figured out a way, he thought. I should at least be able to buy the pirate ride, at least that! I am an *earl*, after all!

Roderick ignored the amused stares he received as he wandered through the area where Adventureland and Frontierland met, and he was enchanted by the warmth which still suffused the park in the gathering dusk. So unlike home! he thought contentedly. He looked cheerfully around at the happy people and the other-worldly series of amusements which presented themselves. It was hard to say which of the rides and exhibits he had enjoyed the most during his week-long stay at the Magic Kingdom, but the Pirates of the Caribbean was certainly close to the top of the list. He found the Peter Pan ride quaint and amusing, and he was astonished by almost everything at Epcot Center—except, of course, the area with the re-created European streets, which was nothing special to him. But the dinosaurs in the World of Energy fascinated him, and the three dimensional film he had seen was delightful.

What was the best? he mused as he walked beside the man-made river and watched the steamboat *Robert E. Lee* chug along happily. The African jungle ride? Twenty Thousand Leagues under the Sea? Space Mountain? The ride through Epcot's Unisphere? So many choices, so many choices.

This evening, as every evening during the past week, he slowed his pace slightly as he drew close to the Haunted Mansion. The ubiquitous lines were rather short this time of day, and he could probably get into the Haunted Mansion in only five or ten minutes. He had never gone into the Haunted Mansion, but every evening he had stopped in front of it.

He looked at the sign which stood beside the entrance way to the re-created Gothic structure. "Inside!" the sign proclaimed. "Nine hundred and ninety-nine ghosts!"

Roderick turned and began to walk back toward the pirate ride. He glanced over his shoulder at the gloomy building which stood high upon a hill beside the man-made river.

"Enough is enough," he muttered. He adjusted his Mickey Mouse ears, took another bite of cotton candy, and walked on.

# ABOUT THE AUTHOR

JEFFREY SACKETT was born in Brooklyn in 1949, and accounts himself fortunate to have made it home from the hospital unscathed. After studying briefly for the ministry, he chose to pursue an academic career, this being preferable at the time to his alternative, which was a year in the Mekong Delta as a guest of the government. He obtained graduate degrees in history from Queens College and New York University, and also studied classical Greek, Latin, and several modern languages. Being thus possessed of a vast fund of fascinating and generally useless information, he became a teacher of history and English, which he has remained until this day. He explored other career alternatives at various times. He worked for a while as a bank guard (during which time the bank was robbed) and as a finder of missing persons (most of whom had disappeared by choice and threatened him with all manner of violent reprisals when he found them). He decided that on the whole, teaching was his safest bet.

*Stolen Souls* is his first published novel. His second novel, *Candlemas Eve*, will soon be published by Bantam Books. He is currently working on a third manuscript.

Sackett lives in a ridiculously overpriced house in Tanglewood Hills, New York, with his wife, Paulette, an artist; their daughter, Victoria Simonetta, an infant; their dog, Paddington, a cocker spaniel; and their lizard, Horatio, a seven-foot-long iguana. Theirs is the only house in the neighborhood with a sign saying "Beware of Reptile" on the fence.

*A special preview of the new novel of horror*

# candlemas eve
## by
### Jeffrey Sackett

*Gwendolyn Jenkins professes to be a witch and she
will demonstrate with deadly power the truth of her
claim. On the following pages is a riveting scene
where Gwendolyn proves she will not be mocked by
mortal science.*

The bouncing melody of "You Are My Sunshine," Percy Campbell's theme song, broke from the speakers, and Campbell himself walked purposefully onto the stage, smiling at the audience and waving. His ruddy, freckled face beamed out at the applauding spectators, and he came to a stop in the middle of the stage and stood humbly, allowing the waves of admiration to wash over him. At last he raised his hands, saying, "Thank you, thank you," and the audience quieted down.

"Hello, everybody," he said. "Welcome to our show. We're going to be trying something a little different today. Instead of our usual assortment of panelists discussing an issue, we're going to have only two—oh, er, I mean three, uh, guests."

He rubbed his hands together thoughtfully. "A few weeks ago we did a show on the use of witchcraft and satanism in rock and roll and in the movies, and about the effects this all may be having upon our young people.

Well, you folks at home seemed to find that topic interesting—judging by the mail we received—so we've decided to present the question once more for your consideration."

He stepped forward, close to the edge of the stage. The hovering boom mike followed him. "Two of today's guests were members of that previous panel. Dr. Ludwig Eisenmann is Professor of Anthropology and History at New York University. A scholar of international repute, Professor Eisenmann is a specialist in the area of comparative religion. He is an authority on the practice and history of witchcraft."

Campbell paused for a moment. "Our second returning guest is Mr. Simon Proctor, well-known rock singer and composer. Mr. Proctor is also, by his own admission, a practicing warlock. Our other guest is Miss Gwendolyn Jenkins, a new member of Simon's band. Miss Jenkins is also a practicing witch. We'll be talking to all three in a moment. Please don't go 'way."

He waited for the engineers to signal that taping had been halted before walking offstage to where Simon and Gwendolyn waited. "Hey, Simon, I've heard your recent stuff," Campbell said. "It's great. A lot different from the stuff you usually do, isn't it? I mean, my kids have some of your records, and none of them sound like that!"

Simon, dressed in his customary performance garb of monk's robe, whiteface, and false goatee, allowed himself a laugh. "That's Gwen's influence. She has a vast repertoire of old songs about magic and wizardry. We've been hard at work adapting them for rock instruments."

"Well, it sounds to me like a good departure for you. Why don't you two go on over to the dais and get ready for the rest of the show? I'll bring Dr. Eisenmann along." His eyes twinkled. "Think you're ready to take on the professor?"

Simon smiled. "I think so," he said darkly. As he took Gwendolyn by the arm to lead her to their seats, which stood beside a desk on the raised platform, he leaned down and whispered, "You look great, Gwen, really great!"

Gwendolyn Jenkins smiled at him warmly. She wore a jet black dress that hugged her torso tightly from bodice to belly and then erupted into streams of tatters and jagged points. The neckline plunged down seemingly to her navel, and the rounded contours of the middle sides of her breasts were clearly visible beneath the fabric. "I am pleased that I have pleased you. I seek to do naught else." She looked around the dais. "Where is the bag I brought with me?"

"Backstage," he said. "I made sure the propmen know to bring it out here before the talking starts. Hey, what's in that bag, anyway? Props for the spell?"

"Materials for the spell, yes," she said softly. As she was speaking, a member of the stage crew walked over and handed her the very bag they had been discussing. It was a plain leather purse, about a foot long, caught together at the top by a strip of thin rope. She took it from him without comment or thanks and placed it at her feet. She and Simon sat quietly, waiting for Campbell to return with Eisenmann.

After a few minutes Percy Campbell came back into view, leading Ludwig Eisenmann toward the dais. The middle-aged Austrian once again wore a silly little bow tie, and once again fiddled with it nervously. Upon seeing him, Simon experienced a knot involuntarily growing in his stomach. As the chubby man walked up the two steps onto the dais and heaved himself into one of the chairs, Simon began to have second thoughts. I hope this wasn't a mistake, he thought. I hope we get the kind of PR out of this that we need.

Simon was distracted when Campbell sat down behind

his desk and said, "Professor Eisenmann, you of course remember Mr. Proctor, don't you?"

Eisenmann smiled his little-boy grin and extended his hand to Simon. "Of course, of course."

Simon shook his hand quickly and coldly and then released it without a word. Son of a bitch, he thought to himself.

"And this is Miss Gwendolyn Jenkins," Campbell said. "Professor Ludwig Eisenmann."

"Charmed, miss," Eisenmann said, nodding politely. He did not extend his hand to her, which was wise, for she would not have taken it.

"Jake?" Campbell called out. "We're ready when you are."

A pause, and then a voice from the control booth said, "Tape on, cue music in five, four, three, two . . ."

"You Are My Sunshine" began playing once again, and as it faded out, Percy Campbell smiled into the camera and said, "Welcome back to the *Percy Campbell Show*. My guests today are Professor Ludwig Eisenmann, Mr. Simon Proctor, and Miss Gwendolyn Jenkins." Each of them nodded in turn at their host. "Professor," he said, turning to Eisenmann with a serious and interested look on his face, "you said the last time you were here that Mr. Proctor and the other entertainers who popularize witchcraft and satanism were—" he turned to Simon, "pardon, Simon," and then resumed, "—that they were not really satanists."

"Not exactly," Eisenmann said. "Whether Mr. Proctor and his friends happen to be devil worshipers or not, I do not know. But the *practices* in his new film—and from what I understand, in his stage show—are pure imagination without any true connection to witchcraft as it was practiced."

"And I still maintain that this is a matter of opinion,"

Simon said heatedly. Gwendolyn patted his hand reassuringly and smiled at him. She was calm, unruffled, confident, much more at ease that he.

"Mr. Proctor, I do not wish to recover old ground here," Eisenmann said, "but surely you must admit—"

"Hold," Gwendolyn said firmly. "Let us not waste words on trifles. May I ask you a question, Professor?"

Eisenmann shrugged, "Uh, yes, well, certainly you may."

"Thank you," she said. She crossed her legs as she spoke, and the long, curvaceous limb distracted Eisenmann from her voice for a moment. As she spoke to him she fixed her eyes unblinkingly upon his as if to master him, and he found himself looking down frequently so as to avoid the penetrating stare. Unfortunately, when he did this, he found himself looking at her chest, and thus became further discomforted. "Allow me to ask you if you believe in witches."

"Oh, of course I do," he said quickly, and then added, "if by that you mean people who practice witchcraft."

She was puzzled. " 'Tis one and the same, is it not?"

"Yes, but I wish to make this very clear. There are indeed people who believe that they have magical powers, and these people are called witches. But that does not mean, of course, that they actually do have such powers. Such beliefs are holdovers from a different age, an age of credulity and ignorance, superstition and fear. Such beliefs are atavisms, like, oh, like a tail on a newborn baby."

"I see," she said easily. "And so when I say to you that I am a witch, and that my master, the Devil, has given me powers in exchange for my worship, you say this is untrue?"

Eisenmann laughed. "Miss Jenkins, I do not wish to offend you, but of course it is untrue! You seem to expect people to hold unscientific beliefs in a scientific age!" He leaned forward and said earnestly, "Listen to me, miss.

Beliefs in magic and sorcery and devils and demons and all of that arose in human civilization because people in prescientific societies could not understand the processes of nature, could not manipulate nature as we can today by the uses of technology—which is, of course, merely applied science—and they thus sought for explanations of things which they could not understand. This is the origin of the belief in supernatural powers."

"Hmmm." She smiled, pretending to consider his point. "And so there have never been true magicians or true wizards or witches? The tales are untrue that are told of Merlin, and Thomas the Rhymer, and old Tam Lin?"

"Well, of course, there was a thirteenth-century Scottish poet named Thomas the Rhymer, but the nonsense about him running off with the queen of the elves?— Untrue, of course. As for Merlin, merely a late medieval addition to the Arthurian legends, without basis in fact. And Tam Lin is just an old story." He paused for a moment, and then added, "Of course, there were people like the alchemists and the astrologers who, without realizing it, were beginning to discover some natural laws back in the Dark Ages. Such people may have been popularly regarded as sorcerers, may even have thought of themselves as sorcerers. But that was because of the time, not because of any magical powers." He laughed and turned to the audience. "For example, I'm sure that most of us here today know how to drive an automobile. But imagine what would be the reaction in, say ninth-century Ireland if an automobile came driving down the road." Laughter from the audience. "You see? This is where superstition begins, with people trying to explain things which they do not understand."

"Do you believe in God?" Gwendolyn asked.

"I believe that there is a creative intelligence to the universe," Eisenmann replied, "but I am not wed to any particular religious perspective. I believe that all of man's faiths hold elements of truth which point beyond to an even greater truth which we as yet cannot understand."

"But how then can you believe in God and not believe in the Devil?" she asked. "And if you believe that God has power to answer prayer, how can you not believe that Satan has power to answer prayer?"

He giggled nervously. "Excuse me, miss, but I think you are deliberately misunderstanding me. I do *not* believe in the orthodox Jewish, Christian, Moslem idea of the heavenly patriarch. I am much more attracted to the Hindu or Buddhist concept of deity as universal mind. I do not believe in prayer, to anyone or anything!"

She nodded understandingly. "I see, I see. So you are saying that my belief in Satan differs not from someone else's belief in Christ, correct? Both are mere superstitions, correct?"

Eisenmann coughed uneasily, and Simon thought, Good, Gwen, good! Get him to equate satanism with Christianity, and we've scored a point against him!

But before Eisenmann could reply, Gwendolyn said, "But enough. 'Tis of no importance."

NO, Simon shouted inwardly, NO! LET HIM ANSWER THE QUESTION!

"I merely wish to make certain that you are quite secure in your beliefs," she went on. "You are absolutely certain that there are no such things as real magical powers? The spells which are cast upon people by witches, these too are superstitions?"

"Well," Eisenmann said, grateful for the change of subject, "if you believe that you have powers, and I believe that you have powers, and you then cast a spell on me, the spell might work in that I convince myself that it is working." Eisenmann fiddled with his bow tie and turned to Percy Campbell. "For example, the Australian aborigines believe that you can sing a man to death by pointing a hollow tube at him and singing a death song through the tube. There is at least one recorded, documented instance of this actually happening, but of course it was the man's belief that he could be killed in this manner which caused him to die."

Gwendolyn smiled. "And you, of course, hold no such belief."

"Of course not!" he laughed.

"So that were I to cast a spell upon you, it would be without effect?"

Eisenmann laughed again. "Really, Miss Jenkins, I am quite certain that so attractive a young woman as yourself can cast many effective spells upon members of the male sex." A few laughs from the audience.

Gwendolyn nodded her appreciation of the compliment and then said, "I am quite serious, good sir. Are your convictions so firmly founded that you could be subjected to a spell, a death spell, say, and not be made nervous by it?'

"Of course," he replied jovially. "I have no superstitions."

She leaned back in her seat. "Then let us conduct an experiment, Professor Eisenmann, right here and right now. I shall cast a spell upon you, and we shall see what happens. Is this agreeable to you? And to you, Mr. Campbell?"

Percy Campbell was attempting to repress a grin. What a great segment this is gonna make! "It's fine with me, if it's okay with you, Professor."

Eisenmann smiled and waved his hand as if to dispel any doubt. "Feel free to do your worst, Miss Jenkins."

The time element, Simon was thinking. Don't forget to say that the spell will take awhile to work. As Gwendolyn reached down for the black leather bag without mentioning this important point, Simon decided to remind her obliquely. "The spell you shall cast, my dear," he entoned ominously, "how long will it take before the effects become evident?"

She looked up at him with amusement as she opened the bag. She knew exactly why he had asked that, and she knew exactly what he expected her to say. "The effects," she said, grinning at him, "will be immediate."

Simon stared at her numbly, unable to believe what he had just heard. "What did—? I mean, the effects—the effects will take a few—"

She stood up. "The effects will be immediate, my dear Simon." She turned from his astounded and infuriated face and said to Campbell, "May I use your desk, Mr. Campbell? And may I ask that the lamps be dimmed?"

"Oh, yes, certainly," Percy Campbell said, standing and moving away from his desk. "Jake, you wanna cut the houselights?" he called out.

Gwendolyn Jenkins took a short candle from the bag and placed it upon the desk top. Then she took a small vial of thick, brown liquid and set it beside the candle. She looked at Simon and said, "A flame, please?"

Simon rose from his seat and took a pack of matches from his pocket. He struck a match, and as he applied it to the wick he leaned close to Gwendolyn and whispered, so low that the boom mike could not pick it up, "What the hell do you think you're doing!"

"Hush, my love," she said calmly. "Sit and behold." He had no choice but to resume his seat and hope that he was not watching the beginning of the end of his career. *I knew I shouldn't have come back on this show*, he thought. *I just knew it! Whatever possessed me to think that I could make up for the last time?* Simon sighed and shook his head.

Gwendolyn continued her preparations. The houselights dimmed but did not go fully dark. She took a small, vicious-looking dagger from the bag, and then a small cloth doll. She turned to Eisenmann and said, "May I please have an article of your clothing? A kerchief, perhaps, or your tie?"

Eisenmann laughed once more and began to untie the bow about his neck. "Really, Miss Jenkins—!"

"This will not take long, good sir," she said amicably. He handed her his tie, and she wrapped it around the torso of the cloth doll. She looked out at the audience and began to speak. There was total silence in the studio. The flickering candle flame sent shadows dancing over her white face, and the flame reflected as two pinpoints of light in each of her green eyes.

"This is a simple poppet," she said quietly, holding the doll aloft and then placing it down upon the desk. "And in this vial is a potion made according to ancient ritual and laws. I shall drink a portion of the liquid, sprinkle a few drops on the good Professor, and pour the rest upon the poppet. This will create a mystical bond between the three of us, and after the appropriate words have been spoken, what is done to the poppet will in fact be done to the man."

"It's like voodoo, right?" Campbell asked. He had seated himself beside Simon in the chair that Gwendolyn had vacated.

"It is witchcraft," she replied simply. "I know it by no other name." She uncorked the vial.

"It is known technically as sympathetic magic," Eisenmann said. "The belief was that powers could be bent to the will of the practitioner by transference of action from a symbol to an object."

"Oh," Campbell said, not understanding what he had just heard.

Gwendolyn said sternly, "Shhh!" There was silence on the stage. She lifted the vial upward as if in parody of the elevation of the Christian sacrament, and then delicately sipped some of the liquid. She brought the vial down to the level of her waist, and tipped it slightly, allowing a small amount of the thick, brown potion to ooze into her palm, and then turned and tossed a few droplets at Eisenmann.

The professor blinked as one of the drops struck his cheek. He wiped off the liquid then sniffed at his hand. Eisenmann grimaced. The smell was putrid, vile.

Gwendolyn poured the remaining liquid over the small cloth doll that lay upon the desk. Taking the dagger in one hand and placing the vial down upon the desk top with the other, she then raised her arms high above her head. Gwendolyn looked up at the ceiling and stood as if frozen for a few moments. Then she began to pray.

"Hear me, Satanas! Hear me! Hear me, master of the World, hear me! Hear me, lord of the flies, hear me! Hear me, father of lies, hear me!" The silence in the studio was so profound that her increasingly rapid and labored breathing was clearly audible. "I am come to bring death. Satanas, hear my prayer! I am come to destroy. Master, hear my prayer! I am come to visit destruction upon the sons of men in accordance with thy commandment, thou harbinger of death! Hear my prayer! Hear my prayer!" A slight chuckle escaped from Eisenmann's lips, but she was too deeply involved to hear it. "Give me the power to slay without touching! Give me the power to kill without touching! Give me the power to destroy without touching! I am thine instrument, open to thee! Flow thou through my limbs and visit death upon mine enemy!"

She stood for a long moment as immobile as a statue, and then moved her arms together above her head and grasped the dagger with both hands. She seemed to freeze once more. Then with all her might she brought the dagger down and plunged it into the doll.

Eisenmann screamed.

Gwendolyn held the doll down with one hand while pulling out the dagger with the other, and plunged it once more into the center of the cloth form.

Eisenmann jumped from his seat, clutching his chest. He stumbled off the dais and fell in the center of the stage. On his back now, he was wracked with tremors.

Gwendolyn continued to stab the doll, over and over again.

Percy Campbell leapt to his feet and ran over to Eisenmann. The professor stared in shock at the ceiling, his blue tongue extruding from his quivering mouth. "Get the lights!" Campbell shouted. "Get a doctor! Hurry!" He pulled open Eisenmann's shirt and then just knelt there, not knowing what he was doing, not knowing what to do.

The dagger came down, pierced the doll, again and again.

People in the audience began to scream as the realization struck them that this was not an act, not a skit, not a rehearsed falsity. They began to rise to their feet, some to come down to the stage, others to flee from the studio.

"I—I think he's dead," Percy Campbell stammered as people from the audience and the studio crew encircled him and Eisenmann. "I can't find—I can't find a pulse. I think he's dead!"

A sudden, stunned silence descended upon the studio. The people stood and looked impotently on as Campbell muttered, "This can't be happening! This can't be happening!"

They turned as they heard Gwendolyn's low, throaty laugh start very softly and then quickly build to a frenzied pitch. Her eyes were wide and mad, and her laughter overwhelming and dreadful. She raised her arms above her and began to cry out.

*"AVE SATANAS! AVE SATANAS! AVE SATANAS!"*

*Jeffrey Sackett's second horror novel,* Candlemas Eve *is the eerily haunting tale of a musician bound to a three hundred-year-old curse. Simon Proctor's adultering ancestor, John Proctor, was denounced as a witch and died on the gallows. Now John's spurned mistress, released for a time from her Dark Master, has come to claim Simon. Gwendolyn Jenkins will marry Simon Proctor by the ancient laws of her evil order—or by all the power in hell, she will wipe all Proctors from the face of the earth.*

*Read* Candlemas Eve, *on sale in February 1988, wherever Bantam Books are sold.*

BANTAM
SHOP-AT-HOME
·C·A·T·A·L·O·G·

# Special Offer
# Buy a Bantam Book
# *for only 50¢.*

---

*Now you can have Bantam's catalog filled with hundreds of titles plus take advantage of our unique and exciting bonus book offer. A special offer which gives you the opportunity to purchase a Bantam book for only 50¢. Here's how!*

*By ordering any five books at the regular price per order, you can also choose any other single book listed (up to a $5.95 value) for just 50¢. Some restrictions do apply, but for further details why not send for Bantam's catalog of titles today!*

*Just send us your name and address and we will send you a catalog!*

---

BANTAM BOOKS, INC.
P.O. Box 1006, South Holland, Ill. 60473

Mr./Mrs./Ms. _____
(please print)

Address _____

City _____ State _____ Zip _____
FC(A)—10/87

Please allow four to six weeks for delivery.